"Emotiona... ...ding and wicked hot."
—Lora Leigh, *New York Times* bestselling author,
on *No Limits*

"[*No Holding Back* has] compassion, interesting family dynamics, troubled pasts, killer fight scenes, and of course, swoon-worthy romance. Highly recommended."
—*Harlequin Junkie*

"No one writes alpha heroes and sexy, swoon-worthy romance like Lori Foster."
—Jill Shalvis, *New York Times* bestselling author

"A must-read!" —*Fresh Fiction* on *The Dangerous One*

"Hot enough to start a fire!... A delicious and dangerous tale that proves why Foster is one of the best in the genre." —*RT Book Reviews* on *Fast Burn*

"Count on Lori Foster for sexy, edgy romance."
—Jayne Ann Krentz, *New York Times* bestselling author

"Teasing and humorous dialogue, sizzling sex scenes, tender moments, and overriding tension show Foster's skill as a balanced storyteller."
—*Publishers Weekly* on *Under Pressure* (starred review)

"Foster is a master at writing a simmering romance."
—*USA TODAY*'s Happy Ever After blog on *Fast Burn*

LORI FOSTER

LET ME BE THE ONE

CANARY STREET PRESS

CANARY
STREET
PRESS™

Recycling programs
for this product may
not exist in your area.

ISBN-13: 978-1-335-00941-8

Let Me Be the One

Canary Street Press
22 Adelaide St. West, 41st Floor
Toronto, Ontario M5H 4E3, Canada
CanaryStPress.com

Printed in U.S.A.

To Lori Edwards, an awesome reader who answered my Facebook request for information on dogs. I often put requests on my wall whenever I'm writing a new book— and I'm always writing a new book. Lori introduced Blu, her beautiful German shepherd to me, and he inspired the hero's pet.

I hope you enjoy the book, and I especially hope you enjoy Blu, his adorable head tilts and his protective nature.

Thank you, Lori Edwards! Give Blu some hugs from me.

Lori Foster

CHAPTER ONE

USING A FOREARM, Tanner Patrick swiped the sweat and dirt away from his eyes. The sun had already set low in the sky, leaving everything in shadows, but the unseasonable spring heat wave remained. Starting at 6:00 a.m. and working through dinner had left him ready for a shower, something more substantial than a sandwich, and then an ice-cold beer.

With Blu at his side, his tools in a wagon, Tanner headed past the trees toward the house.

"It's a freaking horror movie," was whispered somewhere to his right, in *his* woods. After all the recent rains the honeysuckle, black locust, and ash trees made the trails nearly impenetrable.

Giving mixed signals, his German shepherd, Blu, went alert with a low growl, but at the same time swished his tail through the air.

Tanner quickly put a hand to his collar. "Shh."

Obediently, the dog quieted, sat at attention, and perked his ears.

"It's not that bad."

"No, it's worse. The house is probably rat infested. I heard rodents in the yard."

"I think those might have been chickens."

Tanner cocked an eyebrow. Who the hell confused chickens with rats?

"C'mon, Callie. You can't mean to actually live here."

"Actually, I can, because I do."

Live here? On *his* property? Like hell.

"You're always so damned stubborn."

"And you're being a nag. God, Glory, I didn't even ask you to come along."

So, Callie and… Glory? The women clearly didn't understand how voices carried on the evening air.

"Oh, I like that. You know you wanted me here, and you know you're being outrageous."

The intruding voices were most definitely female, and they were getting closer.

"Ow, damn it. My shirt just caught on something."

"Thorns, probably. Did you see the size of those things on that tree?" And then with a grumble, *"I have little sticky things all over me, now."*

Probably the thorns of a honey locust tree, Tanner thought. They were so long and needle-sharp they could be weapons. As a kid he'd been wounded by them more than once. Thankfully, they weren't as plentiful as the black locust or ash trees—though the ash trees brought problems of their own.

The little sticky things had to be burrs. Whoever had gotten into them was going to have a hell of a time getting them out of their clothes.

"It's getting dark and we're in the boondocks. They probably have alligators."

"In Kentucky?"

"I expect to see some crazed person wielding a chain saw at any moment."

Tanner glanced at the large chain saw in his wagon. An evil grin tipped the corners of his mouth and he decided, why not? He had no idea who the intruders were, but the roar of a saw ought to send them running.

"You have a wild imagination, Glory."

"And you don't? Come on, Callie, let's go home."

"No. I want to see the property, all of it. I need to know what I'm dealing with."

"You're dealing with a mess."

"Agreed. Although the mess is Sutter, a wedding I don't want, and everyone trying to tell me what I should do."

There was a moment of silence. *"Don't you think that whole thing with Sutter could be a simple misunderstanding?"*

"No." In the driest tone he'd heard from Callie so far, she said, *"I didn't imagine seeing his dick in her hand."*

Tanner choked.

"Shh. Did you hear that?"

"I hear you trying to talk me out of moving on."

Distracted, the one named Glory huffed. *"He said it didn't mean anything."*

"That actually makes it worse!"

That last impassioned statement gave Tanner pause. Whoever she was, apparently she'd dealt with a creep. He hoped she didn't relent but he also hoped she moseyed off his property so he could wrap up his day.

"If you'd just talk to him—"

"I did—to tell him it was over."

"Callie..."

"No! I've made up my mind—whether anyone else accepts it or not."

Tanner had a pretty low opinion of cheaters. Far as he was concerned, people didn't change their basic natures. So good for her—but she still had no business skulking around on his property.

"Callie," the other woman complained. *"You know what hinges on this."*

"I don't care."

"You're being selfish!" Another heavy silence descended and a charge filled the air before the speaker said, more quietly, *"I'm sorry, Callie, I really am, but a lot of people will be hurt by this."*

"If you're so keen on uniting the families, why don't you marry him?"

"Eew. No, thank you. I have no desire to pick up your leftovers, and in case I need to remind you, there are many."

"No," the more determined voice of Callie said, while loudly thrashing through the woods. *"There are three."*

"Three?" The sound of charging feet followed a disbelieving snort. *"Get real. I know you too well to buy that."*

"Apparently not as well as you think, because the number is exactly three," Callie insisted. *"Buell in high school, and that was nothing grand, believe me."*

Wait a minute. Suspicion loomed hot, bringing a scowl to Tanner's face. There'd been a Buell in *his* high school, too, a major prick with more money than brains. And in fact, Buell had dated…

Sweet little Callie McCallahan, the princess of Hoker High School. Tanner could still see her in his mind, with her silky brown hair and innocent blue eyes. Given how he'd crushed on her back then, he'd probably always remember her. She'd represented everything he wasn't. And of course, she'd never acknowledged him.

"Then there was Warren in college," Callie continued. *"But he went on that testosterone rager that scared me off guys for quite a while."*

"I remember," Glory said quietly. *"That was awful."*

Awful how? An insidious tension invaded Tanner's muscles, making him clench all over. Had she been hurt by some dude named Warren?

Glory pressed her. *"And then Sutter?"*

"Yup. Sutter—who can't keep it in his pants."

"Seriously, that's it? Literally, only three?"

"You say it like I'm unnatural or something."

"Well, no, but...only three?"

"Stop carrying on, Glory. So I don't get around nearly as often as people want to think. It's not a big deal."

"It is when you're canceling all our plans."

Blu looked at Tanner, then back at where the voices loomed ever closer. Despite his arms feeling leaden, Tanner hefted the chain saw from the wagon. It pulled at his already tired shoulders.

"I'm done with Sutter. The rest of you can do whatever you want with him." On the heels of that statement, the woman shoved out of the thick foliage. Her long brown hair sported a few twigs, and her fancy white blouse was ripped at the shoulder over a welt. Clearly disgruntled and oblivious of her surroundings—*of him*—she lifted one foot, eyeing a heeled shoe totally unsuitable for where she'd been.

Ah, hell. It really was her. None other than *the* Callie McCallahan. The one woman who epitomized his tormented past.

A woman who, in the dark of night, still occasionally invaded his thoughts.

Physically, the past ten years had been kind to her. But based on what he'd heard, her relationships hadn't been kind at all. Funny how he'd just caught up on her life without having to ask a single question.

Sucked that she was still so sexy, even more so with the added maturity that now curved her once-willowy figure in all the right ways. A little weight made her hips rounder, her breasts heavier, but those crazy long legs were the same. A man couldn't help imagining them tight around his waist as he rode her hard and deep, or locked over his shoulders while he brought her to a climax with his mouth.

Damn it, she was already stirring him.

A sick sort of dread gripped his guts. He couldn't blink. Couldn't look away.

A second woman appeared, picking her way out of the woods more delicately.

With the devil riding him hard, and desperate to get the upper hand with her for once, Tanner gave the rip cord on the chain saw a hard tug.

The thunderous roar filled the evening air, and quickly snagged the attention of both women.

BEFORE THE UNFOLDING scene could register, Glory flattened herself to Callie's back and let out a bloodcurdling scream that nearly froze Callie's blood. It didn't help that she kept on screaming.

Honestly, Callie couldn't tell which was louder, her cousin or the tool.

It took her a startled second before she spotted the man a few yards away from them, standing in a grove of saplings. Moments ago, a sense of danger had closed in around her, as if someone or something lurked in these woods, but it was nothing compared to the suffocating future she'd left behind.

She'd escaped—that was the only way to describe how she felt.

Catching her fiancé cheating, along with the timely inheritance of a house, had been all the impetus she'd needed to grab for a different path.

This place—spooky woods and all—would be her haven for now.

The chain saw, however, was a little over-the-top. The man wielding it?

Mmm. She knew a really heinous villain could look like a nice everyday guy. But hey, she'd already decided that she would face a den of hungry lions for a week rather than a lifetime of the mediocre existence her family had laid out for her.

So what was one guy with a chain saw?

Hot, that's what he was. Like her most forbidden fantasy...in the flesh.

Real-life men didn't look like him, at least no man that she'd ever met. Did that make him more dangerous, or less so?

Glory gasped, "Oh my God, do you see him?"

Six feet of honed body and piercing brown eyes, staring right at her? Yup, she saw him. Her heart, already in her throat, kicked into a racing beat.

His hair, damp with sweat, curled around his ears and on his neck, somewhat showcasing those broad naked shoulders. Denim-covered legs were braced apart, with sturdy, well-worn brown work boots planted on the ground.

She forgot all about her cousin, and barely noticed

the massive dog beside the man. If she was about to be murdered, well, she'd take that vision with her…

What? No, she wouldn't *die*.

She hadn't come here just to be frightened to death by some backwoods cretin, no matter how gorgeous he might be.

Irritably, she shrugged Glory off, or tried to, but her clingy cousin wasn't going anywhere. Callie frowned at the man, then took one decisive step closer.

The dog shot to his feet, a bushy tail wagging and a look of expectation in his intelligent brown eyes. Nice dog. Much nicer than the man who continued to stare daggers at her and did nothing to silence that obnoxiously loud chain saw.

Shouting to be heard, she asked, "Would you mind?"

He merely smiled, not a pleasant smile, either. More like one that taunted.

Again, she tried to shake off Glory.

The dog's loping approach did the trick. With one final screech, Glory raced off into the thickets, thrashing and crashing behind her.

Abandoned. Oh, well. Glory wasn't being much help anyway. With nothing else to do, Callie knelt to greet the dog. He, at least, seemed happy to meet her. She'd always loved animals, even though she'd grown up in a pet-free home. Whenever she'd visited her friends, she'd spent time with their dogs and cats.

Animals fascinated her, entertained her and didn't leave her blank-brained as the hot lumberjack-looking dude did.

Abruptly, the chain saw went silent.

Thank God for small favors. Her ears continued to buzz while she stroked the dog's thick, soft fur. *Show no fear,* she told herself as she sensed the man's approach. *He's probably just a neighbor. Don't let him intimidate you.*

Right. Easier said than done, especially when those big booted feet stepped directly into her line of vision. He stopped right behind the dog.

When he still said nothing, Callie slowly tracked her gaze up his body—as far as his flat, firm stomach, where she stalled. And stared, and… She might have licked her lips.

Not my fault.

She was used to precisely groomed, nearly hairless men, but there was definitely something to be said for body hair on a sturdy male form. Unlike the hair on his head, his chest hair was darker and tapered down to a silky, tantalizing line that bisected his muscular torso, framed his navel and then disappeared into low-hanging, faded jeans.

"This is awkward as shit, with you down there ogling me."

Embarrassed and possibly a little turned on, Callie cringed at that dark, husky voice. Clearly, that was the wrong reaction, but according to her family and friends, she hadn't had a correct reaction since cutting Sutter loose.

"Sorry." Coming to her feet, she racked her brain for an excuse and settled on saying, "Your chain saw startled me."

"It's not behind my zipper."

Her jaw dropped at the risqué comment, but then she couldn't stop herself from laughing. "No, I'm sure it's not." Peering around him, she saw the tool in his large garden wagon. He was close enough now that she detected the scents of hot skin and clean male sweat. Oddly, it hit her like an aphrodisiac. All the recent changes in her life must've really stirred up her system. Breaking free of lifelong bonds could do that. Maybe. Seemed like a viable excuse for now.

Deciding to change the topic, she said, "I'm afraid you scared off my cousin." She had no idea where Glory had gone, and for the moment she couldn't worry about it. Glory was twenty-five, three years younger than Callie. Surely, she could find her way back to the house.

"I didn't know you had a cousin."

That odd answer took her by surprise. "No, I'm sure you didn't." Since they were strangers, how could he have known anything about her? After brushing her hand on her jeans to remove the dog hair, she offered it to him. "I'm Callie McCallahan. I grew up around here."

Some emotion, maybe irritation, narrowed his eyes, making them even darker. He didn't take her hand. "I know who you are, princess."

Her jaw locked. That was the awful nickname given to her back when her family lived in the area. She'd always hated it, even though it hadn't necessarily been meant as an insult. It made her sound aloof, untouchable. Unfeeling, when she'd often felt too much.

It insinuated that her mother and father were royalty, and to small-town Hoker, Kentucky, maybe they were. Her parents had either owned, or had interests in, nearly every business in town. They had the biggest house, sponsored everything from Little League to prom, and kept company with state politicians.

Until recently, they'd dictated every aspect of Callie's life…and she'd let them.

But no more.

She'd taken a good hard look at her life, at what she wanted, and decided to use the inheritance as the start of a new beginning.

"You don't remember me, do you?"

The question, along with the growled way he asked it, had Callie looking at him more closely. "Should I?" Surely she'd never met him. If she had, no way would she have forgotten.

His short laugh wasn't nice. "No, no reason at all." Abruptly shifting topics, he asked, "Why are you on my land?"

"Your land?" She glanced around at the well-maintained property. Okay, so maybe she'd wandered farther through the woods than she'd realized. "I thought this was my uncle's property."

"He owns exactly ten acres, some of it wooded."

By the second, he grew less friendly, not that he'd actually been friendly at any point. Looking for an ally, she again knelt to pet the dog. "I didn't trespass on purpose. I'm unfamiliar with the setting. I just know Uncle Reggie had some property." Trying to ease the tension, Callie glanced up at him. His sharp gaze was so watchful, she wondered if she should have run off with Glory. "I inherited from him."

"Good for you. So why are you here?"

Definitely antagonistic and she'd about had enough. Standing once more, she smiled at him. "Mr...?"

"Tanner."

"Mr. Tanner—"

"Just Tanner."

She was annoyed enough to quip, "Your name is Just?"

With a roll of his eyes, he said, "Tanner Patrick. No one calls me mister."

"*Mr.* Patrick," she replied with scrupulously polite emphasis. "Please forgive me for daring to step onto your land. I just moved in today, but henceforth, I'll refrain from exploring until I have property lines marked." Giving one last pat to the dog, she turned away, all hyped up for a grand exit. "I'll return to my *own* property immediately." Now if she could figure out how to do that without venturing into the dark, spooky woods again...

In a tone only slightly moderated, he asked, "What do you mean, you moved in?"

Since he sounded more reasonable she glanced over her shoulder. Beneath the edge of her ripped blouse, she saw a deep scratch—and now that she saw it, it burned. Later, she'd worry about injuries. For now, she had to reply to Mr. Nasty. "I'll be staying here."

In one long stride, he brought all that bristling animosity and animal magnetism closer. "For how long?"

"I haven't yet decided." In truth, she thought to rehab the place and then sell it. It was the project she needed to occupy her time while she came up with a more suitable plan. But that was her secret, and she wasn't sharing with anyone—especially not a neighbor who kept glaring at her.

"No."

Both of her eyebrows shot up as she gave a short, incredulous laugh. "I'm sorry, Mr. Tanner, but it's not your decision."

"I've been feeding the chickens. The goats. And the horse is in my pasture."

Chickens? Ha. At least they hadn't been rats, as

Glory had assumed. But goats? A horse? "Are you saying Uncle Reggie had…livestock?" She was *not* a farmer. She would never *be* a farmer.

"How did you get in the house without seeing the chickens?"

She hadn't been in the house yet. With nests and webs around the porch and far too many dead bugs lying around, it had looked intimidating. She'd opted for exploring the yard first, which had led her…here. "I heard them. Clucking, I guess? I couldn't tell where they were."

"They're everywhere, and if I hadn't just fed them a few hours ago they'd have been all over you."

"Really?" What an appalling thought. "All over me as in…attacking?"

One big, sweaty shoulder hitched. "They're chickens."

Whatever that meant. They couldn't be attack chickens because she'd never heard of such a thing. "You also mentioned goats and a horse?"

"Four goats, one horse. Reggie died, no one came to tend them so I've been doing it."

Finally, a redeeming quality. Two, if she counted the ultra-hot bod, though the surly attitude would detract a few points off that. Then again… Her gaze skimmed over him and damned if she didn't feel a bit woozy.

A bead of sweat went down his temple. His brows were flat, his jaw hard, but his lips appeared soft. Really kissable.

"Whew." She fanned her face. "Sure is hot out here. Like a damp blanket thrown over everything." Given her over-the-top reaction to his appeal, she decided she could tolerate him if she tried really hard. "Thank you for taking care of them. No one mentioned animals, at least not that I noticed."

"They'd have starved then, wouldn't they, waiting on you?"

An abhorrent thought. "I'll happily compensate you until the animals can be handled."

Muscles flexed in his jaw, leading her to think he was grinding his teeth.

She tried again. "Tanner." There, that was her sweetest voice. She gave an encouraging smile. "We're neighbors now. Shouldn't we attempt to get along?"

He took far too long thinking about it, before finally giving a tip of his head. "I offered to buy the property, several times in fact, but never heard back."

"My bad." She'd barely paid attention to the Realtor when he'd contacted her. "I've been so busy"—*living a life I didn't want*—"that I'm afraid I didn't make any final decisions until just recently." Before that, she'd been existing in a daze. Once she realized the life that awaited her, she'd been near panicked with the need to get in her car and just start driving.

Thank heavens Sutter was unfaithful.

"You've decided to live here?"

She smiled, not about to admit that she was still undecided on that part. "Will that really be so difficult for you?"

"You're going to tend chickens, goats, and a horse?"

Wrinkling her nose, she said, "I thought I was going to pay you to do that?"

The dog tipped his head in this adorably cute way that made him look super curious, then he glanced at Tanner and sort of murmur-barked-growled.

Tanner nodded and said, "Same, buddy. Same."

The dog looked back at her.

Callie gasped. Had they—man and dog—seriously just had a conversation *about* her, in *front* of her? Sure felt that way. "Well, that was rude." Crossing her arms and cocking out a hip, she struggled to keep her smile.

"Come again?"

She nodded at the dog, then hitched her chin at him. "What was that? That little exchange you two had?"

Amusement—at her expense—curled his mouth, turning his already-gorgeous looks downright devastating. "Blu doesn't know what to make of you, that's all."

Her eyes flared. "And I suppose you don't either? That's what you said, right? You agreed with him. Well, at least I've been up-front with you." She spread her arms wide. "You're the one being all mean and snotty with no good reason at all."

He gave a noncommittal snort, but he was still grinning. "You're offended by what my dog supposedly said. You realize that, right?"

Good Lord, he was right.

She glanced at the dog. He gave her another adorable head tilt. "It's been a long day." She laughed at her own ridiculousness. "Clearly, I'm losing my edge."

His humor eased away, and instead he gave her a look of commiseration.

Oh, hell no. The last thing she wanted from a man, any man, was sympathy. "Again, I apologize for my intrusion. I'll be on my way now." *Before I make an even bigger fool of myself.* She'd just turned away when he spoke again.

"It's getting dark fast. You shouldn't go back through the woods, especially if you're not familiar with them."

"Concerned I won't find my way off your property?"

Okay, that had sounded almost like a sneer. She cleared her throat. Her nature leaned toward being nice whenever possible—and she saw to it that it was *almost* always possible. Certainly, more often than not. "There aren't wild boars or wolves running around, right?" And yet, she did hear a lot of rustling in the woods behind her, which reminded her of how eerie they had felt earlier. Also, yes, it had gotten rather dark.

"No wolves or boars," he agreed. "But there are snakes, an occasional black bear, and often a pissed-off raccoon or two. The bigger problem is that the Garmet brothers are on the other side of you, and they're assholes who are better avoided."

As compared to you? No, she wouldn't say that out loud. "Thank you for letting me know." She'd make a point of finding out more about the Garmet brothers as soon as she could. For now, though… "I'm not quite sure how to get home without going back the way I came, and even then, with it now so dark, I really might get lost. In fact…" She looked around again, seeing heavy shadows everywhere. "I wonder if Glory found her way."

"I'll walk you to the house and we'll see if she's there."

Gallantry, she decided, was another nice quality. Maybe her new neighbor would be tolerable after all.

He went back for the wagon loaded with tools. "Follow me." And with that, he stepped ahead of her.

His dog, however, kept pace with her, continually gazing at her in a friendly way. "Your dog seems nice."

"Blu is smart, but he's not as astute as I am."

Meaning what exactly? "He doesn't bother the chickens?"

Tanner shook his head. "He understands that the chickens are here for a reason. Same with Kam's cat."

"Kam?"

"My brother."

"And he has a cat?"

"Isn't that what I just said?"

"Yes, you did." Her feet were starting to hurt, and that spot on her shoulder stung. "Where does Kam live?"

"Here."

"With you?" She huffed as she tried to catch up to him. Seriously, the man had very long, athletic legs and her shoes weren't cut out for jogging.

"We both live with Addie." He looked over his shoulder at her, and thankfully slowed down.

Once she was at his side he continued on, this time at a more sedate pace. "This was Addie's place when we came here, but we've expanded a lot since then."

When they came there? What did that mean? Sorting it all out would take her some time so for now she concentrated on the basics. "How many acres do you have?"

"Thirty." He glanced at her. "If you sell, we'll have forty."

"And if I'm staying?"

"We'll see." He went back to walking at a clip until they reached a large barn. He slid open a huge door, flipped a few switches, and illuminated it all.

Wow. It was actually nicer than any barn she could imagine. As she followed him inside she craned her neck, looking way up at rafters sporting skylights and then all around at tidy shelves filled with pots, bags of soil and buckets, hoses… She didn't know what half of it was.

The air smelled rich, like fresh soil, but green too, if green had a smell. Combined, it was nice. Earthy.

Sort of sexy…only because he was there, looking so hot.

She couldn't see the very back of the barn but wondered if there might be plants there. Humid air filled her lungs. It was nice, but a little too warm.

Distracted, she asked, "Why would you even need my ten acres?"

"I don't, but that doesn't mean I want anyone living that close either."

Offensive. "You think I'll bother you?"

One brow cocked up as he eyed her standing there, in his barn, while he put the tools from the wagon on specific hooks.

"Okay, so I interrupted your day." Whoop-de-doo. She pinned on her placating smile. "It's my first night here. Going forward, I'll do my best to avoid you."

After shooting her an unreadable look, he went to a utility sink with shelving on both sides, filled his palm with liquid soap and scrubbed dirt from his hands up to his elbows.

Callie waited, but instead of drying his hands, he splashed his face, chest, and the back of his neck until his upper body glistened and rivulets of water ran down his long spine to the waistband of his low-riding jeans.

Lucky water. She wouldn't mind tracing her fingers along that same path. Or maybe her lips. Her tongue…

"You're a complication."

Drawn from her sensual thoughts, she startled. Never in her life had anyone insulted her, much less repeatedly done so. "What does that mean?"

When he finished drying off, he braced his hands on the sink. Shoulders rigid and arms straight, he hung his head.

Callie looked at the dog, who tilted his head and looked back without any answers. For the first time, she saw the exhaustion in Tanner's strong body. He'd washed off the sweat and dirt, but his muscles were still pumped as if they'd recently been strained in hard labor. It was late, and she wondered how long he'd been working and on what. After ten or more seconds had ticked by in silence, she said, "So, Tanner. Everything okay?"

"Fine." Straightening again, he gave her a long look, and then strode past her, leaving the wagon behind. "Come on."

They set out again, this time on a dirt path lined by beautiful trees. In the distance ahead, Callie could see a light shining off the back of a big farmhouse.

"Is that where you live?"

"Nah, I figured we'd visit the Pope."

Okay, that did it. If he wanted to be a smart-ass, then she'd just ignore him. Sooner or later they'd near the road and she could cut over to her own property. Would Glory still be around? She'd have to be, since Callie had driven and she had her key fob hooked to a belt loop.

Unless Glory had gotten lost. Uneasily, Callie glanced behind her. It was dark enough now that it felt like she walked through a tunnel. She dug her cell phone from her back pocket and called Glory.

Her cousin answered on the first ring with a screechy, *"Oh-my-freaking God, where are you?"*

"I'm on my way," Callie soothed. "Just following my neighbor, Tanner Patrick—the dude with the chain saw—to his house, then I'll cut over."

In a horrified whisper, Glory breathed, "You're going with chain saw dude to his house? *Are you out of your freaking mind?*"

Probably. "He's fine," she said airily, knowing Tanner listened. She saw his naked shoulders stiffen and basked in her satisfaction. "He's in a mood, you know? Pouty and stuff."

Now his neck stiffened, too.

"His dog is nice, though." At the word *dog*, Blu glanced at her, then scooted closer and tipped up his face for a pet.

"I thought you were dead, Callie, but I wasn't sure, so I didn't know if I should call the police or not."

Callie missed a step. "I'm very much alive, thank you, so I'm glad you did *not* call anyone." Please, please, please...

"Well... I sort of did."

Damn.

"Call someone, I mean," Glory said unnecessarily.

Callie barely held off her huff. "Who?"

"Now Callie, don't sound like that. I was worried."

Her jaw locked. "Who. Did you. Call?"

Talking fast, Glory said, "I knew you wouldn't want your parents to know if you were being murdered, and I wasn't sure it warranted the police, so I called Sutter."

That did it. She stopped walking. Stopped breathing. Steam built inside her, until she blasted, *"You are no longer my cousin."*

"I'm sorry! If it helps, he didn't answer, so I only left him a message."

"Call him back," Callie demanded. "Tell him you were oh-so-wrong, and make it convincing."

"I will. I promise." There was a pause and then in a smaller voice, "Your house is locked and the car is locked and there aren't any lights on over here. I'm starting to freak out."

Yeah, she could imagine. God, if she didn't love her cousin so much, if she didn't understand everything Glory had been put through, Callie might just tell her to deal with it. Instead, she said, "Hang tight. I'll be there as soon as I can." After disconnecting, she shoved her phone back in her pocket and realized she'd forgotten all about Tanner.

He stood there, his gaze watchful. Blu studied her once again.

Lacing her fingers together, Callie said, "Glory made it. She's at the house but everything is still locked up, so I need to get to her."

"You haven't been inside yet?"

Why did he say it like that, with an expectant glint in his eyes? "No. I wanted to explore the property first." It was possible she'd need to scrape the house and build from the basement up before she could sell it. If property in this area was even selling. Ten acres was valuable where she used to live, but here? Seemed everyone had a spot of land, at least three acres or more.

He shook his head, then said, "Come on. I'll grab a flashlight and walk you over."

They reached his house quickly. It was surprisingly nice—surprising only because the house she'd inherited was so run-down. This house was not. In fact, it was beautiful. Lights glowed all around it, making the white board-and-batten siding look pristine, especially with the black roof.

"Charming."

He grunted.

What kind of reply was a grunt?

Rather than allow Tanner to continue ignoring her,

she started to whistle while attempting to orient herself. Her whistle echoed.

Well, that was creepy. Heavy shadows loomed everywhere, and the night felt far too still, as if even the insects were alarmed.

All she saw around the house was woods, and her sense of direction sucked big-time, but she was fairly certain she just had to go straight ahead to the road, and then to the right. The next house she ran into had to be her own.

With that decided, she made a decision to get on with it. "Tell you what, Grumpy. I'll just bid you goodnight here and figure out the rest on my own. Thanks for getting me this far. It's been…interesting." Using the flashlight on her phone to guide her, she started forward—into that stygian gloom.

"Hold up."

Losing her patience, Callie spun around. "Not another warning, please. I'm over that. The entire day has gone to hell and I really want to find a bed."

From somewhere behind Tanner, she heard, "I've got a bed."

She jumped, Tanner huffed out a breath, and out of the darkness emerged another man, also gorgeous, grinning like the devil with keys dangling from his hand.

Tanner looked at the guy, then said in a too-even voice, "Go on in, Kam. I've got this."

Kam, his brother? Apparently, given how Blu darted forward, his tail waving happily.

More lights came on, almost blinding Callie. She lifted a hand to shield her eyes as a side door opened near the garage. There stood an older woman, probably somewhere in her sixties. Shoulder-length blond hair streaked with gray was tucked behind her ears. Shrewd blue eyes assessed the scene and then snagged on Callie. With her hands in the pockets of a soft pink sweater worn over jeans and slippers, she stepped out. "I thought you boys were past the age of sneaking in girls."

"Don't blame me," Kam said. "I just got home."

"I found her in the woods," Tanner explained. "She's lost."

"Doesn't mean you can keep her." Just as quickly, the woman dropped the attitude. Her grin lifted her rosy cheeks and softened her gaze. "Hello, pretty lady. I'm Addie. What were you doing in the woods?"

Callie took in the three of them standing there as a united front. Even the dog was on their side now.

She should have been disgruntled. Her feet hurt, the scratch on her shoulder burned, and she was starting to think her uncle's house would be a very rude surprise once she got inside.

Luckily for her, the humor of the situation hit and she matched Addie's grin.

Ignoring both men, she stepped forward, hand extended. "Hello, Addie. I'm Callie McCallahan. I'm going to be your new neighbor."

CHAPTER TWO

As STANDOFFISH AS Tanner was, Addie was welcoming. Once she heard an abbreviated version of Callie's plight, she insisted on going along with Tanner to fetch Glory, saying, "You have to see the inside of the house before you make any decisions."

That scared Callie. What exactly was she going to find?

Kam tried to go along too, but with one look, Tanner nixed that idea. Kam had just arrived home from a welding job, which explained why he'd had his keys in his hand. Maybe for that reason, he gave up gracefully, saying, "Fine. I need a shower and food, anyway."

"So do I," Tanner said. "Don't use all the hot water, and leave some mashed potatoes for me."

Addie smiled indulgently at them both. "I made plenty." She confided to Callie, "I always do. But once, back when the boys were younger, Kam devoured all the potatoes and Tanner has yet to forgive him."

Tanner put an arm over Addie's shoulders and pressed a kiss to her temple. "Your potatoes are worth a tussle."

"Are you hungry?" she asked Callie.

No way would she enter the fray over the potatoes, so Callie shook her head. "Just tired, actually. I think I'll make an early night of it." Far as hints went, that wasn't the most subtle, but it did get everyone in the car—including Blu. He sat in the back seat, leaning comfortably against Addie's shoulder.

Tanner said, "One second," and dashed inside the house through the garage, returning with a shirt that he pulled on over his head as he walked to the driver's side. Shame to cover up that fine chest. When Callie realized she was staring at him again, with Addie taking note, she quickly got in the passenger seat.

The SUV was Kam's, he said, and they used it because Tanner's truck was currently full.

Apparently, Tanner was a very hard worker. With his lean, hard body, she believed it.

When the headlights of the SUV cut into her driveway only a few minutes later, they all saw Glory sitting huddled on the hood of Callie's red Ford Escape. She looked petrified.

"Oh, no." Thinking only of her cousin, Callie quickly got out of the car. "Glory?"

Glory nearly fell off the car in her relief. She rushed to Callie, grabbed her in a smothering hug and said, "Thank God you're here!"

"What's wrong?" Tanner asked, already glancing around.

Blu didn't seem worried. He merely tilted his head at Glory.

Addie said, "Poor girl is terrified. What is it, honey?"

"There's something out there." Glory looked at Tanner with distrust, then at Addie with confusion. "Something horrible."

Just then, Callie heard it too and the hair rose on the back of her neck. It sounded like a cross between a demonic cry and a broken wail, the sounds layering over each other in the eeriest way imaginable. "What in the world?"

Tanner cracked a grin.

"That's just the goats." Addie was also amused. "Nothing to worry about."

"Goats?" Glory clearly didn't believe them.

Callie gave her another hug, then released her. "I have chickens, four goats, and a horse."

Glory's eyes widened even more.

To Callie, it seemed like the perfect time to make introductions, and as she did so she explained that Tanner had very nicely taken care of the animals. Hopefully, Glory would catch her drift and be polite.

Addie helped to smooth things over, both praising Tanner as a wonderful "boy" and saying that as neighbors, they were happy to help in any way they could.

"You've been wonderful," Callie said. "Thank you for getting me this far." She even smiled at Tanner. "I know you're ready for your dinner. You should go before Kam eats it all." The joke didn't quite get the reaction she'd hoped for. "It's been a long day for you, I'm sure. I can handle it from here."

He shook his head. "The place has been empty for too long." He looked up at the dark porch. "Addie and I can walk you in, make sure everything is working and that no critters have set up house."

"Critters?" Glory asked, giving the house another fearful glance.

"Raccoons, rats, birds, snakes."

"It's probably fine," Addie said quickly. "But Reggie wasn't much of a housekeeper and I'm not sure what kind of shape he left it in."

"Let's go look, okay?" Tanner patted his thigh for Blu to follow.

It was interesting that the dog wasn't on a leash and didn't wander off. "I have the keys." Callie unhooked them from the belt loop on her jeans and took the lead.

"Careful," Tanner said. "The porch boards might be rotted."

When she hesitated, Glory bumped into her back, then stuck close with one hand knotted in her shirt. Since it was already torn at the shoulder, it ripped a little more.

"Why don't we let Tanner get things opened up?" Addie suggested.

To Callie, that seemed like a great idea, but she didn't want to admit it. She squinted at the entrance. "Are you more familiar with the lock?"

"I am." He held out a hand. "Should be a light switch just inside if you want to wait here for a sec."

Giving up, Callie nodded and gave him the keys. With Addie nearby, he was far more gracious.

The evening seemed even eerier now, with the goats still making their weird noises from somewhere on the property, insects of some kind clicking in the darkness, and an overall sense of impending doom bearing down on her. Glory didn't help, clutching at her the way she did.

Belatedly, Callie realized she should have started her car and turned on the headlights to better light their way.

There was a creak of boards, a metallic clink, and then the groan of a door opening on rusty hinges. Callie held her breath, and a second later lights flicked on inside, immediately followed by the low yellow glow of a porch lamp beside the door.

It was not a pleasant sight. Or smell.

Together, silently, they all stepped in. The house was incredibly stale.

Tanner gave a low curse. "Rotted food. I should have thought of that."

Callie followed his gaze and saw a pizza box, with a bunch of moldy stuff, on the coffee table, as well as other, less identifiable items.

"I dread to know what's in the kitchen," Addie said.

Glory wrinkled her nose. "When you get past the rotten smell, you get hit with the old man smell."

"Glory!" There was a very real chance that Callie might strangle her cousin.

Addie laughed. "She's not wrong. Given Reggie's age and habits, I'm not surprised. He liked to drink and he was a regular chimney. Always smoking. Never saw the man without a cigarette."

"Callie," Glory pleaded. "Please tell me we're not staying here. Not tonight. Not without having it cleaned first."

Weary to the bone, Callie agreed. This independence stuff was hard, especially with a hunk of manhood watching her critically, waiting for her to falter. She drummed up a smile and said decisively, "We'll find a hotel for the night and then I can start fresh tomorrow."

"Nonsense." Addie smiled at both of them. "The nearest hotel is an hour away. We have plenty of room. Just grab what you need for the night. You can get some sleep and tomorrow we can air the place out and see what's what."

"We?" Tanner asked, but he sounded resigned, as if he'd already known what Addie would do.

"I can at least help get her started. That's what neighbors are for."

Tanner went annoyingly silent and Callie felt perverse enough to happily accept Addie's offer. "Thank you so much, Addie. You're a blessing."

THANK GOD BOTH women had declined to eat. It was bad enough knowing Callie was in the house and that she'd be sleeping nearby. Just thinking it made Tanner edgy and almost guaranteed that he'd have a restless night.

Seeing inside Reggie's house should have been enough to send her home. Instead, she'd gleefully soldiered on, determination in every curvy line of her body—a body he'd imagined naked many times over the years.

A body that he still badly wanted to explore.

He drew a slow breath, knowing it wouldn't help, and headed into the kitchen. The shower had refreshed him, but he remained hot around his neck.

Addie immediately put a plate of meat loaf, potatoes, and an ear of corn on the table. "Here you go, honey. All warmed up."

"Thanks, but I could have gotten it." She didn't need to wait on him. Far as he was concerned, Addie already did far too much—for him, for Kam, and now she'd be helping with neighbors.

"Ha! So you could skip giving me all the juicy details?" She pulled out a chair across from him. "Not on your life. You can eat, but also talk."

With a shrug, he dug into the food, then had to groan in pleasure. "No one cooks like you, Addie."

"You know I love it."

Kam, every bit as nosy as Addie, came in and sat beside her. "Let's give him two minutes to eat. He looks starved."

That was something Addie always used to say. *"Honey, you look starved. Here, let me get you something to eat."* In the beginning, when he wasn't too responsive to acts of affection, that had been her way to show she cared.

To a hungry boy, it was a great start.

For years now, Addie had been keeping both him and Kam well fed. Neither of them would ever take her for granted. She was their living, breathing angel, the woman who had delivered them from hell and showed them what life could and should be.

Kam nudged Addie. "He's reminiscing."

"About food," Tanner said.

"And the woman." Folding his arms on the table and grinning, Kam asked, "She's the one, isn't she?"

Tanner went still. Damn, figured Kam would remember.

Addie sat forward. "Wait, the girl from high school? The one who broke your heart?"

"I *knew* her in high school, yes, but she never knew me." Still didn't, in fact. "And my heart was never involved. To her, I'm a stranger."

"Impossible." Addie asked Kam, "Isn't he a handsome young man?"

"Oh, definitely," Kam said, playing along.

"And isn't he tall and well-built?"

Tanner felt his ears getting hot. "Addie, that's enough."

"He's downright dreamy," Kam said, more than happy to keep her going. "No woman could resist him."

"She has no idea we went to school together, which isn't a surprise. It was a long time ago and she was a grade below me." Seeing her still hit him like a gut punch. He remembered everything. The cute little skirts she'd worn. Who she'd dated and for how long. The way the princess had smiled at everyone, all the time, as if she hadn't a care in the world.

Except she'd never smiled at him. She'd never even noticed him.

Tanner shook that off. "More than anything, she was a pain in the ass today. She and her cousin came through the woods like a couple of drunk rhinos." It was mostly true for Glory, but even while he'd held the screaming chain saw, Callie had managed to look composed and polite. It was uncanny how she did that. Must be nice to have such a protected life that nothing ever took away your peace of mind.

Addie frowned. "They came out of the woods together?"

"Yeah."

"So why wasn't her cousin still with Callie when we met her?"

Hiding any sign of guilt, Tanner shrugged. "The chain saw spooked her and she ran off."

"She left her cousin?" Kam whistled. "If she was scared, you would think she'd want to help Callie, too."

He and Kam were big on backing each other up. For them, with how Addie had taught them, loyalty was everything. "Glory doesn't seem to have Callie's backbone. She ran off screaming while Callie just stared me down, smiling." And ogling him. The way she'd looked at him, so absorbed, fed his imagination. It would play big-time in all his future fantasies. "Blu took to her right away."

Hearing his name, the dog's ears perked forward, but otherwise he kept sleeping on a rug nearby. Kam's cat, Percy, was snuggled into Blu's side, but he effectively ignored them all.

"Blu's smart," Kam said. "Pretty women always get his attention."

Tanner shot him a look, but Kam played innocent. "What? Was I not supposed to notice how drop-dead gorgeous she is? That mouthwatering figure? Her super-sweet smile?"

Addie raised her hand. "Well, I noticed. Course Kam would, too. He has eyes, right?"

From the day she'd brought them home, Addie had made it clear that no subject was taboo. She was a woman who encouraged them to share their every thought—even personal observations.

Of course, as he and Kam grew older, they'd started to censor things a bit anyway. Not their likes and dislikes, or their goals and determination. But their interests in sex? Some things a guy just instinctively knew weren't meant for a parental figure.

"Doesn't matter," Tanner countered. "She won't be sticking around. Once she sees the level of work and expense it'd take to fix up Reggie's place, she'll sell it to me so I can level it and get on with my plans."

"Hmm," Addie said. "I don't think so. I got the sense she feels challenged, not discouraged."

"That could be a good thing for you," Kam insisted to Tanner. "With her living right next door, you have a shot now. If nothing else, maybe you can get her out of your system."

That earned a shove from Addie. "He deserves more than that, and so does that nice young lady."

See, that's why they needed to censor things with Addie. The woman had no concept of overwhelming lust, and just how satisfying it could be to indulge.

In fact, now that Kam said it, the thought took root. Have Callie McCallahan for his own? Even for an abbreviated time? The idea had merit. How many times had he dreamed of sating himself on her, and then walking away, proving... What? That her complete indifference to him hadn't mattered? That although he'd fantasized about her, wishing every day that she'd notice him, he'd outgrown that adolescent infatuation?

At least he could prove to himself that none of it had mattered, that his childhood—first devastating, and then later, after Addie, endearing—had gone along just fine without Callie's notice.

The lost youth he'd been in high school had grown into an independent man who handled his shit and didn't slow down for anyone...except Addie and Kam. They were the only people he counted on now and he knew they were rock-solid.

Giving himself another minute to think, Tanner tipped up his milk glass and drank it all. When he finished, both Addie and Kam were still watching him expectantly. He resisted the urge to huff. "Times have changed. Forget high school." As if he could with her so close by, but he drummed up a lie and said, "I have."

"But dude—"

Tanner's scowl discouraged Kam from saying more. If he accepted the prospect of getting close to Callie, of having a brief, no-strings, very sexual relationship with her, it wouldn't do to tell Addie. That'd only encourage her to champion Callie. He and Kam both had firsthand knowledge of how she protected the underdog. And this time around, that'd be Callie.

Addie stood to pick up the empty dishes. "High school was one thing," she agreed. "People change, their perceptions and their priorities change. Important part is that she's noticing you now. The girl could barely keep her eyes off you."

Refusing to believe that, Tanner pushed back his chair. "Let it go, Addie." He took his plate from her, or tried to, but it turned into a tug-of-war. "Addie. I can clean up my own messes."

Smiling up at him, she said, "But honey, you worked all day, and besides, I love taking care of you. Always have and always will. Let me do what little bit I can, okay?"

That attitude was nothing new. He'd left a home where abuse and neglect were the norm, and then was embraced with Addie's unconditional love. It still had the power to emotionally bring him to his knees.

After taking the dishes from her, Tanner set them aside to gather her close. "God bless you, Addie."

"He already did, with you two."

Standing behind Addie, Kam smiled at him. "It never grows old, does it?"

Tanner shook his head. "No." And it never would.

HER VOICE BARELY above a whisper, Glory said, "I can't believe we've ended the day camping out in a neighbor's attic." She glanced around the room with disbelief bordering on awe.

Callie shrugged. "I'm a little bewildered at how it happened, too." Addie was a small tornado who swept everyone up in her path. Mostly, though, it had been her need to thwart Tanner that had convinced Callie to accept the offer. "We have clean beds to sleep in, so don't complain."

The finished attic, or bonus room, as Addie had called it, had a sloping ceiling around the perimeter, though it was high enough down the middle. Twin beds, made up like couches with plenty of throw pillows, were situated beneath the lowest part on opposite sides. Fresh pillowcases and quilts were waiting for them.

The stairs leading up to the room had opened into a small entry that led to a walk-in closet filled with holiday décor. The door had only been haphazardly closed, and inside Callie had seen a giant Santa head next to an electric star, with boxes and boxes of ornaments, some of them clearly homemade. There was also a rack of Halloween costumes in varying sizes, and a large Easter bunny costume beneath a shelf filled with baskets and colorful buckets. There was even some birthday décor.

When Callie had peeked inside, fascinated by it all, Addie had laughed, saying, "I started doing huge parties for the boys when they were younger and I've never stopped. Now it's comical when I put on the bunny costume and make them take baskets to hunt for eggs, or when they have to sit beside me while I'm dressed like Santa." She'd chuckled with the memory. "Gotta have my annual photos, you know, and the boys play along. They're good sports."

In that moment, Callie's heart had begun aching and it hadn't let up yet. A hollowness filled her, making her yearn for new things. Things she'd never had before and hadn't realized were missing.

Holidays at her house were always formal affairs with everyone dressing up to entertain important clients. Never, not once in her twenty-eight years, had either of her parents ever worn a bunny or Santa costume. Someday, she'd love to see Addie's photos.

If she'd be here long enough.

Tanner hadn't made a secret about wanting her gone.

Addie had left them after saying that her kitchen was open if either of them got hungry, and that she'd have coffee ready by eight, but they should feel free to start a pot if they got up before that. No one could be more open, more welcoming than her new neighbor.

Now Callie sat on a bed, rethinking her plans. Because of Addie. And because of Tanner.

Glory, still exploring, said, "Behind that big closet is a bathroom with a shower and on the other side is a small kitchenette."

Addie had said there were bottles of water and cans of cola in the narrow, apartment-sized fridge, but Callie didn't want to impose more than she already had.

"It's spotlessly clean," she noted. "Addie must keep it that way, because she didn't know we were coming."

"Or," Glory whispered, "It's kept that way to remove evidence of past murders. If they lured us here for god-awful reasons, you played right into their hands."

With a roll of her eyes, Callie said, "I hope you're joking." When it came to Glory's overblown imagination, she could never be sure. Honestly, she was jumpy enough after the bad vibes in the woods that she didn't need Glory making her more nervous. "Addie said the boys used to hang out here with their friends."

"I'd hardly call your smoking-hot specimen a boy."

"First, he's not *my* specimen." Which was really too bad. If Tanner were just a little more agreeable, he could make her entire transition a far more pleasant experience. "And I'm sure she meant when they were younger." Couldn't deny the "smoking-hot" description. Tanner had it, in spades. The man was downright fantasy-inspiring, so it was no wonder she was already indulging a few fun scenarios.

Like…what if she did a rehab on the house with the intent of selling it, and along the way she got to play with Tanner? So far, he hadn't seemed interested, but he might change his mind if he knew she wouldn't be sticking around.

Glory shrugged. "I guess if Tanner and his mysterious brother used this space, the foosball table and gaming system on the TV would make sense."

Callie grinned. "Plus those beanbag chairs. I haven't seen those in years." And she'd never seen them in her own home. For just a moment she had a flash of Tanner as a teenager, all long limbs and prominent bones, sprawled in one of those chairs with a controller in his hands. Somehow, the image didn't work, because she couldn't quite imagine anyone as intense as him ever being carefree like that…and yet it felt familiar, too, almost like she could see him.

"I'm going to take a shower," Glory announced. "That is, if you don't mind me going first."

"Have at it. I'll clean up after you." She needed a little time to dig out a change of clothes from her suitcase.

"I'm locking the door," Glory warned, "just in case any of our hosts decide to intrude. If you need to go, now's your chance."

"I'm fine." She shooed Glory away, content to continue her speculation on Tanner. He'd said he knew her. She was from this area. Had they once crossed paths?

Getting comfortable on the twin bed, she plugged in her phone so it wouldn't die, and then did a search of him on social media. Nothing. Seriously, he wasn't on *any* social media? That seemed really odd.

Changing tactics, she looked for family-owned tree farms in Hoker, Kentucky. One business popped up: Willis Tree Farm. Curious, she scrolled through the details and some images, confirming that she had the right place. No photos of Tanner though.

He seemed the same age as her, so she looked up the high school. The website showed only current information with a few alumni from the year she'd graduated. Determined, she checked the class that graduated the year before her...

Bingo.

Tanner Patrick, a graduate who had gone on to sponsor at-risk boys and girls in numerous ways, including with summer jobs, outings for the holidays, and in various sports programs.

He helped kids from the school district. He...cared.

Breathing a little faster, Callie went back to social media and instead of searching for accounts under Tanner's name, she went to each different platform and just searched for mentions of him.

There were plenty.

High school kids shared photos of them in groups at his tree farm on what looked like instructional outings. There were a few shots of Tanner with different boys he'd sponsored in wrestling and track. A group photo of a Little League team with *Willis Tree Farm* on their jerseys.

The last was of him presenting a check to a smiling but exhausted woman at a local shelter for abused and neglected youths. He was surrounded by kids, some of them shy, a few openly happy, all of them staring at him with blatant hero worship. Pressing her fingertips to her lips, Callie tried to contain the well of emotion that quickened her breathing.

The most astounding part of all was that Tanner appeared content. He was devastatingly attractive, no matter what, but with that particular expression on his face? The man could melt an icy heart.

Had she known him in high school? No way. If she had, she wouldn't have forgotten him.

A half hour later, after Callie had finished her own shower, she felt marginally revived, but also exhausted. It wasn't that late, but she was ready to turn in, to explore her private thoughts and consider her current plans.

"I don't know if I'll be able to sleep," Glory said as she paced barefoot around the room. "It helps that the door has a lock on it." Glory peered toward the window. "And if we've blundered into something nefarious, we could always climb out the window, slide down the roof and…fall to our deaths."

Callie spread out the quilt and plumped her pillow. "You watch too many horror movies."

"Very true." Glory came closer for a hug. "I'm sorry I've been a pain all day." She smoothed back Callie's hair, then frowned at the scratch on her shoulder. "Does it hurt?"

"It feels better now that it's clean." Bruising showed

around the scratch and it itched, but tomorrow she'd find some ointment for it.

"I know none of this is what you expected. Thorny woods and grumpy men with chain saws and sleeping in an attic."

To Callie, none of it had been that bad. In fact, most of it was enlightening. Plus, she hadn't thought at all about Sutter, or the canceled wedding, or how her parents were blowing up. If nothing else, Tanner was certainly a nice distraction.

"Tomorrow we'll get it all figured out, okay?"

By "figured out," Glory probably assumed they'd head back home, which was something Callie wouldn't do. No reason to explain that tonight, though. "Thanks. I know it's not that late, but I'm going to turn in."

"I'll be quiet, but I might watch something on my phone. Will that bother you?"

At the moment, Callie didn't think anything could bother her more than her preoccupation with Tanner. The more she thought about it, the more familiar he seemed, as if she'd known him forever. Pretty sure she would dream about him tonight—or at least, she hoped to. It'd be much nicer than focusing on the mess of the house she'd been given. "Have at it. Just keep the lights low, okay?"

"Will do." Glory retreated to the other side of the room and got her own bed ready, but instead of reclining, she propped her shoulders against the wall and scrolled on her phone.

Funny, but even after what they'd been through, Glory looked as beautiful as ever. Her pale blond hair hung smooth and sleek to her shoulders. Her skin remained flawless despite their trek through the woods.

Her cousin fretted about looks a lot more than Callie did, but thanks to her background, she had reason. So many reasons.

Yes, she'd griped a lot, but Callie loved her dearly and accepted Glory as her best friend. More often than not, they argued like sisters. And loved each other like sisters, too.

After mostly being raised together, that made sense.

Callie yawned widely, closed her eyes, and turned on her side facing the wall. Her last thought before she fell asleep was that tomorrow she'd get familiar with her ramshackle house, unseen chickens, spooky goats, a horse—and one very cantankerous neighbor who looked far too sexy in worn jeans and sweat.

All in all, not an unpleasant prospect.

TANNER WOKE EVEN earlier than usual and once he did, he couldn't get back to sleep because he knew Callie was in the house. Probably curled up on the same bed he'd used in his early teens. She'd be soft and warm, her silky brown hair spread over the pillow.

What did she wear to bed? T-shirt and panties? Yeah, that was a nice visual.

He stacked his hands behind his head, stared up at the dark ceiling, and pondered Kam's words.

Was this an opportunity?

Never mind what Addie said—she was clearly bi-ased—he had no idea if Callie would be any more in-terested in him now than she'd been years ago. And even if she was, could he keep it casual? Could he get his fill and then send her on her way?

They'd been kids the first time he'd noticed her, maybe fifth grade or so, and from the start he'd been drawn to her. She'd been standing there, fresh and clean, her long hair curled, her clothes pretty, and her personality sweet.

He'd been wearing torn jeans, a stained shirt, and a black eye.

She was from the wealthiest family in town and he was the son of an obnoxious drunk who people reviled—at least they had back then, before Addie had taken him in the year he turned thirteen. But by then, he'd already become invisible at school. Other kids wanted nothing to do with him, teachers didn't know how to handle his sullen attitude, and counselors had gotten exactly nowhere trying to get him to open up.

As if any kid would want to share about his old man, a dirty house, and all the shame...

Before Addie, he'd missed school more than he'd made it in, and half of that time it had been with bruises. But by God, he'd never failed a grade. Was never held back. In every way, he'd been hell-bent on proving himself...*better.*

Better than his dad. Better than his circumstances. Better than anyone expected.

And still, he'd always known he wasn't good enough for Callie McCallahan.

Thinking back on those torturous days still made him tense, so he shoved the memories to the back burner and rolled out of bed.

Avoidance was his go-to when it came to memory lane. No good came of focusing on what he'd left behind. What he'd never had.

Well, except when it came to recognizing kindred spirits. He'd been there, done that, so he knew how neglected or abused kids felt, and sometimes he knew what to say and do to make it a little better. At those times, he'd gladly go through fresh hell if it made a kid's life even a tiny bit easier.

It was barely 5:30 a.m. when he made his way to the kitchen. Barefoot, wearing only jeans, he went to the counter and switched on the coffeemaker. He hadn't yet decided if he wanted to be around when Callie got up, or if it'd be better to already be out of the house. The sun wouldn't rise for another couple of hours, but he could work in the barn.

Blu, who'd been sleeping in his usual spot near the sliding doors in the great room, got to his feet and yawned, and that disturbed Percy the cat. "Sorry, buddy. It's too early to be up and about, isn't it?"

Percy gave him an annoyed look and sauntered off to another part of the house. He was a lazy thing that liked to sleep, eat, and occasionally prowl outside.

Tanner slid open the door for Blu, then followed him out to the enclosed back porch, where he opened another door to give the dog access to the yard. This early, the air was cooler and a fine mist dampened the air, but Tanner stood there patiently, giving Blu the time he needed. He didn't trust the Garmet brothers, with good reason.

One time, and one time only, he'd found them on his property harassing Blu. Given Tanner's reaction, it was doubtful they'd encroach again, but he wouldn't take the chance. He never did, not with those he loved.

A little voice in his head said: *Callie will be living right next door to them.*

His jaw flexed, because so far there wasn't anything he could do about it. He'd warned her. He might warn her again. The rest would be up to her.

Blu sniffed the air, looked around, and finally found a suitable grassy spot to sprinkle. He'd just finished when his ears went up, but it wasn't anything in the yard that interested him. When he trotted past Tanner and into the house, his tail was already wagging.

Wondering why Kam would be up so early, Tanner followed the dog in through the porch and great room, but froze in the kitchen entrance at the sight of Callie on her tiptoes trying to reach a coffee mug on the top shelf of the cabinet. He should have announced himself, but didn't. Should have looked away, but couldn't.

The dog didn't alert her, either. Blu, standing still but attentive, seemed as mesmerized as Tanner.

Her legs were beautifully bare, her plump ass hugged by a pair of white cotton shorts that didn't cover much more than panties would have, and left little to his oh-so-awake imagination. When he finally dragged his gaze off her stellar behind, he saw that her dark T-shirt was a little roomy, and her rumpled hair hung down her back in silky hanks.

Tanner didn't dare breathe. If he did, she just might disappear.

Giving up on the mug, she watched the coffeemaker as if she could hurry it along, then sighed and rested her forearms on the counter—which better presented her backside to his scrutiny.

Blu had better manners than him, because the dog whined, startling her upright, then came forward in greeting.

Her sleepy gaze landed first on the dog, then lifted to Tanner. Blinking at him, her drowsy gaze going quickly over him, she gave a husky, "Good morning."

He still had trouble breathing. "Morning."

Breaking the connection, she knelt down and rubbed the dog's ears. "Morning, Blu. I hope you slept well."

Blu tipped his head, narrowed his eyes in bliss, and swept the floor with his tail.

Callie kissed the top of his head. "You are such a big sweetheart."

When she straightened again, Blu wandered to his water dish, got a few drinks, then padded back to his sleeping spot and collapsed with a quiet huff.

Tanner knew he couldn't keep staring at Callie, no matter how good she looked all morning mussed and sleepy. He unglued his feet and walked in. "Addie keeps her mugs over here. Easier to reach." He opened a lower cabinet to show her the array of colorful mugs with various sayings. "The ones stored high aren't used that often."

"Oh." She accepted the mug he handed her. "Thanks."

How did the woman always look so rosy and fresh, as if she'd just left a warm shower? Even with her sleepy eyes, her skin seemed to glow and she looked...

Fuck. She looked wholesome.

And why the hell was that sexy?

His scrutiny must have bothered her, because she combed her fingers through her hair, saying, "I didn't expect to run into anyone yet."

"Usually you wouldn't. I woke up early."

"Me, too."

His gaze snagged on hers, speculation running through his brain. "Couldn't sleep?"

With a quick smile, she said, "Actually, I slept better than I have in a week."

CHAPTER THREE

AGAIN, TANNER FOUND himself caught in her gaze. Her blue eyes were just that: blue. Nothing special, damn it. A lot of people had blue eyes. Maybe it was the absorption of her gaze, the way she had of looking at a person, like she saw them. Completely.

Except she'd never seen him. *Am I going to let that bother me for the rest of my life?* No, he was not.

If he took one step forward, he'd be touching close. Kissing close. When he looked at her mouth, her lips parted. He heard her take a breath…

The hiss of the coffeepot as it finished broke the spell.

Get it together.

Easier said than done, but by God, he would do it.

He stepped around her to fill both their cups, and then, as if the moment hadn't happened, as if he weren't affected by her, he pulled out a chair for her at the table. Would she accept the silent invitation, or politely refuse and carry the coffee to the room she'd shared with Glory?

After a moment, Callie joined him at the table. "Thank you."

"Cream or sugar?"

"Both. I can get it if you tell me—"

"I got it." He didn't want her up moving around

again, showcasing those bare legs and drawing his attention back to her ass. It was safer for him if she stayed in her seat. He filled the little creamer pitcher that went with the sugar bowl, then set both before her with a spoon.

"These are pretty."

He gave the dishes a negligent glance. "Reggie gave them to Addie a few years back, after she'd spent some time helping him out when he was sick."

After a long hesitation, she asked, "Was he sick often?"

Tanner snorted. "You're taking the man's house, but you never knew him, never checked on him, or you'd know he was usually sick." The accusation was there in his tone, as if he had the right to accuse anyone of anything.

She surprised him by saying, "You're right, I know that."

Silence ticked by where he felt like a jerk and she looked innocently wounded. Hell, she always looked innocent.

Innocently provoking, most of the time.

"Reggie was my father's younger brother. There's a lot of bad blood there." She waited, maybe gauging his interest.

"Happens in families, I guess."

"I guess. I don't have siblings, but I have Glory, and even though we argue sometimes, I'd never cut her out."

That's how he felt about Kam. Over the years, they'd had plenty of disagreements, a few of them physical. Didn't matter. He'd defend Kam always, whether he was right or wrong. When a person knew what it was like to be without family, he valued what family was gifted to him.

Callie added a spoonful of sugar to her coffee, poured in enough cream to make it pale, stirred, sipped, and sighed. "Perfect."

Looking at that now-weak cup of…whatever, Tanner shook his head. "That's no longer coffee, you know. It's just warmed-up cream and sugar."

Even so early in the morning, with her hair uncombed and her clothes wrinkled from sleeping in them, her smile had a powerful effect. "You sound like my mother."

"Well now, is that a compliment or an insult?" He'd never seen her mother, though he'd heard plenty about her. Most in the town had downright revered her parents, the high and mighty McCallahans who deigned to dwell among them, always improving things—usually for their own fame and publicity.

At least that was how Tanner had seen it.

Her smile widened into a grin. "I'd say it's more insult than otherwise. Mother was forever telling me I'd get *thick* if I didn't watch the sugar—so I always added more, just to annoy her. Now I've learned to like it that way."

"So you're spiteful," he said. "Got it."

Callie laughed. "Next you'll be commenting on my overall sugar addiction, and that my smiles are so big they're going to give me wrinkles."

Something else her mother had said? From what he'd heard yesterday between her and Glory, she seemed at odds with her mom still. "Obviously, you never got thick." Callie had a body that would make most guys salivate. "And your smiles are nice."

Ducking her face, she said, "Thank you."

"Since she was wrong, did your mother ever retract her statement?"

"My mother? Ha!" After another sip, she set down the cup and tentatively met his gaze. "My weight has its ups and downs, and believe me, when it's up she notices. Constantly. I'm not what anyone would call a healthy eater, but I get plenty of exercise and I love my veggies, too, so I've never worried much about it—despite all her dire warnings."

He took a drink of his coffee, then decided, *why not*? "Speaking strictly as a guy, you have no reason to worry." He glanced over her body, but managed—with an effort—to keep it brief. She was still so hot that looking at her made him want to touch. And taste.

And ride.

As if she didn't notice his interest, she said, "Thanks," and wrinkled her nose. "My parents have this thing about perfection, and of course it's impossible to measure up."

With only the slightest touch of sarcasm, he said, "Must've been rough." To him, she'd always seemed perfect. Perfectly styled and behaved. Perfectly kind.

With a perfect body and smile.

"It wasn't so bad for me. I got a kick out of failing, I guess because I knew they'd love me anyway." As if chilled, she cupped both hands around her cup. "What about you?"

Tanner wondered if he made her uneasy, if his abrasive attitude got to her, until her attention slipped, repeatedly, to his shoulders, his chest, and his biceps.

The appreciation in her gaze heated his blood and deepened his voice. "What about me?"

"Do you eat healthy stuff?" Her pretty blue eyes coasted over him once more, deliberately this time. "You seem to be extremely…" She cleared her throat and focused on her coffee. "Fit."

A satisfied, somewhat smug smile curled the corners of his mouth. Maybe Kam and Addie were right after all and he should see this as an opportunity.

When he didn't reply right away, mostly because he was weighing carnal possibilities, she cocked a brow. "Tough question?"

"The way you were looking at me, my mind wandered." He folded his arms on the table and gave her a real answer, instead of grouching at her. "I usually eat whatever Addie fixes. Not a hardship, because she's one hell of a cook. Everything from country meals like meat loaf—which we had last night—to fine dining, like roasted rack of lamb or beef Wellington. Plus the desserts are always amazing. She likes to experiment, so Kam and I benefit."

"She sounds like the quintessential mom."

"Yeah, she has a way about her." A way that had broken through his reserves like a gentle battering ram. As a kid, he'd tried his best to keep her at a distance, but she'd worn away his fear with nonstop understanding and an unwavering routine he could count on. Addie had given compassion, but set it around clear boundaries. And good food. Growing up, he'd been forever hungry, but with her he could always eat his fill.

In numerous ways, Addie had made it clear that his safety, health, and happiness mattered most to her, and then she'd done the same with Kam.

"So she's not only a bighearted woman, but a great cook, too."

Tanner nodded. "In all the time I've lived here, she's only missed cooking a few times. She loves the kitchen, though she says she didn't know that about herself until she got us."

"Us?"

Without thinking it through, still caught in the pleasant memory, he replied, "Me first, and then Kam. She said having boys to appreciate her meals opened new possibilities for her."

Consternation tweaked Callie's slim brows as she tried to follow along. "Not to pry, and I swear you can tell me to butt out—"

Realizing what he'd revealed and knowing exactly what she'd ask, he said quietly, "Butt out."

For a beat of three seconds, she stared at him, then her lips formed a smile. Not a real smile this time, not like he'd seen earlier. This smile was polite…and he hated it.

"Sorry." She took another sip of her coffee, back to avoiding his gaze. "I promise not to go there again."

"Shit." Using both hands, Tanner rubbed his face. He hadn't meant to take his contrariness that far. In fact, he was enjoying this. Enjoying her. "I'm the one who's sorry. Hell, I brought it up. It's just…it's a defense thing, to shut people down." He'd learned the hard way that few people had kind motives. "It's not a secret and since you're here"—*hopefully not for long*—"you're bound to hear all about it."

"No, really, it's—"

He touched her hand. Not something he'd intended to do, but it happened. And then he couldn't seem to draw away. He went still. She went silent. Christ, it was as if he'd touched a live wire and they were both reacting to the shock. It burned through his veins.

He considered it a proof of his strength that he was able, by small degrees, to pull back. "Addie took us in." His voice had gone deeper, rougher, but damned if he'd clear his throat.

Callie hadn't yet blinked. Her eyes were fixed on his, unwavering, slightly flared still from his touch. He noticed that her lashes were thick, dark. Fucking beautiful.

To keep her from more apologies and maybe get back those easy smiles that, finally, after years of waiting, were aimed at him, Tanner explained. "She brought me here first, and then Kam, as foster kids."

Soft color washed over her skin and at last, she blinked. "God, I'm sorry. I didn't realize."

Disbelief and a touch of annoyance had him asking, "Are you blushing?" Women didn't blush around him, and the nice ones sure as hell never apologized.

Callie pressed both hands over her heated cheeks. "I feel like a dunce. It never occurred to me."

"What didn't?"

"That you weren't…that Addie wasn't…"

In a weird way, her stammers amused him. Instead of pitying him, or asking more questions, she blushed and stumbled on her words. "You're not a dunce. You just don't remember me." Hard to remember him when she'd never noticed him in the first place. "It was no secret from grade school on that my dad was a drunken prick who didn't much like having a kid in his way."

"I… I never knew. I hadn't heard…"

"No reason you should have. Though we were both in Hoker, you lived in a different world." Protected, insulated from the ugliness of an existence like his. Seeing the horror on her face, he sighed. "And now you're going pale." He wasn't used to anyone, other than Addie and Kam, giving a shit what happened to him. "When I was thirteen, he got himself killed and Addie took me in."

If anything, Callie looked more dismayed. "Wow, that's…"

"My life in a nutshell."

"Not even," she said, totally earnest. "You're so big and capable now, so confident. And you live here, in this wonderful house, working on this wonderful farm."

"In this wonderful neighborhood?" Tanner didn't know what to make of her. "I'm aware of my size, where I live and work. I think it's pretty great, but someone like you—"

Her chin hitched. "Someone like me?"

"A princess."

"I told you not to call me that."

He remembered, which was why he'd said it. "I imagine if you wanted, you could buy three farms like this and twice as many houses."

"My parents, maybe, but I'm not them."

He snorted. "You're sure as hell not me."

"No, I'm myself, Callie McCallahan, a woman with a plan of her own." She veered off that quickly, and then, as if to convince him of his worth, she said, "Don't you see? It sounds like you had a really rough start but you've built this incredible life and you have people who love you."

"Yeah, I wasn't in need of a pep talk."

Face going hot again, she clammed up, but not for long. With a glance around, she admitted, "I could almost be jealous, except that I'm determined to build myself a good life, too."

"Here?" he asked with skepticism.

It said a lot that she dodged the question. "I assume Addie was just what you needed—which makes sense now that I've seen her in action. She has an aura about her that makes everything feel warmer and more comfortable. Less daunting."

Tanner let her off the hook. No reason to belabor the point. She'd play around a day or two at most before she turned tail and went back to her easier way of life. "That sums up Addie." In part, anyway. "She was definitely good for me, *to* me. I didn't make it easy, either."

"Sounds like you'd been through a lot. It's understandable that you'd be defensive, at the very least. I mean, with your father killed and everything."

Defensive, yes. Scared to death, too. And so God-awful afraid to dare hope. "You're curious how my dad died."

"How could I not be? But seriously, if you don't want to talk about it, I completely understand."

"I don't usually, but right now…" Here with her, in the quiet kitchen with their soft voices and Blu's light snore as the only sounds, it didn't seem like a horrible prospect. "Like I said, you're bound to hear gossip anyway."

"Gossip, *still*? That had to be what, fifteen years ago?"

"Sixteen, and some shit sticks around." Especially the vicious rumors that continued to haunt him. "It's ugly, so you may as well hear it from me."

Eyes solemn, she said, "Have to admit, you've got me on the edge of my seat, so thank you for filling in the blanks."

Thanking him for dumping his fucked-up life on

her? She'd think differently soon. "My old man was the type to get stinking drunk and then get behind the wheel of a car. For some sick reason, he always made me go along. The lousiest bars turn a blind eye when someone dumps their kid near a pool table and then runs up a big tab drinking."

"That's what your dad did?"

Her words were so softly spoken, yet so filled with dread, he barely heard her.

"That last time, he managed to piss off the wrong people. He dragged me out of there in a hurry. He was so drunk that he was all over the road, crossing the line, nearly passing out a few times—then we got hit from behind and the car spun hard. When Dad got it straightened out, he sped home, cursing a blue streak all the way. At the house, he shoved me through the door and into a closet."

Remembered pain, confusion, and fear, all sank into his bones, but he'd long since learned to shake it off, refusing to let himself dwell there. Much.

"I didn't realize I had a broken arm until then. I guess it happened when the car was spinning. Must've hit something."

Callie gave a soft gasp.

"Anyway, he locked the closet and I couldn't get out." They hadn't eaten yet, and he had to use the bathroom, but he knew better than to make any noise. Complaints had always enraged his dad more. "The people who rear-ended us? Guess they had followed him home be-cause I heard shouting, accusations, and then gunshots."

Her hand covered her mouth.

Right. He needed to wrap it up. "Long story a little shorter, Dad was dead, and I was locked in."

Her eyes went huge, filled with sympathy and what looked suspiciously like a touch of anger. He couldn't be sure because he'd never seen that particular expression on her face. Even yesterday, when he'd given her such a hard time, she hadn't looked quite so stormy.

Then her hand slowly left her mouth and curled into a fist. "You're sitting here now, so I know you got through it, but *how*?"

Definitely anger. On his behalf? Should he tell her the accusations from some people? Many people? Nah. Why bother? If she stayed around long, she'd get an earful.

"I waited for what felt like forever, until I couldn't wait anymore." The pain in his arm had grown severe, and he'd had to relieve himself in the closet, soiling the corner and the boxes stacked there. Maneuvering had been difficult, but he'd finally managed. "I sat on a clean spot on the floor and managed to brace my good arm and shoulder against the back wall. I used the leverage of my legs to kick the door until the frame split and it opened."

This time Callie reached out, covering his hand with her own, squeezing as if to share her meager strength. "You must have been a very strong boy, physically and emotionally, to manage that."

She didn't know him and had no reason to care. Her reaction confused the hell out of him, making him want to retreat, except he'd long ago decided he was done retreating. Now if someone insulted him, he confronted them. When they whispered behind his back, he turned around and stared them down.

If they tried to take from him, or they insulted Addie

or Kam, they opened the floodgates of hell and had to deal with the consequences.

One good thing about Callie's touch, it brought him back around, helping him to focus again. It was still that way. Talking about his past, about the shit his dad had done... It would always plague him. He knew it. He worried that he was broken in ways that time wouldn't fix. For that, he hated the man who had fathered him. Never, not once, had he visited his gravesite, and if he ever did it would be to spit on the ground.

"Tanner?" she asked gently, the soft tips of her fingers drifting over his rough knuckles. "What did you do once you were out? You were so young and had to be so scared, and with a broken bone..."

The way she said it, it did sound bad—and at the time, yeah, it was terrifying. He remembered feeling both free, but also utterly lost, so lost that the pain had receded behind other worries.

It was past time to put an end to the story. He hadn't meant to share so many details anyway. "I left the house and started walking. Addie found me on her way home from a late shift and the rest is history." Talk about an abbreviated ending. "I should add that she worked her tail off to get me and then to keep me."

"What an absolutely amazing woman," Callie whispered with awe. "I'm so thankful she's the one who found you that night."

He gave one quick nod because he was damn grateful, too. Now, being older and wiser, he knew that night could have gone in a very different direction. "Addie is a miracle worker, an angel, and a mother down to her soul, all wrapped up in strength and wisdom."

Callie slipped her hand under his, gave his fingers a

squeeze and then retreated. "I think I sensed all that. A tiny bit of it, at least." She sipped more coffee, turned the cup a few times and traced a finger around the rim before saying, "Full disclosure, I walked into Reggie's house and seriously wanted to groan. But Glory was there, already stressing and I knew you were watching, waiting for a single weakness."

The teasing way she said it took the sting out of the words, yet he still felt like a dick. "Not entirely accurate. True, I'd rather you sell to me. Make it easier on both of us, you know?" It was all part of his big plan, a bone-deep need he had to put some good into the world, to give back even a small part of what Addie had given to him. "But while you're coming to the conclusion that you're not cut out for country life, I wouldn't want to see you miserable."

"Good, because I'm not yet certain what I want to do."

Conflicting emotions kept Tanner still. "So you're not planning to stay?" Why the hell did that make his heart sink?

"I wasn't, not until you seemed so set on me going." She gave him a crooked smile. "Like the sugar thing, I tend to dig in and get stubborn when I feel challenged."

Well, damn. Fighting a grin, he asked, "How about if I retract all my initial complaints?"

"Too late. They're already out there and I'm already thinking…things."

Parts of his body took notice of how she said that and what it might imply.

"After Addie offered to go back with me today, I'm hoping she can make some suggestions on a cleaning crew I can hire and a junk hauler to remove a lot of ruined stuff. I'd like to get a sense of what I'm dealing with and I can't until I can see past the trash and filth."

Funny, but the idea of her sticking around wasn't as bad as he'd first thought. "In the end, you'll see. The house needs more work than it's worth and keeping up with the land is a lot for one person."

Grinning, she leaned in to say, "Plus chickens I haven't yet met, and goats that make the creepiest sounds ever."

"That, too."

Her grin settled into a sweet smile. "I might surprise you."

She already had. "Every time I've ever seen you, you're smiling."

"Well…" She leaned closer still, as if to confide in him. "Don't tell anyone, but that's sort of my defense mechanism. I smile when I'm mad or scared. When I'm feeling a little lost or worried. When I'm sad, or when I'm ready to cry. A big smile not only confuses people, but it makes me feel better. And everyone looks prettier smiling, you know?"

He didn't want to think of her crying, but he imagined she'd be pretty even then. At least to him. "How is it you inherited Reggie's house?"

Before she answered, she stood and asked, "Mind if I get more coffee?"

"Help yourself."

She refilled her cup, leaving room for more cream, and offered to refill his, too. Once that was done, she settled back into her seat, and sighed. "Like I said, Reggie was Dad's brother and from what I was told, he was always in trouble. Drunk driving, petty theft, fighting—things that had him in and out of jail. Always needing money. At some point my mother put her foot down and refused to have any more association with him. Maybe Dad was glad for the excuse because he cut ties with Reggie."

"Sounds like most families I've seen—imperfect in one way or another."

"I guess, but I still felt bad for Reggie. Whenever he was around, he was always funny. He'd tell me jokes that my mother deemed improper."

"Yeah, I can imagine. When I was young he told me a few, too. Difference is, Addie laughed with us."

"Ha! I can imagine that. She's much warmer and down to earth than my mother."

Thank God. Taking in two troubled boys definitely required someone earthy.

"I snuck and visited Reggie a few times. When I graduated high school, he sent me a gift card to a fast food restaurant." The memory had her grinning. "I met him there and we had lunch together using the gift card. Same when I graduated college. I told him he shouldn't spend his money on me, but he said he'd 'scored big' and planned to use it all on gift cards as an excuse to visit me."

"Reggie was feast or famine, but his idea of scoring big could have been a hundred bucks or five thousand. He didn't value money the same way other people do." And that included Tanner. He'd been poor, hungry, and dirty, and he knew the importance of every dime.

"He continued to send gift cards, but...then my life got busy. I called him a few times, and we talked about getting together." Her voice lowered. "We never quite got around to it."

"Hey, life happens."

With a shake of her head, she softly admitted, "I didn't even see my parents that often. Honestly, I didn't think about Reggie. How awful is that?"

"I'm sure Reggie understood."

"No, you said he was sick. He should have had some family around him. Even if it was only a weekly visit, I should have made the time."

Tanner didn't want her starting her day with guilt, so he might as well give her some truths. "The last few years, Reggie drank a lot. His liver was completely shot. The doctors told him if he didn't stop drinking he'd die, and still he drank. Couple of times there it got so bad he'd spend a week in the ICU."

Stricken, Callie stared at him. "I didn't know that."

"Wouldn't have mattered. He'd get out of the hospital, last a few days, sometimes even a few weeks, then he'd get back to it. The man had a bad drinking problem and there's not much you could have done for him. Believe me, Addie tried. We all did."

New concern darkened Callie's eyes. "That had to be especially hard for you."

"Because of my dad? You'd think so, right? But Reggie was an all-around nice guy and a funny drunk. He didn't have a mean bone in his body. The worst he did was fall asleep with the chickens." Remembering the day he'd found him there, passed out near the coop, Tanner shook his head. "Drunk or sober, he was generous and a good neighbor. But toward the end there, his liver just stopped working." Reggie had been a mess, suffering and sorry, and he'd given up.

In a way, Tanner was glad Callie hadn't witnessed him like that. "I'm sure your uncle wanted you to hold on to the better memories of him."

Unconvinced, she rubbed her forehead. "I still feel terrible about it, especially since I didn't even know he'd died until Dad told me after he was notified that Reggie named me in his will. He left me his house, a small bit of cash, and everything on his property."

"I don't expect it'll be much. He has an old Buick that runs but is a little noisy. If you decide to sell it, I know a kid who could really use a reliable car." He moved right on from that before she could ask for specifics. He didn't want her to draw a parallel to his own miserable childhood pre-Addie. "Reggie's tractor is in decent shape."

Without much inflection, she asked, "Tractor?"

"To cut the land that's cleared. You could use a riding mower, but it'd take a lot longer. Reggie used the tractor for his garden, too."

"Garden?"

Tanner bit back a smug smile. Those one-word questions showed a lot of uncertainty. He'd give her a week, tops, and she'd be throwing in the towel. "Lots of hauling to do on acreage. There's always a downed tree or two after every storm. We have storms in the forecast right now, you know. Tornadoes sometimes in the spring. If a tree limb hits your house, you'll have shingle repairs—maybe roof repairs. We once had a big tree branch take out a window. Other chores are cleanup for the animals, clearing out the bugs all spring and summer, and you have to watch for critters. Raccoons especially. They're hateful."

After all that, Callie appeared shell-shocked, but she merely sipped her coffee, likely giving herself a second to absorb everything he'd thrown at her.

His conscience was nudging him at that point, even

though running her off would be easier on them both in the long run. He wanted to distract her, maybe get her focus back on him, which might explain why he said, "I heard you in the woods."

"Yesterday, you mean?"

Nodding, he clarified, "While you were talking to your cousin about breaking things off with some asshole named Sutter."

Appalled, she slumped back in her seat. She wasn't overwhelmed now. Nope. She looked embarrassed and annoyed, but only for a moment.

Then she smiled, and damn, it looked mean.

He rubbed a hand over his whiskers, heard the rasp, and wondered if he should excuse himself to shower and shave. He even glanced at the doorway.

Callie asked, "Am I holding you up?"

Had she read his mind? If so, it perversely made him determined to stay. No way would he be the first to retreat. "How could you, when I came to the kitchen for coffee?"

"Not for coffee *with me*, though." She cradled the mug between her hands as she eyed him. "You can run along, you know. I don't mind."

"I can do any damn thing I want. I live here," he reminded her. She was the interloper—an interloper he'd confided in for some damned reason. Now there was an excuse he could dig into. "I told you about me. Turnabout seems fair, so what's with this Sutter jerk?"

"You heard enough to whet your appetite, is that it?"

She really was irked. He could see it on her face, hear it in her deliberately soft tone. Knowing how it felt to be cornered, he relented, but only a little. "I didn't mean to listen in, but voices carry around here. You might want to remember that."

Since he'd turned more congenial, her annoyance eased up, too. "Thinking about what parts you might have heard is pretty embarrassing."

"Something about his dick in someone else's hand."

She sputtered at how he just threw that out there. Quickly, she set down her coffee and accepted the napkin Tanner offered her across the table.

Deadpan, he said, "Guess your coffee went down wrong."

"Actually, your audacity choked me." Her frown faded into a beautiful smile—the kind he associated with her. "So you heard all about Sutter, did you?"

"Afraid so." That and a lot more. But he wouldn't ask her about the pressure, and whatever harebrained plan her family had cooked up for her.

Like a warning, she said, "Just don't think I'm heartbroken, okay?"

"Wouldn't dream of it." But was she?

"When I busted him, honestly, it was a relief."

"Is that so?" He wouldn't pry, but he'd listen to anything she wanted to share.

"We're going to be neighbors—"

"For the time being, anyway."

She made a face at him for his continued insistence.

At this point, he did it more to rile her, and remind himself that it was temporary, than for any other reason.

"For the time being," she conceded. Then she added, "And possibly longer, so it wouldn't be right for me to hold a grudge over you listening in on a private conversation."

"You practically blasted the news on a megaphone."

"Plus," she said, emphasizing the word. "Addie and Kam have been so welcoming. And you've tolerated me. Sort of."

Gesturing at the table and shared coffees, he said, "For me, this is about as welcoming as it gets."

With a sly smile, she drawled, "Well, that's a pity." The second she said it, her eyes went round and she clamped her mouth shut.

Flirting? Yeah, pretty sure that counted. How *welcoming* did she want him to be? He was about to ask, but she rushed into explanations about her bastard ex before he could formulate the question.

"Sutter and I had this idiotic arrangement and it was supposed to be a good way for two powerhouse families to unite. The eldest son of a family with an upscale chain of vacation accommodations, the only daughter from a family specializing in luxury travel, boom, instant harmony, specialized promotion, lucrative for all concerned. When he pitched the idea to me, or to my whole family, actually—"

"Is that a joke?"

"Nope. During dinner with my folks and Glory, he threw out the scenario like a business plan that started with us getting married."

Tanner gave a low whistle. He'd never understand rich people. Pretty sure he didn't want to. "Your folks should have told him to take a hike."

"Are you kidding? They were ecstatic and toasting our impending nuptials before I could even process what had happened."

"Then *you* should have told him to take a hike."

"For real," she readily agreed. "But it took me by surprise, and my parents were so psyched by the idea, going on and on about such a beneficial alliance and how lucky I was. I was already dating him, I worked with his family. Our families meshed and got along, and everyone seemed to assume we were headed for marriage anyway. I didn't despise him or anything. I mean, he was nice enough, affluent, well connected and educated, and we had a decent time whenever we went out together."

It annoyed Tanner that she didn't mention love. Didn't even hint at it. "Sounds like a really hot romance."

Making a face, she admitted, "Tepid at best, but that had been all my relationships. At this point, I'm not sure 'hot' actually exists, at least it never has for me."

CHAPTER FOUR

OH, HOW TANNER would like to show her a hot romance. He could singe her pretty little ears with all the scorching things he'd like to do with her, but since she was talking he didn't want to derail her.

"The idea of marrying him wasn't awful," she said. "And it would have been convenient, not just for our families, but for me, too."

"Spending the rest of your life with someone best described as *convenient* doesn't sound all that great to me."

"Yeah, now I agree. At first, though, it was kind of fun, with a lot of fanfare. Parties to announce the engagement. Publicity showcasing the coalition of families and businesses. Gifts. Invitations." She sighed. "And my parents were happy. Over-the-moon excited, even. I guess I'm shallow enough that, at least for a little while, it seemed like enough."

"I'm not sure that makes you shallow." It sounded to him like the two families had coerced her cooperation. "More like overwhelmed and caught up in the moment."

"Oh, if only it had been a mere moment."

She drank more coffee, and Tanner held silent, giving her time to think, to decide how much she wanted to share.

When her gaze met his again, she winced. "See, actually it was *months*. That's how long I let it go on. Everyone around me was so thrilled and making important plans, that even though I knew it wasn't right, I went along. I didn't muster up the guts to end it until Sutter gave me a good excuse by getting busy with someone else. Even then, I was in shock until a stranger stepped in."

A stranger? "How'd that play out, exactly?"

"We were at an upscale fundraiser. Sutter was late, but I didn't mind." She lifted her shoulders. "Weird, right? Until someone asked about him, I hadn't been missing him at all, wasn't really worried about where he might be or if he'd been in an accident. It dawned on me that I had more fun without him." Her gaze went to Tanner's shoulders, then his throat, before she looked away. "When Sutter was around, he wanted to hold my hand and kiss me, and everyone would look at us."

"Pretty sure no guy would be around you without wanting to touch you."

Her brows inched up, but she didn't ask for clarification. "With Sutter, it always made me feel like a fraud." She went silent again, her body tensed, then she said in a quiet voice, "He was my fiancé, and I preferred for him to leave me alone. I tried to act like I enjoyed his attention, even when I didn't."

"Why?"

"Keeping up appearances?" She shook her head. "It was expected of me, but I felt bogged down by it all, like I needed a month-long vacation with nothing to do except sit in bed and read, eat ice cream, and sleep."

Her parents should never have put her in that position. "Everyone feels like that sometimes."

"Probably, but it hit me like a ton of bricks that I was preparing to marry a man for all the wrong reasons."

"Must have been an eye-opener."

Her short laugh lacked humor. "For sure, especially once I excused myself to step outside where it was quiet so I could call Sutter. It was chilly, so I stopped by the coat closet. The clerk wasn't there but I heard some noises, and then I recognized Sutter's voice so I opened the door—and bam. There he was, pinned up against the wall with a woman I didn't know. Her hand was in his pants, doing… *Things*." She started to gesture, but changed her mind. "He looked…" Color rose up from her neck to her cheeks and all the way to her forehead. "Let's just say it was shocking."

"I can imagine."

"That's the thing, though." She met his gaze with chagrin. "I couldn't. I'd never seen him like that." After a slight hesitation, she said, "Not with me."

Tanner didn't stop to measure his words or to think how telling they might be. "Then he's a fucking fool who didn't deserve you."

Half smiling, she said, "I was the bigger fool. It was horribly awkward to catch him like that. Not heart-breaking or devastating. Just super-humiliating." Her gaze dipped to his mouth, lingered a moment, then moved back to his eyes. "Isn't that odd?"

Not to him. He thought it showed her vulnerability, and it made him want to gather her close—as if she needed his protection, which she most definitely did not. "He embarrassed you and someone should have broken his nose." Tanner would like to do that for her. How dare some jerk treat her like that? "You'd have to be a saint not to be embarrassed to some degree."

Lips twisting, she muttered, "Believe me, I'm far, far from sainthood."

Not quite believing her, he said, "Sucks being human sometimes, feeling things we'd rather not."

Her insightful gaze took his measure, but she didn't put him on the spot. "Very true."

"So what did you do?"

"At first, nothing. I knew my family was going to be disappointed in me. And I was disappointed in myself for just…standing there." With a wince, she added, "Taking it in."

When she looked at his mouth again, Tanner felt a measure of heat building inside. "Until?"

"Until the coat clerk returned and saw what was happening. Now that lady was all action. I remember her lightly touching my arm and asking, 'What do you want to do, honey?' in such a measured tone, almost motherly. I could almost imagine Addie being like that."

More likely Addie would have had some choice words for the guy and his friend. She could let loose like no one else when she witnessed injustice.

Impatient for the part where Callie had finally put Sutter in his place, Tanner said, "And then?"

"The way she asked it made it seem like I had endless choices—and maybe I did." She fiddled with her hair a moment. "I'd ridden there with my parents, and I was supposed to go home with Sutter."

Brows gathering in a frown, Tanner hoped she'd found a solution.

"I wanted to walk out, but we were downtown at night, and it was chilly. Then the woman put a key fob in my hand and curled my fingers around it. She whispered that Sutter had left it in his coat pocket. She was going to ask him if he'd meant to, until she saw what I saw."

"She wanted you to take his car?" The idea had him grinning. "Genius plan."

"I thought so, too. I thanked her, without whispering, and turned to go, but then Sutter realized he wasn't alone anymore. Even with him calling out to me, I kept walking."

"Felt good, didn't it?"

She returned his grin. "It sure did. I'd only gone about ten feet when suddenly it occurred to me that it was the perfect opportunity to end things. All of it. The engagement, the wedding, the future plans."

"The farce?" Enthralled with the story, Tanner waited.

She nodded. "Sutter caught my arm, already apologizing and trying to explain."

"I hope you told him to fuck off."

"My mother would expire if I used that type of language." With an impish smile, she said, "I took off his ring and politely gave it to him with my best smile."

Tanner sat forward. "No way. Tell me you said *something.*"

In lofty tones, her nose elevated, she recited, "Deal's off. You can break the news to everyone. I'm leaving and don't you dare contact me."

That sounded like a very Callie-esque reaction. "Good for you."

Peeking at Tanner, she grinned. "Know what made it even better? The woman who'd given me his fob applauded as I went out the door."

He laughed. "I'm glad she was there."

"You have no idea. She's my hero." Again, her gaze dipped over Tanner, this time to his biceps, down to his forearms, and then his hands. Idly, as if she'd lost interest in the story, Callie said, "He chased me out of there, holding his pants up with one hand, talking a mile a minute. Apologizing and explaining. It was easy to ignore him and keep walking until I reached his car. Every single step I took felt more like freedom. Like I'd just come out of a cave."

Damn, Tanner was proud of her, whether that made sense or not. He offered her a fist bump.

Hesitantly, she tapped her small fist to his. "You're the only person I've told who appreciates the entire thing as much as I do."

"I think it's awesome." Especially the part about her still being single. "No one else has the right to tell you how to live your life."

"Maybe." Subdued, she looked down at her coffee. "But I'm nearing thirty and Sutter's proposition was the only near-proposal I've ever gotten."

"So?" Did she want marriage bad enough to accept an arrangement made by her parents? Another thought occurred to him, drawing his brows together. "Were there other guys you had hoped to marry?"

"Not really." She pursed her mouth, then said more forcefully, "Definitely not. The thing is, most of my friends have gotten married and they all seem so happy. Plus, shallow as it makes me, I wanted the fancy wedding with the beautiful white gown, the ceremony with flowers everywhere, followed by the awesome honeymoon."

Yeah, he didn't want to hear about a dreamy honeymoon for the woman he'd fantasized about most of his life. Determined to let her talk, he blocked that thought. "Doesn't sound to me like the honeymoon would have been all that awesome."

Pretending affront, she said, "Hey. The destination

was great. A really private stay in Costa Rica. Two weeks. Meals delivered…"

He locked his teeth.

"I had so much planned to do there."

"I thought honeymoons were spent in bed."

Making another face, she said, "Yeah, that was the one drawback."

Thankfully, the topic took a different turn, from honeymoon to house goods.

"I loved picking out china and silverware, candlesticks, colorful glass bowls." Her cheeks glowed as she discussed her wish list. "I'd chosen a *gorgeous* bedding set."

"What color?"

"Several colors, actually. White linen quilted with large, watercolor flowers. Stunning. Like a wash of spring for the bed."

"You're a romantic."

"I am, but that's not a bad thing, really. Except that I didn't think about sharing the bed forever with Sutter. I just wanted all this amazing stuff for my imaginary house and my imaginary life."

And then Sutter had gotten himself fondled in a coat closet. What a miserable jerk.

Tempering her smile, Callie said, "It sounds really ridiculous, I know, but at the time, I had myself convinced that it'd all be fine."

He'd thought similar things a few times—not the china and bedding, but a forever home with the right person. "It's not ridiculous to plan a future. You were excited about that part of it, right?"

"Yes." Out of the blue, she said, "I want kids."

If she expected him to laugh or act surprised, he'd disappoint her. "How many?"

Proving she'd given it some thought, she said, "At least two, but I wouldn't mind three. Before Glory came to live with us, I was an only child and it sucked."

He nodded his understanding. "Before I came to live with Addie, I was the only kid." And glad of it. He wouldn't have wished that hell on a sibling, no matter how nice the company might've been.

"Then Addie gave you Kam," she said softly.

"He wasn't exactly a gift."

She laughed. "No, I didn't mean it like that."

"I know." He still remembered meeting Kam, feeling a lot of shit all at once. Threatened, because he'd finally found his place and here was this other punk joining in. Hopeful, because hey, Kam was younger but close enough in age to carry on a conversation, to play ball, to maybe…rely on him. "Kam was a major pain when he first joined our family." There'd been times Tanner had heard him crying at night. Addie would hear too, and she'd spend extra time with Kam, even when he'd curse her and swear that he hated her. "He was this rotten little toughie, always wanting to fight."

"Uh-oh. Awkward."

"Yeah, especially since I'm three years older. Not a big deal now, but there's a lot of difference in size and strength between a boy who's thirteen and one who's sixteen."

"Did you two fight?"

"Sure. Occasionally." That had him smiling again. "There were times Kam didn't give me a choice. He'd just attack and I had to defend myself. But man, Addie would throw a fit. We'd get lectured about brothers and what that meant, and how we should rely on each other.

Guess it finally sank in, because Kam let up, I cut him some slack, and now…he's my brother, period."

A suspicious sheen made Callie's eyes extra bright. "I'm so glad."

Now that Tanner had Addie and Kam as his family, he knew he'd die for either one of them. They were that important to him.

"You also have Blu. I always wanted a dog."

"Blu is my second dog. Addie had a hound when I moved in, and man, I loved that old dog. He was my instant buddy, insisting on sleeping in my bed with me, following me everywhere." Tanner remembered feeling safer with that dog than he had with any human at that point. The dog had helped to transition him into Addie's home, and for that, he'd always have a place in Tanner's heart. "He lived to a ripe old age and passed peacefully at home. At first, I didn't want another dog, but then I found Blu."

"Found him?"

Yeah, that was another shitty story. He was nothing but depressing today. "Never mind. Long story."

"Tell me," she urged.

He got up to refill their coffees yet again. At this rate, he'd be riding a caffeine high all morning. "If we're going to keep talking, I need to make a new pot."

She stood too. "I'll make it. You share how you got Blu."

Leaning against the counter, Tanner watched her. Maybe because he'd always seen her as a pampered princess, he hadn't expected her to be so comfortable in the kitchen. "Not sure I should. It's a downer."

"But it ended well, right? Blu is here, a part of things, and that's a happy story."

Yeah, she was right. Maybe he should rethink how he looked at things. "Fine, but this time I'm keeping it short."

"You aren't enjoying my company?" she asked, just to needle him, he was sure.

"I've talked more this morning than I have all month."

She flashed him a smile before pouring the water into the maker. "Me, too. Everyone is so biased about everything that I can't talk with them."

Remembering how Glory had pressured her, he said, "They have their own agendas."

"Exactly. But you don't know me, and you don't even like me." With the preparations done, she reclaimed her seat. "So yours is a fresh take on things." She nodded at his chair. "Come on, neighbor. While the coffee is perking, come spill the beans."

Funny, but he was enjoying himself. Like she said, the stories sounded different with someone hearing them for the first time. Less traumatic, more manageable, because the happy ending was guaranteed. "All right." He didn't correct her on her assumption that he didn't like her. Truth was, he liked her fine. A little more than fine, and that wasn't a good thing. Keeping her slotted as a fantasy was easier than knowing her as a woman with a sense of humor, her own disappointments, and dreams that mirrored his own—minus Costa Rica. He had no real interest in leaving Kentucky.

"Stop stalling."

From his seat at the table, Tanner glanced over his shoulder to where Blu rested peacefully, his paws occasionally jerking as he went through a dream chase with some furry foe. When he turned back to Callie, she was watching him intently, her gaze soft and interested.

In him or Blu's history?

She tapped her fingers on the table. "Still waiting."

"So on top of being a romantic—"

"And an interloper."

"—you're impatient. Got it."

"Also a neighbor." Her smile taunted as she not-so-patiently gestured for him to get on with it.

How many times in the past hour had she made him grin? Too many, for sure. "Blu was a little guy—just a pup still—and some asshole had him in a filthy outdoor kennel that was way too small. He could barely turn around. No water. I heard him barking and I heard some dude threatening him."

"That happened around here?"

"A mile or so from the main intersection before you turn down this road." Because old habits die hard, he added, "You're not in some ritzy neighborhood."

"Didn't say I was. I grew up here, remember."

He snorted. "Not *here*. You were on the rich side of town."

Her eyes narrowed again. "Being rich is about more than money. From everything you've told me, and having met Addie, I'd say you're doing pretty damn well."

Touché. "Anyway, I saw this old guy storming out to the kennel with a belt." It had struck Tanner like a shock wave what that fucker would do. He knew, because he'd been at the receiving end of a belt too many times himself. "The dog was whining, the guy cursing…" Yeah, this was another memory he hated to relive, except that he'd ended up with Blu. "I intervened."

"Good for you," she said with deep satisfaction. "Please tell me you pulverized him."

God, it had been tempting. Really making it short,

he summarized with, "Let's just say I took the belt from the guy, and I took Blu."

She bit her lip. "Were there repercussions for that?"

"Yeah, there were. He followed me here, and man, Addie was a sight to see. I was holding a traumatized pup, but Addie refused to take him so that I could handle things."

"Hmm. She probably knew how you'd handle it."

"I'd have thrown his sorry ass off the property." It was bad enough how he'd treated the dog, but then to disrespect Addie, too? "I put the dog in the bathroom and got between Addie and the abusive asshole, but she's not one to stay behind a man." He rubbed his mouth, remembering that day only too well. Now he was more amused by Addie's temper than anything else. "To add to the confusion, the cops showed up."

There'd been other times, as a kid, when the cops had come to Addie's house because someone had blamed him for something. It had always scared him spitless, leaving him frantic to shore up his courage while worrying that they'd arrest him, that they'd take him away from the first good place he'd ever had.

But as a man, he'd been more concerned for Addie and Blu.

"She can be a whirlwind and she gave the cops an earful before they even had a chance to say hello."

"Did the cops arrest the man?"

Huh. Funny that Callie made that assumption. For him, still, when cops were involved, his expectations were of dire consequences, not assistance. Callie, with her blessed life, had a different outlook—and he was glad. "Matter of fact, they did. He'd been raging at Addie, kicking at the door, threatening me, and the abuse was visible on Blu. The miserable fuck got hit with a big fine and jail time, plus he had to pay for Blu's vet bills. Best of all, he was forbidden from getting any more pets."

"Perfect." Callie quietly applauded. "You're a real-life hero, and to think I'm your neighbor."

"Temporary neighbor." Damn, that denial was fast becoming a habit. To get her back to talking about herself, Tanner asked, "So your big dream wedding was ruined. Do you have regrets?"

"Only that I won't get the kids, family vacations, or special holidays that I was envisioning." Wrinkling her nose again, she said, "It sounds self-indulgent to complain, since I never had to do without, but I wanted to do things *my* way, you know? Like a real Christmas tree, instead of fake. A mudroom off the laundry room because *my* kids would be allowed to play in the dirt, and I'd need a place to clean the dog's paws when I walked him in the rain."

He liked her vision. A lot. "I think it sounds nice, not indulgent." He couldn't stop himself from saying, "We sell Christmas trees here, so we've always had real. Well, always once I was with Addie." Before that, the only Christmas décor he'd seen was around town. "They smell great and we have fun decorating them."

A wistful expression softened her eyes. "See, that. That's what I wanted and it's the reason I was willing to get married."

"News flash, darlin', you don't need to get married to have a dog or a real Christmas tree."

"Right?" Excited, she propped her elbows on the table and glanced from side to side, as if to ensure they were still alone.

He, of course, was extremely aware of the fact that no one else was around.

"I haven't told Glory this yet, but I went ahead and bought the china and silverware." She grinned. "And the bedding and towels. All the stuff I'd put on my wedding registry."

"For yourself?"

"Why not? I splurged and got my favorites of the stuff I'd picked out for my house. It's in storage right now, but if I settle here—"

When he opened his mouth, she cut him off.

"—or wherever, really, I'll use it. I wanted it and I figured I didn't need a guy to get it."

Enjoying this private glimpse of her character, Tanner gave her a mock frown and teasingly asked, "Guess you're one of those empowered women?"

"Heck yes, I am." After lifting her coffee mug in his direction, she tipped it up and finished it off.

The way she set the mug aside, with so much finality, he knew their quiet interlude had come to an end. Just as well. He'd already shared far too much.

"I should get a move on," she said.

"You just made more coffee."

"For Addie and Kam, since I drank so much of the first pot. I've got a huge day ahead of me with a lot to accomplish."

Reluctant for it to end, Tanner didn't appreciate the reminder that they were, in fact, at odds.

They both started to stand when Addie stepped into the kitchen.

Wearing her well-worn pink robe and slippers, she eyed them both with curiosity. "Good morning." She bent to kiss Tanner's cheek, then looked at Callie, frowned, and turned back to Tanner. "Didn't you offer her a cookie?"

"Didn't think of it," he murmured.

Kam walked in wearing only unsnapped jeans, and said around a yawn, "No doubt you had other things on your mind." He went straight to the counter, pulled a lid off a canister, and offered it to Callie. "Chocolate chip and walnuts. Fair warning, they're addictive."

Doing her best not to look at Kam's body—and largely failing—Callie said, "Mmm, thank you. I'm allergic to walnuts, so just one for me."

"Will you get sick?" Kam asked.

She shook her head. "I'm good at nibbling around nuts."

Silence stretched out with Tanner and Kam both choking.

Addie glared at them in warning. Despite how mean her glares could be, Kam broke first, snickering, trying to cover it with a cough, then outright laughing.

Once he did, Tanner lost it, too.

Even Addie ended up chuckling.

Callie's innocent confusion only made it funnier.

It wasn't even 7:00 a.m. yet, and already he'd had one hell of a good day. In fact, it'd probably go into his top ten best days, and it was all because of his new neighbor.

SEEING THE HOUSE in the daylight, it was even more disheartening. The upside was that the kitchen appliances had been updated five years ago and they were in good running order, but the cabinets and flooring could only be called vintage if someone felt really generous. Addie promised her that once it was cleaned, it'd look much better.

The bathroom, at least, was a pleasant surprise. Yes, it definitely needed a good scrubbing, from the floors to the walls and ceiling, and everything in between. However, a year or so ago Reggie had bought a roomy spa tub. Next to it, he'd situated a small table that still held an ashtray and an empty beer can, but all the tile in the room was neutral, so workable with any color scheme. A nice-sized window, covered with a privacy blind, brightened the room and, when uncovered, gave a view of the backyard.

There were two bedrooms, but one he had used for storage. She'd eventually have to go through everything in there. The other, as Glory had pointed out, had unpleasant smells and a mattress so worn, no way would it be comfortable. Already she was considering sleeping in her car, after she took the time this evening to get online and order some new things.

Despite all that, Callie was determined to make this work, to prove that she had the willpower and independence to make the house a home.

Whether it'd be a permanent home or not, she hadn't yet decided.

She did take the time to document her progress by recording before and after videos on her phone.

Callie had been so preoccupied with the house—and thinking about Tanner—that the entire morning and most of the afternoon passed before she finally realized what had amused her neighbors so much. Her face got hot as she recalled her "nibbling around nuts" comment, but she also laughed. Sometimes she could be such a dork. In her defense, Sutter would have missed the implication, too.

And he would keel over if he could see her now.

Sweaty, her clothes dirty, flyaway hairs escaping her hasty topknot. She was a wreck and didn't care.

She'd spent the day tackling chores large and small, inside and out, working harder than she ever had in her life, and all the while she'd replayed her conversation with Tanner, start to finish, over and over again.

What a fascinating person he was.

What a tough childhood he'd had.

What an impressive man he'd become.

A man she'd really like to get to know. And touch. And... Enjoy.

She had a feeling he'd be *so enjoyable.* The intensity of his gaze told her so. The set of his sensual mouth told her so.

And his body. *Mmm.* He was that yummy. Keeping her attention on his face hadn't been easy, not with his bare chest right there taunting her. A sparse, enticing amount of chest hair decorated pronounced pecs and when he crossed his arms, usually in irritation or challenge, biceps flexed and bunched in a display of pure masculine perfection. Her fingers had tingled with the need to explore that body hair, to test the firmness of all those delicious muscles, to coast over his hot skin. His body was so preoccupying, she'd barely tasted her coffee.

Who had a body like that? No one that she knew, yet he seemed oblivious to how great he looked.

To think that his father might have been that big and strong when Tanner was only a small, vulnerable boy... It made her heart ache.

Thank God his later childhood was made better by a phenomenal woman. It explained so much about him, and yet in many ways he was still such a mystery.

At times he could be incredibly caustic, focused only

on getting his way, which in her case, meant acquiring her property. Yet when he spoke about Addie, Kam, or even Blu, she saw the raw love in his eyes, as if having them was something extra precious to him.

Admittedly, she knew nothing about abuse. Indulgence, yes. Her parents had ensured she had everything she ever needed, and usually whatever she'd wanted. Distraction, too, of course, because affluent people loved to travel with their "set" and showcase all they had. Trips abroad, private cruises and jets; her parents were definitely social climbers who always accepted offers to travel with their "friends," even when it was a holiday, when she was at home from school, or the times that she'd been sick.

Their love was obvious, but so were their priorities: they wanted *more*.

If she'd married Sutter, the "more" would have been immeasurable—for them, but not for her. Thank God she'd finally shaken off the nonsense and taken a stand. She deserved to discover her own happiness.

As did Tanner. Should she sell to him?

Immediately, Callie shook her head. No, not yet. Tanner could be happy without getting *everything* he wanted. And if she stuck around, maybe he'd eventually want her. She certainly wanted him.

How did he know her when she didn't know him?

Over coffee, he'd somehow seduced her just by being himself—and by flaunting that stellar bod of his.

What really got to her was that he'd *heard* her. Things she said, and even things she didn't. Her connection to him was unlike anything she'd ever experienced. Not even with Glory, who was her pseudo sister and best friend in the entire world, did she feel so energized, so...*alive*.

Coffee with Tanner had been more exciting than sex with Sutter. How astounding was that? It reinforced that she'd made the right decision in walking away.

It also explained why, as she'd worked, she'd dissected their every word...until she got to that part about her nibbling around nuts. She laughed again. "Oh, Lord."

"What's that?" Addie asked, as she joined Callie in the yard.

Today, Addie wore her hair held back by a headband. An older T-shirt, faded in some spots, stained in others, covered her to the seat of her loose jeans. She looked comfortably sloppy and happy, even while pitching in at Callie's new house.

Smiling at her, Callie admitted, "I just realized what I said."

"What did you say?"

"At breakfast?" Callie prompted. "Or rather, over cookies?"

An enormous grin creased Addie's face. "Ah, yeah. That was pretty funny. I thought the boys would choke to death on their hilarity. I tried to shush them, but sometimes my evilest, most stern looks have zero effect. Men, you know, can only be wrangled so much."

Callie leaned on the rake she'd been using to clean up the yard. "I love that you see it that way. Like you want to guide them, but within reason." That wasn't really the world today. There were such enormous expectations for some, and none for others. In truth, she thought each individual person had unique potential that should be encouraged without comparing one to another.

It was the philosophy she'd planned to use with her imaginary kids in her imaginary future.

"I had to learn, you know?" Addie stripped off her rubber gloves and tossed them to a rickety wooden table that sat on the back porch before striding closer. "Tanner... Man, I loved that boy from day one. Talk about a heartbreaker." She paused to lean on a tree.

It was one of the things Callie loved about the yard. All the trees, so many varieties, offering shade and beauty.

Dropping nuts, leaves, and branches everywhere. That part was tough, but she'd get the hang of it. "Tanner told me you took him in when he was thirteen."

"He did?" Surprise lifted Addie's brows, then her entire face settled into a warm smile. "Well, guess I'm not surprised. He'd want you to hear it from him before others filled your head with nonsense."

"He said people gossip about him?"

This time, Addie's laugh was short and bitter. "You'll hear it soon enough, but not from me."

Callie wondered about that, but she wasn't sure how to ask, especially with Addie's statement hanging out there. It wouldn't be right for her to pressure anyone, especially after her new neighbor had been so open and welcoming, so incredibly helpful.

"Thirteen," Addie mused aloud, breaking the strained silence. "He thought he was so grown up. Thought he could just go off on his own and somehow make it. And you know what? He might have. He sure had the grit."

More than anything, more than making her house livable or getting to explore Tanner's sexy shoulders and abs, Callie wanted to better understand him. To learn everything about him. All the small and large parts of his life that had knit together such an intriguing guy.

That connection…it was still there, sizzling her nerve endings, keeping her thoughts hopping about, always wondering about him. Now that she was feeling so alive, she couldn't imagine going back to being…well, dormant. Existing, going through the motions but never really taking part. Not with heart. Not like she should.

She'd been living without any real purpose. But this? Being outside and working on the yard and talking to Addie—a woman who had lived with her whole heart—made Callie realize what a shallow person she'd been.

She would have married Sutter. Just because it was easy. Because her parents wanted it. To keep the peace.

And to have her fancy wedding.

Ugh. She didn't like who she was—or rather, who she used to be, because more than ever, she was determined to make herself anew, with better principles and more awareness, and this time *she'd* use her whole heart.

Turning to Addie, she asked, "Feel like taking a break?"

"Right here," Addie said, looking up at the thick branches of a massive oak tree. "With just a little sunlight filtering through and all the fresh air a body could want."

Beautiful sentiment, and it perfectly expressed how Callie felt in that moment. "Just a sec." She set aside her rake, then jogged to the porch to grab a folding lawn chair, which she brought out to Addie. "Right here suits me, too, but you should sit. It's been a long day already. I've never seen anyone work as hard as you do—and for a neighbor you barely know."

"Oh, honey, I've known you—or about you—forever." Gratefully, she settled into the chair. "Isn't this nice, here in the shade? I always thought Reggie had a beautiful yard."

"Agreed." Given the shape of the house, the yard was probably the best thing about the place…next to the nice bathroom. "I love the entire setting." And the more Callie cleared and cleaned and rearranged, the more she enjoyed it.

"I tried to talk Reggie into getting outside more, but he was falling apart and ashamed of how he looked. Poor man hid inside most of the time. Toward the end, he wouldn't even walk to our house to join us for dinner."

"Was the walk too strenuous for him?"

"Nah. See that spot right there?" Addie pointed at some overgrown hedges. "We kept it cleared for Reggie. It's a shortcut right through to our yard. One minute walk or so. When he quit using it, it grew over again. Tanner reinforced the fencing on the other side to make sure the goats didn't wander in and eat our saplings." She confided, "They'll eat anything, you know."

No, she hadn't known, but she was learning, keeping mental notes on every bit of farming wisdom Addie shared. "Do you need something to drink?"

Addie laughed. "Just like my boys, always trying to pamper me. I'm seventy-two, not a hundred." She nodded at the porch. "I left my water bottle up there, but I'm fine for now."

"Seventy-two?" Studying her face, Callie saw the wrinkles, mostly when she smiled, which Addie did a lot, and she saw the tiny veining in her cheeks, a few dark spots, likely from being in the sun so much. Most of all, she saw a woman who enjoyed living. She saw happiness. "I thought you were younger. You're really pretty."

"Ha! Thank you for the kindness, but I'm like a lot of old people, wearing skin that's two sizes too big now." She grinned, showing how her aged skin bunched together. "I don't mind. Getting old is a sight better than the alternative."

Callie smiled, too. "Seriously, I thought you were in your early sixties."

"You're smooth, just like my boys."

"I've met your boys, so I'll take that as a compliment," she said, and they both chuckled.

Despite how hard she'd worked, peacefulness settled over Callie. Odd that the woods had seemed so creepy last night and now they just felt serene. Her stomach was rumbling with hunger, she had blisters on her palms and sweat in unheard-of places, and she hadn't yet explored the attic or basement of the house.

In that moment, it didn't matter.

Chickens, currently roaming free, pecked at the ground, occasionally scratching, and the goats ambled about, often climbing atop everything they could.

The spring sunshine was beautiful, birds were loudly singing, and she was filled with gratitude. Closing her eyes a moment, she imagined the house and how it would be when she finished with it. She wasn't a decorator but she had good taste. She felt certain she could make it not only comfortable, but beautiful.

In turn, her life would become more beautiful, too. She was done with the mundane, done with taking things for granted.

And done trying to please everyone in her life...except herself.

CHAPTER FIVE

TANNER GRUMBLED TO himself as he rummaged in the linen closet, breathing in the scents of bleach and fabric softener. Not unpleasant smells at all. They brought back his earliest memories of staying with Addie, sleeping on a soft, clean bed with a fluffy pillow. The quilt had been worn, frayed in places, and he'd loved it. Long ago Addie had repaired it, but her talents were in the kitchen, not with a needle and thread. That made him grin, remembering the mismatched stitches.

Didn't matter. It was her care that had really touched him.

Using a laundry basket to hold it all, he stacked in two sets of sheets, two quilts, an extra blanket, and lastly, two pillows.

Good thing Addie kept everything so well organized.

He was just about to start down the steps when Blu barked a greeting and a second later, the front door opened. In came Kam, predictably sniffing the air.

From the top of the steps, Tanner said, "Catch," and tossed down the pillows, one after the other.

"Shit." Kam caught them, one in each fist, and held them away from his body. "I'm covered in sweat. It was hot as hell in the shop today."

"Air's not on yet?"

"This early in spring?" Kam grunted. "The owners won't turn it on until we're all roasting midsummer."

At the local shop where Kam worked, he made good money and the hours were usually great, leaving him time to help out around the farm as needed, especially in the busier seasons. The conditions, though, could be grueling. Tanner much preferred the fresh outdoors to being cooped up in a machinery shop with flying sparks singeing both his hair and his clothes.

Kam eyed him as he came down the stairs with the loaded basket. "Moving out?"

The question, asked jokingly, gave him pause. Leave the farm? Leave Addie? Never. His heart, as well as his sweat, was forever bonded to this place. "I can't imagine living anywhere else."

"Ah, so then all this is for our sexy new neighbor?"

Deliberately, Tanner "bumped" him with the basket, knocking him into the wall.

"Hey!"

"Sorry. My bad." Tanner looked at his brother and grinned.

"Again, dude, am I not supposed to notice her?"

That'd be asking a lot. *Sexy* didn't begin to describe Callie. Scorching, sweet, admirable, funny, direct, determined... He ended the litany in his head, knowing he could go on all night listing everything he liked about her.

It was weird, actually. After years of envisioning her as a perfect little princess, now, after one morning of coffee, he knew her as a flesh-and-blood woman. Warm and interesting. He knew what made her blush, what annoyed her, how fiercely she'd reacted to the idea of abuse. Her ex's disrespectful treatment had dented her pride, but he hadn't touched her heart.

Much as she tried to hide it, it was obvious the lack of support from her family was the larger wound. Tanner knew what family meant, and he couldn't imagine how badly it would hurt if Addie and Kam were ever that disloyal.

Best of all, he knew Callie wanted him. She hadn't even tried to hide her interest. The way she devoured him with her gaze, you'd think she'd never seen a grown man before.

"Earth to Tanner. Did I lose you?"

Damn it. He'd been staring into space—and probably smiling. Switching his gaze to Kam, he said, "Maybe keep your observations on Callie to yourself. Or better yet, focus on her cousin."

"Haven't met the cousin. When I left for work, she hadn't yet come down." Kam propped a shoulder against the wall. "Is she sweet on the eyes, too?"

Huh. Mostly what he'd noticed was how late Glory had slept, how she'd come downstairs fully dressed, her makeup and hair perfect. Total opposite of Callie, who was far more laid-back.

Callie had immediately catered to her cousin, getting coffee for her, offering her a cookie, and very deliberately drawing her into the conversation.

Until now, Tanner hadn't thought much about it. "Her name is Glory. She's…different from Callie. More polished."

"And?"

"And what? She's not my type."

"Because…?" Kam prompted.

Fed up, Tanner asked, "What do you want to know

exactly? Blond hair, blue eyes, perfect features." Almost too perfect—although that didn't really describe her, because he thought Callie was pretty damned perfect, too, but in a much more appealing way.

"Now I want to meet her."

That suited Tanner just fine. "Addie's over there now. From what she said, the kitchen, bathroom, and much of the yard has been cleaned up, but you can imagine the shape Reggie's bedroom is in." Just the thought of it gave Tanner the creeps. He'd loved the old guy and didn't mind saying so, but sleep in his bed?

He'd rather camp out with the goats.

When he glanced at Kam, he saw a similar aghast expression.

"Yeah." Laughing, Tanner said, "Don't let your mind go there. If I was Callie, I'd burn that mattress."

"The girls seriously need to just sleep here again tonight."

"The girls? Is that Addie's influence?"

"Probably. She'll end up getting me killed by an enraged woman." Kam smelled the air again. "What's for dinner?"

"Crock-Pot stew."

"One of my favorites." Dropping the pillows on the couch, Kam said, "Give me five minutes to shower and change, and I'll help you carry over everything."

"Only five. I'm already hungry." And although he'd like to deny it, he was edgy with a vague sort of anticipation. He wanted to see Callie again. Maybe a day's worth of work and an up-close view of the undertaking before her had changed her mind about staying.

Then again, maybe it hadn't. He was betting on the latter.

As the sun dropped lower in the sky, Callie's exhaustion settled in. She still had so much to tackle. Her to-do list kept growing. She'd complete one task and think of three more. "It's a lot of land for one person to keep up." Not that she was anywhere near giving up.

"It is," Addie agreed. "But it's manageable. I can give you tips along the way that might help."

"I'd love that." Callie sincerely hoped she and Addie would be friends. She already felt a kinship for the woman unlike anything she'd ever known. It had nothing to do with the fact that Addie was close to Tanner, though that was certainly a bonus.

Addie brushed her foot over a clump of weeds. "Tip number one: the goats are good at clearing out your yard, but if you want any kind of lawn, you'll need the fence repaired to keep them contained."

Callie eyed the faces of the goats with their big ears and funny horizontal pupils and wondered if she'd have the heart to corral them. If not, any flowers she wanted would have to be in front, or up in window boxes so the goats couldn't eat them.

They were all so sweet. Who knew she'd like farm animals?

After checking that the spot near the tree wasn't too messy, she sat down on the ground, her forearms draped over her knees. "I'll get to that tomorrow, if you think it can wait."

"Course it can. Most of it could wait another day if you'd stop being stubborn and stay the night again."

Coming from Addie, the mention of her stubbornness sounded less like an insult and more like affectionate teasing. Callie harked back to Addie's earlier comment, one that had caught her attention. "You said you've known about me?"

"Tanner didn't mention that you went to school together?"

"He did, sort of, only I don't remember him."

With a secret little smile, Addie said, "I know that, too."

"So…what am I missing?"

"He was sweet on you back then. You were his first crush."

"What?" Tanner used to be hung up on her? "How can that be when we never met?" She was certain she would have remembered if they had.

"Hmm," Addie said. "So you never had a crush? Like for some cutie in a boy band or a young actor or something?"

"I guess I did." She tried to think about her high school days, but it was mostly a fog after her tumultuous college time. "I was never star status though."

"No? Rich, pretty girl, out of reach of the boy from the wrong side of the tracks."

Callie winced. There were train tracks that *literally* divided the town.

"When you were off buying dresses for school dances, Tanner was there at the tracks, waiting for the train to pass so he could get home. He wouldn't let me pick him up and he refused to ride the bus. Wouldn't let Kam ride it either. You know how cruel kids can be. Tanner kept his brother at his side as much as possible." Addie rested her head back and closed her eyes. "I remember once, Tanner came home with a horrible black eye and bruised, bloody knuckles. He wouldn't talk about it, but back then, Kam was the weak link. I could usually get anything out of him."

"He tattled?"

"No, never. Those two backed each other up no matter what. But Kam had a hard case of hero worship. Made sense, with him being younger and Tanner being…so much. So proud and tall, so determined and smart." She peeked one eye open to look at Callie. "He wasn't perfect, but near enough to stump me sometimes."

"He feels the same about you."

Smiling, Addie closed her eyes again. "Kam never missed a chance to brag on his big brother, so he was all about telling me how some older boys were giving him a hard time."

Callie imagined that and felt anger tightening her chest. "Did that happen often?"

"Often enough. Neither of them would say what started the fight that day, so I'm guessing it was about me. Some people around here liked to get a rise out of the boys by insulting me since I used to work at a bar. I never minded much for myself. Jackasses are easy to ignore, especially when I'd see them all at the bar, drinking to excess and spending money they shouldn't have. But the boys, man, I had a tough time teaching them to rise above. Especially Tanner."

To Callie, that just made Tanner more impressive. He protected those he loved. Good for him.

She wished her family felt just a tiny bit of that loyalty.

"Kam said that Tanner leveled both boys. He took some hits too, but…" Whatever she was thinking silenced her for a while. When she opened her eyes and sat forward, Callie saw the pain in her expression. Her voice was much softer when she spoke. "Tanner's good at ignoring that sort of thing."

Hating the reality of it, but suspecting it was true, Callie whispered, "You mean…getting hit?"

Abruptly, Addie stood. "Some people in this world leave a bad mark even after they're dead and buried. Then other people pile on, as if a kid has any say in how he handles abuse." She picked up a stick and threw it toward the pile.

For her age, she had one hell of a throwing arm. Callie was impressed.

Subtly, Addie wiped at her eyes before facing Callie again. "Early on in school, Tanner got labeled as something he's not. After that, others refused to see him any other way."

Callie slowly stood, too. She wanted to say, *I see him*, but the words were private, still new and special to her. She'd only known the man a day. Surely there was more to him than what he'd revealed so far. Layers and layers of ugly past and wonderful present, hurt and happiness, broken dreams and future goals. She wanted to uncover it all.

And Tanner wanted only for her to move on, to sell him the house and go away. If she thought about that too much, especially after the impact he'd made on her, she'd get upset. So instead she'd concentrate on anything and everything else.

"I've never thought of people that way," Callie promised. "That someone was all good or all bad. Certainly not bad by association." Her cousin could attest to that. "Or because they lacked money? No, never." She felt confident in that. She might have been a people pleaser, going along to get along in the easiest way possible, but she'd never been mean. Never cruel. To convince Addie, she said, "I had a whole scope of friends in school. Jocks, eggheads, kids in choir and band, arts and athletics."

Addie gave her a look that instantly made her feel chastised. "Were any of them dirt-poor?"

"I don't know." *Liar.* "I mean, I never asked them about their…" Asking hadn't been necessary. She knew her friends were comfortable because they were always ready to shop with her, to dine out, to see a show or concert. Maybe most weren't as well off as her parents, but she couldn't recall any of them ever lacking anything. "I guess not."

"Exactly," Addie said, as if she'd read her mind. "Before God put us together, Tanner was the kind of poor that he sometimes went to bed hungry, and then had to go to school that way, too. Even after we became a family, we sometimes had to pinch pennies, but the boy was always fed. Always."

Taking a good look at herself made Callie feel bone-deep shame. "I hope I never deliberately looked past anyone or excluded them." That she might have done that to Tanner, and in the process made him feel bad, left her stomach in knots.

"I'm sure he never introduced himself, or even said hi. He wouldn't have, not back then. He's a tough one though, don't you worry. Graduated with honors, but had no interest in the ceremony, not even for me."

"He didn't attend graduation?"

"Picked up his diploma from the school office and that was that. I couldn't change his mind. He went to college locally so he could still help out around here. Never mind that I told him we'd be fine. Oh, how I wanted him to go off and have some fun, an adventure or two, maybe fall in love. He's always been too serious and levelheaded though. Got himself degrees in business, agribusiness and forestry."

"Nice," Callie said, though she had no real idea what agribusiness and forestry entailed. Later, she'd look it up and educate herself a little. "There's nothing wrong with staying here. I love it, the business and your home, and especially how close you all are. I'm sure this place brings him comfort."

"The boys spruced up the house. Back when my husband was alive, it was nice enough, but over the years it needed more care than I could give. Almost from the time they could hold a hammer and nail, Tanner and Kam have been adding to it and updating it. Reggie was a contractor once, did you know that? He taught them a lot."

"I didn't know."

"He *retired* early, if you know what I mean." She gave a snort. "More like he simplified his life and enjoyed his vices. But that beautiful kitchen of mine? Six years back, they redid it all and I love it. Reggie supervised and they did the labor. The house was wrecked for months, but in the end it was worth it."

"Wow. So much talent."

Addie nodded. "They added on the rear porch, too, and a big bedroom and bathroom for me so I wouldn't have to use the stairs anymore. Tanner traded labor and landscaping with other local businesses, like plumbing, electrical, and cement work. Sometimes it feels like he works around the clock. Him and Kam both."

Emotion put her close to tears again. "They love you."

"Yeah." Addie's gentle smile showed deep contentment. "God blessed me the day He put Tanner within reach, and then later added the bonus of Kam. I'll tell you, you think life has meaning until real meaning lands. Then you know what you were missing all those years. If it weren't for them, I'd just be another old, weird widow, doddering around in my home alone. Or maybe homeless. Who knows? A gal could only tend bar for so long."

They'd talked so much about Tanner, and some about Kam, but Addie hadn't really said much about herself. Callie moved closer to her. "When did you lose your husband?"

"Years and years ago. We were young. John started out as a salesman and sometimes had to travel. Then he bought us a house and we started a tree farm."

These memories were happy ones; Callie could see it in her eyes and the slight curl of her mouth.

"My John was such a guy's guy, you know? Rough around the edges, sometimes crass, but as a salesman he could smooth-talk anyone. He sure did love me."

"He sounds wonderful."

"My John was a funny guy, always making me laugh, always talking about our future. I believed in him, in us. I thought we'd have a happy-ever-after…until he died and then I didn't know how to live without him."

"You're strong," Callie said, knowing it and needing Addie to know it, too.

"Maybe now, but then? I let the business go under, got a job bartending so I could pay the bills. I lived pretty much day to day, just trudging through without feeling, without happiness. Nothing much mattered. Until Tanner."

Until Tanner. Did he know how much he'd helped Addie, too? It sounded like they were two lost souls who'd needed each other.

"For him, I'd have moved heaven and earth." She gave a short chuckle. "Getting the tree farm going again was a huge undertaking, but I needed to be home more, not out late serving drinks, and Tanner needed someone wholesome, someone he could believe in. We'd work together selling hardwood, and then Christmas trees in winter and saplings in the spring. I cleaned for people while he was in school, and he took odd jobs."

"Sounds like you both pitched in."

"You could say he grew up with the business, took what my husband left me and got it thriving, and he wasn't much more than a boy when he did it. When Tanner wants something, get out of his way. I learned that while I learned about parenting." Another grin, this one self-directed. "Sometimes the heart tells you what's right, and you just gotta listen. That's what I did. Some were saying a gal like me, who'd never birthed kids of her own, didn't know squat about taking on a troubled boy, especially one that was already thirteen and thinking he was a man grown."

"You proved them wrong."

"In part anyway. He really did think he was grown. I can't tell you how many times I tried to guide him and he'd just go about making up his own mind anyway." She gave a soft laugh. "Usually he was right, too, and when he wasn't, he'd own it and try to do better."

"I guess Tanner had to think that way. It sounds like he could only rely on himself—until you."

"That's about it. He came to me with an independent soul, ready to forge a path of his own making." When her eyes clouded with tears, she shook her head. "This is what I used to do to poor Reggie. Carry on and on. But I've never had anyone I could brag to."

"I'm one hundred percent positive that Reggie loved your visits, and I hope you brag to me whenever you want, as much as you want. I think it's beautiful."

"Reggie said the same. He let me share all that motherly pride, and he chimed in. He and Tanner went way back, you know. Almost from the day Tanner came to live with me, Reggie was around, teaching him things, giving him advice, hiring him for odd jobs so he'd have money to get gifts on holidays and stuff like that. Reggie was a good one."

Holding back the emotional excess was getting harder. Callie drew a slow breath. "Please feel free to talk to me anytime. I've never had a heart-to-heart like this. I'm enjoying it, too."

"Not with your own ma? Or even your dad?"

In a roundabout answer, she said, "I guess Glory comes close." But even then, Glory didn't always understand her. Sometimes it felt like she was talking to hear herself, and Glory was busy trying to figure out what it was Callie's parents would want. In so many ways, Glory was far more worried about pleasing them than Callie would ever be.

Fortunately, a goat wandered over to butt Callie's hip, almost knocking her over. It gave her a good excuse to change the topic. "Are they friendly?"

Addie patted the goat. "They sure are, and they're smarter than you'd think, too. Start petting one and the others will get jealous. Gotta spread the love around with them."

She no sooner said it than the other goats showed up. All four of them making noise and wanting attention. Tickled by their antics, Callie used both hands to dole out affection. "They sound like they're crying."

"That's called bleating, and they do it for attention, or to communicate with each other. Goats like companionship."

Appalled, Callie's eyes rounded. "You mean *me*?"

That had Addie laughing again. "I meant other goats, but sure, they'll enjoy seeing you now and then."

There were so many things she didn't know. Maybe she could hire a local high school kid to help her out and teach her more in the process. It was a thought worth considering.

As Callie did her best to keep the goats appeased, she worried. "Do they get along with the chickens?"

"Mostly ignore each other." Addie stretched. "If something spooks the chickens, the goats will run off, too. Luckily, part of your acreage is fenced. You'll just need to check it routinely for holes."

At least Addie assumed she'd stay, Callie thought. She wasn't trying to run her off like Tanner did. "I noticed I had to go through a gate to get into the woods."

"Make sure it's closed tight each time, and secure the goats at night in their shelter, okay? They need to be protected from the weather. You want them separate from the chickens. Chickens leave droppings everywhere and goats don't want it anywhere near their food or water."

"Eww," Callie said. "I wouldn't either."

"Come on. Break is over. I want you to see what I accomplished in the house."

Together, with Callie carrying the chair and rake, they headed up to the porch. It had been a cluttered mess earlier, as if Reggie had only used it to store every broken piece of furniture, small appliance, or bag of garbage that he didn't feel like disposing of properly.

Callie now had it in a neat pile to be hauled away to-morrow. With it was bags of leaves and twigs that had accumulated over the winter and early spring. The porch and the surrounding yard looked much nicer. She was already imagining how the porch would look after a good power-washing, an outdoor rug, and some styl-ish lawn furniture.

Then again, she had goats, so maybe she'd need to keep outdoor décor off the front porch until she fig-ured out the setup.

"I got a few guys who'll come by tomorrow to do some minor repairs, clean the windows, and haul away the trash. You'll be right as rain soon."

Addie's help, as well as her enthusiasm, reinforced Callie's decision to stay. "I can't tell you how much I appreciate everything you've done, and how patient you've been with me." Callie's mother was not a person she could ask about goats, or a broken pipe, or clearing out a trashed house.

She felt silly as she admitted, "I've never had a home of my own. Apartments, sure, but the landlords were responsible for the upkeep on them. If something broke, or overflowed, or whatever, I called them."

Addie slanted her a knowing look. "Feels good to fix up your own place, doesn't it?"

"Amazingly so." As they stepped through the back door and into the kitchen, Callie felt the ache of mus-cles she didn't know she had. "I'm sore, but it's…satis-fying." And then she pulled up short. "Oh, wow." The kitchen was now pristine, with the sink, countertops, and floor all shining. She inhaled the scent of lemon and pine. "It sparkles."

"A woman needs a spotless, well-organized kitchen."

The front door opened, there was some rustling of plastic bags, and Glory appeared in the doorway, arms laden with groceries. She, too, appeared stunned as she looked around the kitchen. "It's like an entirely different room." Giving a deep inhale, she hummed, "Mmm, and it smells so good now."

Callie rushed forward to take two bags from her. "Did you get everything?"

"And then some."

Glory had spent most of her time in the car, first heading out to buy cleaning supplies and heavy-duty lawn bags for all the garbage. Once she returned, instead of offering to pitch in, she'd headed out for food. First for lunch, which the three of them had shared on the front porch, since that had been the least smelly space on the property. When that was done, Glory had again driven off, that time to fill the grocery list Callie made for her.

Because she understood Glory, Callie didn't expect her to partake in manual labor. The very idea of it probably repulsed her cousin clean down to her manicured nails, but it would also terrify her. Neither of them had much experience with that sort of thing, but whereas Callie never minded jumping in to learn something new, Glory always feared messing up and looking foolish.

"You've been a huge help," Callie told her as she checked the cabinets and found them all cleaned. She turned to Addie. "And you! My goodness. You accomplished so much."

"I ran the dishes through the dishwasher, but they won't be done drying for a few minutes yet. If I had more time, I'd stick around and put them away for you."

She glanced at Glory, but her cousin was checking messages on her phone.

Callie sent Addie a smile and a wink. "I can do it."

"You've put in a full day. If you two would just come to stay at my house again, we could finish getting it in order tomorrow."

Glory looked up in hope, but Callie was already shaking her head. "Thank you, but I want to stay here tonight."

"I thought you'd say that. You'll need clean bedding, so Tanner is bringing over some sheets, quilts, and pillows. He should be here any minute."

Her first thought was: oh goodie, she'd get to see Tanner again. Her second thought had her questioning Addie. "When did you arrange that?"

"Before I joined you in the yard." She grinned. "But you're still welcome to come over—"

Callie laughed. "Thank you, no. If I'm going to live here, I might as well start now, but I do appreciate clean bedding." She needed Tanner to witness her resolve, to know she was settling in, not cutting corners and finding an easy way out.

What she'd seen of the bedroom wasn't promising, so she had figured on being up late to wash…well, everything. Now she could put that off for tomorrow.

She'd just started unloading bags when a knock sounded on the front door.

"That'll be Tanner," Addie said, and went to answer.

Callie couldn't deny the sudden tripping of her heart. It was exhilarating, overriding a lot of her exhaustion. Using her wrist, she brushed a hank of hair away from her eyes and smiled at the doorway.

And then kept smiling, but no one appeared.

Glory glanced at her. "What are you doing?"

"We have company. Didn't you hear the knock?"

Twisting around in her seat, Glory whispered, "Who?"

"Good grief, Glory, were you completely tuned out?"

"Sorry. I hadn't checked my phone in a while and I had a lot of messages."

New tension sank into Callie's neck and shoulders. "From my parents? From Sutter?"

Droll, Glory said, "I do have a life of my own, you know."

Yes, she did know. Her cousin was far more social than Callie had ever been, but then, they had very different personalities. "Sorry."

"But some of the messages were from them."

Rolling her eyes and huffing, Callie said, "I hope you're not talking about me."

"Only to say that we're staying here again tonight, and you're fine."

She'd be staying forever, but she didn't want Glory carrying tales, so she just nodded. "I appreciate the loyalty. If I want them to know something, I'll tell them myself. Okay?"

"They're worried about you," Glory countered.

"I'm better than ever, so there's no reason." From the living room, she could hear a few muted voices, one of them Tanner's. Before Glory could say anything else, Callie went to investigate, and found the whole family—Addie, Tanner, and Kam—standing in her small living room, arms filled with linens.

CHAPTER SIX

LIKE AN APPROACHING STORM, Tanner felt Callie was nearby. Automatically bracing himself, he glanced up from Addie, who was doing inventory while he held the basket. His gaze collided with Callie's as she hesitated in the kitchen doorway.

His heart jumped, then began a slow, heavy thudding in his chest. Although the basket wasn't heavy, his thighs tensed. It could almost be alarming, the physical reactions she caused by her mere presence, but then, his thoughts had been churning all day over the things he'd shared with her in the kitchen, things he'd never before discussed with any woman other than Addie, and never in such detail.

What Callie so effortlessly did to him was enough to make him keep his distance, and yet, he knew he wouldn't. Couldn't.

Even wilted, her hair limp and her clothes dirt stained, she was so fucking gorgeous. Maybe more so now. She looked earthy. Approachable.

Like she belonged here.

Glory stepped up next to her, breaking the spell and snagging Kam's attention.

Glad for the distraction, Tanner introduced him. "Glory, I don't think you've met my brother yet. Kam, Glory is Callie's cousin."

Glory lifted one hand and gave a little wave. "Hi."

Hitching a brow, Kam said, "Nice to meet you," and then, arms holding two fluffy pillows, he asked Callie, "Where do you want all this?"

Huh. Had his brother just dismissed Glory? Seemed so. Maybe she didn't appeal to him anymore than she appealed to Tanner. But then again, next to Callie, a supermodel probably wouldn't appeal.

"Not the bedroom," Addie said, answering Kam's question. "Not yet anyway. Let's stack it all in the kitchen on the table, then you boys can drag the mattress out to the yard to air it—"

"Not on your life," Tanner said. "I'm not touching Reggie's mattress."

"Same," Kam said.

Suspicious now, Callie folded her arms and gave one of those not-so-polite smiles. "That's fine. I'm sure Glory and I can handle it."

Glory's mouth fell open. "I, um…" She looked at Tanner. "Why, exactly, don't you want to touch it?"

"It's Reggie's, and toward the end he had a lot of issues."

"Like…?"

Callie cleared her throat. Loudly. "I'm sure I can manage on my own."

Of course, Addie didn't like that. "Come on, honey. I'll help you."

"Thank you." Together, the two women headed down the hall.

Well, hell. He shared a quick look with Kam, who appeared equally resigned. "We'll be right there."

"Ha!" he heard Callie reply, and almost grinned.

Snickering, Kam plopped the pillows on top of the

basket. "Hurry along, now," he needlessly quipped, even as he went to help.

Glory had disappeared, but Tanner found her there in the kitchen when he hastily set the basket, piled high now, onto the table. Standing at the back door, she stared out at the yard, her phone in her hand. Before Tanner could leave again, she got a text. Then another. She was texting back when he left the kitchen and joined the others in the bedroom.

His first realization was that the room wasn't as bad as he remembered. When last he'd been in here, Reggie was all but bedridden, only getting up for the bathroom—when he could. Jaundice had turned him a sickly shade of yellow. All over his face and throat, there'd been patches of red veins resembling spiders. Swelling in his face, limbs, and especially his abdomen made him look like a different person.

Liver disease had devastated him, and even the air had smelled sickly. Tanner had visited anyway, because he loved Reggie. Not like a father, and not in the same way he loved Kam. But Reggie had been kind. He'd taken the time to teach valuable skills to a lost and troubled boy. Those skills had carried Tanner into adulthood.

Reggie's patience had been endless, his manner always friendly.

He'd been…a nonthreatening adult male at a time when Tanner hadn't known that existed.

Just by being himself, Reggie had shared a positive example that helped an angry kid maneuver through life. Because of Reggie, Tanner learned that his father in no way represented men as a whole.

Realistically, he'd already known it; through Reggie, he was able to believe it.

"Wimps," Callie accused, as she studied the room. "This is actually really nice. Lots of space." As she spoke, she went to a window and tried to wrestle it open. It didn't budge.

"Here." Kam stepped forward and forced it up for her. "They probably need the tracks oiled."

Tanner got the other window. "We have a silicone based lubricant I can bring over tomorrow." He'd deliberately offered before Kam could—then he wanted to take it back, especially with the knowing grin Kam shot his way.

"Who stripped the bed?" Callie asked.

"That'd be me." Addie folded her arms around herself. "What the boys weren't so tactfully saying is that Reggie had some serious issues there at the end. Before it got that bad though, he knew where it was headed. When I came by one day to tell him I was heading to the store if he needed me to pick up anything, he requested a mattress cover. It was a simple matter of gathering up all the bedding and throwing it away."

Damn. "You should have told me you were doing that. I'd have helped."

"Oh?" Addie lifted her brows. "Are you the one who just quailed about dragging out a mattress?"

She knew better. He didn't *quail* over anything. "Rather than have you do it alone, I'd have handled it."

"And I'd have helped," Kam said.

"See?" Addie said. "Aren't my boys wonderful?"

Callie pretended to give it some thought before finally nodding. "I suppose they are."

He still would have replaced the mattress before *he'd*

sleep on it, but if she was willing, he could at least drag it outside to air it out. "You want to grab the other side?" he asked Kam.

"I guess that's why we're in here."

Getting it down the hall and out the front door proved to be an awkward endeavor. It didn't help that Reggie's house—now Callie's house—was so cluttered. She ran ahead of them to move things out of the way. After they tilted it against the porch railing, she liberally sprayed both sides with a disinfectant and returned to the bedroom to do the same to the box springs.

"Now," Addie said. "No more arguing. You and your cousin should come over for dinner—"

"Crock-Pot stew," Kam said as enticement as he re-entered the room.

"—and afterward, the boys can help you get the mattress back inside."

Tanner caught the tail end of that invitation, and now he couldn't take his eyes off Callie as he waited for her decision. A big part of him wanted her to agree, but another part of him didn't know if he could take it.

Her gaze skipped to him, then quickly away. "Thank you, but I can't. I still need to shower and get the groceries put away."

Glory stuck her head into the bedroom to say, "I can put away the groceries while you shower." Then with pleading, "Come on Callie. I'm hungry."

Kam glanced at her, frowned, and then stepped forward to sling an arm over Callie's shoulders. "Addie makes the best stew you've ever tasted. Guaranteed, you'll love it."

"Well…" This time she didn't look at Tanner. "I guess I am getting hungry."

"You only had half a sandwich for lunch," Addie pointed out. "The chickens couldn't stay alive on that."

Her grin lit up her entire face. "I was anxious to get back to my chores."

Not liking that at all, Tanner said, "It'll wear thin soon enough."

Addie sidled out of the room, saying to Glory, "Let me help you put things away."

Kam said, "I'll go set the table."

And that left Tanner alone, in a bedroom with Callie. Of course, to his mind, it was still Reggie's room and the bed was now minus a mattress.

Callie smiled up at him. "Was that deliberate, do you think?"

"Leaving us alone? Yeah, it was." He didn't mean to, but he reached for a small dried leaf caught in her hair.

"I'm a mess."

"Hard work looks good on you."

"Is that right?" She tugged at the neckline of her T-shirt. "How about sweat? Are you going to tell me that looks good, too?"

His brows pulled together in a frown. "What's this?" He hooked her neckline in one finger and pulled it out from her body.

"Umm…"

"You're hurt."

"What?" Tucking in her chin, she looked at her shoulder and winced. "I scratched it in the woods yesterday."

"I know, but now it's inflamed."

"What do you mean, you know?"

"I was listening in, remember? And you weren't exactly quiet about it, plus your shirt was ripped there."

Though he probably shouldn't have mentioned that. Now she knew where his attention had been.

"Since you've pointed it out, it's stinging again, but I'm sure it'll be fine after I shower."

Lightly, Tanner traced a fingertip around the scratch. It felt warm, but then, she looked warm. Hot even. "Do you have any antiseptic?"

Shaking her head, she said, "No, but I'll add it to my list."

After dinner, he'd see to it himself. If he didn't feel so protective, he'd just let her use their first aid kit. But he did feel protective. And damn it, territorial. If he just gave her the kit, Kam might step up and offer his help. "Do you at least have soap?"

"Of course I have soap."

For now, that'd have to do. "Clean it the best you can, but be gentle."

"Yes, sir."

The smart response lifted his gaze to hers until he noted the teasing in her eyes. Callie did like to tease.

And he liked when she did it.

Taking a deliberate step back, Tanner put space between them. "Any other injuries?"

"Nope. I'm fine."

He'd bet she had sore muscles already, but if she didn't want to mention them, he wouldn't either. Tomorrow, she'd really be feeling it.

Probably her biggest pain right now was her wounded pride. By working next to Addie when he was young, he'd learned that physical labor in the fresh outdoors had a way of blocking out mental and emotional turmoil. For Callie's sake, he hoped her efforts on the property affected her the same way.

Doing his utmost to banish the image of her showering, he said, "I'll see you soon, then."

"Not more than fifteen minutes, I promise."

Smirking, Tanner glanced at the clock. "I'm timing you."

"Ha!" she said, shooing him toward the door.

He left her with a smile. If he wasn't careful, smiling because of Callie was going to turn into a habit.

Or maybe it already had.

DINNER AT HER neighbor's house turned out to be a blast. Kam was downright entertaining, making everyone but Glory laugh. Her cousin, for some reason, was subdued. It worried Callie. What if it was guilt plaguing Glory... which would mean she'd been sending updates to Callie's family and ex, after all.

To test her, she asked, "Aren't you hungry, Glory?"

A wan smile appeared on Glory's face. "Yes, of course."

"You're not eating much," Addie said.

"I try to eat mostly healthy, that's all."

"What's not healthy about vegetables and meat?" Tanner asked, sounding genuinely confused.

"Gravy, for one thing." When silence fell around them, Glory realized how she'd erred and tried to correct herself. "Oh, I mean, it's *delicious*. Too much so. If I let myself, I could eat the whole pot."

"You'd have to fight me for it." Even as he tossed out that absurd statement, Kam kept his gaze on his food.

Tanner snickered.

Addie smacked at him, but she, too, seemed amused.

Hoping to lighten the awkwardness, Callie said, "I feel the same. It's *so* good, but I'm not as disciplined as Glory." Lifting her spoon in a toast, she said, "This is my second bowl. If I stole anyone's share, you have my apologies, but I couldn't resist."

Beaming, Addie said, "I made plenty, honey, so eat your fill."

Glory glanced from one face to the next, before frowning at Kam. "Thank you, Addie. Your kindness is appreciated."

Ha! Callie hid her grin behind her spoon. Her cousin had a gift for subtle rebuke, not that Kam seemed to notice. Overall, he deftly ignored Glory.

With his bowl now empty, Tanner sat back. Directly across from Callie, he asked, "Did you get the goats and chickens put away before you came over?"

Tension shot down her spine. *How in the world did I forget about the animals?* Not that she didn't already know. She'd forgotten because of Tanner. Whenever he was close—and shoot, even when he wasn't—he plagued her mind.

Callie stared at him, saw the taunt in his eyes, and wanted to throw her spoon at him. A swift glance at the window proved it was already getting dark. *Will I even still have goats and chickens?* She had no idea what animals did in the dark. It's not like they were teenagers.

Glory looked back and forth between them. "Put away where?"

"The chickens go in a coop and the goats have a shelter." Dropping her spoon into her bowl and pushing back her chair, Callie said, "I'll go take care of it now." Though how she was supposed to do that, she had no idea. "I promise to come right back to help clean up."

Addie jumped up from her chair. "But I have dessert."

"I'm sorry!" She skirted around the table, then almost stepped on Percy. The cat seemed to have come out of nowhere.

Right behind her, Tanner said, "Percy's good at that."

"Tripping people?"

"It's his talent." Kam, too, appeared to be following her.

"Guys." Hands on her hips, Callie faced them. "I'll figure it out. You don't need to leave your meal."

"I don't mind," Kam promised.

"But," Tanner said, "you're still eating and I'm done."

Callie couldn't be sure, but there seemed to be a subtle warning in his tone.

Kam confirmed that with a grin. "Down, big brother. I know when my help isn't wanted." He ducked back as Tanner reached for him. "How about I give you twenty minutes or so, then we can get her mattress back inside?"

"That'll work."

Kam winked at Callie, and then casually whistled as he sauntered away.

Having Kam for a neighbor was going to be fun. She lifted her gaze to Tanner's face and caught him watching her closely. Did he think she was attracted to Kam? With *him* around? Not likely. "Seriously, Tanner—"

"Seriously, Callie." As he mocked her, he took her arm and urged her along. "I'll show you how it's done, then you'll know."

A smart girl knew when to give up. Besides, she had no clue what she was doing yet and she liked his company.

With the tall trees everywhere, shadows overtook the area and night sounds filled the air. It had cooled considerably, making her wish she'd grabbed a sweat-shirt instead of one of her cuter tops.

Very aware of Tanner's warm fingers on her arm, she tried to think of something to say. With him so close to her, every breath filled her head with his scent. For real, she'd love to brush her cheek and nose all over him.

"Just a second." Tanner stopped outside the garage, opened his truck, and located a small first aid kit that had been stored under the seat.

Her heart beat faster. "So."

"So?"

Right. For a conversational gambit, that failed. "I hope you won't think badly of Glory."

"Because she didn't like Addie's stew?"

"But she did. That's the thing. She worries overly about…well, everything. Especially her figure and stay-ing healthy and doing the right thing."

He shook his head. "And eating stew is the wrong thing?"

"I didn't think so, but then, I never count calories or worry much about consequences—like gaining weight. I think it's why she insisted on coming along with me. In a lot of ways, we're like sisters, and she's the re-sponsible one."

Instead of replying, Tanner just kept walking, lead-ing her across the yards.

"You're awfully quiet."

"I don't want to overstep."

That made her laugh. "Seriously? You tell me to leave with every other breath, but now you're circum-spect?"

In the dim light, she could see his half smile. "Fair enough, but it's different when it comes to family.

Someone could insult me all day and I wouldn't give a damn. Insult my family, though? That crosses a line."

They reached her front porch. Callie wished she had turned on the outside lights, but she hadn't thought of that either. She'd add automatic light sensors to her ever-growing list of things the house needed.

In the distance, she could hear some rowdy laughing and foul curses.

"Garmet brothers," Tanner groused. "Stay away from them."

It wasn't the first time he'd given her that warning. As she went up the porch, she asked, "What were you going to say about Glory?"

"You want to have this conversation?"

"If you're going to insult her, I'll need to reprimand you."

He huffed—especially when she opened her door.

She stepped into the house and flipped on the light, only to see the angry incredulity on Tanner's face, and that ignited her own temper. "Hey, look, if you're planning to say something awful about her, you can turn around and leave right now."

Instead, he stepped in, crowding her back, and closed the door behind him. "You didn't have it locked."

Wait, what? "You're talking about my door?"

"Yes, your door." He moved her aside and set the first aid kit on the coffee table. "Wait here."

"Not a chance." She caught his shirt as he started to walk away. "What do you think you're doing?"

"Checking your house, *because you left your door open.*"

More umbrage rose up. "No one uses that tone with me."

"You're not in Kansas anymore, sweetheart. I told you that, but apparently it hasn't set in yet. Around here, you damn well lock your doors." Again, he turned to walk off.

Again, she stuck close. A different kind of nervousness plagued her now. "It's actually dangerous? We were right next door!"

"Out of sight, inside where we wouldn't hear a thing. Yes, it's dangerous. Especially with Dirk and Lang Garmet next door."

It wasn't just the creepy woods surrounding the houses, or the night sounds in the air, or an unfamiliar setting. His worry became her own.

Tanner glanced through the kitchen first, then strode across that room and locked her back door, after shooting her another disbelieving frown.

She shrugged. This, clearly, was another thing she needed to learn.

Next he looked into the bathroom. Thank God she'd put her dirty laundry into the hamper. All he saw was her damp towel hanging over the rod.

The storage room got a quick glance, but she was confident nothing and no one else could fit in there. Reggie had left it packed. Even the closet stood open, filled with junk.

The living room had been obviously empty, so that left only her bedroom.

Staying close to him meant she bumped into his back every three or four steps. He didn't mention it, and she wasn't about to give him more room.

The bedroom looked the same as she'd left it. No mattress. Bare box springs.

But they both heard a noise.

Honest to God, her breath stalled in her lungs, especially when Tanner pointed to one open window and the bent screen now on the floor.

Keeping his gaze on the room, Tanner reached back, his hand landing on her hip. He pressed her to the hallway with the silent command for her to wait there.

Right. She could do that. Gripping the doorframe, she peeked in to watch him.

He stepped forward and listened again, his attention jerking to the closet where a quiet rustling sounded. The closet door was ajar.

She badly wanted to grab Tanner and make a run for it, but she was living independently now—sort of, or rather, just barely—and she supposed that meant she—or rather he—should check on anything out of place. This time, anyway.

Next time, she'd know what to do.

Next time, she'd damn well lock her doors and windows.

When he swung open the closet door, an enraged raccoon shot out, snarling and hissing, and even barking like a dog.

Tanner quickly backed up, giving the vicious critter a little room. It lunged at him but didn't make contact. "Get me a broom or something," he said quietly.

She raced off to the kitchen, located a broom in the pantry, and sprinted back.

Tanner now stood in the hallway with the bedroom door mostly closed. He took it from her with an offhand "Thanks," and an order to "Wait here."

Yeah, this time she wouldn't argue. "Be careful." Keeping one hand on the doorknob, she listened.

"Yah! Go on. Out you go."

To which the raccoon offered more threatening sounds…and finally it was quiet. The thud she heard was, she hoped, the window closing. Peeking in, she saw Tanner checking the closet again, top and bottom, and he even used the light on his phone to look in the dark corners. With that done, he set the broom aside and closed her other window.

The second he turned to her, she held up her hands. "Lessons learned. No unlocked doors or open windows."

He gave her a frown and stepped past her. "Raccoons are predators and they consider chickens an easy meal."

Horror froze her to the spot as she envisioned slaughtered chickens filling the yard she'd only cleared today. Tanner had reached the kitchen before she ran after him. She'd gotten in more running today than she usually would in a month.

He flipped on the outside lights and opened the door.

Holding her breath, Callie followed him out.

The yard was quiet and still, and that scared her even more. Were all the chickens murdered? She'd already gotten accustomed to them milling around, occasionally making faint clucking sounds that, to her, sounded quite pleasant.

When a goat suddenly screeched, so did Callie, and she startled Tanner.

He turned on her with a glare. "Don't do that!"

A nearly hysterical laugh bubbled out, even as she clutched his arm. Before this very moment, she never could have imagined badass Tanner Patrick jumping like that. "Where are the chickens? Please, *please* tell me they aren't all dead."

Rolling his eyes, he drew her close and put his arm

over her shoulders, which made her feel better as they crossed the yard. "Settle down. They're likely in their coop."

"They...what?" She would have halted but he kept them moving. "I thought you said—"

"They'll go in on their own." With a squeeze, he reassured her. "But you need to make sure the door is securely latched. Raccoons are clever about opening everything. Their little hands are stronger than you could imagine."

While another horrific scene flashed in her brain, one of stealthy raccoons opening doors and latches, she released him so he could peek into the coop first.

After sticking his head inside, he said, "They're in there."

Her panic receded, the relief so great that her legs went wobbly.

Until he stepped out and said, "Minus one."

Callie noticed that he didn't seem particularly worried about the death of a chicken, but it was destroying her. The birds relied on her and on her very first day, she'd failed one of them—"Ack!"

The chicken dropped from a tree with a lot of wing fluttering and excitement. It raced past her, up the ramp to the coop, and disappeared inside.

"They go in trees?" she shrieked, incredulous. "No one told me they go in trees!"

"A lot of people clip their wings so they can't. Reggie didn't feel right about that."

Heart still hammering, she struggled to catch her breath. "I wouldn't feel right about it either."

"Reggie named that particular bird."

His nonchalant tone told her this was a trap, and still she asked, "What did he call her?"

"Callie—because she's *flighty*."

Okay, so that was a little bit funny, prompting her to laugh with him. "You just made that up."

"I did, but she really is the only one who seems fond of getting into the trees. You'll have to check on her each night before you close up the latch."

"She doesn't fly away?"

"She knows her territory. They all do. They don't venture off too far." He led her over to the coop to show her how to properly secure the complicated latch. "If you don't do it right, sooner or later a raccoon will get in there."

And that would make for an awful surprise. "I need to let them out early?"

"As long as the sun's up." On their way to check on the goats, he gave her a rundown on how and when to feed the chickens, on keeping their water clean and fresh, and the upkeep of their coop. Then he surprised her with an offer. "I can come by in the morning and walk you through it, if you want."

His voice had lowered, gone rougher as if the words were grudgingly forced from him, but she didn't care. Every minute with him, even if they sniped at each other, felt like more. More than she'd had with a man in a long time. More intuitive and understanding. More warmth.

More *important*.

How that was, she didn't know, but she figured it had something to do with Tanner. Maybe chemistry between them. Or just good old-fashioned lust on her part, because no one could deny the man was *fine*.

The mature, responsible side of her had her asking, "Do you have the time for that? I know you keep a busy schedule."

Typical of Tanner, he shrugged. "I wouldn't have offered if I didn't."

"Such a grumpy Gus."

With a quick scowl, he opened his mouth, likely to withdraw the offer.

Callie didn't give him a chance. "I accept, thank you."

After holding her gaze for three heart-stopping seconds, he cracked a smile and looked away.

It felt like a victory, until the goats gave another eerie scream and she clenched all over. "I am *never* going to get used to that."

"You'll be gone before you have to."

This time he said it lightly, and she took that to be progress. "We'll see." The goats had already bedded down, piled close to each other in the shelter.

Tanner gave her a quick accounting of the space. "The fresh straw is stored up there in bales." He pointed to the rafters of the oversized shed. "You'll need help getting more down." His gaze landed on her again. "So did Reggie, so don't think that's a dig. Kam or I can pull down a bale when you need it. The floor is dirt, then gravel, and a nice layer of straw." In quick order he explained what she'd need to know about the goats.

After that, they went back inside. Callie was ready to wilt, but it was still too early for bed and she had promised Addie that she'd return.

At the front door, Tanner picked up the first aid kit. "Let's take a look."

Her brain ran away with that, leaping into a scenario

where he meant her clothes, all of them. And his own. Yup, she'd love to take a look. Pretty sure she'd enjoy him looking at her, too, as long as he didn't expect perfection. That was Glory's forte, not her own.

Hers was... Comfort? Ease? Overall, the ability to appreciate herself and what nature had given her. Imperfect, with hips a little wide, a curve to her stomach, but fortunately breasts to match. Glory forever worried because she wasn't quite as big-busted, and Callie hadn't yet been able to convince her that it didn't matter. Her cousin, unfortunately, tended to see everything about herself as a lack.

Realizing that her mind had wandered and Tanner was watching her, waiting, she grinned at herself. "Sorry. My thoughts took off in a whole different direction."

"Care to share?"

She shook her head and reached for the kit. "I can do it," she offered, though she'd definitely enjoy his efforts more.

Lacing his fingers with hers, he tugged her along. "I won't hurt you. Let's go."

Go where, she didn't know, but she followed anyway.

He urged her into the bathroom, where he flipped on the bright overhead light, then he opened the kit on the counter.

To be helpful, Callie pulled the neckline, as well as her bra strap, to the side and hooked them over her shoulder so he could see the scratch again.

He zeroed in on her, staring at her shoulder as if she'd bared a breast. With his expression so hot, she felt exposed. Silly, when her bathing suit showed a lot more skin and she wore that on the beach in big crowds.

The difference was that no other guy had looked at her with so much heated concentration, almost anticipation.

Touching her with just the tip of a finger, Tanner again brushed the skin around the raised, broken welt. His gaze never left her body, but his mouth tightened. "It's warm. Is it painful?"

"Only a little," she whispered, and it surprised her that she could say that much with him so near and so gentle. The absorbed way he studied her, as if memorizing her in detail, sped up her heartbeat. *Get a grip. He's not the first man to touch you.* "I did a rush shower," she said, though he already knew that since she'd made it within the allotted fifteen minutes, as she'd promised. "But I was careful to clean it well."

With the light graze of his finger touching her collarbone, then the side of her neck, he continued to scrutinize her.

"Tanner?"

"I'm going to go over it with an antiseptic swab, too." The low stroke of his voice drifted over her skin as gently as his physical stroke. It primed her in an unfamiliar way. Like foreplay, but with words, a tone, his attitude.

She tried to breathe normally and failed. She tried not to stare at him, but everything about him captured her sharpened interest. This late in the day, the rough texture of whiskers along his jaw and upper lip made her want to feel them. Her fingers wanted to tunnel into the thick hair hanging over his brow and curling slightly at his ears.

The shape of his mouth…how his lips moved as he spoke…she wanted to feel them against her lips.

While she grew hotter, he opened a little packet and pulled out an already-moist pad. "It'll sting," he warned gruffly, "but scratches from the woods run the risk of a fungus infection, same with rose thorns, moss, and hay."

The low murmur of his deep voice was the sexiest thing she'd ever heard, but the second the pad touched her skin, she hissed. No kidding, it stung. Badly.

"Sorry," he said, sounding like he meant it. After carefully swabbing the entire area, he leaned closer and gently blew on her.

With a deep, quiet inhale, she breathed him in. Still, he heard, and his eyes met hers. *Kiss me.*

As if he'd heard her thoughts, his gaze dropped to her mouth.

Hoping to encourage him, Callie put a hand to his chest. Through the soft cotton of his T-shirt, she felt the heat of him, the firmness of his body.

She tipped up her face.

His breath, warmer now, meshed with her own quickened breathing. By reflex alone, her fingers curled into his shirt, knotting the fabric. Anchoring him so he couldn't move away.

He made a rough sound and his mouth touched hers, tentatively, maybe waiting for permission.

Melting against him, she slid both hands up to his shoulders. "I'd really like it if you—"

Closing his arms around her, he turned his head and took her mouth like a starving man.

Whoa. Okay, *this*. Tanner's mouth, his possessive hunger, would go a long way toward obliterating all worries about the days ahead. She could feast off this one moment for weeks.

Loving how it felt to have her body against his, she

pressed closer. It could only be better if they were skin to skin. In a bed. God, he had a ripped body. Her hands explored as he devoured her mouth—

Suddenly he set her back, his gaze incendiary, his breathing ragged.

Confused, even a little lost, Callie concentrated on staying upright.

After staring into her eyes for an extended moment, he dropped his hands. "This probably isn't a good idea."

He was rejecting her? No, she wouldn't accept that. "It's a *great* idea." She tried to kiss him again. *More, more.* She wanted, needed, more.

"Callie, listen…" He caught her hands and continued to hold her away. "You're on the rebound."

No way had he just said that. Her brows drew together even as her lips continued to tingle. Seriously, she wanted more.

And he didn't.

Well, thank God for indignation. It was a far more comfortable emotion than dejection. For his obnoxious comment, she jerked her hands free, but in case he mistook the gesture, she clutched his shirt again and went on tiptoes to speak right into his face. "Don't think to tell me who I am, or what I'm doing. Only I get to do that."

"Okay," he said cautiously, eyeing her stance as if she might attack.

"Damn it, don't use that placating tone with me either."

His brows lifted high. "What would you have me do?"

In a near growl, she said, "Keep on kissing me."

He half laughed, then dropped his head forward a

second before cupping her face. "Honey, there's nothing I'd rather do. Well, other than a lot more."

Yes, please. More, more, more.

"But," he said, stressing the word, "you just busted your fiancé getting handsy in a coat room, right? Broke off a big society engagement. Bailed on a fancy wedding. Became the owner of a run-down house, goats and chickens, and a horse you haven't even met yet. Tell me if I'm missing anything."

He was missing her resolve, her free will to enjoy a stellar moment with an electrically hot man who made her yearn for things she'd never thought about before.

Clearly he didn't recognize her determination to have it all, on *her* terms, regardless of what her parents, Sutter, Glory, or anyone else wanted.

Looking at his set features, she knew there'd be no relenting on his part—and it infuriated her. Why did men always want to be noble at the worst times? "You're missing that I'm an adult who can choose what I want to do and when I want to do it. Right now," she flagged a finger back and forth between them. "With me and you? I was having a great time. Actually, I've enjoyed every minute with you." There, let him stew on that. "If that makes you uneasy, hey, that's your issue. At the moment I don't really care."

Instead of appearing uneasy, he gave her a slow, wicked grin. "A great time, huh? So I'm the balm for what's-his-name?"

Dropping her head back, she groaned out, "Ohmigod, you're being impossible." Then she took a determined step away from him, even though she'd have rather plastered herself to him and demanded…what?

If a man tried to make demands of her, she'd cut him off at the knees.

He waited, equal parts annoyed and unsure.

"Sutter was the farthest thing from my mind. To me, there was just us and a lot of sexual compatibility."

His brows lifted again, proving she'd surprised him. Score one for her.

"Fine," she said at last. "Play hard to get." She'd do her best to be fair, but she didn't have to like it. "I won't beg, or even try to convince you. If somewhere along the way, before I get too busy"—*as if*—"you decide you'd like to see where the chemistry takes us, you know where I am." She tilted closer to taunt him. "Here, with my goats, and my chickens, in *my* house, where I damn well intend to stay."

After a long, pointed look, he said, "Funny, Callie, but I don't see that ever-present smile of yours."

Eyes narrowing, she forced her lips to lift at the corners just the tiniest bit.

He didn't return the smile, but she saw the amusement in his dark eyes and even that, his never-ending attitude, made her want to touch him all over.

She was trying to think of something calm and reasonable to say, but Kam chose that auspicious moment to rap at the front door, saving her the trouble.

"We'll bring in your mattress," Tanner said on his way to the living room. "And then we'll let you call it a night."

Meaning she was no longer invited over to help clean, or to have dessert? Actually, it was a moot thought because Glory was with Kam, she had a plate of dessert from Addie, and Kam informed her he and Addie had already put the dinner stuff away.

Meaning Glory hadn't helped? Seemed likely.

She wouldn't worry over it. People were who they were, and she wasn't likely to change any of them tonight. But she did understand them. Somewhat.

Kam was a charming character, always ready to tease without ever really sharing himself. Addie was a caretaker, through and through, anxious to mother one and all. Sutter, her ex, was a product of his wealth and influence, selfish and entitled. Glory was steeped in her insecurities and doing her best to hide them, which often made her seem standoffish.

And Tanner... Mmm, Tanner. She watched as he and Kam wrestled the mattress back down the hall.

Tanner was a challenge, a steamy temptation, and a man who just plain did it for her. Never mind her broken engagement, her change of plans, or her unknown future. None of that was what made Tanner so appealing.

It was deeper than that. An innate connection. A gut feeling.

It was worth exploring.

She'd do her best to be patient while he figured it out. After all, she wasn't going anywhere, no matter how he'd prefer it.

CHAPTER SEVEN

THE NEXT FEW days were something of a routine, and Callie took comfort in knowing what to expect—in the short run, anyway. Each morning, Tanner or Kam had showed up to make sure she had the hang of caring for the animals. Addie visited her during the day. Glory alternated between complaining about wanting to go home, and looking at her phone.

She could have told Glory to go home, but that would mean she was at the house by herself. At night. Daytime was fine, but those pitch-black evenings with wailing goats and intrusive raccoons, not to mention the bugs, tended to weird her out a little. It was easier to sleep with Glory in the bed right next to her.

In between the never-ending chores, Callie immersed herself in recording her progress so they could post it later. She also fixed up the house so it'd be more livable. And in between those things, she dreamed up ways to seduce Tanner.

Twice more, she'd accepted Addie's invitations to dinner.

She was supposed to dine with them again tonight.

Addie swore she loved the female company, and Kam joked enough to keep her entertained, but each time Tanner grew more remote.

The third night, he wasn't even at dinner. She'd been

looking forward to seeing him again all day, especially
since Kam had visited her that morning instead of Tanner. Now he wasn't here, either.

Even to herself, Callie refused to admit how much it
bummed her. She decided to ignore his absence, as if it
didn't matter at all. "I don't know how you do it every
night, but the dinner is incredible."

"Chicken Marsala," Addie said. "It was a new rec-
ipe for me."

"It's perfect with the rice," Glory said. "I've never
had better."

Hmm. At least Glory was making the effort to atone
for her first performance at dinner. Now, she was all
compliments and an occasional shy smile at Kam, which
he ignored.

Unfortunately, after a few bites, she seemed to realize they were missing someone. "Tanner isn't joining us?"

"Nell called," Kam said, as if that explained it. He
went back to eating without elaborating.

It immediately made Callie wonder who Nell was
and why Kam was quiet about it.

I will not ask, I will not ask, I will no—

Addie huffed, appearing disappointed in her discretion. "Nell is sixteen, soon to be seventeen, actually.
She's a real sweet girl, but she has some difficulties at
home."

"Difficulties?" Callie asked in concern.

Kam frowned at Glory. "That doesn't leave this table
though."

"Oh, I wouldn't… I mean, I don't even know anyone
here. I wouldn't say anything even if I did." After all
that, she clammed up and glared back at Kam.

"Goats and chickens put away?" Addie asked, which was now her habit.

"Yes, and I ensured the latches were secure." She'd also locked her door.

"You get that extra room cleared out yet?"

Callie smiled. "Mostly, and no, I don't need you to finish it. You've already done more than enough for me, especially with dinner again. You work too hard."

"Amen," Kam said. Then he offered, "But if you run into anything heavy, or need any help, just let me know."

Glory flushed, maybe because she was the only one not offering.

To help her out, Callie said, "I'm going to enlist Glory to help me finish going through the last few boxes. Once that's all done, I hope to make it a proper bedroom."

Blinking fast, even smiling, Glory looked up at her. "*Oooh*, new furniture?"

"I think so." Callie hadn't told anyone yet, but she'd made plans to get some of her stuff out of storage, especially her beautiful bedroom set. "I want to get both bedrooms painted first."

Glory touched her arm. "I'd love to help."

Like it was an honor? Had Glory wanted to pitch in, but hadn't known how? Knowing her cousin's history, Callie should have considered that. "I was also hoping you'd help me with my videos."

More excited, Glory turned to face her. "For your channel?" This time the color blooming in her cheeks was enthusiasm. "I would love, love, *love* it! It's my specialty, you know."

Yes, Callie did know it. "Awesome."

"How do you have a specialty in online videos?" Kam asked, his skepticism plain.

Of course, Glory froze up, but only for a couple of seconds, then she turned back to her plate, cleared her throat, and composed herself. "I've studied audio engineering, sound design, and audio production."

"Plus she has hands-on experience."

"Only with family stuff."

"And it always looked beautifully produced and professional." Whenever she could brag on Glory, she did.

"Fascinating," Addie said. "Why don't you tell us more about that?"

See, that just made her adore Addie even more. The woman knew how to bring out the best in people.

While they ate, Glory modestly shared what she'd learned and what she could do with even the simplest recordings. They were almost finished with dinner when suddenly Blu, who'd been sleeping within view in the great room, jumped to his feet and gave a joyous bark. Everyone looked up.

Addie left her seat. "That'll be Tanner." She went to the stove and began preparing a plate.

Blu charged out of the room, and when he returned, Tanner was with him, talking softly to the dog and stroking his neck. He met Callie's gaze first.

Addie bustled over and gave him a hug. "I'm heating up your meal now."

He embraced her, his cheek to the top of her head, holding her gently…for an extra-long moment. Callie felt like she was intruding and yet she couldn't look away. Kam clasped Tanner's shoulder in brotherly concern, then he took over where Addie had left off with the food. He covered the plate and put it in the microwave.

With one last squeeze, Tanner released Addie, saying low, "She's okay."

"Thank God," Addie murmured.

Glory shared a quick, concerned glance with Callie.

Nodding, Callie pushed back her chair. "The food was incredible as always. Thank you."

Addie said, "You're not leaving, are you?"

"Actually, I have a dozen things to do yet tonight." She looked at the kitchen. "I'd like to help with the dishes before I go."

"You always help," Addie said. "Take tonight off."

She couldn't resist glancing at Tanner again, but he was busy accepting his plate from Kam, hot from the microwave, and sharing a few hushed words. Deciding not to interrupt the men, she said softly to Addie, "Thank you again for everything." She nudged Glory forward and the two of them left after giving Blu a pat. They passed Percy, the cat, who was sprawled out asleep on a chair in the great room. They exited through the back door.

It was another cool evening with the scent of rain carried on a heavy breeze. Tree leaves stirred overhead and the goats started their nightly bleating.

"I wonder what's going on," Glory whispered.

"With the goats?"

She rolled her eyes. "No, with Tanner and the mysterious Nell."

Callie shook her head. "I don't think she's mysterious. It's probably just a private matter, as Addie said."

"And young." Glory stuck to her side. "I don't even know her, but I already feel bad for her."

Callie hooked an arm through Glory's and pulled her closer as they walked. "I understand."

"I know. You're the only one who ever has."

Sadly true. "We're sisters, right? Even if we weren't born from the same parents."

After biting her lip, Glory asked, "Do you really feel that way? Still?"

"Of course I do. No matter what, Glory, that will never change." As the skies grew darker, Callie was glad she'd remembered to turn on the outside lights. "I know there have been a lot of changes."

"So many, and I...well, I need to confess something to you."

Dread gripped Callie, but she kept her tone calm. "Oh? Does this have something to do with my parents and Sutter?"

She nodded miserably. "They contact me constantly wanting updates on you."

"I figured. Sutter, too?"

"A few from him. Remember I called him that one night?"

"Yes." And in annoyance, she'd told Glory she wasn't her cousin anymore. "You know I was mad, right?"

"Yes!" Glory turned to her, stopping them both at the end of the driveway, where the porch light didn't quite reach. "I don't blame you, I swear I don't. I wanted to convince you to go back—I mean, I *still* do."

Slowly, Callie grinned. "No you don't."

"I do!"

Callie just looked at her, waiting. It got darker by the second, and she could almost feel the rain moving in.

Shoulders slumping, Glory grumbled, "All right, fine. It's what your parents want. And Sutter says he's still madly in love with you."

"Sutter was never in love with me, madly or otherwise."

Huffing a breath, Glory glanced around. "At first I didn't get it. This place is awful, the animals are possessed, and bugs are everywhere."

"At first you thought that?"

"I still think it—mostly. But it's sort of growing on me." Glory hugged her arms around herself. "I've slept better here than I ever have, and listening to you, Kam, Addie and Tanner all talk…it's so peaceful and easy. And personal, in such a nice way."

"It is, isn't it?" Going forward, Callie would ensure that she drew Glory more into the conversation. "Most importantly though, no matter where I live, or what anyone else wants, I'm not marrying Sutter. I've told all of you that often enough."

"So then why?" Holding out her arms, Glory asked, "Why all this fuss?"

"What do you mean?"

"Your parents sent me along to 'talk some sense into you,' as if I've ever had sway over you. They insist, constantly, that I need to do my duty and bring you back. Even when I told them it was useless, that I wanted to come home—"

Glory had wanted to leave her?

"—they said I *had* to stay. They said…" Her voice broke, but Glory rallied. "They said if I didn't bring you back with me, I might as well not return either."

Of all the nerve! "What the hell does that mean?" Glory had lived with them forever. She was, or should have been, like a daughter to them.

Playing it off with a sad smile, Glory lifted her hands.

"Pretty sure it means I won't have a job, or family, if there isn't a wedding."

Fury lit a fire through Callie's veins. "I'll take care of it." The words emerged calmly enough, but they were forged with steel. Glory *was* her sister. *Better* than a sister. No one, not even her own parents, could treat her like that.

"Don't you see, Callie? Your parents are frantic and acting out of character, and Sutter, I swear, is nearly apoplectic with the need to get you back. To all of them, it's critical or something. I mean, I know it was going to be a big society to-do and all that, and uniting the families was a big deal for the business. But is there something I don't know?"

Callie was starting to wonder the same thing. Just then they both heard voices coming from *her* house. Male voices that didn't sound like Tanner or Kam.

Glory huddled closer. "Who is that?" she whispered.

"No idea. Come on." Together, they inched along the driveway until Callie could see her front porch. Two men were there, and one was peering through a window. With Tanner's many warnings ringing in her ears, she wasn't sure what to do.

Getting out her phone, she pulled up Addie's number but didn't yet hit the call sign. Hoping to make a strong stance instead of appearing as a wary woman, she took a hard step closer and immediately drew their attention. "Gentlemen, can I help you?"

Both men slowly turned to fully face her. They were not ogres. Opposite of ogres, even. *Almost* as gorgeous as Tanner and Kam.

"Holy shit," Glory whispered in a very uncharacteristic loss of decorum. Then even lower, she murmured, "They're growing some really fine guys around here."

No lie. "Must be the country air." These two men weren't as tall as Tanner, and they weren't as shredded with muscle, but they were lean. Almost too lean. The taller of the two at maybe five-nine, or five-ten, visibly sized her up. Bracing his hands on her porch railing, he replied, "And who are you, darlin'?"

"I live here." That's all she'd tell him at the moment.

His eyes narrowed slightly. "Try again. This here's Reggie's place."

Surely this wasn't one of the Garmet brothers. "It was, yes. Reggie passed away."

"I'm aware. But the house never went up for sale."

"Naturally, since he left it to me and I'm not selling."

One man looked at the other, and they both grinned.

"You find that amusing?"

"Very." His gaze shifted to Glory. "You both livin' here?"

Glory surprised her by hefting her chin and saying succinctly, "We are."

"Well now. Reggie only had one bedroom. The other was piled high, from what I remember."

"So?" If Reggie had something of theirs, she'd get it for them and end this awkward visit.

Wearing a lecherous grin and sliding his gaze over Glory, the second guy came forward. "So since there's only one bed, does that mean you two will be sleeping...together?"

Of all the... Infuriated, Callie stepped in front of Glory. "She's my *cousin*."

He lifted both hands in mock surrender. "Hey,

don't say it like that. Can't fault a man for the way his thoughts go."

"Actually, I can." Most definitely when he acted like a pig.

"Oh, gawd," he groaned dramatically. "Don't tell me you're one of those."

They were insufferable. Callie crossed her arms and cocked out a hip. "Those being?"

"Women who twist every word, who get insulted over every little thing."

"What you were implying wasn't a little thing, and no, I don't get insulted easily." Let him make of that whatever he wanted. "I think it's past time for you two to go."

"Ah, now, darlin', don't be like that," the taller one said. "We're neighbors."

Damn. Sincerely hoping she was wrong, Callie guessed, "The Garmet brothers?"

"None other." As if settling in, the taller guy propped his forearms on the top rail. "I'm Dirk, and this is my brother Lang. We're harmless, I promise, so let's get acquainted."

In her mind, Callie couldn't help contrasting Dirk's nauseating attitude to Tanner's when they'd sat at the kitchen table joking about her independence. Tanner had teased, not insulted, and not once had he leered at her in such a disgusting way. "Not tonight." Yet they stood on her porch, so how could she get in her house without getting closer to them?

"Come on up," Dirk said. "We don't bite."

Lang laughed.

Callie didn't know what to do. When a growl sounded behind them, she turned—and God bless him, Tanner was approaching at a fast clip with Blu beside him. The dog immediately stepped in front of Callie and Glory, his ruff up, ears flattened and body stiff.

As Tanner passed them, he shoved a plate of cookies at her, which she automatically accepted. "Stay," he said, and Callie seriously hoped that abrupt command was for the dog and not her, because she'd had enough of hardheaded men for one evening.

She passed the cookies to Glory and, much more sedately, followed Tanner.

The men on the porch straightened, their expressions uneasy.

Dirk said, "Hey Tanner, what's up, man?"

"Leave."

Dirk and Lang both went rigid. "We were just introducing ourselves to the women and—"

"And you're done. Leave *now*."

"Fucker," Lang muttered, but he skulked down the steps.

Dirk, deliberately provoking, took his time. "Staking a claim, are ya?"

Tanner bunched up even more. "Say it again."

"Just asking, dude."

"No, you're insulting her and in the process you're pissing me off."

Callie remained just a few feet behind him. If things erupted, she didn't want to be in the way, but she hoped to smooth over the confrontation before that happened.

"Does she know you're a killer?" sneered Dirk from the porch. "Does she know how your mama had to mortgage her house just to keep your sorry ass out of prison?"

Showing no reaction to the taunts, Tanner shrugged.

"I have no idea what asinine rumors she's heard from the local lowlifes."

The complete lack of emotion in his tone alarmed Callie and clearly irritated Dirk. "If I may interrupt," she said, "it's getting late and I'd really like to call it a day." To ensure Tanner knew the dismissal wasn't for him, she stood at his side and gave all her attention to Dirk and Lang.

Dirk accepted it, loping down the steps, but with caution. "Maybe I'll see you tomorrow then." He glanced at Tanner. "Or maybe not." Pretending he didn't care, he backstepped away, keeping Tanner in his sight.

Tanner stood there, his body still tense, his gaze watchful as if he thought the brothers might attack at any moment.

Callie appreciated his rescue, but wasn't sure how to feel about his methods. He'd been antagonizing before he even understood the situation. Still, if it would deter Dirk and Lang from menacing her again—because they had been menacing, she wasn't oblivious to that—then she'd accept Tanner's influence.

While the other men were still near enough to hear, she said, "Tanner, would you and Blu like to come in for a few minutes?"

One of the brothers guffawed, and then they disappeared into the shadows at the side of Callie's house.

After drawing a slow, deep breath, he gave an abrupt nod. "Blu, come on."

The dog calmed, but he didn't leave Glory's side, sticking with her as she carried the cookies up the driveway, her expression bewildered. When she reached Tanner, who hadn't yet moved, she whispered, "I don't know what that was, but thank you."

For Glory, he softened. "Welcome." He took the plate from her and gestured for her and Callie, which included Blu, to precede him. "You might want to put my number in your phones. Kam's too, because no way is that the end of it, and the Garmet brothers are a hell of a lot worse than a raccoon or two."

Callie didn't realize she was shaking until she tried to get her door unlocked. She fumbled the key twice before getting it right and finally opening the door. The house was dark inside, so she took the plate from Tanner and, as she carried it to the kitchen, she flipped light switches. On her way back, she even turned on the hall light.

Blu took that as an invitation to explore, something she appreciated, especially when the dog returned without alarm, sniffing the floor, the couch, the walls.

"Probably looking for Reggie." Tanner patted his thigh. "Come here, Blu. You won't find him, buddy."

The dog immediately trotted over, then tipped his head in question.

Callie had the urge to cry. She even bent to hug Blu. "You are such a good boy, Blu." Swishing his tail, he nuzzled her, then stepped away and dropped down to rest in front of the door.

The house fell silent, the only sounds that of Glory pacing and Blu huffing out a tired breath as he settled in.

Tanner looked at Callie, ran a hand through his hair, and said, "Sorry about that."

She shook her head, unsure what he meant.

"Escalating things. Looking for a reason to take Dirk apart. The brothers set me off every damn time I see them."

Glory said, "Well, I can see why. They're disgusting."

"Agreed." Callie badly wanted to get closer to him, but she didn't want to press him. Ever since they'd kissed, he'd kept his distance. "I got the feeling they were going for charm, but missing it by a mile."

"They have zero respect for women. Honest men, either. Don't ever be fooled by them."

"We weren't." No, from the first sight of them, she'd sensed something was off—especially with them attempting to peer in her windows. "Were they friends with Reggie?"

"Hell no. Reggie didn't trust either of them. He'd busted them stealing from him plenty of times over the years, and once, when they were late teens, he found them shooting his chickens with BB guns."

Callie fumed. *"Cretins."*

"Their dad, before he passed on, thought it was hilarious and tossed ten bucks at Reggie, as if that'd solve it. Reggie punched him in the mouth and told him if he saw either of his boys around his place again, he'd call the police."

"He should have anyway!" Callie insisted.

"Wouldn't have done any good. They have cops for kin, so somehow they always skate by." Tanner studied their enraged faces. "Not to alarm either of you…" He stopped and shook his head. "Scratch that. You should be alarmed."

Glory put a hand to her head and groaned.

Callie said calmly, "Let's hear it."

"You need dead bolts on the doors, and probably on the windows, too." He hesitated only a second, then said, "I know a kid working an apprenticeship with a contractor. He's handy and always looking for extra cash. If you can afford him—"

"I assume he wouldn't cost any more than anyone else I hired?"

"Less, I'm sure. Liam's just turned nineteen and trying hard to make it on his own. He's the kid I told you about who needs a car."

And Tanner was trying to help him? Her admiration grew every time she was around him.

"I could bring him by tomorrow, after I do some deliveries," he offered. "Late afternoon, probably. You could meet him then."

"Sounds perfect." She'd be happy for the extra security, and for another visit with Tanner. "While you're both here, we could check out the car, make sure it still runs and everything."

Nonplussed, he blinked at her. "You haven't started it yet?"

She shook her head, and gave a ridiculous admission. "Don't you dare laugh, but I haven't even been in the garage yet." It was a detached building, and to her it didn't look at all inviting.

"Basement? Attic?" he asked.

"No to all that. I wanted to get my living space in order before I did anything else, though I planned to venture downstairs tomorrow because Addie said the washer and dryer are down there." And she already had plenty of laundry to do, especially with Reggie's bedding, towels, and dish towels that had gotten musty over the last couple of months.

"They are, among other things." He crossed his arms and watched her.

With a sigh, Callie said, "I can tell you're just dying to explain that cryptic comment."

"Glory might faint if I do."

"Oh God," Glory said, dropping to sit on the edge of the couch. "It's that bad?"

Tanner had the gall to laugh. "Lots of cobwebs, spiders, and other creepy crawlies. That's all."

A shudder ran over Callie. There was no guarantee that things in the basement would stay down there. "So I need an exterminator. Got it."

His taunting smile faded to one of gentle amusement. "Tell you what. While I'm here with Liam, I can check out the basement, make sure it's clear of the worst stuff."

She would love to agree, especially since he was being so nice about it. However, that would mean she couldn't handle it. Two big male strangers looming on her porch was one thing. A few spiders or other bugs was another. Surely, single women dealt with that sort of thing, and worse, on a regular basis.

So she sucked it up and declined with a grateful smile. "I appreciate the offer, but I can handle it."

His brows drew together in concern. "Okay, but would you mind waiting to go down there until I'm here, just in case?"

"Just in case I chicken out?"

"No, just in case a snake has taken up residence, or anything like that."

Her stomach bottomed out. Pretty sure she went pale, too. "Oh." Her effort to sound blasé failed. "Snakes." Yeah, she sounded sick.

"Most around here are harmless. Rat snakes or garter snakes, no big deal. But we have pit vipers too, and I wouldn't want you to run into one of them."

Yeah, that pretty much ensured she would not step foot in the basement.

He elaborated anyway. "They're venomous, in case you didn't know. Copperheads especially like to take up in abandoned buildings, and since it's been two months—"

Thrusting up a hand, Callie shushed him. "Say no more. Perhaps when Liam is here, he can also install a dead bolt on the basement door."

"Not a bad idea, since there are two windows down there."

"Well." Glory flopped back on the couch as if wilted. "If I hope to get any rest after all these dire warnings, I'm going to need a sleeping pill tonight for sure."

Looking genuinely contrite, Tanner said, "Sorry, but it is a concern." Taking Callie by surprise, he stepped closer and cupped a hand to the side of her neck. "I'm serious about you having my number. Keep your phone near you and call if either of the Garmet brothers gives you any trouble."

"Or if a snake intrudes?"

The corner of his mouth hitched up a notch, but his voice emerged as a husky rumble. "Even a raccoon."

The warmth of his hand on her skin had a lulling effect, as did his dark eyes staring into hers. She intrinsically trusted him, regardless of whatever had happened with the mysterious Nell today, or what that horrid Garmet brother had insinuated about murder. Already, Tanner knew things about her that no one else knew, not even Glory, and definitely not her parents.

Given that he'd talked with her about his childhood, she felt certain that he'd also shared things with her he would normally keep private.

However it had happened, they'd connected, even bonded, and not just in a "nice to date" or "sexual chemistry" type of way. There was that, for sure. Never in her life had she been so physically drawn to a man. Yet it was more, especially for her because she'd been looking for someone who would accept her choices, let her test her own boundaries.

Just let her *be*.

Oh, he grumbled, but he also encouraged her and when necessary—as it had been tonight, and previously with her raccoon intruder—he stepped up to make sure she was safe without ridiculing her.

Even when Tanner did criticize her, it didn't feel condescending. It felt teasing, sometimes automatic, as if he did it by rote, and occasionally self-serving and deliberate. After all, there were things he wanted with her house, so he had his own agenda.

"Thank you," she whispered, leaning a little closer.

Abruptly coming to her feet, Glory said, "I think I'll get a shower. Thank you for the help, Tanner. And the cookies."

Without looking away from Callie, he replied, "No problem."

Blu glanced up, watching Glory disappear down the hall, then he checked out Callie and Tanner, but he must have decided everything was fine because he put his head back on his paws and dozed off again.

The second they heard the bathroom door close, Callie went on tiptoe to kiss Tanner. From the moment he'd showed up, some part of her mind had wanted her mouth on his. If she thought of him, kisses were involved. When she looked at him, her lips tingled. Now he was here, in reach, and he wasn't exactly resistant.

But then, neither did he deepen the kiss.

His hand slid from her neck to her shoulder, then down her back so he could nudge her closer by small degrees until they were in full body contact.

Her senses rioted. How did she even stay upright? The scent of him, the feel of his solid body, his strength and warmth...so intoxicating.

Being held by him offered contentment, acceptance, and safety, all together in an incredibly stirring mix. She was twenty-eight years old and she'd never felt anything like it.

However, he wasn't devouring her mouth as he had last time, and in fact had turned the kiss so tender, their lips were barely touching. That was special in its own way. Sighing, she rested her cheek on his chest. "Kissing you is so, so nice."

His hand stroked up and down her back. "I wanted to talk to you."

Hm. So he'd rather talk than kiss. She could handle that—barely. "Okay." He sounded so grave, she emotionally braced herself.

"I had to miss dinner. I didn't want you to think I was deliberately dodging you."

"Kam mentioned someone named Nell." She waited, not releasing him, in no hurry to break physical contact with him.

His arms tightened around her. "I have no idea why I want to explain this to you."

At that, she pressed back to see his face. "Right? How long have we even known each other?" In case he misunderstood, she said quickly, "It just feels right, though, to share, I mean?"

"It does." He cupped her face in both hands. This kiss

was deeper and more thorough, but still far too brief. "Though I've known you for a long time."

Ouch. She was still smarting over that when he took her hand and led her into the kitchen.

With a glance around, he said, "The place is coming together."

She practically beamed. "Coming from Grumpy Gus, that's quite the compliment."

He hedged his big topic by saying, "You've done things faster than I expected."

"Oh?" She got out two mugs and a jug of milk, setting them on the table with the cookies and a decorative napkin holder that she used as a simple centerpiece. As she dropped into a chair, she asked, "What did you expect?"

He looked back at the kitchen entrance to ensure they were alone, then said, "That you'd be more like Glory, and no, that's not an insult to your cousin."

Sure sounded like one to her. "Then what is it?"

"An observation." He took the seat opposite her. "I assumed you'd look at a mess, hire people to clear it out, and otherwise stay clean."

"Clean?" she repeated.

The look he gave her almost brought on a blush. As far as she could remember, no man had ever looked at her like that, as if she was both the sexiest and most wonderful woman he'd ever known.

"That's what I always noticed about you. How 'fresh from the bath' you always seem." His gaze traveled over her cheek, along her neck and then the top of her chest. "Even sweaty, you glow." His voice dropped. "Makes me want to breathe you in all over."

You can. Name the day. Now would be fine. He was

so serious, though, she didn't want to derail him. "I look at you and see strength and compassion." That didn't quite cover it. "Protection, too."

His gaze sharpened. "For yourself?"

"No, not necessarily. For anyone who needed it, I guess." A dog, a brother...a girl named Nell. "In case you can't tell, I admire you, Tanner. A lot."

"I was getting a whole different vibe."

She grinned. "Yeah, well, I want you, too." And she didn't mind saying so. "But fine as you are, I wouldn't get all hot and bothered around you if I didn't admire you, too."

His laugh was quick and rough. "Hot and bothered, huh?"

Fanning her face dramatically, she said, "Very much so." There, she'd said it. He could make of that what he would.

CHAPTER EIGHT

BEING AROUND CALLIE had turned into one enormous, endless struggle. He wanted her, but he needed her to move on.

She was a longtime fantasy in the flesh, and a huge distraction.

He didn't want to care for her, but he couldn't help himself.

She admires me. For a man like him, that was better than pure desire. He'd been wanted before, by plenty of women over the years. But admiration? Far as he knew it was only his family, Addie and Kam, who offered that.

When she poured two mugs of milk, he accepted one, and the cookie she offered on a napkin.

Once they were both settled, he said, "You might meet Nell. She comes around to the farm for the occasional odd job. Mostly grooming Blu, but she'll help Addie plant flowers in the spring, or lend Kam a hand when he's washing our equipment."

"What's she like?"

Giving it quick thought, he said, "She's…sweet sixteen going on a jaded thirty."

Wearing her patented friendly smile, Callie said, "So, she's complicated?"

So complicated that she often made his head spin.

Boys he understood. Girls, not so much. Especially not at that age. "She's had one hell of a hard life that's left her cynical, tired, and looking for a reason to hate everyone, including herself."

"Rough. Teenage girls are hard enough on themselves when they're not dealing with anything major. Just growing up with peer groups and expectations can take a toll."

Was that how Callie had felt? He'd always assumed that she'd coasted through life without a single worry.

Envy of someone's money, social standing, and family could give that impression. Loosely, Tanner clasped his hands on the tabletop to keep from reaching for her. Holding her went a long way toward making a hellish day better.

Actually, just being with her did that, too.

"One minute, she'll be like a kid, happy about something." Concern gnawed at him. "Then it's like her world was upended and all she wants to do is run away."

"That sounds…" Callie studied his face. "Scary, actually. And a good reason to worry."

Glad that she understood, he did a fast rundown. "Her dad has always made her feel like dirt, blaming her because her mother took off to find a new man."

Callie winced.

"Her maternal grandmother tries, but at seventy-nine, she's too old to keep up with a teenager. At least with her, Nell has a place to live, food to eat, but guidance? Understanding?"

"Where's her dad now?"

"In and out of her life. More out than in." Thankfully. "There's an uncle who moved back home and it seems that he takes pleasure in making her life more miserable. Strange that he's her mother's brother, but he's a lot like her dad. Nell told me that there must be something about her that makes men feel that way."

"You corrected her? I mean, I'm sure you did," Callie said decisively, as if she didn't have a single doubt. "You and Kam would treat her with respect."

He nodded. "Respect, with a little guidance offered up. With her seventeenth birthday around the corner, Nell thinks she's all grown up and can just take off on her own." Much as he had at thirteen. Where he'd have ended up without Addie's help, Tanner couldn't say. All he knew was that he could do no less for Nell. "It takes some tricky juggling."

"Firm but kind?"

Sounded like Callie actually got it. "For someone who already feels unwanted, who's been treated badly most of her life, a single insult can overshadow a dozen compliments. One barb has a way of digging in."

"And festering," Callie said softly. "Is that what happened tonight?"

He sat back, already feeling better now that he was getting it off his chest. "The little fool hitchhiked out of town, but got dumped off at a restaurant." Biting into a cookie gave him a second to tamp down his renewed worry—and to corral the anger that accompanied it. After a drink of milk, he said, "Two guys were coming on heavy and she got spooked."

"Wow. I'm guessing she had the good sense to call you?"

Using both hands, he rubbed his face. "Yeah." Fear had hit him first, followed by bone-deep frustration. "I have zero problems helping out, but it's dicey because

I'm a grown man and she's an underage girl, so I can't just put her in a car alone with me."

"Not without possibly getting a lot of rumors started."

"The Garmet brothers already say plenty about me, but if they slandered Nell…" He left that open-ended, because when it came to Dirk and Lang, he never quite knew what he'd do, only that he would absolutely act.

He'd been living with rumors his whole life. He didn't want the same for Nell.

"I heard them," she said, as she dunked a cookie into her milk, then ate half in one bite, followed by a drink of milk.

Her appetite amused him. The lady really did love her sugar. "You don't seem concerned that I'm a murderer."

"Not in the least." With a fast smile, she moved past that without asking a single question. No, instead she just finished off her cookie.

Her easy attitude soothed him like a balm. "I went straight to her, of course. The second I walked in, the other men—and they were grown men, the bastards—took off. But then we had to wait for my friend at the halfway house where I…" Well hell. From the start, he should have known that this, too, would get around. Nothing much stayed private in Hoker, and definitely not in his life.

With Callie right next door, she was bound to notice a few things. Like teenagers helping out around the tree farm, and occasionally camping in the yard like a field trip. Educational seminars when he worked on trees. Seasonal outings.

Possibilities, he'd found, were endless when dealing

with young people who craved a little care and attention, as well as a positive outlet for complicated emotions.

"The halfway house where you help out? Where you sponsor?" She switched to the chair next to his so she could rest a hand on his forearm. "Full disclosure, I googled you that first night I was here."

"I'm not on social media." He dodged all that as much as he could.

"I know, but you put yourself out there helping others, especially kids, so others have info on you." Her fingers curled over his arm, then slid down to his wrist. "I saw some photos."

On occasion, he had to remind himself that Hoker wasn't all bad. Addie and Kam lived here, and there were a score of other caring people who also stepped up to help kids who were struggling, boys and girls going through hard times in their lives or with their families. Kids who needed a friend. Someone who would listen.

Firming his mouth to keep from making more confessions, Tanner nodded. Beyond that, he wasn't sure what to say.

"You got Nell somewhere safe?"

That was a question he could answer. "The halfway house for tonight—where she promised to stay until we can sort things out. I reminded her that she didn't want her grandma upset, so she called her and told her where she was."

"It's happened before?"

"Let's just say social services are aware."

Callie bit her lip, then leaned in to give him a quick hug. "I'm so sorry. You'd already had that to deal with, then you ran smack dab into the Garmets and all their nonsense."

What the Garmet brothers dealt out wasn't nonsense. It was danger. Intrusion. Often a menacing combo of both. Dealing with them had been his pleasure, a way to release some tension. A good old-fashioned brawl would have been even better, but then Addie would have had a fit, and it would have scared Blu, and who knew what Callie would think about it.

So far, most of her reactions were unexpected. "Take my number."

Appearing happy to do so, she got out her phone and opened up her contact list. "Go."

He recited his number, and then Kam's. "Make sure Glory has both numbers, too." When it came to Dirk and Lang, they weren't above using either woman to get to him. Or just to take what they wanted. It was how they'd always operated, for as long as Tanner could remember.

"I'll share with Glory." She touched his hand. "Do you want mine?"

If he had it, it'd be so tempting to call her, even when he knew he shouldn't. She was a city girl with a city job, and probably a city fiancé just waiting for his chance to lure her back.

It was that last thought that rankled the most. He needed her to go, but not like that. Not to the dick who'd hurt her.

He got out his phone. "Ready."

When that was done, they each finished off another cookie before Callie got up to put things away. She covered the cookies and stored them in the microwave to keep them fresh, saying with a grin that she hadn't yet bought a cookie jar, but she would.

Because to her, she thought this place was her new home. A place for nesting—cookie jars and all.

He knew better. Much as she appeared to be settling in, she wouldn't stay. He couldn't let himself believe that. Not only would it throw off all his plans, it'd make him think… No, he wouldn't go there, not even in his thoughts.

"I promise to return Addie's plate tomorrow."

Seemed every day she or Addie found an excuse to be together. From Addie's perspective, he got it. Having another woman so close was nice for her. What was Callie's angle? Sure, Addie had a way of winning over everyone she met, even princesses from the rich side of town who'd long ago moved on. Would that be enough for her? Did Callie enjoy Addie's brand of motherly nurturing?

Far as he knew, she'd always had the best of everything. Well, except fiancés. Her fiancé had apparently sucked big-time. And maybe her parents weren't so great if they still expected her to marry the guy. Even her cousin, who Callie clearly loved, had hassled her over this Sutter jerk.

Other than that though, Callie had scored big in life.

Even to himself, that reasoning sounded absurd. How sweet could her life have been surrounded by people who didn't prioritize her emotional well-being?

Tanner almost snorted. For most of the troubled kids he knew, Callie's wealth and privilege would be a huge boost. They needed love and attention, definitely, but they also needed clothes, good food, and the occasional gift.

A beautiful woman like Callie would have no problem finding a guy—hell, twenty guys—who'd give her all the love and attention she could bear.

So for her, what was the lure of small-town living?

"You've gone awfully quiet, Tanner. It's like I can feel you stewing." She cast him a flirty glance over her shoulder. "Or dissecting my character."

Watching her bustle around the kitchen sent tension spiraling through him. "Just noticing that you move with the practiced ease of someone who grew up wiping crumbs off a table and washing coffee mugs to stack in a drainer."

Laughing, she said, "Thank you. I try," as if he'd given her a huge compliment.

Shaking his head, Tanner accepted that she worked in her yard the same way, and when she fed the animals, she looked… Happy. Content.

Like she belonged here and nowhere else.

That wouldn't last. *It wouldn't.* But his tension mounted until it felt like he couldn't breathe.

"Take a picture," she quipped while hanging the dish towel just so, as if it mattered. "It'll last longer."

That last taunt proved his undoing. Tanner rose silently from his seat, then came up behind her to loop his arms around her waist and drag her into close contact with his body. Definitely, that helped. He filled his starving lungs with a deep breath, filling his head with Callie's unique scent. "*Have* you worked in a kitchen before?"

Her laugh was pure delight without a hint of affront. "I've had my own condos and apartments—without staff, so yes. Heck, when we lived here, Mom and Dad were just making their mark in the world. We had cleaning people who came twice a week—"

"And landscapers, painters, designers, pool maintenance, accountants… Your family employed half the town."

"True, but my daily chores included making my own bed, putting away my own laundry, and sometimes helping in the kitchen, since we often had dinner at home."

"You poor child," he whispered with clear irony.

"Stop it," she said around a light laugh. "I know I was pampered. Don't rub it in."

He wouldn't mind rubbing... No. Better to ban that thought.

"Like I said, I had my own place. When there wasn't a dinner meeting, I usually picked up something, but in a pinch I could grill a cheese sandwich, or fry an egg and bacon, and you already know my love of all things sugary." She lifted her shoulders. "So cleanup was a necessity."

"Well, you look great doing it." Doing *anything*, really. He'd always thought so. Being dressed down and "roughing it" it was no different.

"Oh, fun. I'm glad to hear it because that will be part of my video podcast series. How to look good while working with chickens. Or goats. Or weeding the garden." She flagged a hand in the air. "Basically, how to feel good about yourself no matter what. It's catchy, don't you think?"

He didn't want to think about her shooting videos of herself and sharing it with the world, so he switched topics on her by saying, "I think you smell indescribable." He brushed his nose along the side of her neck and the slope of her shoulder, a little amazed that he was here with Callie McCallahan, flirting, touching, and kissing in what used to be Reggie's cluttered kitchen. "I always knew you'd smell this good."

She leaned into him, even tilted her head a little to make it easier for his mouth to explore. "Tanner?"

"Hmm?" Her ears were small, each with double piercings, but currently without earrings.

Lacing her fingers over his, she kept his hands at her stomach. Not that he was moving them, but now she'd locked him in place—unless he forcefully pulled away. "I don't want you to give a single thought to anything Dirk or Lang might say to me."

Automatically, he started to step back—then he realized why she held on to him. "They're assholes. I never pay attention to them."

"Be that as it may," she said, her tone proper enough to defuse his reaction, "I wanted you to know that I put no stock in what I hear, unless I hear it from you."

Well hell. Did that mean she trusted him? Completely trusted him? Already?

Awful rumors had always been his curse, tainting the judgment of others before they'd even met him. Now Callie had heard them, but discounted them, and it left him feeling primed.

She turned in his arms and smiled up at him. "I haven't been here that long. You owe me nothing, not defense against other pesky neighbors, and definitely not explanations that you aren't ready to share." Kissing him quick and firm on the mouth, she added, "I plan to be a no-pressure neighbor, as long as you understand that I already like you. A lot. In many ways." And with that, she said, "Oh look, Blu came to check on us."

Which was her way of saying their visit was over. Sure enough, Blu was there, but typical of the dog, he hadn't made a sound. When he wanted, Blu could be as stealthy as a ninja.

Tanner stepped back. "Wedge a chair under each door, and call me if anything spooks you."

"My, my," she teased, looping her arm with his and walking him back to the living room. "You are the absolute best, most attentive and caring neighbor ever—especially for one who would rather see me packing up to leave."

Caught in his own mixed messaging, he made a sound, half laugh and half growl.

"I see your concern as yet another reason for me to want to stay. Permanently."

THAT BIT ABOUT Tanner being a murderer and how Addie had to mortgage her house played over and over in Callie's mind as she got through her morning and early afternoon chores. Had someone accused him of murdering his father? At thirteen? Absurd.

Although, given the abuse she suspected he'd suffered... *No.* She refused to imagine awful scenarios. She trusted Tanner, so unless someone told her something concrete, she'd do him the courtesy of ignoring accusations.

After she showered and changed into a cute halter and shorts, she and Glory did a quick makeup video. In the backyard. With curious chickens meandering into the frame and the goats putting in a few cameos.

Glory had a much better eye for lighting and background, and she occasionally prompted Callie on which way to turn, or how to tilt her face.

Throughout the video, Callie teased about the country life, the fresh air, the importance of sunscreen—at Glory's insistence—and how invigorating it was to be her own boss. She ended it with a double coat of mascara, batting her eyelashes at the camera and teasing that soon they'd be weeding the garden, and how fun would that be?

Even Glory laughed, though she covered her mouth to muffle the sound.

All in all, Callie was pleased with her performance and she trusted Glory to edit it in a way that would make it more interesting.

While Glory got more footage of the yard and the animals, Callie forced herself not to check the time. She'd already done so, repeatedly, but Tanner hadn't specified exactly when he'd be by other than later afternoon, and counting off the minutes wouldn't make it happen any sooner.

Glory said, "I'm heading inside now. I want to do some editing while my ideas are fresh. Do you need anything before I get started?"

"Nope." Callie knew that once her cousin dug in, she'd be involved for an hour or more. "I'm good, so take your time. And thanks."

"It's going to be great." With that, Glory went into the house. Her laptop, which contained her editing programs, was set up in the bedroom on a folding table they'd located in the spare bedroom. She'd use a kitchen chair until Callie could get new furniture, which would include a desk and office chair.

To keep herself busy, Callie headed out to the detached garage to see the car that Tanner had mentioned. If he thought Liam could use it, she'd be more than happy to give it to him. She had no need of a second car. Her red Ford Escape was still fairly new.

Weeds had grown up around the outside of the wooden building, though the apron and foundation were

concrete. Her gravel driveway, running along the side
of the house, led right up to it, except that a fence had
been installed to keep the goats in the yard. To use the
garage, she'd have to get out and open the gate, then
drive through and get out again to close the gate.

She wasn't at all sure it was worth the effort. However, the storage would be nice. Circling the building,
she checked it out from every angle. It appeared sturdy
but in need of fresh paint and, like the rest of the property, a good cleaning.

The afternoon sunlight couldn't penetrate the grimy
windows on two walls. On the third wall, she found a
regular entry door, but it was locked. The wide garage
door wasn't, but it was surprisingly heavy. She struggled to get it halfway open, then levered her shoulder
under it—a mistake, given how dirty it was—and used
her legs to lift.

Just as she heard a car door in her driveway, she also
saw movement from the corner of her eye. Barely main-
taining her hold on the door, she looked into the dim
interior, and she saw something slither.

That something was a *snake*!

Screeching, Callie stumbled back. The garage door
landed with a loud bang, and she landed on her butt.
She didn't stay put though, still screeching, she shot to
her feet and turned to run.

Right into Sutter.

His arms automatically went around her. "Callie?"

She screamed again, this time—at least partially—
in frustration. But hey, a snake was near and she was
determined to find safety, even if that meant with her
ex. She tried to duck behind him, but he was laughing,
hugging her.

He said, "I missed you too, honey."

Turning so she could see the garage, meant turning Sutter as well, since he continued to hold her, but she got them both shifted around. Going on tiptoe, bracing her hands on his shoulders, Callie looked behind him, relieved that no snakes were in sight, at least not that she'd spotted yet. That didn't mean one wasn't near, though. The thing had seemed huge. Long and black and... She almost screamed again.

Sutter kissed her hair, then her cheek, before embracing her tightly and turning her in a half circle. "God, I'm so glad to see you. I should have known coming here was the right thing, that you've missed me too. But with the way you walked out on me... I wanted to give you time to realize that it was a mistake to leave."

Wait—*what*? She pressed him back, and then, just beyond him, saw the frozen faces of Tanner and a young man. Liam, she assumed.

Sutter cupped her face. "Tell me you missed me."

"No." Damn it, Tanner would definitely get the wrong impression. She'd only grabbed Sutter because... Remembering the snake, she looked around wildly again, this time spotting it in the grass.

Screaming once more, she ran to Tanner. "Snake. *Huge*. It came out of the garage."

With a fierce frown, he set her aside and started forward for a closer look.

"Tanner, no!" With both hands, Callie caught the back of his shirt. "It could be poisonous."

"Venomous," he corrected, already stopping when he spotted it. "That's a rat snake. Big, yeah, but harmless."

Liam jogged forward. "I'll get it."

"Good Lord." Callie seriously thought she might

faint. She tucked her face against Tanner's back, unable to watch. What a terrible impression she was making on his young friend, screaming and carrying on. She hid anyway.

That is, until she heard Sutter's voice, much closer now, demanding, "Who the hell are you?"

"Neighbor," Tanner said, his tone flat but not antagonistic. "I take it you're Sutter?"

Callie peeked out to see Liam disappearing in the woods, his hands full of—*gulp*—snake.

Sutter smiled widely. "She's talked about me?" His gaze moved to Callie and he opened his arms. "Come here, babe."

"Ah, no." But she couldn't continue to cower behind Tanner or that might cause strife while, currently, there was none. At least, not between the men. The "insta-rage" Tanner had exhibited for the Garmets was thankfully absent now. "You shouldn't be here, Sutter. If you had called first, I would have told you that."

"Callie," he said, his tone mildly chiding, almost playful. "I know how stubborn you are. You wouldn't have answered."

"So instead you just show up?"

He waggled his fingers in a "gimme" gesture. "Let me hold you again."

Gritting her teeth, Callie said, "Absolutely not."

"Excuse me." Tanner stepped away for the garage. "I'll make sure there aren't more snakes."

Shuddering, Callie did her best to be brave. "I'll be right there," she told him, astounded and pleased by his careless attitude. Sort of. *No*, she definitely was. She didn't need a caveman getting all territorial. It was great that Tanner was behaving reasonably.

Or…maybe he really didn't care? Could that be? Had the connection she'd felt been all one-sided? Her side? Ugh.

While Callie stared after him, Tanner lifted the heavy garage door—perhaps with a bit more force than necessary, he certainly didn't struggle with it as she had. Pronounced muscles moved over his shoulders and biceps.

Sutter touched her back, then slid his hand to her neck and tipped up her face. "You've gotten too much sun."

The stark differences between the two men hit her anew. "No, I haven't." Prioritizing, she stepped out of his reach and, for the moment, gave all of her attention to him. "You need to go. Right now. We're done. Over. There's nothing to talk about."

"Callie," he chided again, making her realize how much she hated it when he said her name like that. "We can still go…where was it you wanted to go for our honeymoon? The Cayman Islands?"

"Costa Rica," Tanner called from inside the garage.

Shaking that off, Sutter said, "Right. I knew it started with a *C*." Then his expression softened. "We can still go. And all those beautiful things you put on the registry. There was some kind of bedding you loved, right?"

"Floral," Tanner said offhand as he walked out with yet another snake. He shot Sutter a look. "Linen."

It struck Callie that her fiancé hadn't listened, but Tanner had. *What a precious thing it was to be heard.* Her heart started rapping hard and wouldn't let up. She didn't know if it was the fear of the snakes, or the sudden surge of emotion for a particularly irascible neighbor. "Floral linen," she confirmed softly.

Tanner didn't go far, definitely not out of her sight, and then Liam was there to take that snake from him. He reentered the garage and started moving things around.

After anticipating his visit all day, Callie didn't want to waste another single second on her ex. In a lowered voice, she said firmly, "Listen up, Sutter. We are one hundred percent done. No do-overs. No makeups. No second chances. I will not, *ever*, marry you."

Desperation, then a touch of anger, altered his congenial expression. "This is ridiculous. Plans were already made. You know that. You can't back out now."

"I already did!"

"No, you had a little fit because I did something stupid. I regret it, but that doesn't mean you get to ruin everything." He leaned into her space, which meant bending down because he was similar in height to Tanner. "Our families—your parents, *my parents*—invested in each other. You can't just fuck everyone over because you're pissed."

Wow, okay, she hadn't seen that one coming. Never before, not once, had Sutter used that tone with her. She'd seen him annoyed at others, not her, and even then he'd kept it together.

It made her stomach churn to have him speak to her like that. "You need to leave now."

"Not," he said through his teeth, taking a step closer, "until we talk."

Her own temper spiked, quickening her breathing, narrowing her vision. "That's where you're wrong." She turned to walk away, but he caught her arm, making her gasp.

Before he'd even turned her around, Tanner was

there beside her, his gaze pinning Sutter. "Think hard," he said, the softness of his voice somehow more commanding, "how you want this to play out."

Sutter released her, but didn't relent. "She's my fiancée, and we have things to discuss."

"No, I am *not*," Callie said, even more frazzled now that Tanner had interceded. "And no, we don't. I have nothing to say to you." In a precautionary measure, she stepped partially in front of Tanner. "I'll talk to my parents, but I'm not talking to you."

"Damn it, Callie—" He reached for her again.

"No," Tanner said. Just that, again quietly, but it landed in the space between them like a thunderclap.

Scowling, Sutter withdrew his hand and curled his lip. "Neighbor, my ass. There's more going on here."

She hoped that was true, but Callie wouldn't verify anything for him, and she definitely wouldn't speak for Tanner. "Will you please just *go*?"

"For now." He looked at the house and snorted. "Where's Glory?"

"Why?"

"I need to talk to her."

Callie got out her phone and sent Glory a quick message, unsure if she'd even see it while editing the video.

Seconds later, the back door opened and Glory, wide-eyed, stepped out. Cautiously, she looked at each of them, and then Sutter. "What are you doing here?"

"They want to see you. In person." He barely looked at Glory as he turned to go. "I'll wait five minutes and then I'm leaving."

"Five…" Glory turned to stare at Callie, shocked and unsure.

Her heart broke for her cousin. Far too many times

her parents had done this to her, acted as if she somehow owed them total obedience because they'd taken
her in. "Ten minutes, and if you leave before that then
you can explain to my parents."

Jaw tight, Sutter nodded.

Glory looked off to the side, breathing hard, then
she ran back inside.

Furious with the situation, Callie looked up at Tanner. She touched his jaw. "Thank you for being amazing."

His eyes narrowed.

Hating to impose even more, but knowing it was
necessary, Callie asked, "Could I be an even bigger
burden and take a few minutes to help Glory? I promise I'll be right back."

Taking her off guard, he held her face and bent to
give her a very soft kiss. "I'll show Liam the car. We'll
be right here."

Yup. Amazing. She smiled at him, then headed in.
Unlike Glory, she didn't race, but she did use long
strides.

Glory was in the living room, perched on the edge
of the seat, her laptop and purse beside her, but not her
suitcase or toiletry bag. The second she spotted Callie,
she shot to her feet. "I want to come back. Is that okay?"

Until Glory said it, Callie hadn't realized how much
she was dreading being alone. "Yes!" She hugged her
hard. "Yes, of course. I told you, you're always welcome to be with me."

Glory caught her shoulders. "Promise me you'll be
careful."

"You first."

After sharing a laugh, they hugged again, and Glory

faced her with new optimism. "I need to get my car anyway, right? And more clothes. Other…stuff. I'll talk to your parents and I'll try to make it clear that I can't be the go-between."

"You don't have to do that." Callie knew the pressure they put on her. "I don't care if you update them. With Sutter showing up here, I plan to talk to them anyway."

"I'll tell them I support your decision." Glancing toward the window to ensure Sutter was still there, she added, "It's past time I broke those chains. It's just… I've gotten so dependent on them."

Very true. Callie's parents, her mother especially, had always made Glory feel beholden, as if they'd rescued her instead of simply loving her. They set conditions on everything they gave, including their approval.

In turn, Glory had worked endlessly to show them how much she appreciated being part of their lives. So often, she'd seemed to feel that she didn't have a choice. "We both know how they'll react. If you truly feel that way—and I'll love you regardless—it'd be better if you slowly and gently break away. It doesn't have to be a big, bold statement."

"Do you think so?"

"Yes. Do what you're comfortable doing. I can hold my own, and as soon as you're ready, come back."

"It'll probably only be a few days."

"I'm already missing you."

CHAPTER NINE

AFTER GLORY AND Sutter drove off, a very bad mood descended on Tanner. He hid it, knowing Liam needed his positive influence, not his distraction with one very beautiful, determined and fascinating woman. Seeing what Callie was up against though... It had taken greater restraint than he knew he had to keep from flattening Sutter.

After the summons given to Glory, more pressure would be on the way.

Would Callie give in and resign herself to a life with that prick? God, Tanner hoped not.

Yes, he still needed her to go. Being with Liam today reinforced that, but he didn't want her to be unhappy.

He didn't really *want* her to go.

It was for the best, he reminded himself over and over again. Back when he'd been lost and alone, when he'd about given up on the world, he'd received what he needed most: encouragement, someone who cared. A purpose.

Now he knew a dozen kids facing the same turmoil he'd once faced. How could he let them down?

"Day-yum," Liam murmured, once he'd uncovered the car.

The awe on his face should have been reserved for a Rolls Royce, not a twenty-year-old, two-tone Buick

Rendezvous. Granted, Reggie had kept it in good shape, but still...

With the way Liam ran his hand over the old Buick, his handsome young face split with a smile, he already loved it in a way nearly exclusive to nineteen-year-old boys.

"She's in sweet shape, isn't she?"

She? Yup, definitely a young dude thing. "From what I remember, she runs great, too."

From outside the garage, her caution evident as she looked all around, Callie asked, "Would you like to take it for a drive? I brought the keys." In her hand, she held up a goofy peace sign keychain that used to be Reggie's. The car key, and several others, dangled noisily.

Round eyed, Liam asked, "For real?"

Callie actually laughed. "Fingers crossed it runs!" She tossed the keys to him, then backed up. "Forgive me, but I've had enough snakes today."

Did that include the kind that stood on two legs? For Tanner, it did. Her ex was far, far worse than any rat snake, or even a copperhead.

Quickly, Liam cleared the way to ensure he could pull straight out. Tanner helped, then waited until Liam got inside and started it up. The car purred as Liam caressed the steering wheel.

Making a split-second decision, Tanner opted to let him go on his own. He stepped back. "How much gas does she have?"

"Quarter tank."

Nodding, he said, "Don't go too far, maybe just around the block a few times."

Like a kid on Christmas morning, Liam put it in Drive. "I'll be extra careful."

"I know." Tanner had taken him to get his license a

few years back. Whenever possible, he let Liam drive the truck. He was a good, hardworking, independent young man, largely because he hadn't had other options, at least on the hard work and independence. The good…that came straight from Liam's heart. "Let me open the gate." He jogged across the yard and pulled the gate wide open.

Wearing a tempered smile, Liam slowly pulled through.

Callie came to stand beside Tanner while Liam went down the driveway, passed alongside her car, paused before turning on the road, and then drove out of sight.

"That was pretty awesome," she said. "Thank you for letting me share it."

Always with her, it was the unexpected. "It's *your* car."

"No, it was Reggie's. Mine is that cute red Escape in the driveway." She grinned. "Seriously, I have no need of another car. As far as I'm concerned, that's just another place for snakes to hide. If he still wants it, you can consider it Liam's."

"Just like that."

"I mean…yes? I'll have to find the title and sign it over to him, but it made me happy to see him so happy."

Not crushing her to him for a long, deep kiss proved difficult. Every single time Tanner saw her, she said or did something that made him want her more. Sharing in Liam's happiness was a biggie, one that hit him right in the heart.

Locking his hands at his sides, Tanner stepped away from enticement. "We can discuss it with Liam when he gets back." Time to put a little more distance between them. "The title should be in a box with Reggie's other important papers, stored in the spare bedroom."

"You know that, how?"

"He told me. Since he didn't have any close family—and no, that's not a dig at you—he said he needed someone to know where to find things in case anything happened to him."

Callie still looked wounded with guilt.

"Hey. Phones work both ways. He could have called as easily as you could have." To keep from consoling her—with a hug, or a kiss…maybe more—Tanner headed back to the garage.

"Who taught him to drive?" she asked, hustling to keep up with his long-legged stride.

"I did."

As if she'd already known the answer, she looped her arm through his in an awkward still-walking hug. "That's what I figured."

Scrubbing a hand over his mouth didn't lessen the need to kiss that smile off of her beautiful face. He stopped outside the garage. "Do you think it's a good idea for you to stay here alone?"

"Yes," she replied immediately. "It's a great idea." Almost daring him to disagree, she stated, "It's my home, after all."

For now, he reminded himself. "Sounded to me like your folks are expecting something different."

"When it comes to me, they usually do." Her sigh held not a hint of real regret. "In one way or another, I've been a disappointment to them my entire life."

"No way."

"Sadly true—not that I'm all that broke up about it, really. They have expectations but most of them are based on me being someone I'm not."

Tanner crossed his arms. "I remember you as a straight-A student."

"That was me. I'm still an overachiever." Holding out her arms, she encompassed the property. "Now I choose to overachieve here, with my goats and chickens."

"And a horse you haven't met yet."

She tucked back a loose wisp of hair. "Yeah, I need to do that, I guess." Tapping her head, she said, "Adding it to my ever-growing list."

Whether she was trying or not, she charmed him. Always had. Back then it had been her looks, her smile, and her overall upbeat attitude. Now it was more about what she physically took on and her iron resolve that affected him.

Plus, yes, she was still gorgeous. "I remember you being a cheerleader, too."

"Now I'm cheering you. And Liam. Probably Nell too, if I ever get to meet her." She tilted her head back, eyes closed, and drew in a deep breath. "Me, too, I guess." Opening her eyes again, she met his gaze and grinned. "I'm cheering myself on because I'm going to make this work."

His huff of exasperation sounded more like a laugh. Made sense, because her happiness was contagious. "So good grades, cheerleading, always polite—how are you not meeting mommy and daddy's expectations?"

"That was high school. Wasn't really different in college though. If I do something, I want to do it right. Except I don't want to marry Sutter. I don't care about uniting the businesses. I don't really care about the pampered life I had. I mean, wait, I *sort of* do. Like I still want my leisurely soaks in a jetted tub every so often."

He did not need to hear that. Or imagine it.

"And I love the occasional salon trip. Facial, pedi, maybe a massage."

Nope. He propped his tingling hands on his hips and pretended impatience.

"I love good food. Well, all food, I guess." Wrinkling her nose, she patted her hips with both hands. "I often have a big appetite."

Insinuating it showed? He could tell her that her ass was perfect, but he wouldn't. "So the big conflict is… what? You don't want to work for them? You didn't like your job?"

"Correct on both counts. Plus I'm sick of bossy men who see me as arm candy because my dad is important, but they don't really see *me*."

Scoffing, Tanner said, "There's not a hetero man alive who doesn't *see* you."

"I doubt that's true, but if it was, then maybe it's in how they see me. Clearly, Sutter sees me as a connection. That's all."

He couldn't argue that one. It was downright bizarre how Sutter had plowed right past her objections as if she hadn't spoken. "He's a rare breed of fool, that's all."

"You heard him, Tanner. You saw how he is. Do you have any idea how humiliating that is? I swore after college that I'd never again let a guy take advantage of me, and then Sutter came along and my parents liked him, and—"

"Whoa, wait." He touched her lips to interrupt her. They were soft, like the rest of her. He got so involved in tracing her lips that he almost forgot what he wanted to say. Dropping his hand and putting the space of a big backstep between them, he said, "Back up. To college."

"It's not a great story and I'm kind of on a roll here." Moving in, she ran her hands up his chest.

It'd be so easy to cave, to get wrapped up in wanting

her that he forgot everything else. Except Liam would return soon, and for now Liam was the priority. Whenever Tanner was with one of the kids, he made sure that they had his entire focus.

But until Liam got back… "We'll have a teenager showing up any minute now, super psyched about the prospect of a car, so let's put this"—he pressed a firm smooch to her mouth—"on hold for a bit."

The corners of those irresistible lips tipped up in pleasure. "Right. On hold. This is me." She laced her fingers together. "Being patient."

It was her being pure temptation, but at least she wasn't sliding those small, soft hands all over him now. He could resist a lot, but not that.

"What happened in college?" He'd heard mentions of it twice, once when she'd first arrived in the woods with her cousin, and then again just now. He sensed it had been a game-changer for her, something that had affected her deeply.

Tension firmed her jaw and she looked away.

So maybe he shouldn't press her. If it was difficult for her to talk about, he didn't want to put her through it with his nosiness.

"Sorry," he said, meaning it. "I shouldn't pry."

"No, it's my fault for bringing it up." She squared her shoulders and met his gaze. "Plus, I've dug into your life plenty, right?"

"A little here and there." She often made him feel comfortable enough to share. That, too, must be one of Callie's unique qualities.

"I'm going to condense it because if I start going into the nitty-gritty, well, I still get worked up over it."

His curiosity expanded. "Whatever you're comfortable with."

"In college I started dating a guy—his name was Warren, but everyone called him War. It wasn't until later that I realized how apt that was. At first he seemed like a nice guy. Attentive, available despite playing sports and a decent class load." Her voice faded off. Seconds ticked by, and she shook her head. "One night we were supposed to go to a party but I wasn't feeling it. I wanted to stay in, just watch a movie and relax, maybe order in pizza. Warren was disappointed. Then insistent. His attitude irked me because I figured I deserved a down evening if I wanted one. I told him to go without me."

"Did he?"

She shook her head. "At first he was all about it, saying he would, like it was a threat. I was tired enough that I snapped back." Her lips pressed together, her brows pinching. "He hit me," she whispered. "Out of the blue, he went from the guy I knew to someone else."

Every muscle in Tanner's body snapped tight with unreasonable rage, a rage that he felt clear through to his soul. *He hit me.* As that statement echoed like a gong in his head, not a single word could edge out past his clenched jaw, probably a good thing because he knew he couldn't speak gently. Not about some asshole putting hands on her.

"It went out of control fast," she whispered. "I had my own apartment, we were there alone, and I knew there was no way I'd make it to the door." Her eyes flinched away, as if she were reliving it all.

That was too much for Tanner. Carefully, he gathered

her close, finding some gentleness in his touch at least. He pressed a kiss to her temple, words still beyond him.

With her face tucked to his throat, she said, "Sorry. I hate talking about it."

"Shh." He smoothed his hand over her hair, then along her back, half-afraid to find out how it had ended, but also desperate to know.

Her hands knotted in his T-shirt. "Thank God I've always been close with Glory, because I'd already told her I was staying in. She showed up to check on me in case I was sick, but she found Warren trashing my apartment and me scuttling behind the couch." Easing back from him, Callie found a smile. "Glory has quite the set of lungs on her. No one can scream as long and high as she can."

He remembered that from the night he'd first met her, when he'd started the chain saw.

"I think half the apartment building showed up. It took three guys to hold Warren down while someone else called the police."

It didn't surprise him to see that his hand was slightly shaking when he cupped her cheek. "Your cousin just got elevated. She's now among my favorite people."

Genuine amusement turned up her lips. "Mine too. Always."

And that was why she didn't mind Glory's ways, even though they were different from her own. He got that. You loved certain people for reasons that others might not immediately understand. "Did he hurt you?" Tanner frowned at his own inane question. "Of course he did, but I mean..."

This time she touched her fingertips to his mouth.

"I know what you mean, and no. Other than that first hit, which put me on the floor—"

Christ, he hoped someone had demolished the guy.

"—I was fine. Rattled, for sure. Jumpy for a few weeks. I think he backhanded me, though I didn't see it coming. I just know if he'd used his fist, he probably would have broken my jaw."

Or killed her, and knowing that destroyed Tanner. There wasn't enough air in the sky to relieve the constriction in his chest.

Callie touched her cheek now, as if remembering the pain. "I stayed with Glory for a month. Then I got rid of my apartment and moved."

"Tell me there were severe consequences for him."

"I guess it comes down to perspective. He spent a few days in jail, lost his scholarship for using steroids— as if the coaches hadn't known—and got fired from his job. He tried to apologize but I wanted nothing more to do with him."

Tanner told himself to release her, to step away again, and instead he drew her closer. "How can you stay here alone now after going through that?"

She replied, "How can you be so good and caring after what your father put you through?"

Damn it, this wasn't about him. "Not the same thing, honey, and you know it."

"I do. What you lived with for years is a million times worse, but overall you've conquered it to be the person you want to be. What happened to me was a one-off, and it was years ago. Sutter is oblivious to me but he's not abusive."

Tanner was of a different opinion. The bastard had abused her feelings.

"I'm wary with unknown guys, now," she admitted. "But I refuse to let Warren's drug-fueled lapse affect me long-term."

What rang loud and clear in Tanner's head was that she'd never been wary with him. What that meant, he didn't know for sure—but he liked it.

Just then, they heard Liam returning, the tires rolling slowly up her gravel driveway. Together, they went out front to greet him, with Callie saying, "No reason for him to park back here when he'll be taking it with him, right?"

Tanner suppressed the grin, saying instead, "Ask him—and then find the title." He already knew what Liam would say, but he felt like this should be Callie's doing since the gift was coming from her.

She took up the challenge, greeting Liam the second he stepped out by saying, "So what do you think? You want to keep it?"

Liam contained himself, just barely. "It runs nice, no problems that I could see." He looked to Tanner for guidance.

Feeling about ten feet tall—thanks to Callie's generosity—Tanner said, "I know Reggie took care of it, until he couldn't anymore. There shouldn't be anything major but if something does come up, Kam or I could help you with it. It'd just be the cost for used parts."

Liam cleared his throat.

He looked so damned young that Tanner wanted to mess up his hair, but he remembered himself at nineteen, how serious he'd been about everything, especially his independence, so he afforded Liam the respect he deserved.

"I'd love to have it," Liam said. "If I can afford it."

Callie clapped her hands. "Awesome! Consider it yours. No charge. I'll just have to locate the title."

Eyes going wide, Liam said, "Wait...what?" with a touch of panic. He wasn't used to getting gifts, or consideration. His Adam's apple bobbed in his throat. "Ms. McCallahan—"

"Callie, please." She held out her hand. "The snakes kept us from a proper introduction."

Liam immediately took her hand, held it a split second, and then withdrew. "Thank you, but I can't just take it from you."

"You'll be doing me a favor, getting it out of my way. Plus..." She crossed her fingers. "I'm still hoping you'll help me with getting the locks changed and dead bolts added."

"I... I mean..." Liam's mouth snapped shut so he could grin. "Yes, ma'am. I'm happy to do that for you. Tanner already picked up what we'd need."

"Oh." Callie gave him a level look. "He did, did he?"

With a shrug, Tanner said, "Liam starts work early tomorrow. I figured I'd save him some time."

"Well." She looked at each of them. "I guess we should go inside." Callie led the way around the house to the back door.

Deliriously happy, Liam followed her.

For a moment, Tanner merely stood there, watching the two of them as they chatted, probably about the car or the chores Callie wanted done. Liam was a hard worker, always ready to pitch in, but right now he was floating over the amazing generosity of a woman he'd only just met.

The car would make Liam's life so much easier. Getting to and from work, grocery shopping, hell, everyday life would now be simpler because of Callie. That realization worked against Tanner, making him want to reach for more.

More than he should.

He had an agenda and whatever it took, he'd stick to it.

That meant for the foreseeable future, he'd have to keep his distance from Callie, unless the two of them had company. Alone with her, no way could he keep his hands to himself, especially when she didn't. Knowing she was interested and willing made it hard enough. When she touched him his resistance melted like ice on a griddle.

He'd still check on her—with Kam. Or Liam.

Somehow, he had to avoid falling in love with her... all over again.

GLORY'S "FEW DAYS" turned into a few weeks.

At first it hadn't been too bad—especially since they talked often. Glory was a genius, her execution of the final edited videos both amusingly entertaining and, Callie hoped, educational. With each new video added, her audience grew. More and more questions were popping up in the comment section, so once a week she tried to set aside time to answer a few. Glory claimed that keeping the content personal was what would ensure its success.

Overall, Callie would have felt encouraged with her new life, except that her fear of more snakes had expanded. Liam, who was a remarkably wonderful young man, went above and beyond to ensure her property was kept clear. Refusing to simply accept the car for free, no matter how she'd tried to insist, he'd instead bartered for work, and work he had. Such a proud young man and so determined to be better than his own father.

At one point, Liam had confided that his big goal was to be more like Tanner. Mission accomplished, as far as Callie could tell.

First he would finish his day job, then he'd come over early evening and do odds and ends for her. She'd added a routine sweep of the area for snakes or bugs.

Liam would puff up like a hero-in-training—very much like Tanner—and meticulously search everywhere, which included her basement, the garage, the porches, and the animal shelters.

He taught her more efficient ways to complete her chores. Anything she didn't know how to do, Liam was willing to teach her. He'd spent a lot of time on an actual farm with his grandfather, whenever his own father got to be too much, so he knew all the best methods.

Now she truly did feel empowered. More capable, more independent.

Except that missing Glory wasn't her biggest issue. It was that she saw Tanner only in company. Never alone.

He came by to visit with Liam on occasion, or with Kam to assist her with something heavy. She saw him a few times at dinner with Addie.

But it was never just the two of them and Callie knew it was because of a choice he'd made. She'd come on too strong, been too up-front, and while he might have been interested in a casual hookup, the proximity, no doubt, would make it awkward for him. He didn't want her as a neighbor, so he definitely didn't want the added pressure of a romantic relationship.

She'd acted like a fool, but it didn't change her feelings. Tanner interested her more than any man she'd ever met. And now he was dodging her.

"You'd think, just once, I'd get it right," she mumbled.

"What's that?" Liam asked.

"Nothing. Just talking to myself." It was a Friday night but Liam had spent it with her. Together, they'd cleaned out her gutters, trimmed several long tree branches, and weeded the garden. It was another reason for her to feel guilty. "How come you don't have a date?"

He flashed her a grin. Little by little, he'd gotten more comfortable with her. "I do, about an hour from now."

"Liam! You should have said something." She'd kept him over without realizing.

"It's fine. I just need to get home in time to shower and change."

Being tall with broad shoulders and an air of calm confidence beyond his years, Liam was a good-looking young man. She imagined he could do plenty of dating if he wanted, and instead he worked overtime.

"Anyone special?" With a glance at the darkening sky, she began gathering up their tools. The forecast had predicted heavy thunderstorms and already the air smelled of rain. Hopefully her roof would hold up.

"Nah. I have no interest in getting involved. Too much I still want to get done."

"Like?" she asked, as she quickly led the way to the garage. It was now clutter free, with everything neatly organized. Without the car taking up space, and most items stored on shelves, it didn't seem nearly so much like a snake haven.

Liam dropped a bag of debris into the largest can, then hung the saw on the wall. "I'd like my own set of tools like the ones I use with the contractor. He's great, but someday I'll want to branch out on my own. People around here are getting used to me being with him. They're trusting me. When it's time, I want my own contracting business."

That was the most he'd ever divulged to her and it made her feel special that he had shared. "It's a great goal. Have you gotten anything yet?"

"Sure. At my little apartment I pay extra for the garage space so I can store everything. Though to run my own business, I still need a lot."

Just then, a blinding streak of lightning split the sky. "Wow." Seconds later, thunder rumbled, sending a tremble along the ground. "I need to get the animals put away."

"I'll help you," Liam said.

"No, it's fine. I'm sure I have a few minutes yet before the rain starts." Thanks to her recent practice, she was proficient at handling the animals now. "They're probably all in their shelters already. I'll just double-check." Often they put themselves away and all she had to do was secure the door. "You go on so you're not running late."

He stopped, hands on his hips as he studied the sky. "The lightning doesn't seem close yet."

"It's not." Another thought struck her and she asked, "Would you like me to pay you early?" After his first generous week, she'd insisted on paying him for his continued help. When she'd finally gotten his agreement to take the amount she offered, he'd asked to be paid on Mondays after a full week and weekend.

"I'm still good with Monday, but thanks."

"You're *sure*?"

His grin went lopsided. "You and Tanner are two of a kind. I'm good though, so no worries."

The mention of Tanner made her heart sink, but she worked up a smile for Liam. "Off with you then. Have fun and be safe."

Jokingly, he said, "Yes, Mom," and then jogged away.

There. That sweet exchange fixed her heart right up. Who needed Tanner? Not her. She was just fine and dandy without him.

A gust of wind whipped her hair into her face, reminding her that she had to hurry. Concentrating on the animals would also help her put Tanner in perspective. Seriously, she didn't need to get hung up on a guy right now anyway. Her broken engagement wasn't that long behind her, and her parents were apparently still irate with her. She'd called her mother once, with no answer. Then she'd texted her twice, and still nothing. Whatever her mother thought of Callie's "cease and desist" requests, she was keeping to herself. Knowing her mom, that meant she wasn't ready to give up.

Unfortunately, Sutter had called her twice, but both times she'd kept it short and to the point. They had nothing to talk about, period. She wasn't cruel or hateful, but she left no room for misinterpretation.

Talking with Glory was Callie's only contact with her family. Yet even that was…cautious.

Knowing how susceptible her cousin was to pressure, and knowing not to trust her parents or Sutter, Callie kept many of her most private feelings to herself.

Her loneliness, her fear, that sense of being adrift—not fully settled anywhere—ate at her, especially at night when she tried to sleep. She didn't belong at home with her family and old job, she didn't have a meaningful relationship, and even in her new home she wasn't quite fitting in.

Stopping at the chicken coop, Callie found all the hens huddled inside, most of them comfy in their nesting boxes, one on a perch, and one getting a drink. She counted twice to be sure. "Good girls," Callie murmured low, before securing the door.

Farther back, she looked around for the goats but didn't see them. Usually where there was one she found the others. Feeling the first drop of rain, she hustled to the shelter, peered inside, and found…three goats. Not four.

Her heart dropped like a stone in a pond. "Oh, no." How did a person misplace a goat? Frantic, Callie secured the door to ensure the other three stayed inside, then jogged from tree to tree, bush to bush, looking for the fourth. Her pulse pounded in her ears, so she stopped to drag in a few deep breaths and tried to calm her panic. She had to think about this logically.

The front gate had remained closed while Liam had helped her work, so she knew the goat hadn't gone that way. With the size of her property, that still left a lot of room to roam with thick weeds and brush making ideal hiding places for a cantankerous goat.

"I should have named them," she said aloud, just to break up the sound of the approaching storm. "Then I could call for him, though who knows if goats come when called." Another thing she would research, she decided. Alone every evening, she had nothing better to do than research absurd things.

At a brisk pace, she scoured the expanse of the entire yard, but stalled when she found the back gate standing open. She had ten acres in all, much of it dark woods, and it butted up to her neighbors—on both sides. Sadly, she'd yet to mark her property so there was a good chance she would blunder beyond what she owned.

No problem when it came to Tanner, Kam, or Addie.

But Dirk and Lang Garmet? She didn't want to trespass with them. Unfortunately, the goat wouldn't hesitate.

Staring out beyond the trees into dark recesses, hanging vines and tangled honeysuckle, it seemed so eerie, made more so by the static of the storm and the time of day. What choice did she have though, with her goat missing?

The urge to call someone made her fingertips tingle, but she'd left her phone in the house as she and Liam had worked. All she had on her was the keys to the back door.

And damn it, she'd left it unlocked.

Decisively, Callie stepped through the gate and secured it behind her. She'd hunt for the goat right now, before the storm started in earnest. Surely, the critter hadn't gone far. Once she found him, she'd get him put away and then, only then, would she get safely into her *own home*.

The place where she would stay.

Where eventually she would belong.

It was ridiculous for a grown woman to fear a little storm, the woods, or… Being alone.

"Goat," she called out, hoping that if he heard her voice, he'd come to her. In the distance, she heard a sound that, to her beleaguered ears, sounded like that of a creepy goat wail. It certainly sent shivers down her spine.

A smattering of raindrops turned into a steady

sprinkle. An *icy* sprinkle. Thankfully the honeysuckle was tall and thick, shielding her from much of it. She wrapped her arms around herself and picked her way forward, doing her best to venture in a straight line without wandering too far toward the Garmet property.

Her unruly neighbors continued to plague her on occasion. Wolf whistles, loud parties—to which she was occasionally invited, but always declined—and casual drop-ins, as if she hadn't been clear enough already. From an early age, she'd had good manners pressed on her so she dodged the brothers without being rude, finding polite excuses galore. Yet they persisted.

On the other side of her property, Addie wanted to see her more often, Tanner clearly didn't want to see her at all, and Kam was annoyingly upbeat about it all, as if he found it endlessly amusing.

Oh what she wouldn't give to have Kam out here with her now. He'd help her look for the goat while also teasing her. Never, not once, did he act as if he was doing her a favor. He treated everything like a lark, not a chore.

She really liked that about him.

The way he'd taught her to collect the chicken eggs would always be a favorite memory. He'd alternately instruct her and then heckle her for her nervousness, until she'd gotten it right. Kam was the type of brother she envied; she wished she'd had him for her own.

When Callie heard a laugh, she froze. It came from somewhere nearby. Then she heard parts of a conversation and knew the Garmet brothers were close. Had she encroached on their property?

Or were they on hers? Honestly, she wasn't sure.

"Tanner's away," one of the brothers said, his voice

traveling even through the steady rain. "She can't call him, and I doubt she wants Addie out here in the rain."

"Doesn't mean she'll come out," said the other.

Another chuckle. "She will. Feels all responsible for those fucking goats, you know."

So… They had taken her goat and they assumed she'd come look for it—and she *had*. Now what? Had they lured her out here? To what end?

She didn't know and she didn't want to find out. But if she moved, they'd hear her. If she didn't move, they'd find her.

Realizing her vulnerable position made her start to tremble. Her heart tried to punch right through her chest, especially when she heard the goat again. The animal didn't really sound distressed, but then, she had no idea what a distressed goat might sound like. To her, they always sounded weird.

In so many ways, she'd messed up. In even more ways she was out of her element.

Pity party later, she sternly told herself. *Now get your butt in gear.*

Right ahead of her was an enormous oak tree with branches that stretched far out in different directions. Some of those limbs dipped lower, almost within reach. Not that she'd ever climbed a tree, but surely she'd be safer up there.

Of course, if she could get in the tree, so could the brothers, she reasoned. If she was already up there, though, anyone who tried to follow could be kicked in the face.

Brush moved around her. Footsteps closed in.

"I can't believe you talked me into this," Lang said.

Dirk answered, "Playing the hero once won't kill you. And think what we might gain."

Knowing they'd run into her any second now, alarm bells began clanging in her head to the tune of *do something, do something, do something.*

And then, they stepped out to her right.

Spotting her, Dirk's frown turned into a smile. "Ah, Callie. What are you doing out here in the storm?"

Without another single thought, she spun around and took off running, reached the tree, and lunged. By some bizarre miracle, she caught a low-hanging branch. Her work boots slipped on the trunk before she caught enough traction to help lever herself up. It took a lot of absurd fumbling and straining and surely laughable acrobatics, but she finally hooked a leg over and hauled herself up.

Huffing every breath, precariously perched, she dared to look at Dirk and Lang. The two of them wore identical expressions of awed amazement.

After a few dazed seconds, Dirk moved forward. "Darlin', what the hell are you doing?"

Staying out of reach. But she said, "Looking for my goat." It infuriated her that they'd put her in this position. Well, not the position in the tree, but a position of feeling like she had to be in a tree.

"Thought I heard a goat," Lang said with absurdly feigned confusion. "But I wasn't sure." He, too, moved closer.

Callie scampered up higher, just in case.

Laughing, Dirk said, "I know you're a city girl and all, but your goat isn't up there."

Feeling ridiculous, she said, "I know goats can't climb trees." How absurd. "I can see better up here," she lied. With all the leaves and twigs, not to mention the rain and the dark, she couldn't see a thing, not really.

"Actually, goats do climb trees, but if you stopped to listen, you'd know your goat is deeper in the woods."

Goats climbed trees? No, she refused to believe that. Like many things since moving here, she'd look it up later. For now, she said, "Kam is coming to help me look, so in the meantime I was trying to spot the goat."

"No," Dirk said. "Kam isn't coming."

"He is," she insisted, hoping to convince them. "Should be here any minute."

The brothers exchanged a look. "Sorry, darlin', but Kam is out on the town. Don't expect he'll be home tonight at all."

Lang added, "They're twitchy about bringing women around Addie."

"Respectful," Callie corrected, assuming that was the reason why Kam and Tanner didn't bring home casual dates. "They love and respect Addie, as they should."

Dirk lost a bit of his "good old boy" routine. "Sure, whatever. They're fucking choirboys."

She wouldn't go *that* far.

"We're all getting soaked," Lang pointed out. "Come down from there and we'll help you find your damn goat."

Right. Go *deeper in the woods* with the two of them? Not happening. "I'm fine," she said inanely, uncaring that her hair stuck to her face in wet clumps, while rivulets of rainwater ran down her nose and dripped off her chin. A combo of cold and fear made her tremble so badly that "fine" sounded like three syllables. Embellishing her lie, she said, "Kam cut his date sh-short once I t-told him a goat was missing." Damn her chattering teeth.

Warily, Lang glanced around.

The brothers wore rain slickers with the hoods up, so other than wet boots, the weather wasn't affecting them much, not like it did her. Already it had saturated her shirt and jeans, and chilled her to the bone.

"This is dumb," Dirk barked, startling her. He came forward with a scowl and a purpose. "You can't sit in a damned tree during a thunderstorm. You'll get hit by lightning."

The goat cried out again, further rattling her, but what could she do? As Dirk advanced, she felt the same fear she'd experienced in college when Warren had nosedived off the deep end of rage. It stole all the breath from her lungs. Back then, Warren had started destroying things and in the process he'd thrown things out of his way—including her. His strength had been terrifying, especially since she'd assumed that once he finished attacking her apartment, he'd turn on her.

"Callie?"

The sound of her name, called out from a slight distance, sent a surge of hope and happiness through her. *Tanner*. How he was here, she didn't know, but her relief was enough that she let out a sob.

"Callie?" Kam called next, turning her lie into truth. "Where are you?"

In that moment, she loved both men, and as soon as she was safely back in her home she'd tell them so.

Getting it together, she shouted back, "Here! In a tree." Looking down at her dumbfounded neighbors, she called with warning, "And the Garmet brothers are here."

CHAPTER TEN

TANNER POUNDED THROUGH the woods, every awful scenario he could imagine slamming into his brain. Had Callie said she was in a tree? The storm had intensified and with the downpour and whistling wind, he couldn't be sure.

The name of the Garmets had come through loud and clear, though.

Whatever situation she was in, he hated knowing they were involved.

When he finally spotted Callie, her arms and legs wrapped tight around a sturdy oak limb, she was alone. Sopping wet.

And *crying*.

Her face was too wet to see any tears, but he could hear it in the broken way she gulped air, see it in her panicked expression.

Before he could reach her, she started explaining. "The Garmets were h-here, but they took off. They had my g-goat. They wanted me to come down, but I didn't know…"

The tumble of words continued while he went to her and Kam started looking around.

"They're g-gone now," she said, her words shivering together. "And I'm stuck in a tree!"

"You aren't stuck," Tanner said calmly, sensing she

didn't need to see his anger right now, even if it was aimed at others. He'd left Blu at home rather than risk the dog in the storm, but now he wished he'd brought him along. If Dirk or Lang were still around, Blu would pinpoint them.

Knowing Kam had his back, Tanner ignored his surroundings and reached up for Callie. "Honey, can you swing your leg over? I promise I won't let you fall."

Lightning crashed overhead, alarming him. A creek bed that ran through the woods had already filled with the spring rain. The sound of the water rushing past mingled with the downpour and consistently rumbling thunder. The branches of the tree, large and small, swayed from the force of the storm.

A tree was a terrible place for her to be. Then again, on the ground in the darkened woods with Dirk and Lang might have been worse, so he silently applauded her resourcefulness.

She shifted cautiously. "It was e-easier getting up."

"I know." Fear had probably provided the impetus she'd needed, and it killed him to think of her being so terrified. "Just bring your foot over the side—that's it. A little more." The second her leg was free, he held her above the knee, steadying her, providing a foundation. "See, I've got you. Now the other leg."

"My hands are cold and the limb is w-wet."

"I swear to you, Callie, I won't let you fall."

She stared down at him, chose to trust him again, and then nodded. Once she went to move her other leg, she started slipping and let out a horrified gasp.

Tanner scooped her up, catching her against his chest, cradling her close to his body. He wished he had thought to get a jacket, but he hadn't. His T-shirt was wet through so even if he offered it to her, it wouldn't do her much good.

"We have to get out of this storm," Kam said.

"My g-goat."

They both listened, heard the near-continuous cry, and Kam took off. "I'll get him."

"Watch your back," Tanner warned. Later, he'd settle up with Dirk and Lang. If they'd hurt the animal, there'd be hell to pay. He'd see to it.

Callie squeezed him in a death grip. "I'm s-sorry I'm such a bother."

"Shush. You're not." He kissed her temple. "I want to get you inside, but I don't want to leave Kam alone if those bastards are around."

She nodded, burrowing closer to steal his warmth as they waited.

Less than two minutes passed when Kam came back bare-chested. He'd removed his shirt to create a leash, which he used to lead along the anxious goat. "He was caught up pretty tight in some vines." His gaze met Tanner's. "Nearly hobbled."

"Oh," Callie said, lunging away and dropping to her knees on the muddy ground to embrace the wet goat. "I'm s-so sorry, baby."

"He'll be happiest in his shelter with the others," Tanner said, catching her upper arm and urging her back to her feet. "We need to get out of the storm. Come on." Together, two men, a shaken woman, and a frazzled goat, they made their way back to Callie's property.

Kam secured the gate, then got the goat settled in with the others. "I dried him off with some straw. He has a few abrasions on one of his legs."

"Oh no," Callie whispered, her tone filled with horror.

"He's fine for tonight," Kam assured her. "We can check it out tomorrow."

"But—"

"He's already huddled in with the others."

Tanner had to fight the urge to lift Callie in his arms and carry her in, just to get her out of this damned weather, but he knew she wouldn't appreciate that. Through the woods, while shivering and upset, she'd doggedly put one foot in front of the other. She'd watched the goat in front of her but avoided his gaze.

Now that she was in her own yard and the goat safe, she was already bucking up, standing a little straighter and holding herself more tightly.

No longer leaning into him.

"Thank you. I'll ch-check him first thing in the morning." Still with chattering teeth, she said, "My back door is unlocked." She stood there, watching Kam wring the rain from his shirt. "W-when I saw the gate was open, my first th-thought was to find him."

Without her phone. Without her keys. A woman alone going into the woods. In a *thunderstorm*.

How many times had he warned her? But, he reminded himself, she'd been alone with no one to call, even if she'd had her phone. That was on him. Anyone could see that she truly cared about the animals.

"I understand," he said, determined to get her inside where she could warm up. "Could have happened to anyone."

Kam kept his worried gaze on Callie and her averted face. "Why don't you two go in?" He said to Tanner, "I'll run home and get you some dry clothes."

Tanner started to nod, but Callie stepped away, further separating herself.

"I love you b-both for the rescue. N-no idea what

I'd have done if you hadn't shown up." With a shaking hand, she shoved back the sodden clumps of her wet hair. "You can both go h-home, now. I'm fine. Thank you for your help."

Her flat tone sounded like anything but love. More like dread. Guilt. Self-recriminations.

Tanner turned back to Kam. "I appreciate it. Thanks."

Nodding, Kam ignored what she'd said, acting only on Tanner's agreement. Callie didn't look up to debating it with him. Already she was trudging forward, her every step weary as she tried to leave them behind.

Reaching the door before her, Tanner opened it. Callie could be stubborn enough that she might lock him out.

And maybe he deserved that.

As they stepped inside, she asked, "They'll be okay? My ch-chickens and goats? The storm won't frighten them?"

"They're outdoor animals, so they're used to it."

Accepting that, she locked the door—belatedly, to his mind—and then bent down to strip off her short, sturdy boots. They were meant for outdoor work. A good choice, but the soaked laces wouldn't give.

"Here." Tanner pulled over a kitchen chair and gestured her into it, then he knelt down and, with a little effort, got the laces loosened enough that he could tug off each boot. He set them on the rug by the back door, and then removed his own boots, too.

After peeling off her socks, Callie murmured, "I'll get some towels," and she started out of the room, barefoot, dripping, still shivering.

"Callie." Catching her hand, Tanner gently turned her to face him. "Could you do me a big favor?"

Her downcast gaze lifted, searching his face. With

her lashes spiked, her lips pale and her nose pink, she said, "Of course," like a vow. "Anything."

Anything was one hell of an offer, but he took it as she no doubt meant it. Now was not the time to tease her. "Since the door was unlocked and the Garmets were already around, let me check the house with you." When she started to speak, he acted on impulse, putting a quick, firm kiss to her chilled lips, lingering just long enough to add a little warmth. "I can see how it happened. No explanation necessary, but I'll feel better if I take a look around."

Her shuddering inhale nearly did him in. "Okay. If you insist."

"I do. Thanks." Taking her icy fingers in his, he went through her house. The basement door now had a dead bolt, thanks to Liam. Front door was bolted too. There was no place to hide in the kitchen or living room, and he made quick work of peeking into the bathroom, the two bedrooms, and the closets.

There was definitely something to be said for a small space.

Back to the bathroom, he found some towels, handing one to her before he stripped off his shirt, wrung it out over the tub, and then laid it over the side before briskly drying off.

Callie watched him so closely that awareness warmed his skin.

"You have dry clothes, honey?"

She paused in the process of using the towel to squeeze rainwater from her hair. "Why are you calling me that?"

Grateful that her voice now sounded steadier, he asked, "Honey?"

She nodded.

He hadn't even thought about it. Treating her gently, reassuring her, had been foremost in his mind. "I guess because it scared me, finding you out in the storm like that."

Blotting the dampness from her face gave her a second to hide. When she lowered the towel, she appeared resigned. "How did you even know?"

"Glory tried to reach you." He took the towel from her and briskly dried her arms. At least her teeth were no longer chattering, but shivers continued to chase over her skin. "When she couldn't, she called Addie to see if you were there—since you often have dinner with us. Because it was storming, Addie ran over to make sure you were okay, and you were nowhere to be found but your car was here. She called me, I called Kam." He lifted a shoulder. "Kam and I both came straight home." And good thing. What if they hadn't? Would she still be in a tree? What would the Garmets have done?

What had they intended to do?

Groaning, Callie dropped against him, her face ducked beneath his chin. "So much trouble for me."

"Hey, you're worth that." And more. "We look out for each other around here. Addie knew how careful you were being and she said you never leave the door unlocked unless you're right there. Only this time, you weren't."

"She's right. Both Liam and I were in the yard after we finished cleaning out the gutters and downspouts. With the first raindrop, I insisted that he head out for his date." She paused. "Did you know he had a date? I was so excited for him. All he does is work."

Tanner smiled at her enthusiasm for Liam. "He's determined."

"I know. I worry about him."

Of course she did. Because she cared, about everyone and everything, and he'd left her alone.

Before he could get annoyed with himself, she got back on track. "After Liam left, I went to make sure the animals were in their shelters. That's when I realized one goat was missing."

And of course she'd acted on instinct, immediately going to investigate.

"I thought I'd find him in the yard, but he wasn't there. I looked everywhere." Her shoulders tensed, her voice lowered. "The back gate was open."

He'd bet money that neither Callie nor Liam would have left it like that.

As if he'd said it aloud, she shook her head. "We were nowhere near that gate, Tanner. If the goat got it open, I don't know how. I fastened it the way you showed me."

"How about we figure that out later?" Goats could be clever when they saw something tasty on the other side of a fence. Usually, though, they tended to stick together.

"Poor Glory," she said, switching tracks yet again. "I shouldn't have left my phone inside, but I didn't want notifications going off while I was working with Liam."

"I'm sure by now Kam has told Addie, and Addie has told Glory, so she knows you're okay."

Her groan was more humor than misery. "It's like a sick phone game with me at the center of it all."

No, it was like a woman alone who had a history with aggressive assholes, and now had two of them living next door to her. "Come on." With an arm around her, he led her to her bedroom. "Get changed into something dry, okay?"

Looking miserable, she nodded.

As he started to step out, he noted the way she went

rigid, bracing herself to be alone. Fuck it. He couldn't do it. "One more favor?"

She closed her eyes. "What?"

"Don't complain when I stay right here while you change."

That had her eyes flaring wide. "Here?"

Truthfully, he said, "I need to be close to you." He would never forget the fear he'd seen in her face as she'd clung to that tree. "I'll turn my back," he offered. "How's that?" The subtle easing of her shoulders told him he'd made the right move.

"Okay. Just…give me one minute." Now in a rush, she opened drawer after drawer, pulling out a shirt, shorts, socks…and panties. Tiny panties, made of silky material and lace in a frosted peach color.

Tanner wanted to look away, but he hadn't yet talked himself into it. Callie was pale and still shaken, her wet clothes clinging to her body, her brown hair hanging in heavy hanks down her back and over her chest. And even now, so disheveled and unsettled, she had the ability to twist him into knots.

When she dropped everything on the foot of her bed, he got himself together and faced away. Unblinking, he stared through the bedroom doorway to the hall. "Kam will be here shortly."

"I'm hurrying," she said.

"I didn't mean that." He'd just been speaking to keep from thinking so much. Envisioning her as she changed. Imagining those wet clothes peeling away from her naked body. He ran a hand over his face. "I only meant we'd both be dry soon. Then I'd like to talk to you."

Sounding grim and defeated, she said, "All right."

Outside, the storm continued to rage. Loud rumbles of thunder reverberated throughout the house. Strobes of impressive lightning danced through the blinds. Steady sheets of rain lashed the windows.

Heavy storms weren't uncommon in Kentucky this time of year, but tonight felt different. Maybe because he was in Callie's bedroom. Every crack of lightning lifted the hairs on the back of his neck. Never in his adult life had he been so attuned to a woman, hearing her every breath, feeling her every movement.

Sensing her continued upset.

It made *him* want to rage as violently as the storm— not against her, but for her.

"Kam shouldn't come back out in this," she whispered.

The muscles of his arms contracted, tightening in his shoulders and neck. Already she wanted to send him away when they both knew she'd prefer not to be alone.

Then she suggested, "You could just wrap up in a blanket or towel, and we could put your clothes in the dryer."

His tension eased, just not enough. With Callie so near, he was bound to stay rigid and on alert.

"No way am I doing that." It'd be far too tempting to pull her close and lose the insubstantial barrier. She wasn't herself right now, so he'd stay in his wet jeans before he added to her uneasiness.

Then it no longer mattered because Kam texted him to say: Driving stuff over. Be there in 2.

"He's already on his way." Tanner returned the thumbs-up emoji to his brother, then cleared his throat. "Need any help?"

"No, I'm done."

Slowly, he turned to see her sit on the end of the bed. Her T-shirt was big, her shorts tiny, and over both she wore a man's flannel shirt with the sleeves rolled up.

He wondered where she'd gotten it, but it didn't exactly look like Sutter's style. More like something she'd picked up at a discount department store.

As he watched her, she pulled on thick white socks.

It was far from a stylish outfit, not at all what a rich princess would wear, but it looked comfortably cute.

On her, it also looked sexy.

Callie gathered up her wet clothes and held them away from her body. "I could put these in the bathroom."

She could, but he guessed she wanted him to go with her. His heart squeezed, seeing her like this, with big solemn eyes and a stoic attitude. "Good plan." He took them from her and, together, they went into the bathroom and arranged them to dry over the shower rod, tub, and even over a towel bar. Her panties she dropped into a hamper.

Back in the living room, he lifted away the blinds to see her driveway. "Kam should be pulling up any second."

Silence stretched out, then she whispered, "You could just ride back with him. Who knows how long this storm will last."

Glancing over his shoulder, Tanner saw that she'd averted her face again. "I'd rather stay with you."

For the longest time she didn't move. Tanner didn't either.

Then, as headlights flashed in her driveway, she looked up and said, "I'd rather that too, but I've been enough of a nuisance."

"You're not. Ever." He opened her front door. "Watch for me. I'll be right back in." Holding on to the image of her pale face, he dashed out into the rain to save Kam from getting soaked again.

If Callie wasn't going to use the garage, she'd need a carport. Otherwise, in the next storm, she might get caught in a downpour.

That is, if she was going to stay.

At the car, Kam said, "I'd have brought it in."

Thankfully the rain was blowing from the other direction, so it didn't pour into Kam's open driver's side window. "Then we'd both be drenched." Without a shirt, the rain stung and still Tanner hesitated. "The storm isn't letting up."

"Nope," Kam replied. "Forecasted to go all night."

Glad to have a viable excuse, Tanner nodded. "I'm probably staying here then."

"Good." Kam glanced to the door. "I was hoping she'd let you."

"I haven't exactly asked yet." But he was hoping the same. "If I decide to head home, it won't be for a while."

"I'll take care of Blu."

"Thanks. And tell Addie not to worry."

With that exchange wrapped up, Kam held out a large plastic bag stuffed full. "Clothes and food."

"Appreciate it." Half curved over the bag to protect it, Tanner dashed back to her porch. His bare feet slid over the wet grass, got pricked by random weeds, and he winced as he landed on a few sharp rocks.

When he reached the door, Callie was just putting away her phone.

"Glory?" he asked.

"Yes." She looked him over. "I'll get you another towel."

He watched her for signs of stress, but she moved more freely now. Without as much anxiety, she hustled into the bathroom and returned with one of the towels they'd already used, plus a clean one.

She dropped the used towel on the floor.

He handed her the bag. "It's heavy. My clothes and some food that Addie sent." Quickly, he dried his feet on the used towel.

"Such a sweetheart."

As he ran the fresh towel over his neck, shoulders, and chest, he asked, "Kam or Addie?"

"Both," she teased back. "But I meant Addie." After carrying the bag into the kitchen, she dug out his neatly folded jeans, socks, briefs, and shirt, putting them on a chair, then took out a few covered dishes. "Tanner, this smells like fried chicken." She peeled back a lid and inhaled. "Oh, *heaven*. It is."

Smiling at her appreciative tone, he picked up the change of clothes and asked, "How about I change in the living room while you get the food together?" He'd be close enough to hear her but with some privacy so he didn't embarrass her—and didn't tempt fate.

"A solid plan," she said, but before he walked away she touched his arm. "Thank you. For everything. And for…understanding."

"It's not a big deal, okay?" He was glad to be here for her.

"It embarrasses me." Then she shook her head, as if that word didn't suffice. "Not that I lost a goat and forgot my phone and left my house unlocked, bad as all those things are. Not even the part with being in a tree." Her next breath sounded forced, her words pained. "The freak-out, though? God, how I wish I could…not do that."

To his mind, it took a lot of guts to face your embarrassment, to admit to it and own it. Callie had more grit than she realized. "Some things take longer to conquer. Some things," he added softly, "stick with us forever."

As he well knew. "Kam and I were both impressed with how you handled yourself."

Her short laugh was slightly broken, and he noted the fresh sheen of tears in her eyes, but also her slight smile. Such a conflict.

"I hate that I fell apart on you." Angrily, she shoved back her hair.

"Not *on* me," he said softly, though he wouldn't mind.

"I don't do that." She took a step away, but pivoted right back. "No one other than Glory has seen me cry. I'm usually good at holding it together, saving it until I'm alone."

"Hey." Holding the clothes in one arm, he tugged her close and bent his knees to look directly into blue eyes wounded with disappointment—in herself. "I hate that you were upset, and I wish you never had reason to cry." He cupped her cheek, feeling her cool skin against the warmth of his palm. "But if you do, I'm here. You can always lean on me, okay?"

For a long moment her gaze held his and he could almost hear her thoughts. He hadn't been there, not for the past week—because he'd been avoiding temptation.

Her sad little smile let him off the hook. "Sure," she murmured, briefly nuzzling her cheek into his hand before stepping apart from him. "I appreciate it."

"Always," he reiterated, without knowing how long "always" might be. Not with Callie.

Tense seconds ticked by in silence. There was nothing more he could say; they both knew his preference was for her to sell him the house.

For her to return…to what?

To parents who pressured her? An ex who didn't deserve her? Divided on many levels, he shook his head—to her and himself—and he retreated to the living room to change into dry clothes. What he wanted long-term, and what he wanted at this particular moment, were at complete odds.

Urge her to go, or convince her to stay.

Point out the many ways that she was out of her element, or praise her for all she'd accomplished already.

Hinder her, or help her.

For tonight, at least, help was the only thing on his mind. Callie needed him and so he'd be here.

The future, whatever it held, could be figured out later.

Rarely had he ever warred with himself like this. He liked to make a decision and stick to it, seeing things as black and white, right and wrong, progress and regression.

The last time that he could recall was when he'd struggled to resist Addie. He'd wanted autonomy, without all the emotions mucking with his head. Yet Addie's love had been impossible to refuse.

Callie was proving just as difficult…and in many ways he liked it. Because he liked her. More than he'd thought possible in the short amount of time she'd been here.

With his thoughts still bounding everywhere, he pulled up his dry jeans—and suddenly everything went pitch-black and utterly silent. No hum of the fridge or ticking of a clock. No blue light from the small TV or appliances. The only sounds were that of the perpetual wind and pummeling rain against the house.

Giving himself a few seconds for his eyes to acclimate, Tanner called out, "Stand still. I'll come to you."

"I'm already here," Callie said, her searching hands landing against his throat and shoulder.

It seemed the most natural thing to pull her close and hold her. "Is your phone in your pocket?"

She nodded against his chest, then shifted around to pull it free and turn on her flashlight. "Blast. My power is already low. How about yours?"

"It's charged." Using the light from her phone, he located his wet jeans and retrieved his phone and wallet from a back pocket. To be safe, he double-checked that the front door was locked, took his discarded jeans to the bathroom—which was now full of wet clothes—and was back to her in under thirty seconds. She hadn't moved. "Got any candles?"

Surprised, she said, "Yes! Reggie kept them in the kitchen and when Addie reorganized it for me, she put all that type of stuff into one drawer." She snagged his hand and took him along with her as she went to the cabinet and got them out. "No candle holders though."

"Not a problem. We can put them on a plate or something." Stepping around her, he asked, "You mind?"

She waved at the cabinets. "Help yourself."

He found a shallow but thick white bowl shaped like the bottom of a chicken. Made him wonder if it had a top somewhere, but for now it'd do. In the same drawer where she'd gotten the candles, he found a box of matches.

After a little more searching, he was able to light three candles, one already in a jar, so at least the kitchen was illuminated. He set the jar on the table and, trying to put her at ease, said, "A romantic dinner by candle-light."

The worry left her gaze and her smile slowly crept into place. "After the past couple of hours, doesn't that sound perfect?"

Yeah, it did—since it was with her. "I'll grab my shirt if you can get the food together."

With a pouting glance at his chest, she said, "Spoilsport," but then she shooed him away. "Go on, dress if you must." She started darting around for plates and silverware, drinks and serving forks. "I don't know about you, but I'm famished."

As Tanner pulled on his shirt and socks, he realized he was smiling, too. Honest to God, he couldn't think of anywhere else he'd rather be right now. Sitting in a darkened house in a vicious rainstorm, Callie dressed in mismatched clothes and her wet hair drying in clumps, about to eat Addie's fried chicken by candlelight, yeah, that seemed like the perfect night to him.

"I'm ready," she sang out, to urge him along.

For now, he was just going to enjoy himself. Pretty sure he couldn't do anything else. Not when it came to Callie McCallahan.

Funny how a woman could go from a mundane life of contentedly dining at the trendiest restaurants, wearing designer fashions without real appreciation, and hanging with affluent friends who didn't truly know her all that well, to having far, *far* more fun in a rustic kitchen setting with a large, very alpha and often cantankerous guy, eating incredible home-fried chicken with only an unscented candle for light.

Never mind that fear had stripped a year off her life and she was still worried about her goat and his possibly injured leg, not to mention that she'd made a colossal fool of herself in front of all her male neighbors. Somehow, when Tanner was around, even a destructive storm and a terrible experience turned into an incredible day.

The man was pure magic.

It helped that the food was so good. It took her and Tanner little time to consume fair portions of everything. She was still frazzled, her hair was beyond wrecked, and face-burning mortification poked around the periphery of her contentment, but she was no longer hungry or afraid.

Great progress by anyone's measure.

"What are you thinking?" Tanner asked, his last forkful of potatoes paused in front of his mouth. "You're just sitting there staring at me."

Holding back a sigh, she explained, "I can't help it. You look good in candlelight. All the shadows show off your cheekbones and the golden glow is reflected in your dark eyes." When he tucked in his chin to scowl at her, she had to grin. "I mean, you always look hot, built as you are and all that."

He snorted.

"Seriously, Tanner. Do you even realize how off-the-charts gorgeous you are?"

Setting his fork on his plate, he met her gaze. "Are you trying to keep me off balance?"

"No." She liked that he was the steadiest person she'd ever known. It didn't seem likely that she could offset him.

"I know what I look like, honey. I'm not an ogre, but I'm rough around the edges, not at all slick like your Sutter."

That jibe stung. "He's not *my* Sutter, so don't say that."

At her firm tone, he gave a nod. "You get my drift."

"Sutter is handsome enough, but he's…" *Not you.* The realization hit her like another clap of thunder. Her lips parted but nothing came out.

No one else was Tanner.

No one had ever gotten to her like this.

If some other guy had avoided her for a week, she'd have told him to take a hike. She would *not* have shared dinner with him. She absolutely would not have clung to him for comfort, no matter the situation.

Yet with Tanner, it all felt right.

It wasn't just that she understood his reasoning for wanting her to move on. She knew he had his own plans for her house—and it *was* her house. Now that she loved it so much, no way would she budge, not even for him.

But it was so much more than mere understanding. It was an inferno of spiking sensations—both physical and emotional. Tanner made her feel things that until now—until him—she hadn't known existed.

Callie shook her head, trying to clear it, but the confusion remained.

Somehow, in a super short time, she'd gotten completely hooked on a guy who would gladly tell her good-bye tomorrow.

Heck, starting tomorrow, he might go back to dodging her.

That thought made her breath catch.

Tanner's frown intensified. "What?"

Blinking out of her fog, she repeated, "What?"

He half laughed. "You said Sutter was handsome, then you just trailed off and started staring at me again."

Heat slid up her neck and slowly filled her face. Thank God for low lighting. "You said he was slick, but slick isn't all that great, especially on a pretentious jerk like Sutter. You're genuine and he is not. And besides, he's not a specimen like you."

"So why does it feel like you just censored that? What were you really going to say?"

"I don't know."

He cocked a brow. "Oh, I think you do."

"Fine." Deciding he could just deal with the truth, she said, "Everyone I know says Sutter is gorgeous, but his eyes don't make me forget myself. He doesn't smell good enough to eat."

Tanner abruptly sat back in his seat, a fire starting to smolder in his eyes.

On a roll, Callie continued. "He doesn't openly love his mother and brother the way you do. He doesn't want to help people—that is, anyone but himself. He doesn't growl in a way that amuses me, or argue in a way I enjoy. Never, not in a million years, would he know what to do if he found me in a tree during a rainstorm. And I can guarantee he wouldn't give two flips for a dog, or a goat, or this mysterious horse you keep claiming is mine."

As she spoke, she breathed faster. Tanner breathed deeper.

Gripping the edge of the table, she leaned in, unable to stop the flow of words. They'd been building the entire week that he'd stayed away. "I never missed sleep thinking about Sutter when I was already exhausted. He would hate having a meal here, in this house, this setting, without power." The more she said, the more clarity she had. "I could never, not for any reason, suffer through marriage with him."

The word *marriage* put Tanner on alert. She couldn't tell if she'd intrigued him or made him want to escape into the storm.

"Relax," she snapped, peeved by his attitude given the wealth of emotion imploding inside her. "I don't know you well enough to propose, but I like you enough that I can imagine it." That sounded absurd so she tacked on, "Not that I have been." She could say that with complete honesty. "I've had my hands full just getting through every damned day." Standing, she picked up her empty plate and went to the sink. Heavy shadows lurked in the corners, shifting with the candle flames, but she knew her way around her own kitchen.

Disposing of the scraps, she scraped her plate and then put it and her fork in the sink before returning to the table. "Snakes," she muttered, feeling very put out. "Bugs and new locks and weird noises and things that don't work when they should. Animals that I don't yet entirely understand." She snapped up the dishes Addie had sent and sealed the lids over them, before carrying them all to the counter.

"Don't open the fridge yet," Tanner warned, his voice calm and even. "Wait until you have everything ready to go inside. That way you'll only open it once and it'll stay colder longer."

"See, you know *everything* and I know almost nothing, but you don't rub it in. Sutter would. That is, he'd be all condescending and superior and I'd want to punch him in the throat."

Seeing Tanner's grin only amped up her frustration. Especially when he stood and pitched in.

Stepping back, Callie gestured. "And that! Doing kitchen chores like it's nothing. Big, bad Tanner can work a full day, save a loony neighbor out of a tree, stick with her because she's falling apart, then smile and help clean up."

"I didn't—"

Whatever he was going to say, she didn't care.

She threw up her hands. "It's freaking unnatural! What man does that?"

"The good ones?"

Oh, sure—with the insinuation being that she'd

LORI FOSTER   225

picked nothing but the *bad ones* for her entire life? "And then be all jokey-jokey about it?" Even knowing she was being unreasonable, she still wanted to tackle him to the floor and devour him.

She wasn't sure if he'd let her though, so instead she filled her lungs, clenched her hands, and tried to bring all the excessive feelings under control. Not an easy task in her current frazzled state. "Before coming here, before you and Addie, goats and chickens, Liam and the Garmets, I was a sensible, even-tempered person. People liked me because I was easy and fun, not ranting and irrational." She jabbed a finger at the table and her voice pitched higher. *"In candlelight!"*

Tanner watched her like she might start screaming any moment. Or maybe she was already screaming. God, what a day it had been.

"I need a shower," he said, still in that casual, even tone.

Every muscle in Callie's body seemed to lock up. Did he mean to shower at her house, or had she just driven him away? If he decided to go, she would not ask him to stay. Absolutely not.

After swiping a cloth over the table and then giving a glance at the dirty dishes in the sink, he faced her. "So."

So *what*? She stiffened her spine, belatedly trying to find her pride.

As if nothing much had happened, like he'd had a normal day with a normal woman who hadn't just gone off on a tirade, Tanner gently rested his heavy hands on her shoulders.

The simple touch felt so good—human-to-human contact. Even better, contact with Tanner, a man she admired, a man she wanted. Scented heat poured off his body, luring her closer. It took a lot of effort to hold her ground.

"Callie?"

"Hmm?"

"Would you like to shower with me?"

Her mouth opened again, but at least this time she managed to properly function. "Yes." She nodded for good measure. "A hot shower in candlelight"—*with you*—"sounds like a terrific idea." The *best* idea.

"We can get the dishes tomorrow. The power should be back on by then."

"Okay."

After the slightest pause, he asked, "Can I sleep with you tonight?"

Not knowing if he meant *sleep*-sleep or smoking hot sex, she nodded fast, because the answer was a resounding *yes* to either one. Hopefully both. "Absolutely." In case that wasn't affirmative enough, she said, "I'd like that."

The corner of his mouth kicked up in an amused grin. "Pretty sure I'm going to like it, too."

CHAPTER ELEVEN

IF TANNER KNEW of her high expectations, based on her previous delicious—even sometimes unnerving—reactions to him, he might have been intimidated. Then again, she'd yet to see him apprehensive about anything. His usual mode seemed to be confident forward momentum, no matter what.

Whether trying to run her off, save her, or anything in between.

He jumped into that mode again by scooping her up. "Grab a candle."

"Oh, um…" This was a first for her. In her world, men didn't just scoop up women like it was nothing. If he was any other guy, she might have been annoyed, or she might have found the action hilariously ridiculous. With Tanner, it felt natural. Again.

She reached out and took the jarred candle from the table.

As he carried her closer to the remaining two candles, he said, "Blow them out so we can save them."

She obligingly huffed a breath.

"Good." With her holding the only lit candle, and him holding her, shadows closed in around them. If she'd been alone on a night like this, the atmosphere would have felt ominous.

Instead, as he carried her to the bathroom, she felt…

special. Pampered. As if she really mattered to him. It was so unexpected, a nervous giggle escaped her when she seriously wasn't the giggling kind.

At the look he slanted down at her, she cleared her throat and said, "I could have walked."

In a tone devoid of haste, he said, "We got here faster this way." The second he put her back on her feet, he took the candle from her and set it on the sink. "One second." Moving all the damp clothes away from the tub, he turned on the water, pulled the shower curtain and lifted the nozzle to start the shower.

Efficient, that's what he was. And maybe in a bit of a hurry regardless of how composed he appeared.

She, on the other hand, was already antsy. Big-time. Give her half a second and she could have him naked. Bummer that all they had was candlelight, but she'd make do.

Was there a flashlight somewhere in the house?

She was considering that, trying to remember if she'd seen one somewhere, when he stepped behind her and stripped away her open flannel shirt.

"Mind if I ask where you got this?"

Unsure what he meant, she turned to face him and found him scowling at the shirt like it offended him. "I guess it was Reggie's. A few of his things were stored in the basement in a big chest." Lifting a shoulder, she explained, "It looked cozy so I washed it and added it to my own stuff."

For unknown reasons, that answer pleased him enough that he stole her breath with a consuming kiss. His hands moved over her hips, along her back, up and under her T-shirt, and as he put a marginal amount of space between them, he stripped that shirt away, too.

In the silence of the room, she heard his deeper breaths. As dark as it was, she could swear she felt the heat of his gaze moving over her breasts. With an inarticulate sound of hunger, he kissed her again, but not for long.

"Your water heater is small so we'll need to rush through the shower before the tank empties and you're out of hot water."

Never before had she given a thought to where her hot water came from, but an icy shower didn't appeal to her at all. "Race you." She stripped off her shorts, panties, and socks in one quick movement, and while Tanner gave a heartfelt groan, she grabbed a clip off the shelf behind the toilet to hold up her hair, and then she stepped into the tub. The water was already tepid so she washed with haste and was almost done when he stepped in behind her.

Unfair! She had a most spectacular naked male in the shower with her and she couldn't linger. "It's too dark to see!"

Laughing, he moved around her, hogging the spray for a moment. It was an erotic push and pull as they each hurriedly washed and rinsed, and when the water suddenly went cold, Tanner gallantly blocked it with his body so she could snatch up a towel and step out.

Shivering, she said, "Hurry," knowing he had to be freezing.

He shut off the water, pushed back the curtain, and gave her a candlelit view of his body. The awesome sight sucked all the oxygen out of the room, forcing her lungs to labor.

Her avid gaze moved over his wide shoulders, solid chest, down a firm abdomen and... Reluctantly, she held out a soft, dry towel for him to use. He was already hard, despite that cold water, and suddenly she wanted to fan herself.

Mine, mine, mine, her brain silently chanted. It wasn't something she'd say out loud, yet the territorial instinct grew.

So many parts of her life were currently uncertain, but not this. Not what she felt for him, how intrinsically she reacted to him. It was new and exciting, practically overwhelming, and she wanted more.

As Tanner absently dried himself, he made it clear that he liked what he saw, too. He didn't care that her hair was wrecked and she was without makeup. In fact, Callie couldn't recall ever wearing makeup around him.

This was not the time for comparisons, but it struck her that no other man had seen her like this—stripped down to the most elemental version of herself.

Yet Tanner considered it enough.

Completely undone by that realization, she grabbed up the candle and headed out of the bathroom. Thankfully, Tanner was right behind her. In the bedroom, she set the candle on the dresser.

With a suggestive smile, Tanner moved it to the nightstand so that the glow fell over the bed.

A flush of excitement warmed her. Getting in the bed seemed a priority, but Tanner caught her hand, keeping her on her feet. He removed the clip from her hair. Gently, despite the still-damp tangles, he finger-combed it, lifting it over her shoulders, smoothing out each long lock.

With a soft kiss, he said, "I get the feeling you don't realize how sexy you are like this."

"I'm a wreck," she replied, amused that their thoughts

seemed to be running along the same rail. "But even on my best day I'm not the physically perfect example you are. Don't misunderstand," she added, "I'm content with how I look."

His smile made a sexy promise. "Be content all you want, princess."

For once, the nickname didn't offend her, not the way he said it.

Using just the backs of his fingers, he brushed a heated path over her shoulder, her chest, down and over her left breast. "But I'm going for a hotter reaction." And with that, he took her down to the bed and showed her how much he appreciated every single inch of her skin.

Callie wasn't inexperienced, but with Tanner every touch felt special. Every kiss seemed like her first.

And yet, it all felt incredibly natural, too, as if it was meant to be. Novel but familiar. Unbearably exciting and still comfortable.

Everywhere she touched him made her want more. From his sleek, hard shoulders, to the crisp dusting of chest hair, the deep furrow of his spine and the solid muscles that flanked it.

She let her hands trail to his backside, but before she could truly appreciate the firm muscles there, he slid down in the bed to kiss a path along her body. He lingered at her breasts, first nuzzling, then licking, and finally sucking. Her body arched as sensation washed over her in tantalizing waves. He drew on her until she was gasping every breath.

"So close," she gasped, unable to believe that she was on the cusp of an orgasm from only this.

"Not yet," he replied huskily, taking her mouth in

another hungry kiss. He curved his rough hand over her thigh, gently squeezed, then brought his fingers higher—between her legs.

Callie caught her breath and held it, anxious for his touch, *needing* it. It felt like a lifetime ago that she'd first come out of the woods and found him standing there. Six feet of scorching temptation. She'd wanted him then, and every second since. Getting to know him, caring about him, had only sharpened the desire. She didn't think she could take any more.

"Tanner…" she pleaded.

"Shh." He kissed her again. "Let me enjoy you."

Enjoy her? Well, that sounded nice—if he'd only get on with it. Instead, he kept playing, teasing his fingertips over her, lightly stroking, ratcheting up her tension. She widened her legs, silently demanding.

With a murmur of appreciation, he pressed one finger to her, parting her, finding her hot and wet.

Callie wanted to touch him everywhere. Never had she felt more alive, as if every nerve ending was sparking. She gripped his back, licked his shoulder, lightly sank her teeth into the rigid muscle there.

With a groan, Tanner worked another finger into her, pressing them deep, then sliding out to tease her clit before thrusting in again.

Once more, Callie found herself on the ragged edge. *Please, please, please.* She needed this release. Needed it so badly.

Without saying a word, still with his fingers stroking, Tanner began kissing his way down her body, past her breasts again—and of course he paused to tease again—then down to her stomach, over to her hip…

Knowing where this was going, anxious for it, she tangled her fingers in his thick hair.

And then he was there, right there where she needed him. With a wet kiss, he left her undone. Every groan he issued, every lick of his tongue, left her ready to combust.

She understood sex. This was something else.

This was... *"Tanner."*

Her entire body coiled in acute pleasure, wringing a husky moan from her. She was unable to stop herself from riding up against his mouth, twisting until he settled a firm hand on her stomach to hold her still.

That, too, was unbearably exciting.

"Tanner," she whispered again and again, hoarsely, then somewhat shrilly.

He drew her in, sucking, licking—and she came apart. Over the top of her own cries, she heard his hungry groan.

After that, Callie wasn't sure what she said or did. The unbelievable pleasure wrung her out.

Just as it started to fade, Tanner came over her, his hands cupping her face. "Are you protected?"

Callie gulped air, barely hearing him through the haze of pulsing sensation that remained.

He kissed her hard. "Babe, do I need a condom?"

Trying to bring him into focus, she whispered, "I'm on the pill, never missed a dose, and we're both healthy."

Kissing her again, his hold possessive and firm as if he knew she was floating, Tanner nudged her legs wider—and thrust into her in one long, easy glide that filled her up and caused her body to clench yet again.

Rarely had she ever indulged without a condom in

use. Sutter preferred them, because as he often said, he wouldn't take chances.

Tanner, apparently, trusted her—as much as she trusted him. She felt him and only him, driving into her in delicious friction.

She needed to catch her breath, but he only deepened his kiss, and… Who needed air? Callie wrapped her thighs around him, trying to hold him tighter. Wishing she could hold him forever.

Locking her arms around his neck, she countered his thrusts with the rhythmic roll of her hips, earning his growl of approval.

Astounding her, another orgasm built in a rush. Her body tightened around his erection, squeezing, and suddenly he pressed his face to her neck. "Now," he ordered. "Now, babe. Now or never."

His thrusts were hard and fast, and again she gave herself over to it.

Her release was debilitating in the best possible way. Never before had her body felt so foreign, so relaxed and limp. Utterly spent.

As their combined breathing eased and Tanner levered up to his elbows, she couldn't even get her eyes open. Smiling, because she was happy and replete, she let her limbs fall away from him.

Tanner gave a quiet, gruff laugh, and nuzzled his mouth to hers. It was nice. Sort of an afterglow smooch, haphazard and lazy.

"Mmm," she said, knowing full coherent words were beyond her.

He continued to play at her mouth while they both caught their breath. When at last the haze had lifted, leaving her lethargic, he gently pressed his lips to her forehead, her cheek, and the bridge of her nose.

"Stay put," he whispered. "I'll be right back."

Still, she didn't speak. Wasn't sure she could anyway.

When he returned a minute later with a damp wash-cloth, she was barely awake. Even when he rearranged her, tucking her under the quilt and climbing into the bed beside her, all she could do was drift on the residual pleasure. A gal could easily get addicted to something so phenomenally satisfying. Maybe she already was.

Pulling her against him, Tanner breathed in her ear, "Sleep."

After the day she'd had, that sounded like a grand plan.

CALLIE SLEPT FOR a few hours, then woke with a start. Tanner held her closer, reassuring her with a murmured, "Easy." Knowing she might have forgotten, he said, "Lights are still out—and I'm still with you." In fact, he never wanted to move.

"Mmm," she whispered sleepily. "Sorry I dozed off."

"You could have slept through the night and it would be okay with me." She'd gone out so quickly, he knew she had to be exhausted. Apparently, the sleep she'd gotten had rejuvenated her, because she immediately got busy seducing him.

It was a uniquely pleasurable experience to be the recipient of Callie's sexual greed.

A man could get addicted.

This time, he was a little more thorough, a little less rushed—but Callie still raced to the finish line. She was so sexually explosive that he couldn't hold back as long as he would have liked.

Not that it mattered. It was still the best carnal experience of his life. Would always be, in fact. He had to wonder if he'd ever be the same. Doubtful.

Warm and sleepy, her fingertips drifted over his chest. "Could I ask you something?"

Since he'd passed the point of keeping much from her, he replied, "Anything."

Her long hesitation warned him, and then she whispered, "What the Garmet brothers said early on about Addie almost losing her house because of you... They made it sound like you'd done something wrong. Not that I believe them," she assured him, tightening her hold as if she thought he'd surge away in anger.

The question was so far removed from their current position—naked and entwined in bed—that for a moment, it stymied him.

"Tanner," she persisted. "I trust you."

"I know that," he said, stroking her in reassurance. From the start, even when he'd been standing there with a roaring chain saw, Callie had trusted him. It had defied reason, and started the deconstruction of his resistance.

"I shouldn't have mentioned it," she said, and pressed a kiss to his sternum.

Knowing it was bound to come up sooner or later, Tanner had considered different angles to dodge the question. In the end, he'd known spitting out the truth was the only way to go. Now, here with her in the dark, seemed like as good a time as any. "I was accused of killing my father."

Anger brought her upright, but he tugged her back down. Nice that it was anger on his behalf. He didn't have a single doubt about that.

"I was a suspect for a while," he explained. "Something like that gets around, especially in a town this size."

"Tanner." She hugged him tight. "I'm sorry I brought it up."

"I'm not." It would be better to clear the air, especially if she'd be staying.

"Good," she stated firmly. "I don't want any secrets between us and I don't want you to ever worry that I'll believe rumors."

Take-charge Callie. That's what he should call her. Sharing one of his biggest shames was never easy, but with her, it wasn't as difficult as he'd imagined. "Relax."

Gradually, she eased, her body melting against his again.

He loved how they fit together. Few things had ever felt so right. "Addie had already claimed me, and now that you know her a little you can imagine how she reacted."

"I'm sure she was fierce."

"Yeah." That described her perfectly: fiercely protective, loving, and determined. "She told me that she'd believe anything I told her, and if I had in fact killed him, she'd still back me. I think I fell apart, as dramatic and panicked as a boy that age could be."

The entire scene played out in his head. He could still feel the tight lock of Addie's arms around him, the reassurance in her voice as she'd promised him over and over that he was safe, that she'd never let him be hurt again.

Emotion prickled his nostrils and thickened his throat, forcing him to take a moment, to swallow, to breathe.

Callie said nothing, but she pressed her lips to him again, just above his heart as she patiently waited.

"Addie decided I needed good legal representation, so she took a second mortgage on her house. At the time I was young enough that I didn't understand what that meant." Though others had ensured he knew, doing their utmost to shame him over it. For years he'd carried that blame. So much of it that without Addie's love, and later Kam's, he knew it would have crippled him. "She fought tooth and nail for me, and in the end it was proven that I'd been in the closet the entire time." Other abuse had been uncovered too, and that was a unique shame all its own.

Callie forced her way up despite his mild effort to dissuade her. Folding her arms on his chest, the tears in her eyes visible in the candlelight, she smiled at him. An intimate, meaningful smile, one he'd never seen from her before.

Grateful for the darkness, Tanner didn't bother to hide his own expression.

"I never doubted that you were innocent or that Addie would move heaven and earth for you. Knowing you even a little, meeting her that first time, it was all clear to me."

Impossible, yet she looked so sincere.

"Something else I want to ask if it isn't too personal. Why don't you and Kam call her Mom? Not judging, because I'm sure there's a reason. I'm just curious." Her smile went crooked. "Now that you've knocked my world off its axis with phenomenal sex, I want to know everything about you." Cautiously, she admitted, "The more you're with me, the more questions you're bound to get."

Not knowing what the future held for them, he didn't want to dwell on that. "Ask me anything you want. If I can answer, I will." The fall of her hair drew his fingers. Here in the dim light, her brown hair cast intriguing shadows over the side of her face, exaggerating her eyelashes, adding softness to the curve of her cheek and the corner of those impossible-to-resist lips. "Kam and I talked to Addie once about calling her Mom." Remembering, he barely suppressed a smile. "We were worried, wanting to know if she minded that we didn't, if we'd hurt her feelings for not calling her Mom. One thing about Addie, she always gave it to us straight."

"She's an up-front, honest person."

To the core of her being. "She told us, all serious-like, that we could call her anything we wanted. She said she loved us like a mother, but also more than a mother ever could. She'd chosen us because we owned her heart, every single beat of it, and that would never change."

"Aww," Callie said softly as a tear slid down her cheek. Smiling, she brushed it away and sniffed. "I *love* that."

"Yeah, we'd loved it, too." He stroked his hand over her messy hair, from the crown, down the warm length and to her slender back. "Kam said his mother wasn't much to speak of, so to him Addie was more than a mom. I guess that inspired me—hard to explain the reasoning of boys that young—but I confessed that my mother had skipped out and left me with an abusive dick for a father. I agreed that Addie was better than any mom I'd ever seen."

The candlelight found more tears in Callie's eyes, but they weren't tears of sadness. He loved that she didn't try to hide them from him. She just whisked them away again, and with her silent interest she kept him talking.

"Addie had cried," he said, catching a stray tear off Callie's cheek with the side of his thumb. He drew her down for a kiss that lingered. "She'd laughed, too. Kam and I were so confused. We'd never seen anyone bawl and laugh at the same time." He grinned, remembering how they had looked at each other, unsure what to do next. "She'd grabbed us both into an unbreakable embrace and swore, over and over, that we were the best things to ever happen to her. So to us, she's always been Addie. Better than a mom." Tanner tunneled his fingers into Callie's hair. "Better than anything we'd ever known or dared to hope for."

Funny, but at that moment, Callie did that confusing chuckling and crying thing that had so bewildered him as a boy. Now he understood though, and he hugged her close. "Any other questions?"

"Not just yet," she promised, breathing out a shaky sigh.

"Then how about we get some sleep?"

She cuddled down against him. "It's not raining anymore."

"No, it's not. But it's the middle of the night."

"You can still stay? If it's a problem, I understand, but I'd love it if—"

"I'm not going anywhere," he assured her. "Earlier, before you started eyeballing me over dinner, I'd been trying to figure out the right way to ask, but then you did your kitchen routine—"

She lightly poked his ribs for teasing her.

"—and that changed things."

"I beat you to it."

She'd beat him to a lot of things. But hey, it had gotten him here, naked in a bed, sharing life-changing stories…with Callie McCallahan, who, as it turned out, was far better as a real woman than she'd ever been as a fantasy idea of perfection.

WHEN THE KNOCK sounded on Callie's door, she stirred from a heavy sleep, instantly aware of the warmth of Tanner hugged up to her back, how his scent enveloped her, and the smile that bloomed on her face. Last night had been the stuff of romantic dreams and sexual fantasies mixed up with heart-filling emotion.

She was waking up as a new woman. Whatever happened next between her and Tanner, she'd always have the very best night of her life to remember.

Sunlight streamed in through the blinds and a hum filled the air, telling her the electricity was back on. Tanner's hand, completely engulfing one of her breasts, contracted just a little.

It would be so incredibly easy to linger, but…there was that knock again.

Thinking it would be Kam or Addie, she nudged Tanner. Instead of taking the hint, he pulled her more tightly into the curve of his body, her back to his front, and she felt the unmistakable rise of his interest.

There could be no better way to wake up than this.

"Hey," she said, her voice froggy with sleep. "Tanner?"

"Mmm?" His mouth touched her shoulder. "Damn, you smell good."

Snickering, she turned in his arms to face him. "None of that. Someone's at the door."

From one moment to the next, his dark eyes flashed

open, instantly alert, not a single sign of sleepiness remaining. "You're sure?"

Mindful of her morning breath, she tucked her face against his throat. "I heard the knock."

Tanner jerked upright. "Who the hell is calling on you at…" Twisting to see his phone on her nightstand, he added, "Seven a.m.?"

"I assume your brother?"

Snorting, he threw back the covers. "Kam knows better."

For a couple of seconds, she was awestruck again by his powerful body, the fluid movement of muscles flexing, and the obvious strength. *Sinfully* gorgeous, and no matter how she'd fawned over him last night, he still didn't seem to realize his physical impact on her senses. "I like you in the morning light." She bobbed her eyebrows. "If I could take a photo—"

"Not in this lifetime."

While he snatched up his jeans, she said, "Maybe it's Addie."

The incredulous look he threw over his shoulder made her grin.

"No?"

"Addie is an intelligent woman, so no, she wouldn't show up here this early, knowing I stayed over with you. The only way it would be her or Kam is if…" His expression darkened. "Something could be wrong." Expression grim, he started out of the room.

Unsnapped and unzipped.

"Wait!" Callie jumped up too, but he hadn't paused and as she pulled on shorts and a shirt, she heard her front door open.

Then heavy silence.

Oh crap. She finger-combed her absolutely hideous hair as she darted down the hall—only to find Tanner standing in front of the open door, staring daggers at Dirk. What in the world?

From the porch, Dirk asked, "So it's like that, huh?"

"Exactly like that," Tanner growled back.

Like *what*? Callie wanted to ask, but instead she cleared her throat, which immediately gained her the attention from both men.

Dirk's gaze took a quick dip down her body, then respectfully returned to her face. "Didn't mean to intrude."

Tanner gave another rude snort.

"That's okay," she said. "I need to get started on chores soon anyway." When both men just stared at her, she asked, "Did you need something?"

Shifting, glaring at Tanner, then back to her, Dirk said, "You were…upset yesterday."

Meaning: *you were up a tree.*

He cleared his throat. "Just figured I'd stop by to make sure you're okay."

Even knowing she was a wreck and clearly recognizing Tanner's antagonism, Callie still smiled. It disarmed people and kept them guessing what she thought.

Truthfully, though, she was surprised by his concern. He even managed to look sheepish, as if he didn't make these type of neighborly calls very often. "I'm fine now, thank you."

"As you can see," Tanner stated.

It was already clear that they'd slept together. He didn't need to drive it into the ground.

Tanner glanced back at her. "How about some coffee? I'll be right back." And with that he started to step out.

Stunned at his audacity, Callie surged forward. "I don't think so." She caught the doorknob before he could pull the door closed behind him. Taking matters into her own hands, she asked Dirk, "What were you doing out there? And why did you take my goat?"

Dirk stared at her so hard, her skin prickled in unease. "I didn't take your goat. I was trying to get it back for you."

"I heard you talking to Lang."

"Yeah?" After absorbing her accusation, and seeing Tanner's attitude, he discarded his concern and instead copped an attitude. "What the fuck did you hear?"

Wow, that turnaround had happened lightning-fast.

"If you know what's good for you," Tanner growled, "you won't curse at her."

"But she can sling accusations at me? Fuck that. I'll say whatever I want."

Uncertainty crept in on Callie. She put a hand to Tanner's arm, letting him know she didn't want or need his defense on this. "I heard you say that Tanner and Kam were away and I was home alone."

"All true!" Dirk threw up his hands. "And your goat was out in a storm."

Tanner asked, "How'd it get out, Dirk? You want to tell me that?"

"How the hell should I know? I'm not the keeper of her animals. I heard the damn thing carrying on and thought to help her out. So fucking sue me."

"Enough with the language," Callie said, before Tanner could react again. "Why were you in the woods?"

"Same reason you were." He thrust his chin forward

and repeated with annoying enunciation, "Hunting a goat."

"Right. You and Lang, dressed in rain slickers, just tromping through the woods during a storm?"

He had the nerve to laugh. "Sounds better than you, without a rain slicker, climbing a fu...*freaking* tree."

To show her appreciation for his censorship, she dipped her head. "I counted the goats and realized one was missing. I was already looking for it when the drizzle turned into a storm."

"Lang and I were hunting morel mushrooms along the edge of our property and heard it." He lifted his hands. "Next thing I know, you're up a tree and panicking."

"Er... I wasn't exactly panicked."

"Bullshit. I thought you'd faint and fall to the ground. Why do you think I got closer to you?"

"To catch me?" she guessed, feeling a little sick.

"I'd have tried." He narrowed his eyes. "What the hell did you think was happening?"

Nervously twisting the ends of her hair, she said, "I guess I... I heard you and Lang, and I thought..."

Dirk glared at Tanner. "And you've painted us as pure evil, haven't you, you motherfucker?"

Good Lord. Expecting fireworks at any moment, Callie tried to tighten her hold on Tanner, but it proved unnecessary. Once again, other than his mouth curling in a small, taunting smile, he showed no signs of being provoked. "I've given her an accurate representation of you." He took one step forward. "And now it's time for you to go."

"Yeah, it is." Sneering, he glanced at Callie. "Believe me, I've learned my lesson on being a concerned neighbor. I won't make that mistake again." He stomped off before she could think of anything conciliatory to say.

If only she'd gone in and made coffee as Tanner had suggested, instead of confronting Dirk. Her heart lay heavy in her chest. Disliking the Garmets on principle was easier than admitting she'd badly overreacted.

"They were trying to get the goat back for me." Color washed from her face as she realized her own misjudgment. "And I climbed a tree." Feeling sick, full of regret, she watched Dirk until he disappeared behind a wall of thick honeysuckle that ran in a tangled line between their properties.

Taking her arm above her elbow, Tanner urged her inside, and then to the couch. He crouched down in front of her.

Given he was barefoot and bare-chested with his jeans undone, it was an enormous distraction.

"Listen to me, Callie."

Right. She'd messed this all up and she needed to pay attention, so she forced her gaze to his.

He surprised her by saying, "Never, under any circumstances, trust Dirk or Lang. Do you understand me?"

"But—"

"But nothing. If you got a vibe, then you were smart to act on it. God gave you instincts for a reason."

And her instincts had been clamoring. Was that an actual issue she had with them, a residual fear left over from her college experience with Warren, or something instilled by Tanner and his dislike of the brothers? She frowned over the thought. "I climbed a tree."

"A big one, I know." His mouth twitched. "I'm proud

of you. Couldn't have been easy, but you got up there and took yourself out of harm's way."

His attitude helped to lessen her embarrassment. "I think I might've flown."

He laughed. "No, you did what you had to and that was smart. If you'd stayed within reach, who knows what they might have done?"

Today, with the skies clear and the sun bright, she had a feeling they'd have helped her find her goat. Tanner's earnestness kept her from admitting that out loud, but it didn't eradicate her guilt. "I'll keep my keys and phone on me from now on."

"Probably not a bad idea, even when Liam's around. He's a capable guy, but only nineteen."

"I wouldn't want to put him in the position of thinking he had to protect me."

"If I told him you said that, he'd be mighty insulted."

No doubt. She looked at Tanner, at his thighs spread on either side of her, his hands now holding hers, and she felt…things. Too many to decipher all at once, especially after the stunning night she'd had with him.

Tipping forward, she rested her forehead on his bare shoulder. "What now?" She felt his slight stiffening.

In a carefully neutral tone, he said, "I have work to do, and you have critters to tend."

So that's where they were. Back to business as usual.

It saddened her, but she'd already decided she wouldn't push for more. Neither of them was going anywhere and with their off-the-charts chemistry, this sort of thing was bound to happen again. She'd bide her time until then, and probably miss him every minute. "I understand."

"I doubt that." Standing, he said, "Sorry, honey, but

I need one minute." He went down the hall and into the bathroom. The door closed with a quiet click.

And of course, that made her need to go too, but she only had the one bathroom. Confused, unsure how to take his back-and-forth mood this morning, she curled up on the couch and waited. After the flush of the toilet and the sound of running water, Tanner emerged.

Completely cavalier about their morning-after, he bent to give her a quick kiss, leaving her with the scent of her mouthwash. "I'll get the coffee started."

It bugged her a little that Tanner coasted through the inevitable awkwardness like it was nothing, while she was left floundering. "Thanks."

Deliberately, she took longer than he had, brushing the tangles from her hair, splashing her face, and cleaning her teeth. Lastly, she pulled on socks to protect her feet from the cold floor and shrugged back into her flannel shirt.

When she got to the kitchen, Tanner had just sat down at the table, with two mugs of steaming coffee at the ready. He'd even prepped hers for her.

He was awfully good at making himself at home. And at winning her over.

If Sutter's life was on the line, she doubted he'd be able to say how she liked her coffee, yet Tanner had remembered.

After she took her first sip, she admitted—only to herself—that she liked how he settled in and got comfortable. It'd be far too easy to imagine him moving seamlessly into her life on a regular basis. Sleeping with him each night, the hot sex, the tender hugs, sharing coffee on a cool spring morning… They'd discuss everything big and small, then he would go off to do whatever landscaping jobs he had, and she would…

Her thoughts paused there. She'd never done the home and hearth before. Looking around now, she saw that she still wasn't doing it. This house remained Reggie's home, without her décor, her preferred arrangement, or her personal touches. Probably why Tanner was comfortable; he'd been here innumerable times.

She hadn't made it her own yet, but still, she'd been so content.

Was she settling? Or so intent on proving something that she was willing to be "less than" everything she could be? She feared it might be the latter.

After a few fortifying sips of her coffee, she faced Tanner across the table. "So…" How did you ask a man where they were headed *without* outright asking? Was there a casual way to find out if this had been a one-off? Or would Tanner want a repeat performance?

Maybe she could start by asking him about dinner.

Except, Addie loved cooking dinner. Callie wouldn't rob her of that—*if* she even could, which seemed doubtful. She took so long trying to figure it out, Tanner took over.

"Want me to help you with your chores before I take off?"

Hmm. No mention of later. Callie shook her head. "No, that's okay. I have a routine." And she should probably get to it. "I know you do as well?" She said it more as a question than a statement.

He nodded. "I'll have a lot of cleanup to do. Storms always bring a mess and longtime clients ask for help in saving damaged trees and plants."

That made sense, plus it sounded better than him

claiming last night had been a mistake. "What about your own trees?" So far she'd only seen a portion of his tree farm, but with thirty acres she imagined he'd have damage, too.

"We have a few part-time employees who work the land farther from the house when necessary. I give them a schedule, though it might change now. I'll go out on the tractor later to check on things."

"You have a tractor, too?"

"A compact residential tractor. Makes it easier to dig up and plant trees." He sipped his coffee, then added, "The job varies from week to week, season to season. I'm mostly doing landscaping now, but maintenance is a year-round job. Much like tending your animals."

"Speaking of that, I'll need to check on the goat to see if he's okay, too."

"I'll give Nell a call. She's studying to be a vet tech, but she's always had a way with animals. She grooms Blu for me."

Which, Callie felt sure, was another way for Tanner to show Nell that she was needed, he trusted her, and she had options. He was backup when necessary and always a reliable friend.

It was so, so easy for him to steal her heart just by being himself. "I'd love to meet her," she said softly. "Thank you."

He upended his mug to finish it off, then pushed back his chair. "You'll be around all day?"

"I don't have any plans except the usual, so yes, I'll be around." Was he going to ask about seeing her again? Hopeful, and irked at herself because of it, she waited.

Tanner collected his shoes at the back door. "Then I'll tell Nell to stop by when it's convenient for her."

Determined that he wouldn't leave without at least one more kiss, she stood as well. "Okay, thanks."

They stared at each other.

The knock on her door—now for the second time—made her want to groan at the interruption. Surely Dirk wouldn't return so soon?

Possibly having the same thought, Tanner scowled and stormed that way.

Callie had to hustle to keep up. "I can answer my own door, thank you."

As if that hadn't occurred to him, he paused.

She skirted past him, unlocked the door, swung it open and—good God.

Her parents. A bucket of ice water to the face wouldn't have shocked her more.

CHAPTER TWELVE

SEEING HER MOM and dad standing there in the humid morning air took the strength from Callie's knees. Bracing herself, she wheezed in a big breath that, admittedly, sounded more like a horrified gasp.

In complete silence, her thoughts going everywhere all at once with a tinge of panic, she gapcd at them.

Grinning hugely, her dad stepped in and enfolded her in a big, warm hug. "Sweetheart, you had us worried."

"Worried," she squeaked, supremely aware of big, bold, shirtless Tanner standing right behind her.

"Your mother texted and called repeatedly, but you didn't answer."

She'd forgotten all about her phone! "Oh, um…" He set her back, his congenial smile still in place as his gaze moved over her. "Look at you. My little country girl," he teased. "You look cute as hell."

At least her dad seemed happy to see her.

Tanner remained silent.

The sound her mother made, exasperated and impatient to be invited in, brought Callie back to reality with a snap and she started rambling. "We had a big storm last night. I lost power. My phone was ready to die when I went to bed, but I couldn't recharge it and I guess I slept late, then didn't give my phone a thought because I needed coffee so badly. Luckily, the power had come back on—as you can see. I mean, I do have coffee now." Forcing herself to *stop*, she opened the door wider and stepped aside to welcome them. More calmly, she said, "I'm sorry that I worried you."

Staring past her, her mother zeroed in on Tanner. "Who is your undressed guest, Callie? And why is he carrying muddy boots?"

Liz McCallahan didn't exactly say it in accusation, more like curious confusion. She, too, gave Callie a brief hug, very brief, in fact, using only one arm, because her gaze stayed glued to Tanner.

Not that Callie blamed her. A woman at any age would appreciate the sight of him. Most guys, too. No way around it, Tanner was impressive.

But how in the world should she introduce him? *Oh, hey, this is the hot guy next door who just rocked my world. I learned things about sex I'd never suspected. Naturally, I want more.*

No, definitely not. "Um, Tanner, is a neighbor."

Her mother's perfectly arched eyebrows lifted in a respectful demand for more detail.

Tanner, thankfully, covered for her. "Tanner Patrick." He held out his free hand to her father, and then her mother. "It's nice to meet you, Mr. and Mrs. McCallahan. I remember you both from my school days."

His smile was perfectly polite, but not very warm— at least, not to Callie, who'd seen him genuinely amused. Her parents seemed to buy it, though.

"Oh?" Frank McCallahan said. "You're from here?"

"I've never lived anywhere else. As Callie said, I'm in the house next door."

"The tree farm?" Liz asked.

"Yes, ma'am. It's been years, I know, but you might

remember how many houses lose power during a storm. Since Callie is new here, I checked on her. With all the rain, though, my boots got muddy walking over."

Glancing at the porch behind her, Liz asked, "You didn't just leave them on the porch?"

"Came to the back door, ma'am. There's a path that cuts through both properties." Tanner glanced at Callie. "I was just leaving though."

Damn it, she didn't want him to leave like this.

"Through the front door now?" her mother asked with a small provoking smile.

Callie finally recouped enough to say, "Mother! Stop badgering him." She could have explained the true situation to her parents, but she didn't want to involve Tanner in family drama—and she was fairly certain there would be drama aplenty. "He walked to the front door with me because you knocked."

Not the least bit deterred, Liz said, "Just sorting it out, Callie. We're here to talk about Sutter, after all, so finding a near naked man was a bit of a surprise."

Callie's mouth fell open, but she took a second too long to find words.

"And," her mother smoothly continued, "since you didn't do a proper introduction, I'll tell Mr. Patrick that I'm Liz McCallahan, and my husband is Frank."

He nodded. "Feel free to call me Tanner."

Smiling, her father said, "Nice to meet you, Tanner. Hope we didn't interrupt?"

"Frank," her mother chided. "She's engaged."

Blanching, Callie corrected, "No. I'm most definitely not."

"Well, that will get sorted out during our visit, I'm sure." Liz wandered in, dismissing Tanner. "I haven't been here in years. I'd nearly forgotten Reggie's house, though it hasn't actually changed much."

Yes, Callie wanted to say, it has. *Because now I live here.* But she'd just acknowledged to herself in the kitchen that other than being clean, nothing had changed all that much.

Disturbed by that thought, she instead focused on Tanner. "Thank you again. I'd have been lost without you." Sleepless too. And still edgy, though he'd taken care of all of that and now she felt almost liquid with satisfaction.

Or rather, she would have if she knew where they were going with this and if she didn't have her parents and their unexpected visit to contend with.

Tanner gave her a very neighborly nod. "Any problems, just let me know."

Such a lackluster goodbye. Frustration mounting, she said, "I'll walk you out." She could steal one minute more with him—

"No need." He nodded at her parents again. "I'll let you get back to your visit." He stepped out, shoved his feet into his boots and walked away.

Pretty sure he just took her heart with him. Who knew a heart could get attached that quickly? It never had before. She wasn't the type to get clingy. Except with Tanner, she was discovering new things about herself. She wasn't at all sure she liked this new, encompassing need. Or maybe she liked it *too* much.

Closing her door, she turned back to her parents. Only they weren't there.

Dear heavens, if they went through the house they'd see the discarded clothes in the bathroom, the messy bed...

From the kitchen, her mother said, "We're helping ourselves to coffee."

Oh, thank God! "Go ahead, Mom. I'll be right there."

Darting for the bathroom, Callie decided she'd put her house to rights before she joined her parents. That would also give her a little time to gear up for whatever they had planned.

First, she gathered up an armload of clothes and stuffed them into the hamper. With Tanner's jeans included, they barely fit. Hmm. She could wash them, then return them with Addie's dishes. That would give her an excuse to…

No, no making excuses to see him. The next move would be his.

So why did that decision feel so awful?

She knew why. There were no guarantees with Tanner. She could see him tonight, or weeks could go by without a word. So far, nothing with him had been predictable.

Even the sex had taken her by surprise.

But liking him? Laughing with him, enjoying him? Yes, far, far too easy.

Growling at herself, she went to her bedroom and quickly tidied up the room. She even fluffed the pillows and spread out the comforter. There. No one would know they'd slept together—in any context.

Except that the room still held Tanner's scent, and it made her want to crawl back into the bed, press her nose to the pillow and think about…

Pivoting away from temptation, she strode through the hall and to the kitchen. "Sorry to keep you waiting."

Her father stood on the back porch, breathing deeply of the morning air, but her mother was braced against a counter, her expression thoughtful as she stared at the mugs on the table.

Let her stare, Callie decided. So she'd enjoyed a mug of coffee with her neighbor? Big deal. She was allowed. "I'll need to head out to take care of the goats and chickens."

Her mother ignored that to say, "Sutter is coming by, too. I thought we'd all talk."

Figuratively, maybe literally too, Callie staggered. "You invited him *here*? Without asking me?"

"There's more at stake than you realize." Calm personified, her mother sipped her drink. "We need to settle some things."

Shrill and unable to level her tone, Callie said, "*It's settled*. Sutter and I are *over*."

Her mother frowned. "Is that what you're wearing today?"

Frustration imploded. "*Yes*, this is what I'm wearing," she reiterated sharply through her teeth. "I have animals to tend and chores to do."

Sticking his head in the door, her father gave her a commiserating smile. "Come on, honey. I'll help you."

"Frank," Liz said. "You'll ruin your shoes."

"I'm sure Callie has a hose. I'll clean them off later." He reached out a hand to her, waggling his fingers to get her moving.

With a slow, deliberate inhale, Callie stepped forward. She picked up her own muddy boots and stepped out on the back stoop, then took a seat on the top step. While her dad closed the door behind them, she tugged on the boots with more force than necessary, silently fuming.

"Don't let your mother rile you." He took a seat beside her. "I remember this place well. Reggie and I grew up tending animals, did you remember that?"

Callie wanted to hold on to her annoyance, she really did. But the pleasure in her father's tone, the wistful way he looked around, drained away some of her irritation. "You'd both told me. Reggie said that you, as the oldest brother, caught the brunt of the workload."

"True enough, but it didn't do him any favors being the baby." He grinned and confided, "He hated when I called him that."

The affection was clear, prompting Callie to say, "Reggie loved you a lot, you know that, right? Even more than that, he was proud of you. Always."

Looking out at the yard, her dad nodded. "Your mother and I grew up around here. My childhood home was similar to this, maybe smaller. Reggie and I always shared a room."

"I bet that was fun," she said facetiously.

He snorted. "It had its moments." As if remembering his wife, he glanced warily at the door, then stood and offered her his hand. "Let's talk while we work."

Conspiring with him, Callie whispered, "You mean away from here so Mom can't listen."

"Exactly."

Even as she smiled, Callie wondered what her dad had to discuss that was private. Overall, he tended to side with her mom on anything—including cutting off his brother at a time when, from what she'd learned, Reggie had needed them all the most.

The sun came out with a vengeance, turning the soggy yard into a sauna. The goats didn't seem to mind. Callie was relieved to see they were all walking just fine, even the renegade who'd gotten into the woods.

She didn't say much, because then her dad might want to hear the whole story and no way was she sharing those details.

The chickens were thrilled with the amount of worms and bugs they could now find, thanks to the overnight storms. For a while, she and her dad worked in companionable silence, feeding, cleaning, and refilling water stations, and ensuring their shelters were still dry. She saw that he was still a pro, doing the chores without direction from her.

While she collected eggs, he walked the property, commenting on how nice it looked and what a great job she was doing on the upkeep. It was like throwing a shovelful of guilt onto her head, because a goat had gotten out, possibly injured, and she'd acted like a fool. Not a great job, at all.

"Dad," she said, to give herself something to concentrate on other than the previous night, "Why are you and Mom here?"

"I'm here because Liz is here."

Typical answer for her dad. "And Mom insisted?"

"Afraid so." He drew her toward the garage. "You can't tell your mother this, but I sent money to Reggie. Every month, in fact. He always sent it back. Didn't matter how I cajoled, he told me it wasn't money he wanted from me." A grimace of remorse tightened his jaw. "I should have come to see him. Nothing should be allowed to interfere with family."

Callie agreed but didn't say so. "I feel so horrible that I stopped visiting."

"You had a busy life," her dad said. "Reggie understood that."

She wished she could excuse her actions so easily.

"I still talked with him often."

"On the sly?" Callie asked.

"It was the only way. He loved getting updates on you." With a shake of his head, her dad said, "He continued to adore Liz. Said she was a wonderful woman and only wanted the best for her family. He understood her drive."

Callie cuddled into his side, loving him even more in that moment. "You never gave up on him."

"He was my brother," he said simply. "For the sake of my marriage and because Reggie really could be a royal pain in the ass, I bowed to Liz's wishes. Her memories of childhood aren't as fondly remembered as mine. Liz was ambitious when I met her and that hasn't changed."

No, it hadn't. "I'm not reuniting with Sutter, Dad."

"I want you to be happy." They stepped into the shady interior of the garage. "No matter what, remember that, okay?"

Callie tipped her head as she stripped off her work gloves. "What does that mean, exactly?"

"Liz is going to tell you all about it, but the truth is, the alliance would have saved us."

Dazed, Callie stared at him without a single blink. "Saved us?"

"We're overextended." He waved a hand. "Suffered a few losses and all that. I don't mind so much. I could happily sell off half of what we own and never miss it." Picking up a hoe, then swinging it like a golf club, he said, "I could even move back here to Hoker and be happy with a simpler life. But your mother... She knows there will be talk and her reputation means everything to her."

More than her daughter's happiness? "I don't understand."

"I screwed up. That's the long and short of it. I got a little too comfortable with the life of leisure. Lost my edge—and my hunger." His mouth tightened with shame. "I didn't supervise the accountant closely enough, took foolish financial advice, and made too many bad decisions." Carefully, with precision, he replaced the hoe in its designated spot. Looking at his hands, now dirty, he said, "I speculated on travel to places where no one wants to vacation. With the economic downturn, we're strapped. Uniting our family business with the Griffin family business through marriage with you and Sutter... The association and their investments might have given us new life, or at least kept the wolves at bay long enough for us to shuffle a few things, redirect and recover."

"Dad." Having never suspected, Callie felt sick with dread. She naturally stepped into her dad's waiting arms. "I'm sorry. I never guessed."

"No reason you should have. And no reason for you to marry to fix it. That's what I wanted you to know. Your mother is going to bluster and explain, and she'll try to convince you. That's just how she is." He held Callie back and gave her a ridiculous grin that didn't do a thing to hide his agitation. "That's how she shows her love."

Callie snorted, but it was more with humor than disagreement. She thought of her own investments, the profits she'd made the last few years. She couldn't think of a better way to use them. "Dad, I have some money of my own that I would happily give—"

"No." He shook his head. "I would never do that."

"But—"

"It wouldn't help, anyway. No, this is a lifestyle problem butting up to a changing market. A loan, or even a gift, wouldn't help. It's big, but I have faith in your mother. She'll come around."

"You really think so?"

"I've learned the hard way after living five decades that family is what matters. Nothing else is as important."

And her family needed her. Such a depressing thought.

"Callie," he chastened. "Don't misunderstand. I've loved your mother from the day I met her. The two of you have been the world to me. I want you to have that same kind of love. Nothing less."

His little speech humbled her. "Thank you, Dad."

"Just remember, no matter what I say—or don't say—during your mother's arguments, I want you to be happy. If it's not happening with Sutter, then that's the end of it."

After everything her father had just confided, it hurt Callie to speak the truth, but he deserved that much. "Not Sutter." She couldn't, especially now that Tanner had showed her what she'd been missing. "Not ever."

He gave her a bright smile. "Then that's that."

Her stomach twisted. "Couldn't you and the Griffins work out something else?"

Shaking his head, he explained, "You know their entire hotel business is run by family. They're old-fashioned and not very trusting of outsiders."

Yet their son was a flagrant cheater. "Are they aware that you've had a financial downturn?"

"No. God, no. And I'm hoping they don't find out. So far, both sides have only concentrated on how mutually beneficial it would be to combine efforts. Sort of a legacy for any offspring you'd have together."

Eww. She did not want to have Sutter's children. Someday, sure, she'd love to have kids—but not yet and not with Sutter.

So many plans had been made around her. If only she'd been paying attention.

"I'll figure out something else," her dad promised. "But I won't have a chance to do that if they find out about our situation. They'd kill all business with us and the end of the company would come even sooner."

Feeling like she carried a lead weight in her chest where her heart should be, Callie nodded. "I see."

He caught her shoulders. "It's important to me that you not pay for my mistakes. Understand? This isn't on you." He tugged her in for a hug. "I'd be a failure as a dad as well as a businessman if I let that happen."

"You're not a failure," she stated with firm conviction. "You've run a successful business for years, and you're a wonderful dad."

"You're a wonderful daughter, so you make it easy. I'm so proud of you, Callie. Never forget that." He hugged her one more time, his hold tight, a little desperate, before he straightened again. "Let's not keep your mother waiting any longer. She's liable to start going through your things."

Alarmed by that possibility, Callie agreed. She needed to deal with her mother, but she also needed breakfast and time to sort out this new mess before Liam or Nell arrived.

Most of all, she needed to be free.

The odds of attaining that were starting to look pretty slim.

AFTER A FEW hours spent helping clients, Tanner was muddy, sweaty, irascible, and he couldn't stop thinking about Callie. In his head, he could still picture her under him, her beautiful face twisted in pleasure, the way her body had cradled his, the sounds she'd made, the scent of her skin and hair…

More than anything, he'd like to spend a week in bed with her, until finally she didn't plague his brain any longer.

But then, the idea of *not* wanting her was bothersome, too. He liked the way Callie put his senses on alert. Around her, he felt like the best version of himself.

Judging how the morning had gone so far, with the unwelcome intrusion of her parents, it didn't seem likely that he'd get to visit with her again anytime soon. And maybe that was for the best.

He was headed back home now, and with any luck her parents would have finished their visit. She could be at his house when he pulled up, having the excuse to return Addie's dishes.

When she wanted to see him, she'd reach out. Until then, he didn't want to pressure her. She had more than enough going on.

Blu rode in the back seat of his truck, his snout and tongue stuck out the partially open window. The unseasonably hot spring weather had returned, with a thick blanket of humidity.

It had nothing on Tanner's mood.

He couldn't stop thinking how Callie had accepted the introduction of him as only a neighbor, and that should have suited him just fine. What had he expected? For her to introduce him as something…more?

He'd felt like more, at least for a few hours.

When he was forced to stop at the railroad tracks, waiting for a train to pass, he spotted a fancy car in the lot of a sandwich shop nearby. Because the car reminded him of the slick BMW Callie's folks had left parked in her driveway, he gave it a second look.

And there was her ex, Sutter Griffin, standing by the hood.

Even more surprising was seeing the Garmet brothers talking with him.

What. The. Everlasting. Fuck.

If there'd been any room for him to maneuver, he'd have turned around and backtracked to the shop. Nothing set him off like the brothers, but seeing them with Callie's cheating ex? Yeah, that tipped the scales.

Blu had spotted them too, and his tongue was now back in his mouth, ears forward and body tensed.

"Sorry, bud," Tanner murmured, still watching the men through his side-view mirror. "We can't check it out today."

Blu tilted his head to listen, but as the men separated and Sutter got back behind the wheel, the dog went alert again.

"What do you want to bet he's heading to Callie's?"

Another whine. Sure sounded like agreement to Tanner.

Since Sutter pulled into the line of cars waiting for the train tracks to clear, it made sense that he was headed that way. "Her parents want them back together." Why did they want her to tie herself to the jerk?

Finally, the caboose went past and moments later, the gate arms lifted. Tanner finished the drive with his common sense warring against his basic urges. Realistically, he knew he couldn't pull up to Callie's house and wait for Sutter to arrive, just to tell the prick to leave.

For one thing, Callie could be embarrassed with the scene he'd cause, especially if her parents were still around to witness it.

For another, she'd be severely pissed. He'd figured that out this morning when he'd started to answer the door for her. Good thing she'd stepped past him too, since it was her parents knocking.

Her father, Frank, had barely changed from what Tanner remembered a decade ago. Maybe he had a little silver in his hair now, but the man was still tall, lean, friendly to everyone he encountered. Seemed to Tanner that her father had summed up the situation in a single glance. Oddly, Mr. McCallahan had been more amused than affronted by Tanner's presence so early in the morning, and wearing no more than jeans.

At least he'd buttoned up and zipped at that point.

Tanner half grinned with cynicism, recalling the expression on Mrs. McCallahan's face when her gaze had landed on him. Not that she'd been rude. She was too much the polished businesswoman to ever lower herself to outright rudeness.

In some ways, she reminded him of Callie, especially in her coloring. Her hair, similar to a shade of Callie's but lightened with salon effects, was shorter and framed her face in a fancy style. Her tailored clothes looked crisp and uncomfortable to him. Her astute gaze missed nothing.

In a single glance, she'd made note of him standing there, no shirt or socks. Not for a second did Tanner believe she'd been fooled with the "neighbor checking on neighbor" story he'd pulled out of thin air, but finding him there hadn't fit her agenda so she'd dismissed him as unimportant.

In the end, would Callie do the same?

He just didn't know. Until they settled a few things—if there was anything to settle—Tanner decided he'd be cautious.

Instead of pulling down his driveway, he paused in front, his right forearm resting over the steering wheel as he watched the side mirror. Blu leaned over the seat to snuffle his ear, requiring him to lift a shoulder and laugh. "Hold on, buddy. I just want to see what happens. I'll let you out in a sec."

Less than half a minute later, Sutter went past and pulled into Callie's driveway. Tanner was weighing what he wanted to do with what he knew he should do when Liam pulled up beside him in the older Buick.

Rolling down the window, Tanner asked, "Boss didn't need you today?" He worried endlessly that Liam might somehow lose the job he loved to someone more experienced.

"It was too muddy to do much on the site, so he let me off early," Liam said. "Since I had free time, I figured I'd come by to see if Callie had any damage."

A perfect solution. "I'm sure she can use you." He glanced back to Callie's now full driveway. "Park on the street. She has company."

Liam frowned. "Maybe I should've checked with her first."

"No, you made the right call. Just give her the option to see what she thinks." He was betting Callie would keep him around. "If she doesn't need you, let me know."

"You need a hand with something?" Liam immediately asked. "I'm always willing. I owe you."

"No, you don't." He and Liam had been through this

many times. "But I appreciate the offer." Mostly, he wanted to grill Liam to see how things were going. "Her parents dropped in on her and now her ex is here. She could probably use a friendly face right about now."

One brow lifted, making Liam appear far more mature than his nineteen years. "A friendly face other than yours?"

"Exactly." Then he thought to add, "Though if you think she needs me, send me a text."

Liam cracked a grin. "Will do." With a quick wave, he pulled up to Callie's and parked at the curb.

Tanner wanted to linger, but he was layered in sweat and Blu was restless. It was time to put Callie from his mind—or at least, to function properly while thinking of her nonstop.

WHILE HER MOTHER droned on and on, Callie silently counted things she'd rather be doing. She was up to about a hundred. Clean out the gutters again? Sure. Play with the goats? Definitely. Sweat off a few pounds weeding the garden? Right now, even that tree she'd climbed was starting to sound like heaven.

With a glance to the window, she wondered what Tanner was up to.

"Callie! Are you even listening to me?"

No. "I'm sorry, Mom," Callie said for the tenth time. "I really am."

Her mother gave her a look that was both fond and exasperated. "Just not sorry enough?"

Callie snorted. "Tell me something I can do to help—other than marry Sutter—and I'll try my best, I promise."

"Let up, Liz," her dad said, which was his very passive, very rare method of going against his wife. "You can see she already has her hands full."

Dramatically, her mother took in the shape of the living room. "This is the same furniture Reggie had the last time I saw him."

"Not so," her father countered. "That was a two-cushion olive-green couch."

Callie glanced at the dingy three-cushion beige corduroy couch that took up part of the room now. It was clear which seat Reggie had preferred, because that cushion was smashed, with a clear indent where he'd sat. Parts were worn thin, edges frayed. *At least it isn't olive green.*

"I suppose you're right." Her mother pinned her with another look. "You'll need a little time to absorb everything I've told you."

She'd absorbed it already. The situation wasn't good. Her mother had pointed out that if they started selling houses, people would assume they were in a financial crisis. And at the core of it, they were. If they lost one contract because of rumors, others would follow and that could lead to the domino effect.

Her dad tried to brighten the situation. "I wouldn't mind retiring early."

Appalled, her mother frowned at him. "We're only in our midfifties!"

"So?" He drew her in, and then danced her across the floor. "More time for us to enjoy our lives."

Fussing at him, her mother pulled away. "We won't have a life if we don't figure this out." Once again, her gaze landed on Callie.

And so it continued.

The first hour had been the worst, fending off repeated mentions of how she should do the right thing, how the family needed her, how she'd been raised better than to go backward when she should be going forward—backward being Reggie's house in their old neighborhood.

Forward, apparently, meant marrying Sutter.

It had her throat tight, thinking of the possible financial ruin of her parents' business.

Thinking about marrying Sutter was worse. *Far*, far worse.

Now, especially.

Realizing that she'd never loved him had been bad enough. Accepting that she'd gone along for all the wrong reasons had made her question her character.

But now, after knowing Tanner, after experiencing what intimacy should be between a man and woman? No way would she settle for Sutter, not ever, not for any reason.

Whether things progressed with Tanner or not, it didn't matter. She would not involve herself with Sutter. Just the opposite. She wanted to cut all ties with him beyond professional courtesy.

Now if her mother would just put her brain on finding another workable solution, they could, possibly, salvage this visit. Or her parents could leave, disappointed in her—as usual—and she could forge on with her plans, flimsy as they seemed to be.

Trying to gain another topic, Callie asked, "Where is Glory, anyway? Why didn't she come with you?" *Or return yet, as she'd promised?*

Flitting her fingers in the air, her mother said, "I sent her off on a little trip."

Suspicion stirred. "A trip where?"

"Research, really."

"That's not her job," Callie pressed. "What kind of research?"

With a delicate huff, her mother gave in. "I wanted her away from you. She's been negatively influencing you, encouraging you in all this…" The wave of her hand encompassed everything. "Nonsense."

Gritting her teeth, Callie replied, "She's not a lackey, Mother. She's your niece, and she's like a sister to me."

"Don't worry about her. She'll return soon enough."

"When is she due back from her trip?"

Her mother glanced at her father. "Currently undecided."

Meaning Glory would be kept away indefinitely with whatever nonsense her mother had cooked up?

Callie was gearing up for an explosion when yet another knock sounded on her door. Later, she decided, she'd get hold of Glory and find out what was going on. Until then…

Popping to her feet, her mother smiled in relief. "That must be Sutter." She grabbed Callie's hand and pulled her up from her seat. "For heaven's sake, smooth your hair." Her mother did that for her until Callie brushed her hands away.

"Stop it."

Not in the least bothered, her mother smiled. "Try to be *nice*."

To the man who had cheated on her? Unbelievable. Callie was just cross enough to say, "Ha!" right before she swung the door open.

And there was Sutter, hands in his pants pockets, expression sheepish. "Callie," he said softly. "God, it's good to see you again."

Before she could snort, her mother interceded. "Sutter, hello. Since you're here, would you do me a favor? We brought Callie a gift, but it's in the back of the car." Sotto voce, she added, "I didn't want Frank to strain himself. His age, you know."

"Ah." Sutter nodded. "We don't want him to have any undue stress."

The two of them conspired to make it sound like her dad was old and frail. Callie made a point of staring at him and caught his grin. Her dad was healthy as a horse, in shape from golfing and tennis, and he was as handsome as ever. "Dad," she warned.

He winked at her. "It's a giant plant, Callie. Massive. Might need a forklift to get the thing in here. Sutter can handle it though, I'm sure."

Sutter balked. "It's that big?"

"Already in a heavy clay pot. The dirt alone must weight fifty pounds."

Callie almost laughed at her dad's shenanigans. Sutter, though in shape, was not a physical man. He didn't lift heavy things.

He didn't use chain saws.

Or play with dogs.

He had no interest in helping at-risk kids…or rescuing a neighbor when she got herself stuck in a tree.

Folding her arms, Callie waited. It'd be interesting to see what Sutter might do. Would he go along with her mother's scheme to make him look manly, or would he balk as she expected?

Before she could find out, Liam stuck his head in the door. "Wow, you have a full house. Should I come back another time?"

"No!" Callie said, thrilled to see him.

Her mother, however, was not as welcoming. "Who are you?"

Country charm personified, Liam said, "I'm just the hired help, ma'am."

"And a friend," Callie corrected. She could use an ally who didn't want to sacrifice her to Sutter.

Sutter, forever an ass, got out his wallet and handed Liam a twenty. "Get the plant out of the car, okay?" He looked to Callie. "Where did you want it, sweetheart?"

"Not your sweetheart," she corrected smoothly as she stepped past him to join Liam. "Let's see the plant and then I can decide."

"Sure." Liam handed the money back to Sutter with a smile. "I work for her, but thanks."

As the two of them stepped away, Callie said under her breath, "Well done."

Liam nodded at the car. "Sweet ride."

Yes, it was. Her parents had always had expensive taste in vehicles. Her red Escape was one more thing her mother had frowned over. Apparently, McCallahans should buy black cars. Liz deemed the color elegant.

In the next second, Liam said, "Your cherry red Ford is cool, too." He elbowed her. "And I'm loving my Buick."

Callie laughed. "Are you a little car crazy?"

"No way. The things I want…they aren't that easy."

No, they weren't. On impulse, she squeezed his shoulder. "You're getting there."

"One step at a time." He opened the hatch and they both took in the enormous size of the plant. Liam lifted a brow. "That's a tree."

"It's tall enough to be." Five feet of leafy plant filled the back of her parents' SUV at a tilt, with some leaves spilled over to the front seat. "I love it, but it does look like it weighs a ton."

Grinning, Liam lifted the entire awkward thing out, and then, holding it like it was nothing, he asked, "Where do you want it?"

She laughed again. From the time of her parents' arrival, she'd been in an awful funk, but already Liam had lightened her mood.

"You make it look so easy." She hustled ahead of him to the porch. "For now, let's leave it outside by the door." Plans were forming in her head, and she wanted time to think them through.

Unfortunately, the second they stepped inside, Sutter drew her in for a tight hug. Didn't matter that she kept her arms stiff at her sides, or that she leaned away as much as she could.

Her parents had disappeared, probably back into the kitchen, but Liam was still right there, and as she glanced at him over Sutter's shoulder, she saw him cross his arms and lean on the wall.

Clearly, he wasn't budging unless she asked him to. God love the young man, she owed him something special for his loyalty. Maybe, if Tanner gave her a chance, she'd talk to him to figure out something good. He knew Liam better than she did, and he'd probably have some great ideas for a surprise.

CHAPTER THIRTEEN

"AHEM." WEDGING HER hands between them, Callie pressed Sutter back. "Don't do that again."

"Come on, Callie. Talk to me."

"I can talk without being plastered to you."

"Fine." He held up his hands. "If you want to talk, we'll talk."

Wait, what? "I *don't*. You're the one who—"

"I've been thinking that we could work on our problems."

"*Our* problems?" Damn it, she was getting shrill again.

"Neither of us is perfect, right? A professional counselor could help with that." Despite the promise he'd just made, Sutter cupped her shoulders, his hands massaging. "You'd been so distant, that's why I sought solace elsewhere."

Unbelievable!

"Things can be fixed," he insisted. "If we *both* work on it."

If it wasn't for Liam snickering, she might have lost her cool. "No, we're not perfect. That much is true. But I am *perfectly* happy here, in Hoker, Kentucky. I'm *perfectly* happy being single, too."

Gently, even with a touch of pity, he crooned, "You know that's not true."

She seriously felt like punching him. "I know my own mind, Sutter."

"Sure you do. But you are fooling yourself. You're out of character. And I know why."

Oh, this should be good. She gestured magnanimously. "Go on. Let's hear it." The sooner she got this over with, the sooner she could toss him out.

"I hurt you and I'm sorry. If I could go back and undo the damage, I would."

He sounded almost sincere.

"And now you're trying to hurt me in return. I understand that, Callie. I really do. But *you* need to understand, it's not just me. You're hurting your parents, and Glory. You're hurting my entire family."

Guilt crept in again, but she refused to show it to Sutter. "I see. Have you explained to your family why I broke things off?"

He stiffened. "They know you saw me with someone else, but that wasn't my fault. You were ignoring me. With all the wedding prep, I barely saw you." He pulled a sad face. "I was lonely."

"Ah. So I'm the one at fault?"

"No, of course not." He reached for her again. "I love you. You know that."

She was starting to feel smothered. "So not your fault, and not mine." She lifted her brows. "The other woman's?"

"Yes!" Jumping on that excuse, he cupped her face and smiled. "Not yours, not mine. It was a bad outside influence."

Fed up, Callie slapped his hands away. "You're thirty-six years old, Sutter, not ten. If you're still susceptible to female pressure, then you're far, far too weak for me." After she said it, and seeing Liam wince, Callie almost felt bad for the brutal honesty.

Except that Sutter continued as if he hadn't even heard her. He rarely did. "She'd been flirting with me forever, you know. Maybe if *you'd* been paying attention, you'd have noticed."

Callie laughed, but not with humor. "Ah, but I wasn't and I didn't," she said with mock sympathy. "Now why would you want a wife who was so uninterested in you?"

"And you didn't even give me a chance to explain! You just took off. Do you have any idea how awful that was for me?"

"Poor Sutter," she crooned with mock sympathy. "Standing there with your pants open, looking guilty. Yes, I'm sure you were devastated."

On a roll, Sutter paced away. He was oblivious to Liam's presence. Uncaring that her parents were near enough to hear every word. Honestly, he was oblivious and uncaring about her, too. "You humiliated me, Callie."

Yup, and she was about to do so again. She opened the door. "Get out."

That tripped him up. "What? *No.* We have to talk!"

"You're doing all the talking, most of it accusations. I agree, I was a terrible person. You'll be much better off without me. Now *leave.*"

Her mother hustled back in. "Callie…"

"You, too, Mom. If you can't respect my wishes, then you should also go." The mad thumping of her heart seemed to quake her entire body. Never, not in a million years, had she ever envisioned throwing her mother out of her house. But damn it, she didn't like being cornered, not by anyone.

Apparently, there was a first time for everything.

Her mother stared at her, appalled.

"I love you Mom," Callie said, hoping to deescalate the situation. "But this is all wrong. Can't you see that?"

Her father stepped up behind her mother, whispered something in her ear, and her mother's expression softened. "We'll be back to visit later then."

"Later…when?" Hopefully not later today. She couldn't take a second visit so soon.

"We'll see how it goes," her mother said, and breezed out the door.

"Enjoy the plant," her dad added, then he kissed her cheek—and stepped out around Sutter, who stood there with his hands locked into fists and his face red.

Callie didn't relent. "You, too, Sutter. Out."

"This isn't over," he practically snarled. "Not by a long shot."

Whoa. Never before had he been so forceful. Callie stiffened her spine. "Beg to differ." She held the door wider.

"Big mistake, Callie, but then you're making a lot of those lately." As he passed through the doorway, he grabbed the doorknob, yanking it from her hand to give it a good slam.

The abruptness of it all lingered in the still air. Not only was her heart thumping, but her stomach cramped.

Liam cleared his throat. "You okay?"

"Yes," she whispered, trying to find her bearings. None of that had gone as it should have. Callie knew it would be a day she'd regret for a very long time.

"So…" Liam watched her closely, as if she might cry. "What's on the agenda for today?"

Forcing a slight smile, Callie attempted to reassure him. "What do you know of horses?"

His shoulders relaxed and he gave her a grin. "Ready to meet Rebel, huh?"

"That's the horse's name? I love it." Focusing on the horse was much easier than facing the debacle she'd just played out.

"Were you wanting to ride him?"

Callie shook her head. "A lot of my friends had horses, but my parents have never been animal-oriented so I know nothing about them."

"Tanner does. They have three, including your horse."

Her jaw dropped. "No way. Tanner's never mentioned having horses."

"That's why he took yours after Reggie passed away. Horses are social. They don't like being alone. Rebel was often with his horses anyway." Liam's mouth quirked. "Reggie first took Rebel in because a buddy of his moved away, but Tanner's always been the one to take care of him. Now that spring is here and the landscaping business is busy, they have a groom who does the daily upkeep, but Tanner, Kam, and Addie still visit the horses often. They all ride."

"How did I not know any of this?"

Liam laughed. "There's probably a lot you don't know about them. Tanner doesn't realize how many people in this town respect him and Kam, and they all love Addie. Most around here have benefited from them in one way or another."

So they weren't all like the Garmet brothers? Wonderful. "Can you give me an example?"

Liam sat down on the couch, getting comfortable as if he had a lot to say. "The groom I mentioned is a retired guy. He couldn't afford to keep horses, but he still loves them." Offhand, as if it wasn't big news, Liam said, "He has a small place on the other side of the tree farm. He rides over in his golf cart every day to tend the horses. He feeds them, checks their hooves, stuff like that. They'll go out in the field while he mucks out the stalls, then he rubs them down and sees them bedded each night."

"He enjoys it?"

"Sure. He was alone all the time before Tanner hired him. Now he sees one or all three of them often, and Addie is forever sending him baked goods. They're like family to him. Plus he told me that with what Tanner pays him, he doesn't have to get his groceries from the food bank anymore." His grin went crooked. "You never saw anyone so happy to hit up the grocery store."

Emotion filled her chest. "Remarkable."

"Kam and Tanner both volunteer time with the kids from the halfway house. They sponsor holidays and team sports, outings and movie nights."

Callie dropped back against the wall. She'd known he was involved, but not to that extent. "Wow."

"Tanner has an apprenticeship where he teaches job skills, like landscaping, but also lawn maintenance. Kam does the same with welding." He added more quietly, "Tanner takes on a lot."

Did he ever take time for himself? "Sounds like he has multiple projects."

Liam nodded. "I started as one of those projects."

Callie wasn't sure what to say to that.

"We're friends now," Liam assured her. "He's like the big brother, or maybe a favorite uncle that I never had. At first though... I didn't want to trust Tanner."

He frowned. "I didn't want to trust anyone. But Tanner has a way of understanding, you know?"

Because he'd been through those awful times himself.

As usual, when talking about him, her heart went squishy. "He's pretty amazing."

"I can't disagree." Liam stood again. "So what do you say? Want to meet your horse?"

She did, but she also knew Nell would be visiting. "How about tomorrow? Will you be busy?"

"Nah. That works for me. Usual time?"

"Yes, but don't tell Tanner."

Liam gave her a long look. "Because…?"

"Because he's been keeping the horse for me, feeding him, including his care in what he pays the groom." Making a firm decision, she said, "That should be compensated."

"You know Tanner would disagree."

Yes, she did know it. For now, she let that go and instead grilled Liam on everything, from the cost of keeping a horse, how to take care of it, and boarding fees in the area.

At first, she suspected he was fudging the costs, so she threatened to research it online.

Liam gave up and told her what he knew. He claimed that costs were cheaper in Hoker, because, well, everything was cheaper in Hoker. She couldn't refute that logic.

She started to say more, but then Nell arrived. She was a lovely young woman who looked closer to twenty than not-quite-seventeen. Thick, shoulder-length dark hair and blue eyes framed by nearly-black lashes. She shyly introduced herself, but when she spotted Liam, she blushed.

Liam, for his part, couldn't take his eyes off her. They were already acquainted, and obviously interested in each other. Callie almost felt like the third wheel until she remembered why Nell had stopped by.

While they went out together so Nell could check the goats, Liam hung back to tick a few items off her to-do list.

"I love your goats," Nell said, kneeling down to greet each one, then giving them quick checks. The chickens came over to visit her too. Nell greeted them like friends, saying, "Hello, girls. How's the feathers flying?"

Callie laughed. "My gosh, they adore you!" If chickens could purr, hers would be.

"I have this thing with animals. They're sometimes easier than people." Nell ended up on her butt in the mud, but she just grinned. "This is why I always bring along a change of clothes."

"Smart," Callie said. "Tanner told me you're good with animals, but it's like you're magic or something."

"He's the best, right?" With the sun hitting her in the face, Nell squinted up at Callie. "You two got something going on?"

She wished. "Neighbors," Callie said with a shrug. "That's all."

"Uh-huh," Nell replied with teasing skepticism. "Pretty sure there's more to it than that."

"What makes you think so?"

"I don't know. Tanner sounds different when he talks about you."

"Oh? How does he sound?"

"Just different. I've known him a while now and he's never been like that before."

Like...what exactly? Annoyed? Interested? Frustrated—maybe as frustrated as Callie herself? She would love to grill Nell, but that would be awkward. "You know how he is. He and Kam are both helpful."

"Oh, for sure. I swear, I think Tanner is happiest when he's being the hero."

"Right? And apparently, he's heroic pretty often."

"*All* the time," Nell said. She let out a breath. "He's saved my butt more than a few times."

Callie wasn't sure what to do with that info, so she admitted, "He's done the same for me now, too." Was that when Tanner was happiest? If so, that could stem from his childhood, too, when he'd so desperately needed a hero.

Then Addie had shown up in his life, so he certainly knew all about heroes and the impact they could make. She wondered if Addie fully understood the influence she'd had. Or for that matter, did Tanner even understand?

He'd had choices in life, to stay angry, to give up, or to act out. Instead, he'd taken his cues from Addie and turned into one of the nicest, most understanding and caring men she'd ever met.

While carefully checking over the renegade goat's legs, Nell said, "I've seen your videos. They're cool."

"Seriously?" Callie joined her in the mud. "I didn't know if anyone around here had caught my channel yet."

"You have a lot of followers. You don't check it?"

"A little here and there, when I have time. My cousin,

Glory, edits and uploads the vids for me." Oh, how she missed Glory.

"There are a lot of girls at the home—you know, where I'm staying right now? It's like a halfway house. Whatever." Nell skipped right past that. "We watch you."

"I had no idea." Callie's thoughts scrambled as she tried to remember the various episodes. Had she been appropriate for teenage girls? God, she hoped so. Until this very moment, she hadn't given a lot of thought for her audience. "I mostly record stuff because it's… I don't know. Cathartic for me."

"I don't know what that means."

"It's a way for me to express myself and shake off some tension." It was nice to have another girl to talk to, especially with Glory away. "Moving here, uprooting my life, trying something new. It's all different for me and I could so easily get overwhelmed." More often than not, she *was* overwhelmed. But she was twenty-eight years old and she had options open to her.

Nell was only sixteen and her choices were limited. Callie had no idea what it might be like to live in a group home, but if her silly videos helped to entertain the girls, well then, she was honored. "I record the stuff I'm struggling with. When I'm laughing at the camera and admitting how bad I am at learning new things, it somehow makes it easier."

"Huh. I didn't know that."

"Boring, right?"

"No, I think it's interesting. Right now, I'm sharing a bedroom with three other girls. We watch you together at night when we're supposed to be sleeping."

Callie barely withheld her wince. Four girls to a room? "You're all friends?"

"We were strangers at first but we're friendlier now." Nell was matter-of-fact about it. "You know our favorite episode? You did that thing with your hair once and everyone loved it."

"Thing with my hair?"

"Yeah, when you were working in the garden. It was like you just… I don't know." Nell put her own hands in her hair and gathered it to the top of her head. The silky hanks immediately fell loose again. "You twisted it up somehow, but it looked awesome. We all said so."

Flushing with pleasure, Callie smiled. "Really?" Only half-jokingly, she said, "Maybe I should do more hair videos."

"That'd be great. I'd love to see them." Giving the goat a hug, Nell said, "They're all fine. No injuries that I can find."

"Wonderful news. Thank you." Though she'd already suspected as much given how easily the goats had moved around, Callie still said, "You've put my mind at ease." Together they stood and, almost at the same time, they each glanced at their backsides—and then laughed. "Luckily, with the sun, it isn't as bad now as it was this morning. When I first got up the yard was a swamp. If I'd sat down I might have sunk to my chin."

"The whole town is muddy right now. I can't wait for summer."

Would she still be in the home then? It saddened Callie a lot. Girls her age should be cherished, encouraged. Loved and protected by their families. Knowing Nell didn't have that made Callie want to hold her close and promise her the world. "So," she said, trying to sound lighthearted. "How much do I owe you?"

Startled, Nell laughed and said, "Nothing."

"Oh, no way. I have to pay you, otherwise I won't be able to ask you for help again if anything else happens and I'd really like to know that I could call on you if necessary."

"Yeah, I'd like that, too."

"Then…how much?"

"I guess… Whatever you want to pay is fine."

Callie smiled at that offer. She'd make it well worth Nell's effort. "Deal."

As they started in, Nell stared at the house. "Do you think Liam is still here?"

"He should be." In a friendly gesture, she nudged Nell. "You two already know each other?"

"Sure. It's a small town." Without being asked, Nell added, "Liam has big goals. He doesn't waste time on girls."

Callie didn't mean to, but she snorted.

That caused Nell to crack a smile. "Well, not much time, and not on me. He's told me a dozen times that I'm too young for him."

"You turn seventeen soon, right?"

"Why?"

Ideas buzzed through Callie's mind. "Do you have plans?"

"What do you mean?"

Oh now see, that almost broke her heart. She did a quick edit in her head, then suggested, "If you won't be too busy, I'd love to visit with you again. Maybe share some birthday cake and ice cream."

As if she didn't understand, Nell looked at her curiously. "Birthday cake?"

"Hey, I'm always looking for an excuse to eat cake. Oh! Maybe we could get our nails done, too! I know I must seem ancient to you, but you're the only girl I've had to talk to since my cousin went off on a business trip." No way would she burden Nell with her family issues.

Nell laughed. "You definitely aren't ancient."

Well, that felt like a boost to her ego, especially considering her hair was currently a mess, her nails were short, and the seat of her jeans was damp with mud. "Awesome as Addie is, she doesn't count because anytime I'm around her, she waits on me and I don't want to add to her workload."

"Yeah, Addie is sweet."

"So what do you say? Is there a salon around here anywhere? It'll be my treat, of course, for your birthday."

On a deep breath, Nell stopped and dropped her head. Then she looked away and all Callie could see was her profile. "You don't even know me."

"Not well, but you're nice and you're good with animals, and you're easy to talk to. I've enjoyed chatting and I'd like to get to know you better."

Her brows came together. "Did Tanner put you up to this?"

It broke Callie's heart, seeing so much distrust in someone so young. "Of course not. When I thought my goat might be injured, Tanner said he could ask you to take a look. He said you were great with animals."

"He didn't... Tell you about me? About my uncle?"

She still didn't face Callie. "About my whole useless life?"

Lying to the girl didn't feel right, but Callie didn't want to betray Tanner's confidence, either. She touched Nell's arm until she got her full attention. Then she smiled, hoping her sincerity would shine through. "I invited you back and asked about a salon because I'm sometimes lonely. I'm close with my cousin, but she's out of touch right now. Fitting in here… Well, I'm completely out of my realm. Tanner and Kam are great, and I have massive respect for Liam, but they're guys." Wrinkling her nose, Callie added, "I doubt I could talk any of them into a salon visit with me."

Nell grinned. "Probably not."

"So what do you say?"

"I've never been in the salon, and to be honest I can't say I'm anxious to go either."

Even deflated, Callie kept her smile in place. "Okay, I get it."

"I'd like to visit again though." Nell bit her lip, then said, "And cake sounds great. Honestly, I can't remember the last time anyone remembered my birthday."

Then by God, Callie would make this year memorable. "Birthday cake it is! And ice cream." She thought ahead and said, "If we just visit here, I could invite Addie, too. Just an intimate little gathering. Is that okay?"

Nell grinned. "It's your house, your rules. Invite anyone you want." Then her confidence slipped. "If you get busy though…"

"Pfft. I'm already looking forward to it." There was no way Callie would be one more broken promise. She'd bet Nell had suffered enough of those in her lifetime. "So let's see. When can we do this?"

They were still setting up their plans when Liam stepped out.

"You two done?" he asked.

Nell's demeanor changed from cautiously optimistic to flirtatious—and her blush was back.

Callie had to fight her smile. "Yup. The goat is fine."

When Liam looked at Nell, there was more than kindness in his eyes. More than curiosity and friendship as his gaze lingered. "Want to help me with something then?" he asked her.

"Depends," Nell said with teasing attitude. "What did you have in mind?"

He smiled back. "Behave."

"Now what fun would that be?"

He laughed. "I'm cleaning screens. I need someone on the inside while I lift them up to the windows from the outside."

"I'm glad to help."

And just like that, Callie was forgotten.

She didn't mind at all.

As she watched them both go into the house, she couldn't stop grinning. Oh, Liam was most definitely getting invited to the birthday shindig.

Her heart felt full. And more than ever, she wanted to see Tanner.

Sadly, the hours passed and he didn't call. She ordered a pizza and shared it with Liam and Nell, enjoying their company—and again feeling like the interloper in her own home, but in an amusing way. She'd forgotten how intense young adults could be. Watching the two of them subtly flirt was eye-opening.

Callie tried to remember herself at that age, but her life had been so vastly different from theirs, she couldn't quite pull up the memory. She assumed she'd been skimming around from one prearranged activity to another, always busy, always secure, and always protected.

Even with her recent breakup and move, she'd led a truly gifted life.

After Nell and Liam left, she wrote out a check with "Rebel upkeep" in the memo, then she put it in an envelope with Addie's name on it—not Tanner's—and made plans to slip it in the storm door of their home at her first opportunity. She'd go when Tanner was more likely to be gone for the day. If needed, she'd use the excuse of returning his clothes and Addie's dishes.

Feeling better now with that decided, she double-checked the gates on her property—with her keys and phone on her. Looking up at the sky, she realized that the sun was setting later each day. Shades of vivid pink and tangerine blended into a purple horizon. She breathed deeply, enjoying the coolness of the evening after the hot day.

The woods didn't appear menacing now. Instead, she appreciated the cacophony of animal sounds. The rustling of squirrels, chirping of birds, and a faint breeze that teased the treetops. The sweet scent of honeysuckle hung thick in the air. Somewhere in the distance, she heard a chain saw and wondered if it was Tanner, still at work.

The animals had already gathered in their shelters. To the goats, she promised, "We'll figure out names tomorrow." To the chickens, she praised them for being so sweet and not flying into the trees.

Back in the house, she indulged in a long leisurely bath that relaxed her muscles, but not her mind. At least a dozen times, she checked her phone.

Finally giving up on Tanner, she got into bed, but she was still too antsy. Instead of trying to sleep, she sat up against the headboard, held her phone against her raised knees, and did a quick video.

For a moment or two, she just looked into the camera, then with a sigh, she said, "Hello, everyone. I know I'm recording this later than usual, but it's been one of those days and I'm not yet ready to turn in." She gave herself another brief moment to think about what she was doing, then she explained to her audience about her runaway goat, how worried she'd been, and how she'd gotten herself caught in a storm.

Rather than mention the tree and the Garmet brothers, she omitted those humiliating details.

By the time she finished, she was actually grinning about it. Hopefully, anyone watching would also see the humor involved and not just think she'd gone off the deep end. "I've decided that I need to name the goats. Something cute and easy to say, but goat-like, you know? When it's necessary, I want to be able to call them just like we would a dog or a cat. I'm open to suggestions."

It would be fun to involve her listeners. She wondered if Nell would watch.

Would Tanner? Doubtful.

"I guess I should sign off and at least try to sleep. I hope you do, too. Toss out those names in the comments. I'll choose from your suggestions tomorrow." After making that promise, she sincerely hoped she got some good ones. "Oh, yeah, I should probably tell you that they're girl goats, four of them, and they're real sweethearts." She thanked everyone for visiting her, blew out a few kisses and then, while still recording, she turned out her light. Into the darkness, she whispered, "Good night, everyone." Then she ended the video.

It struck Callie that now, finally, she felt a little better. What she'd said to Nell was true. Doing the videos was like keeping a diary. Getting her thoughts and worries out, sharing them with strangers since she couldn't share with family or friends, made them a little lighter.

Still in the darkness, with only the light from her phone screen, she sent the finished product off to Glory, hoping her cousin would see it soon and that she'd like it. It was more personal than anything she'd done so far, but she was in a personal mood.

A few minutes later she was still sitting against the headboard, lost in thought when her cousin called.

Badly startled by the buzz of her phone, she jumped, then pressed a hand to her thumping heart. "Good God," she muttered to herself as she checked the screen and saw it was Glory. She answered with, "Did you get the video?"

"Yes," Glory said, "and I *love* it! You're perfectly relaxed and the limited light from your screen is soft and pretty. It was almost like sitting in bed with you, talking to you in person. I'm sure your followers will feel the same. I'm uploading the video as soon as we finish talking. But first… Are you okay?"

"Hello to you too, Glory," Callie said with a laugh. It felt great to connect with her cousin again.

"The video really was perfect, but to me you seem down."

"Maybe just introspective." Callie sighed. "We haven't talked in forever."

"I know," Glory said with dramatic exaggeration. "Texts just don't cut it, but your parents have had me traveling almost nonstop. Miami, Denver, New York. I've either been running through the airport, sitting on a plane, or passing out in a hotel room. I'm worn out."

"You didn't say anything."

"I know, I'm sorry. It's why I called—but it's so hard to explain." Voice going lower, Glory said, "I know you don't understand…"

Actually, she did. She wished she could help Glory to stand up for herself, but so far, her efforts had failed. All she could do, all she really wanted to do, was love her. So instead of pressing her, Callie asked, "Why all the travel?"

With relief in her tone, Glory explained, "Overall, they have me compiling a list of the best new restaurants, hotels, and nightclubs in each area so they can make new contacts."

"They've expanded your job scope, then?" Knowing her parents' financial woes, maybe they'd cut back on other employee positions. She hated that thought.

"I guess so, though your mother didn't really explain her reasons. She just gave me an itinerary and told me what she expected."

Figured. Her mother was an authoritative woman who rarely felt the need to explain herself. Gently, Callie suggested, "You could just say no."

Instead of reacting to that, Glory said, "I've been in a bar nearly every night with plenty of interested guys making sure I feel appreciated. That part has been nice, but I am exhausted." After a brief pause, she added,

"I was thinking that when I get home from Boston, I won't even tell them." Another hesitation, and then Glory declared, "I'm going to repack, grab my car, and head your way. After I'm there, *then* maybe I'll send in my final report."

Callie had missed her so much, she couldn't keep from saying softly, "I love that plan."

With obvious relief, Glory laughed. "Good. I'm ready for a break and I can't wait to see how you're doing there. Watching the videos hasn't been enough. Can you believe it, I've actually missed the goats? And I keep thinking about you and that super-fine neighbor of yours."

"Tanner?"

"Yes, him. Unless you have something going on with the other one now. The bossy brother?"

Callie grinned. "Kam isn't bossy, at least not compared to Tanner." She wanted to tell Glory all about Tanner and the amazing night she'd spent with him, but it still felt too private—especially if it was a one-off. So instead, Callie told her about her parents visiting, and how they'd included Sutter in their trip.

"They didn't!"

Appreciating her cousin's outrage, Callie confirmed, "They did. And I'm afraid I lost it there at the end. I literally told my mother to get out."

Gasping, Glory whispered, "Was she furious?"

"Honestly, she acted like it hadn't happened. You know how Mom is. She ignores anything that conflicts with her plans."

"That's how she is with you," Glory specified. "She would have annihilated me on the spot."

Probably true, though mostly because Glory had always allowed her mother to be that bossy. "I'd stand up for you," Callie promised. She always had.

Remembering all the ways Glory had pressed her to marry Sutter, Callie asked, "Did you know they're struggling financially?" The silence stretched on so long, Callie thought the call had dropped. "Glory?"

"Sorry, I'm here." She released a short sigh. "I found out that same day that I left your house with Sutter."

"*He* knows?"

"No," Glory rushed to assure her. "After I got home, your mom and dad told me, but swore me to secrecy. They insisted that no one could know, and at the time, that included you."

It stung that Glory had sided with her parents.

"All along, from the time you and Sutter got engaged, your mom talked about what a huge difference it would make to the company. She'd said it would advance all our prospects, on both sides of the marriage. I thought of it as a big deal, a way to grow, but I didn't realize…"

Hurt by her cousin's deception, Callie said, "You could have told me when you found out."

"I should have, I know, but your dad asked me to give Sutter a chance to convince you. He said you were strong-willed and smart, and you'd only take Sutter back if you wanted to."

At least her dad had faith in her.

"I figured that was true…to a point. But if you'd decided to get back with Sutter, I'd have told you then."

Feeling guilty about it, Callie said, "I'll never take him back." Maybe before she'd met Tanner, before she'd been intimate with him… Now she knew exactly what she would be missing in a marriage to Sutter.

"Not even to save the company?" Glory quietly asked.

The question bothered her. Was she being selfish? Probably—but Callie didn't change her mind. "No, not even for that."

"Good." With a touch of pride, Glory said, "I wouldn't want you to."

They talked for almost an hour more, all about Glory's trips and the guys she'd met, her hopes to be back in Hoker soon. When Callie started fading and Glory sounded half-asleep, they ended the call with a promise to be back together soon.

Callie disconnected, plugged in her phone to charge, and then snuggled into the bed. It wasn't easy, but she accepted that the previous night might have meant a lot more to her than it had to Tanner.

That idea bothered her enough that she didn't fall asleep for a very long time.

CHAPTER FOURTEEN

FOR A WEEK, Tanner stayed so busy with jobs created from storm damage that he didn't have time to dwell on Callie. Much, anyway.

Damn, he missed her.

A dozen times he thought about calling her, but he never did.

She hadn't reached out either. At least, not to him.

He knew Addie had seen her a few times. And Liam told him that Callie had taken to visiting Rebel—but only when he was away. He was disappointed that she hadn't asked him to show her the horse. It was something he'd actually anticipated after all their teasing back and forth.

After Sutter and her parents had visited her, it was as if things had changed. Right there, on the spot. They'd left the bed, hell broke loose, and everything from the night before had just evaporated. Partially his fault—but she had a hand in that, too.

And damn it, he was thinking about her again. It irritated him that his thoughts remained on a perpetual loop that sooner or later, centered back on Callie.

It was well past dinnertime when he got home. Eight days since he'd slept with Callie. It felt like a month. Or longer.

He was barely inside the house when Addie and Blu

joined him in the kitchen, the first greeting him with a kiss to the cheek, and the other with an enthusiastically wagging tail.

Tanner knelt down to shower love on the dog. "Sorry I couldn't take you with me today, bud. It was a long job and way too damn messy."

"Go shower," Addie suggested as she pulled containers from the refrigerator. "I'll heat up your dinner so it's ready when you're done."

As always, he said, "I could heat it up myself."

She sent him a look. "You know I want to, so go on."

Something in Addie's expression warned him. "Everything okay?"

"Everything is fine, but we do have stuff to discuss, which we can do sooner if you'll get on with it."

He half grinned. "Yes, ma'am." Blu followed him from the room, then stuck near the shower door while Tanner let the hot water wash away the sweat and dirt, and unkink his tired muscles. What a day it had been.

He'd talked to Liam earlier, so he knew Callie had been busy all week redecorating. It amused Liam that every single day, Callie found something new that she wanted to change. It kept Liam working and helped give odd jobs to others in the area. Tanner didn't know all the details, and he didn't want to grill Liam on it, but he was curious.

Maybe he'd find an excuse to check on Callie and from there he'd see how things progressed.

If they went from "how've you been?" to another overnighter, he'd be fine with that. Now that he'd had her once, he wanted her again. Always. Every damn night—and during the day, too.

After he'd finished his shower and dressed in jogging pants, a T-shirt, and sneakers, he took Blu out and then joined Addie in the kitchen. Percy the cat was there, presumably waiting for Blu to settle so he could snuggle. "Something smells good."

"Grab a seat," she said, then proceeded to serve him pot roast, potatoes, carrots, and corn bread with a tall glass of iced tea.

Sure enough, when Blu sprawled out next to Tanner's chair, Percy curled up near his hip.

"I missed lunch." Tanner dug in, then hummed his appreciation and gave his usual heartfelt compliment. "No one cooks like you, Addie."

"You're biased, but thank you." She took the seat opposite him. "I saw Callie again today."

"Oh?"

"She wanted me to know that she's having a little birthday gathering for Nell next Saturday. We're all invited."

"A birthday gathering?" As he ate, Tanner wondered what had brought that on. "I didn't know they were close."

"Nell won her over with one visit. I think she's been back there every other day." Sitting forward in her seat and crossing her arms on the table, Addie asked, "Did you know Callie does videos?"

He recalled her saying something about it. "Documenting her progress on the house or something, right?"

"Or something."

Feeling Addie's amusement, he asked, "What am I missing?"

"Only that she's turning into an influencer."

"A what?"

"I didn't really know either, but Nell was here today to groom Blu. You know how he sheds in warmer weather. She was singing Callie's praises the entire time." Hearing his name, the dog tilted his head, ears perked, and swept his tail over the floor, disturbing Percy. The cat stretched, but otherwise didn't bestir himself. "You love her, don't you, boy?"

Tanner almost choked—until he realized Addie was talking to the dog. "Blu has loved Nell from the day he met her. She has a way about her. It's uncanny how animals trust her." He reached down to rub Blu around the scruff. More fur floated out, but Nell had done a great job.

Percy opened one eye, so Tanner also gave a gentle scratch to the cat's chin before brushing his hand on his leg to remove the fur and then getting back to eating.

Thankfully, none of them were squeamish about fur. They all loved Blu and Percy too much for that.

"They're a good judge of character," Addie agreed. "Might be why Blu is so fond of Callie, too."

Rather than weigh in on that, Tanner just made a sound of agreement and concentrated on cleaning his plate.

"I told Callie we'd all be there for the shindig."

"We?"

"Me, you, and Kam. She's insisting on doing it all herself. She has this plan of decorating the kitchen to surprise Nell. Balloons, streamers, and all that. I'm loaning her some of our decorations. Should be fun. We haven't done up a real birthday party since you boys were teens."

"Not that you don't try," Tanner said with a grin. Addie still went overboard, but they'd left the balloons behind.

With a shrug, Addie said, "She's ordering a fancy cake and no matter how I argued she wouldn't agree to let me bake it."

"Callie knows you work too hard already."

"I could have made the cake," she grumbled, but then got back on point. "It'll just be Callie, us, and Liam."

Not a surprise. Anyone who saw Liam and Nell together knew they were interested in each other. So far,

Liam had steered clear though. His plans for the future didn't leave a lot of free time, and in many ways Nell was fragile—not something Liam would miss. No one wanted to see her hurt again. Once, not long after Nell had turned sixteen, Liam had explained that she was too young for him. He'd already turned nineteen a few months before, and at the time, Tanner had agreed.

"So you'll be there?" Addie pressed. "Kam has already confirmed."

Tanner tried to sound casual when he said, "Sure. Should be fun," but his thoughts had jumped ahead to seeing Callie again. He glanced at the time, but no, it was probably too late to call her. "I wonder if there's anything she'd like us to do to help." Tomorrow, before getting to work, he could ask her.

"I doubt it. Lately, she seems to be on a crusade to do everything, all at once, all by herself."

That didn't sound good. As Tanner gathered up his last bite of food, he remembered how shaken Callie had been in the storm. Thankfully, the foreseeable forecast had only the usual spring rains. "What do you mean?"

Addie nodded to his plate. "Seconds?"

"No, I'm full." She'd already given him double portions, but then Addie had often showed her love through food. He understood. Just as he'd been ill-equipped to understand a mother-figure, she'd had little experience caring for a kid. "Thank you. It hit the spot."

They both stood at the same time.

"I'll clean up." Insistent, Tanner grabbed the plate before Addie could get hold of it. For once, she didn't debate it with him. Instead, she went to the refrigerator and lifted a magnet to free a check she'd put there.

"I want to show you something."

"What is it?" He scraped his plate and then put his dishes in the dishwasher

"A payment from Callie."

A payment! "For what?"

Instead of answering, she waved the check at him.

Forcing himself to be casual, Tanner rinsed and dried his hands before taking it from her.

Confusion hit him first, then anger. "What the hell?" Callie had written a hefty sum, made out to Addie, with a note for "horse upkeep."

"My reaction, too," Addie said. "Kam just laughed."

"He would." His brother found Tanner's current predicament hilarious. Every damn day, he egged him on, telling Tanner to man up and go see her. But damn it, he knew her parents wanted her back with Sutter, and he knew Sutter had visited her.

Liam, apparently, was aligned with Kam to force him to make a move.

"I tried to give it back to her," Addie said. "She kept insisting that I keep it because we're taking care of Rebel. Then she asked if we wanted the horse—as a gift. She said she'd still continue to pay for him, but she knew she didn't have the knowledge or the time to do it herself and she thought we might be attached to him." Addie folded her arms and gave him a frown. "Tell me you'll take care of this."

"Yeah," he said, knowing he now had the excuse he needed. "I will." Tanner folded the check and stuck it in his pocket. "Where is Kam?"

"He worked late, stopped here to shower, and then headed out for a date. Said he'd be home around ten."

So Kam wasn't around to heckle him. "Has Sutter been back over there?"

Addie lifted one shoulder. "Since you and Callie have

started avoiding each other, I haven't seen as much of her either."

"I'm not avoiding her." Hell, he *had* been busy. More than anyone, Addie knew that.

She also knew he was full of shit.

Huffing out a breath, Tanner asked, "She's dodging you?"

"Just not coming around like she had been. Last two times I invited her to dinner, she thanked me but declined. Then today she said she didn't want to keep you from your own table."

What the hell? "You told her that wasn't the case, right?"

With a nod, Addie said, "We can't take money from her."

"No, we can't." Tanner glanced at Blu. As if the dog anticipated his next move, he jumped to his feet. Percy, put out over it, sauntered away to find another spot to sleep.

"When will you take care of it?" Addie asked.

Blu went to the door and whined. Smart dog. "Right now." And with that decision made, Tanner already felt better.

CALLIE STOOD IN the hallway, staring up at the attic. The scraping noise she'd heard while showering came again, making her pulse race. It was far too late to bother Liam, who would have to be up early tomorrow, and no way would she call on Tanner or Kam.

The past week had been a lesson in endurance.

A dozen times at least she'd wanted to call Tanner, but over and over again she'd reminded herself of how he had left. How *he* hadn't called.

At the end of the third, lonely day without a word from

him, Callie told herself to snap out of it, then she took steps in that direction by throwing herself into home repairs.

In very little time, she had completely transformed the interior.

For a reasonable price, Liam and a few of his friends had helped her put fresh paint on the walls. With the house so small, they'd accomplished it all in rapid time. Bright white in the bathroom and kitchen, pale grayish blue in the bedrooms. Light, neutral sand tone for the living room and hall.

She'd bought new window treatments, which were already installed, and she'd sent for her beautiful bedding, but it hadn't yet arrived.

Surprisingly, the house had hardwood beneath the worn carpet. Though Liam insisted he could tear it out, without charge, Callie had hired men to come in. Since they came at a time when Liam couldn't be there, Kam had dropped in, claiming no one wanted her home alone with strangers.

Very sweet, but she assumed that "no one" meant him and Addie. Tanner had been suspiciously absent even when she went over for dinner once.

After that, she didn't go again. She loved seeing Addie, but it was just too awkward for her right now.

To continue her home decorating spree, she'd even gotten a new couch and chair. After adding new lamps, a throw blanket, and pillows, it looked like a brand-new house. At least on the inside.

Eventually, she'd like to have the floors refinished, but it wasn't top of her list at the moment.

No, right now she was concentrating on being brave enough to find out what was making that awful noise in her attic.

The house wasn't cold, but her skin prickled at the

thought of going up there. Still, this was *her* house and she damn well needed to learn full independence.

With that decision made, she dragged a chair from the kitchen and climbed up to reach the rope hanging from the attic door. It pulled open and she saw the stairs that Liam had described to her earlier. Still hearing that odd sound, Callie imagined a rat, or possibly a raccoon, just waiting for her to stick her head up there.

But that's exactly what a man would have done, and she didn't have a man, so *she'd* have to do it. Damn it, this was one adventure she didn't want.

Cautiously, she unfolded the wooden ladder, then went back to the kitchen to return the chair and to get both a flashlight and a broom. Awkwardly carrying them both, she slowly ascended the stairs, one step at a time, all the while her ears were straining for a sound.

The fact that it had now gone curiously silent did not reassure her.

Her chest went tight, her breathing shallow, her palms clammy. She shined the light into the opening, and found that the attic was surprisingly clean. Pausing, she forced oxygen into her lungs, then quickly went up another step and flashed the light all around.

All she saw were boxes, most of them cardboard, others wooden, along with old suitcases, some trunks, and a few pieces of broken furniture. One trunk was open, with balled-up newspaper spilling out.

At the far end of the attic, she located a window that, until now, she had only ever seen from the outside. It had always been closed, but now she noticed a broken pane in the bottom corner. Pieces of jagged glass littered the attic floor. Could a tree branch have done that? It might explain the sound she heard.

Frowning, she listened—and something moved to her right.

When she jerked around and shone the light there, she came face-to-face with an enormous snake coming out of the open trunk.

With a startled scream she dropped the broom, lost her hold on the ladder, and half slipped, half fell down, banging her arms and legs on each rung until she landed on the floor with a painful thud. For a stunned second she just lay there, shocked, the flashlight still gripped in her hand.

Until the hideous snake dropped down beside her.

Screaming again, Callie scrabbled to her feet and raced, limping, to her front door. Without daring to look back, she wrestled with the lock and just as she was turning the knob, the door was shoved open, half knocking her back.

Hard hands grabbed her upper arms. *"Callie."*

She almost screamed again—until the furious barking of a dog penetrated her fear.

Somehow, Tanner was here and that was all well and good, but she wanted out. "It's in the house!"

Tanner tugged her out and stuck her behind him as he turned to face the threat. "Blu, stay."

The dog immediately sat beside her, even leaned against her, which absolutely helped.

Gasping every breath, aware of a sudden throbbing that radiated up her thigh, her hip, and especially into her left arm, Callie pressed her face against Tanner's back and tried to find some composure. "Snake. Attic." Her voice shivered. "I fell."

"Jesus." He looked inside, taking in the scene. "No one else is in there?"

She shook her head, then said again, "Snake."

He turned to hold her. "Babe, it's another rat snake, that's all."

Callie covered her mouth, shaking all over, hating herself and hating her newly spiffed-up house, and most especially hating freaking snakes.

Tanner was calm personified. "I'm going to take it out back, okay? You stay right here with Blu."

"My chickens…"

"I'll make sure it's out of your yard. Now promise me you won't move."

She nodded, swallowed hard, and said, "Thank you." As he disappeared inside, she badly wanted to sink down and just sit…but with snakes still on her mind she didn't dare.

It was dark outside with her porch light only reaching so far. Insects buzzed around her, and in the distance she could hear music playing where the Garmet brothers lived. Off and on through the week she'd encountered them. Each time they'd briefly shared greetings, but it was clear they weren't interested in being friends. Not after she'd wrongfully accused them.

It wasn't until Tanner returned that she realized she was favoring one leg, cradling her hurt arm—and wearing only a T-shirt and panties.

His gaze swept over her, his brows down in a concerned frown as he eased his arm around her. "You're turning black and blue. Come on."

"It's gone? You're sure?"

"I moved the snake well away from your house and stuck it through the honeysuckle toward my house."

If she lived to be a hundred, she'd prefer to never see another snake. An unrealistic hope given where she lived, so she needed to get over her fear. *Later.* "There's a windowpane broken in my attic. I think that's how it got in, but what did it do? Climb a tree? *Where are all the snakes coming from?*"

"Shh." Tanner got her inside and helped her to the couch.

Blu was already busy scouring the place, his nose to the ground as he searched everywhere.

"What's he doing?"

"He knows you're upset and he's finding out why." Tanner lifted her legs up to the coffee table, slipped a throw pillow under her feet, and urged her to relax. "If there's another snake anywhere, he'll find it."

Glancing at the dog, Callie said, "Good boy, Blu, but be careful."

"Why were you in the attic?"

"I kept hearing a scratching noise. Snakes don't scratch. I wasn't expecting it. I was thinking rat or something equally awful, but not something worse." A shudder rippled over her, making her breath catch again. "My uncle has a trunk packed with wadded-up newspaper. The snake was moving in that and I guess that made the scratching sound."

He gave her that endearingly crooked smile. "Don't budge. I'll be right back." First he locked the front door, then he headed down the hall. When he returned, he had two hand towels that he set on the cushion beside her. Next he went into the kitchen and she heard him rummaging around before he returned with a bag of frozen diced onions, and a plastic bag of ice. "I'm going to put one on your arm, one on your thigh. Okay? It'll sting, but it'll help with the swelling and bruising."

On the verge of verbally rambling again, Callie forced herself to just nod. She didn't yet look at her arm or leg, afraid that if she did they'd start to hurt even more.

"Try not to move okay? I'll check out the attic, make sure there aren't any other critters up there, and then I'm going to check you."

Check her? "Where's Blu?"

"Here he is now." To the dog, Tanner asked, "All clear, bud?"

For an answer, Blu jumped up on her couch and got comfortable, settling close beside her.

Tanner started to stop the dog, until she put her un-injured arm around him.

"You got new furniture," Tanner said, concerned.

But Callie shook her head. "Blu is fine." Staring Tanner right in his dark, sexy eyes, she said, "Anytime Blu is here, he's welcome to get comfortable anywhere he wants. The couch…the bed. Doesn't matter to me."

"Okay, then." His mouth hitched in another smile. "I'll be right back. Try not to move too much."

Callie nodded. With the pain settling in, she wasn't sure she could. "Tanner? Please be careful."

He nodded. Holding her flashlight, he headed up.

Grateful that she had Blu with her, Callie hugged the dog. He snuffled her, gave her a lick, then turned back to watch for Tanner. Body alert, Blu waited, but he didn't really seem worried and that helped Callie not to worry. She could hear Tanner moving around up there and imagined that with the shorter ceiling it was an awkward exploration for him.

Thankfully, he wasn't gone long, maybe ten minutes that felt like a lifetime, but when he came down the lad-der, she immediately pounced. "Well?"

"No snakes," he promised. "But I'll need to secure that window tonight. You don't want a bat to get in."

No, she didn't.

Tanner crouched down in front of her. "Have you been in the attic at all?"

"No. This would have been my first time, but it was a spectacular failure." Seeing his expression, she frowned and asked, "Why?"

"There's a rock in the attic. I think that's how the window got broken. Also, the latch on the inside is opened."

It took a second for the implications to sink in. "You think someone deliberately broke a pane of glass and got into my attic? But for what reason?" An incredulous, nervous laugh escaped her. "To toss in a snake?"

"That's the big question, right? Actually, rat snakes are good climbers and they're sometimes drawn to attics if you have a rat or mouse problem."

"Okay, full-fledged freak-out coming on."

"I looked around," Tanner assured her. "No sign of rodent droppings and nothing was chewed up."

Hopeful, she asked, "So no rats?"

"No signs of even a cute little mouse."

Callie dropped her head back. "Finally, some good news."

"Here's the thing, though. Somehow that rock got in there. I'd think the rock was just thrown in to scare you…"

"Except for the open latch."

He nodded. "I didn't want to rummage through your uncle's private things. That's for you to do. There could be something valuable up there." He shrugged. "But I doubt it. From what I could tell, it just looked like old photo albums and stuff from childhood."

From Reggie's childhood—and maybe her dad's too? "I'd like to see them."

"Tomorrow I can bring them down."

So she'd see him again tomorrow? Meeting his gaze, Callie gave him an out. "I could pay Liam to do it."

Tanner pretended to take that on the chin. "Ouch." Expression softening, he said, "We have a lot to talk about, don't we?"

She'd thought so, until he'd disappeared for a week—again. "You tell me."

Cupping a hand to the side of her neck, he leaned in and put the gentlest of kisses to her lips. "We definitely do. But tonight I just want to take care of you."

"I'll be fine."

Tanner withdrew. For a few seconds, he appeared to struggle before he turned direct. "Is that your body talking or your pride?"

Callie said, "Both?"

"Babe, I can see you're hurt. If I had those bruises, *I'd* be hurting." He lightly touched her leg, and true enough, his expression was pained.

Swallowing down emotion, Callie gave him a full truth. "It would be nice if just once you wanted to be with me because you like me, not because I need help."

"Christ." He stood to tower over her, his expression fierce. "How can you even think…" Agitated, he paced away. Or more like stormed away. Every step a stomp.

It fascinated Callie. "How can I think what?"

He spun to face her and threw out his arms. "That I don't like you? I fucking *more* than like you. That should be obvious."

Wow. Okay, that sounded genuine. And calm, in-control Tanner, unraveling and having a fit? She liked it. How twisted was that?

She wished she could get to her feet too, square off with him face-to-face for this discussion, but she plain didn't feel like moving yet. She settled on saying, "That's odd, since you're always trying to get me to move away."

Almost immediately, he shuttered his expression. "We shouldn't ignore that broken window. Something else could get in."

So much for liking her.

One look at the ladder and Callie knew there was no way she'd go back up there—if she even could with her arm and hip throbbing.

"I can temporarily cover it," Tanner offered.

The very last thing she wanted to do was impose on him, and yet, she sensed it would hurt him more if she refused. "Okay, thank you." When his gaze locked to hers, she smiled. "Seriously, I hate bothering you, but—"

Abruptly, he turned away.

Message received. He didn't want her gratitude. For the next twenty minutes, Tanner was busy getting tools from her garage, along with scraps of plywood, while she stewed in silence.

So he more than liked her, but he didn't want to talk about it? Men were so damned complicated.

It made a racket when he went up again and began hammering the cover into place. When he finally finished and put the pulldown ladder away, she was relieved. On top of the aches and pains in her body, her head was starting to pound.

"It's not pretty," he said. "But it's secure. Liam can probably recommend someone to replace the glass if that's what you want, or you could permanently board up the window."

"I like the second idea." She did not want any more snake surprises. It was bad enough finding them outside.

Tanner patted his thigh and Blu got down. "Good

boy." He petted the dog, then eased into his place beside Callie and lifted the compress off her arm with a wince. "It could be broken."

Cautiously, she wiggled her fingers. "It's sore, but not enough pain to be a break."

"Can you straighten it?" Tanner helped by supporting her wrist and elbow.

Very carefully, in small degrees, she moved her arm, bent her elbow, and turned her wrist. Yes it hurt. Fiercely. But not the way she assumed a break would hurt. "Some aspirin and rest, and I'm sure it'll be fine."

Though he clearly didn't want to, Tanner accepted that. "Let's check out your leg."

"I'm not wearing shorts."

"Believe me, honey, I noticed." He lifted away the ice. His voice went a little hoarse when he said, "God, that looks awful."

"I bruise easily." Although she'd never had bruises like these. It was easier to see her thigh than her arm. Yup, it did look horrid—a swollen hot-pink splotch the size of her fist, surrounded by purple that faded into dark blue. "Looks like the galaxy, right?"

He was not in a teasing mood. "You could have broken your neck."

If he hadn't whispered it, she might have been offended. "It's not like I meant to fall. The snake startled me."

"Good thing I was close."

True, but that led to a new question. "It's late, so why are you here?"

Tanner got to his feet. "We'll get to that, but first let's see if you can stand."

"Of course I can. I ran outside, remember?"

"You were riding on adrenaline then. Come on."

Again with care, she slowly got to her feet. Tanner's supporting arm around her back helped, and it wasn't too excruciating, even when she put weight on her leg. "See, no real damage, just colorful."

"You're going to feel it tomorrow."

More than she felt it now? Not an uplifting thought. Determined, she started to limp her way to the kitchen. With a full day tomorrow, she'd need to get to bed soon.

There'd been a time in her life when thoughts of sleep wouldn't have occurred to her until at least midnight. Clearly, those days were long past.

Tanner carried the makeshift ice packs in one hand so he could keep his other arm around her.

So much for her show of independence.

In the kitchen, he replaced the ice in the plastic bag, and substituted the frozen diced onions for frozen French fries. "Be as pissed at me as you want—you still need to keep icing both spots, okay?"

"I'm not pissed." Not anymore. Mostly she was confused, and she wanted to hear more about him liking her, but she didn't want to badger him for the info.

At the refrigerator, she reached for the milk but Tanner got it before her.

"You're hungry?" he asked. "What do you want? I'll get it for you."

Exasperation overwhelmed her and that turned into a frustrated laugh. When she looked at his frowning face, it amused her even more. "I haven't seen you for over a week, Tanner. Eight whole days. Not a peep."

"I know how long it's been."

"Perfect. So give me a reason for your visit tonight, and then give me some privacy so I can tend my bruised body without an audience."

The way he stared down at her, those brown eyes searching yet unflinching, put Callie on the defense.

"Well?"

Tanner pulled her check from his pocket. He showed it to her, then ripped it in half, then into four pieces and tossed it in her trash can. "Addie doesn't want it. Kam and I don't want it. We're happy to have Rebel though, so if you really don't mind us keeping the horse, then we thank you for the gift."

She'd forgotten all about the check and tonight she didn't have it in her to fight about it. "Fine. The horse is yours. He was already yours, really. I appreciate how you've cared for him. Now I need a cookie"—or two or twelve—"with my milk, and I need to be alone."

Leaning back on the counter, Tanner said, "The check was a great excuse, by the way."

Oh, that did it. "I did *not* give Addie the check as an excuse to see you! I waited until you wouldn't be there."

"I'm aware, which means you were dodging me, not the other way around."

Her eyes flared. Damn it. She wouldn't let him put this on her. "You made yourself clear—"

"Apparently not." He touched her cheek oh-so-gently. "What I meant was that returning it to you gave *me* a great excuse to see *you*."

If her body wasn't aching, Callie would have thrown up her hands. He had her interest, so instead she drew a calming breath and said, "A cup of milk please, and just bring the whole pack of cookies. I'm going to need them."

Tanner's mouth curled in the barest of smiles. "Thank you, Callie."

She didn't bother replying. For real, she needed to get off her feet. With Blu keeping pace at her side, she

returned to the couch and managed to get settled with
only a few groans of misery.

HE'D MISSED HER so much. Even more than he'd realized.
Being with her now was like coming out of a dark cave
for the first time in a week. Didn't even matter that she
kept trying to kick him out.

Yeah, right. Of course it mattered. No way could
Tanner convince himself otherwise.

At the same time, he reasoned that if she hadn't
wanted to see him, she wouldn't be so angry now. Plus
she'd shared that bit about wanting him to like her. As
if he wasn't already half in love with her.

Sucked that he didn't better understand her. However, he had a chance to change that tonight.

With everything on a tray, including the refreshed ice
packs, Tanner rejoined her. She was putting up a good
show, but he could tell she was shot, hurting, tired, and
overall miserable.

Hoping to ease into things, he got her situated,
watched her devour a cookie in one bite, and then
looked around again. "The house looks great."

The compliment took the edge off her attitude.
"Thanks. I think so, too. With everything spiffed up,
the charm is coming through."

"Before your changes, I didn't know the place had
charm. I see it now though." He ran a hand over the
fabric of her new couch. "With this warmer weather,
Blu is going to shed."

She leaned over and kissed his dog. "I don't mind."

"Then would it be okay if I put down a bowl of water
for him?" With any luck, he and Blu would be around
a while.

"Of course." She hesitated one second, a cookie

dunked in her milk, then said, "I picked up some treats for him, too."

Blu was quick to catch that word, his eyes hopeful.

Grinning, Callie kissed him again. "I thought I'd be seeing more of you, bud." She shot a mean look at Tanner. "Didn't know your daddy would dodge me."

"I'm not his *daddy*." For God's sake, he didn't think of Blu as a son. "We're...friends. And we already established that you were the dodger."

Callie snorted. "Fine. Whatever. Get your pal a couple of treats, will you? I put a variety in the pantry."

Pleased that she'd planned on seeing him and disgruntled that she hadn't reached out, Tanner returned to the kitchen. Getting things set up for Blu gave him a minute to sort out his thoughts.

He wanted to stay with her. Obviously, he'd have to clear up some misconceptions first. Maybe it was time to be up-front with her.

After finding the treats, including a chew that would keep the dog busy for a little while, he whistled. Blu stuck his head in the kitchen with a "what?" look on his furry face. Tanner grinned. "Come here, Blu." Once the dog sniffed the water bowl and got assurance that it was for him, he took a long drink. "I know you'd like to stick close to Callie, but how about leaving that to me for a bit?" He offered the chew. "This might help, right?"

From the living room, Callie said, "I can hear you."

"I don't mind," he called back, glad that she didn't deny his plans.

Blu accepted the treat, but he carried it back to the living room. Instead of getting on the couch with Callie, he curled up on the rug in front of the door.

When Tanner carefully seated himself next to Callie, she asked, "Want a cookie?"

"No, I'm good. Thanks." He did another check of her arm and thigh, then got down to business. "I've missed you."

Her beautiful blue gaze lifted to his.

"So damn much," he admitted.

She took a second, then whispered, "I missed you, too."

A big admission, considering her earlier anger. He figured he might as well go for it. "Since I'm here and Blu seems settled, how about another overnight?"

Callie was quiet a long moment, then she put down her cookie. "I'm trying not to be a wimp, but I'm not up for anything physical tonight."

It wasn't easy, but he didn't grin. "I just want to be near you." If she needed anything, if it turned out her injuries were worse... He wanted to hold her. "I'm a light sleeper so I promise not to hurt you during the night. Blu will be fine sleeping on the floor at my side of the bed."

To his surprise, she didn't immediately refuse. "If I agree, are you going to assume I'm still shaken up over a snake?"

"I'll assume that, like me, you prefer not to sleep alone."

Callie rubbed one eye. "If you prefer that, you could have said so at any point over the last many days."

So she would have been fine with him making nightly calls? Nice. He could hopefully build on that. "You could have said so, too. Last I saw, your parents were visiting and your ex was coming over, and then...nothing."

"You already knew how I felt about Sutter!"

"But I didn't know how you felt about me."

Frowning, she grabbed up another cookie and muttered, "I came to dinner when Addie invited me, and you weren't there."

"Because I had a longtime customer with an enormous downed tree blocking his driveway." He watched her devour the cookie. "I wanted to be there, to see you."

"Oh."

Warming to his grievance, he said, "And I would have liked to introduce you to Rebel, but instead you had Liam do it."

Sounding grumpy, she said, "Liam doesn't confuse me."

"Callie." With a touch to her stubborn chin, he turned her face toward him. "You were a grade school crush, then a high school fantasy. Having you here, right next door, threw me hard."

"You wanted me to leave."

"At first, because I thought that would be easier." He slid his hand to her jaw, then let his thumb brush her downy cheek. Fortunately, she hadn't hit her face in the fall. She could have broken her nose, or shattered a cheekbone. He braced himself against those disturbing thoughts. "Now I know different."

"Now...you want me to stay?"

"The things I want with you..." It was difficult to put them into words. "Even though we didn't see each other, I knew you were here." *Not* back with Sutter. She hadn't returned to her old, easier life.

If he told her that he hadn't trusted in her convictions, her anger would return so instead he leaned in and kissed her. With his mouth lightly touching hers, he said, "I like having you here."

She pressed closer, and the kiss she gave him was not that of a wounded woman. He accepted—he couldn't have done anything else—but he didn't let it get out of hand. Whether she realized it or not, she was badly hurt. For certain, she'd feel every ounce of pain tomorrow.

Already in his mind, he had rearranged his schedule. Hell, he'd rearranged Addie's and Kam's, too.

The second she let up, he said, "Let us stay the night."

"Us?" she breathed.

"Blu and me. I promise we won't be in the way." He practically held his breath...until she nodded.

"I'd like that." She yawned. "For now, I think I'm ready to go to bed."

Not surprisingly, his body had ideas that his brain knew weren't possible. "I'll take Blu out first. Do you need help into the bathroom?" The sooner they got done, the sooner he could hold her.

"Not in this lifetime." She popped the last cookie into her mouth, and then let him take the tray and ice packs. "I'll leave out a spare toothbrush for you if you want."

"Thanks." Tomorrow, he'd talk to her about bringing over a few things—and food for Blu. He wasn't moving in on her, he told himself.

But he'd damn sure take advantage of the time she gave him.

CHAPTER FIFTEEN

TANNER'S PREDICTION THAT she'd feel worse in the morning proved true. It took all of Callie's concentration just to stand upright and move.

"Told you so," Tanner said low as he got up to help her.

"Shush it." After a very sound sleep with Tanner curled around her and the soft sounds of Blu's snores filling the air, she was more sluggish than usual. Still, she managed to shuffle into the bathroom mostly on her own steam. Tanner stayed at her uninjured side and Blu kept pace behind them.

"I'll make coffee. Give a yell if you need me."

God willing, she wouldn't have any drop-in visitors today. This morning, her entire body felt broken, though she knew it wasn't anything that serious. It took an effort to clean her teeth and pull up cotton shorts. No way could she brush her hair or manage socks with the dull pulsing pain in her arm.

When she entered the kitchen a few minutes later, Tanner helped her into her chair and set a mug of steaming coffee in front of her.

"I'm going to take a quick shower. Blu's already been out back. While he did his business, I took care of the goats and chickens."

In disbelief, Callie stared up at him. "I was only in the bathroom five minutes!"

"Ten," he said with a smile, then he bent down to kiss her lightly on the mouth. "Let me help out, okay?"

A little slow to process this morning, she nodded. "Um…okay. Thanks."

He kissed her once more. "Drink your coffee, then you'll need to use those ice packs again."

That alone was reason to groan. "I hate being cold. Wouldn't heat work, too?"

He shook his. "Not yet. Ice first for swelling. Maybe tomorrow, depending on how it looks, a hot soak in the tub would be okay."

"That sounds like experience talking."

"Between Kam and me, we've had our share of mishaps." One more kiss and a quick "Be right back," and he was gone.

True to his word, Tanner took a speedy shower. He reentered the kitchen shirtless, wearing only the loose jogging pants from the night before. They hung low on his hips, making her think he'd skipped boxers.

Barefoot, with stubble darkening his jaw, upper lip, and chin, he was sexier than ever—and as usual she looked like death warmed over.

Her gaze went all over him. She imagined he'd taste even better than her coffee, and that was saying something.

In short order, he took her mug to refill it, then handed her two aspirin and got the ice packs arranged against the worst of her aches.

Sliding into a seat beside her, he asked, "Did you find even more bruising today?"

How unfair that he was once again here, looking like original temptation, and she was down for the count. Seeing no reason to lie about it, she admitted, "They're everywhere, but I didn't do inventory." None of them were as bad as the two main injuries.

"I figured." He smoothed her hair, brushed the backs of his fingers over her cheek, and got down to business. "Will you let me stay?"

Because she hadn't seen that coming, she almost choked on a sip of coffee. When she caught her breath, she asked, "Here, with me?"

"Today, tomorrow, until you're back to one hundred percent." Lifting her right hand, he kissed her palm. "I thought about trying to do this in stages, pushing for a few hours, then the night, taking it one day at a time. But I want to be here, Callie, and that means I need to get a few things together."

"What things?"

"Food for Blu, my razor and toothbrush, change of clothes." He shrugged. "Your soap and shampoo smell like you and I love the scent—on you. On me…? Somehow I don't think it'll be the same."

"Probably not." It dawned on her that he meant stay-with-her as in *stay-with-her*. Around the clock. "I…" Her voice croaked, so she cleared her throat and tried again. "I see. Won't that be an awful imposition on you?"

"Having to be away from you for long would be the imposition." He was quick to add, "Not that I'll be here around the clock. I have a couple of things scheduled today that I can't get out of, but I want to come back and I want to be here after work. I want to sleep with you again."

"Oh." He'd already said that he *more* than liked her and now he wanted to stay over? And keep sleeping with her? She really wished she understood how in-volved he planned to be.

As if he'd read her thoughts, his mouth curled. "For now, I want to sleep with you in case you need any-thing, but as soon as you're ready count me in for more." He leaned forward, his expression intent, ready to say something...

And a knock sounded on the door.

Frustration hit her hard. "Damn it, if that's my par-ents again—"

"It's probably Addie. I called her first thing so she wouldn't worry."

Considerate, but Callie had a feeling he'd been about to open up to her and she wanted to hear it. Unfortu-nately, he'd already left to answer the door and when he returned he had not only Addie with him, but Kam, too.

Without even a greeting, Kam lifted the ice pack from her shoulder and gave a long whistle. "Damn, girl." Next he looked at her leg and grimaced. To Tan-ner, he asked, "She can walk?"

Callie answered. "Yes, she can walk. It's sore, but nothing's broken." Then she became aware of Addie standing there, a hand covering her mouth, her eyes rounded with worry. "I'm fine," Callie assured her. "I promise."

Tanner took some packages from Addie. "She re-ally is. Here, sit down." He got Addie in a seat, but she didn't stay there. She popped right back up and then carried on like a horrified mother, doing everything in her power to put Callie back to bed.

Callie resisted because deep down she believed she had to keep moving or the aches would overtake her.

"No bed," she insisted. "But admittedly, I wouldn't mind taking it easy today."

"Of course you're taking it easy! I'll take care of meals. Kam can check on the animals. Tanner, you're going to stay with her?"

"He has a job to do today," Kam said, as if it had already been decided. "I'll check in a few times, though."

"And Liam will be over," Tanner said.

Callie started to laugh and that hurt. She moaned and laughed some more. She'd always been a somewhat passive person and now she was smack dab in the middle of a pack of alphas, all of them trying to take over at the same time.

Tanner's mouth quirked. "Tickled you, did we?"

"I think she's hysterical," Kam said, teasing her.

Addie swatted at him. "Leave her alone. You can see she's in pain."

And so it went.

When Nell came by that afternoon, she was horrified by the sight of the bruising, which had spread and darkened. She actually wanted to cancel the upcoming party, thinking Callie wouldn't be up to it, but Callie refused. "I've got everything ready. Party supplies are in the spare bedroom. The grill is set up and the burgers bought. Drinks are in the fridge and ice cream is in the freezer."

"But you're hurt."

"I'll be fine by then. All I need to do is the—"

"Cake!" Popping up from her seat and nearly dumping the potatoes she'd been peeling for a soup, Addie said, "Now I can bake it, right?"

That brought on more laughter. The last thing Callie

had meant to do was make Addie feel slighted. "I was going to say get the decorations in place."

Nell said, "I don't need decorations."

Addie said, "Yes you do, and I'll help with that—but I also want to make the cake."

Callie had a cake on order. She'd planned to pick it up early on the day of the party, but seeing Addie's hopeful expression, she caved. "I love everything you bake, but I didn't want to give you more work."

"Oh honey, I *love* baking."

"Then by all means," Callie said gently. "Please plan on baking a birthday cake. Thank you."

With excitement dancing in her pale eyes, Addie turned to Nell. "What flavor do you want?"

Watching them make those decisions, Callie couldn't help but smile. Addie treated Nell like a granddaughter and Nell was soaking it up. It was a great relationship for both of them, and she'd been included in their awesome circle. It made her feel a special part of something bigger, a feeling she'd never experienced before.

This amazing family unit held greater meaning than a thriving multimillion-dollar company, or clout in the travel industry.

In a way, Sutter had done her an enormous favor when he cheated, because if that hadn't happened, if she hadn't literally walked in on him in the act...

She might have gone through with the marriage.

From the inside out, gratitude filled her and put a smile on her face. When Nell and Addie wound down, Callie said, "Thank you, Addie. I hope you know how much I adore you."

Addie flushed. "I adore you right back."

"Me, too," Nell said. "Both of you."

Such a remarkable gift. "I swear, with this family even being black and blue is wonderful." And that had the three of them laughing again.

Tanner was in and out all day, checking on her between jobs even when she assured him it wasn't necessary. She found that the more she moved, the less she ached—as long as she took it easy. Slow walks and a little flexing of her arms after ten minutes of ice did wonders.

Once Addie went home to put on the soup, Liam arrived. He scowled at the attic as if it had attacked her, and then he brought down two boxes of photo albums and three boxes of memorabilia from her dad and uncle's younger days. For now, Callie had him stack them at the end of the couch.

With a glance at her bruises, Nell asked, "Will you tell your viewers about falling?"

She hadn't thought about it. "Should I?"

"They want to see you again, but I don't think you're up to doing much."

Liam came over to her, wincing in concern. "One thing is certain, they'd know how hard you're working and that this isn't all a lark."

That struck her. "You know, you're both right. I think it'll be interesting. Something different from me." Far more inspirational than sloppy hair tips.

While Nell recorded, Callie explained about her fall, mentioning that anyone living alone should be extra careful. "I'm fortunate that I have wonderful neighbors who are helping out. If they weren't here, I would have had to figure out a way to feed my girls." Nell panned out to the chickens who were busy pecking at fresh feed. "And you know Daisy, Poppy, Rose, and Daffodil would miss me." She nodded at the goats. "They haven't recognized their names yet—which, by the way, were Katie Ann's recommendations from one of my earlier videos." Callie grinned when the camera centered on her again.

Off to the side, out of view, Liam stood with his hands outstretched as if he thought she might totter over at any moment.

"My point is that I'm learning, as someone living alone with others depending on me, I have to use extra care. And you, my dear viewers, male and female alike, have to do the same." One of the goats—Daisy, she thought—wandered into view and did one of her weird, lengthy bleats. With a laugh, Callie said, "I guess that's it then. Until next time, keep being awesome everyone."

Nell ended it and said, "Wow, I *loved* doing that! I hope I kept the camera steady enough."

"You did great. Thank you." Callie took one step and winced.

Liam immediately slipped his arm around her, his expression stark with worry. "I can see that you're hurting. Come inside now. You need more aspirin."

In that moment, Callie learned something new about herself; she did not like being babied. In her mind, she figured Liam, Kam, Addie, and especially Tanner, would have pushed on.

Nell was watching her though and she didn't want to alarm her, so she smiled and gave in. Back in the house, Callie watched the video, laughed at the ending with the goat, assured Nell that she'd done an incredible job as videographer, and sent it off to Glory.

Not long after, Tanner finished up for the day. He came in freshly showered and changed, with Blu at his side. He looked at Nell and Liam. "Addie says she made enough soup for everyone if you two would like to join us."

A look passed between the young people.

Liam said, "I already offered to get Nell a burger."

Nell cleared her throat. "Um…the burger sounds great—unless it's going to hurt Addie's feelings?"

Wearing a half grin, Tanner promised her it was fine.

With that reassurance, Liam and Nell left together. Callie couldn't stop grinning. She just loved seeing the two of them together.

Sitting down beside her, Tanner asked, "Do you want to join Addie and Kam, or would it be easier for you if I brought the food here?"

"Let's go there. I'm already restless. I haven't had this much leisure time since I moved here." She started to rise, but Tanner caught her and practically lifted her to her feet.

"Easy."

She loved him for caring, but after being pampered so much throughout the day, she needed some freedom.

Wrapping her uninjured arm around his neck and pressing her lips to his, she took him by surprise. He had to bend down to accommodate her, but he didn't resist. Instead, he carefully gathered her close, his hand gentle as he cupped her cheek.

Heaven. *This* was what she'd needed.

Unfortunately, Tanner ended the kiss too soon. "Ah, way to torture me, babe."

"That should be my line to you."

He leaned back to playfully frown at her. "You do realize you aren't up for sex, right?"

She did, but she wished it was otherwise. Sighing, she said, "I guess not."

"I know not, and while I could easily take care of you—"

She perked up. "Yes?"

His sexy mouth lifted in a full-fledged grin. "Getting off generally requires stiffening, clenching..." He nuzzled her neck. "Twisting a little—arching a lot." He kissed the corner of her mouth, then the bridge of her nose. "You did all that, you know, but now it would be damned painful with your arm and leg so banged up. Those are deep contusions and they need time to heal."

"Total bummer."

"Let's give it a few days, okay?"

"You promise you won't vanish on me again?"

The smile faded from his face, and his eyes grew darker, more serious. He brushed his thumb over the corner of her mouth, then kissed her again. "I'm not going anywhere."

That was more of a promise than she'd ever gotten from him. For now, she'd have to take it. "All right then, let's go eat."

TANNER WOKE WITH Callie's warm weight still nestled against him, and of course he was already hard. Her scent alone was enough to do that to him, but her hair, her skin, that perfect backside pressed to him? Pure, hot temptation.

Not that he'd even think about doing anything sexual right now. She'd had a restless night, flinching awake every time she'd moved. It wasn't until he'd convinced her to try something different that she'd finally gotten some rest.

After he'd helped her to put a smaller pillow under her bruised arm, he'd scooted close to her, aligning his legs behind hers, curving his arm around her and holding her securely so she couldn't inadvertently shift too much. He'd surrounded her as much as he could—and within minutes her breathing had grown deep and even.

At one point the arm he had under her head started to tingle, but there was no way in hell that he'd move and disturb her sleep. For a time, he'd just rested there in the dark, listening to her steady inhale and exhale. The scent of her always made him think of sunshine. The reality of her as a strong but gentle woman was better than any of the fantasies he'd concocted throughout his lifetime.

Blu had snored, occasionally yapping in his sleep as he dreamed of chasing rabbits or squirrels, but thankfully it didn't wake her.

And eventually he'd faded out, too.

When the rude knock sounded on her door, he'd automatically glanced at the time. Barely 6:30 a.m., way too early for visitors.

Why did that keep happening?

She stirred but didn't awaken, at least not until she started to stretch, then an agonized groan ripped from her.

"Careful," he murmured. "Let me get up first so I can help you."

For an answer, she shifted slightly and gasped.

Blu had heard the knock, too, and he was already on his feet, his body rigid as he stared at the hallway.

"Blu, stay."

Reluctantly, the dog sat but didn't give up his vigilance.

When a harder knock thumped the front door, Callie muttered, "Damn it. Again?"

"My thought exactly." Now that he was on his feet, Tanner helped her to sit up. He hated the discomfort he saw on her face. "Want me to get it?"

"Yes." Gingerly cradling her arm and keeping weight off her leg, she managed to stand with his help. "But can you promise to be nice?"

"To you, sure. Come on." He helped her into the bathroom, then said, "Take whatever time you need." She was already limping toward the toilet.

He didn't want to leave her, but he knew she wouldn't let him help, so he gave her privacy. Wearing only his boxers, with Blu at his side, he went to the living room.

A peek out the window showed Sutter—who was trying to look in. They stared at each other, Tanner with sharp annoyance, Sutter in surprise.

In two seconds flat, Tanner moved away from the window and jerked open the front door.

Blu shot out, but he was a well-trained dog and did no more than offer a growl.

"Blu, no."

Blu shot him a look that clearly asked: Are you *sure*?

Damn, he loved his dog. As he stepped out with the dog, Tanner instructed, "Go do your business, bud."

Reluctantly, Blu went into the grass but he kept an eye on Sutter the entire time. It was almost humorous to watch the dog piddling while mean-mugging Callie's ex.

Finally, Tanner gave his attention to Sutter. The other man wore a petulant scowl; obviously, he'd expected to find Callie alone. "What do you want?"

Sutter drew himself up with umbrage. Teeth locked, he said, "My fiancée."

"Sorry, dude, but that ship not only sailed, it sank."

Crossing his arms, Tanner leaned against the outside of the doorframe. "Anything else?"

Eyes narrowing, Sutter insisted, "I want to see Callie."

"I'm here," Callie said, shuffling slowly into view.

Incredibly enough, Sutter didn't seem to notice her bruises. "I woke you?"

"It's not even seven and I had a rough night." She stepped onto the porch beside Tanner.

"Oh?" Sutter's gaze shifted to Tanner in accusation. "Let her down, did you?"

"No, he didn't," Callie said. "Why are you here?"

Finally, Sutter's gaze dipped to her exposed thigh and the kaleidoscope of blue and purple bruising. His brow lifted, but not an ounce of real concern showed in his expression. "What happened to you?"

"I fell out of my attic."

"Callie," he chided softly. "This is why you shouldn't be here alone." He opened his arms to her.

In disbelief, Callie huffed at him, then leaned into Tanner.

Sutter slowly lowered his arms and frowned. "What is this?"

"Exactly what you think it is," Tanner said, not about to make that same mistake twice. He slipped his arm around Callie to offer support.

Pulling back, Sutter shook his head. "No."

"Oh, yes," Callie said with happy conviction.

Okay, so despite dickhead dropping in, it was turning into a great morning for Tanner. Especially when Blu came up to sit with them. Now it was three to one—if Sutter could even count for a whole human being.

He needed to get Callie inside, give her some aspirin and coffee, and possibly more ice for her aches. But first Sutter would have to go.

As casually as he could manage, Tanner said, "If that's all then?" He started to turn.

Sutter surged forward a step, infuriating Blu who stiffened and showed his teeth in a snarl.

The way Sutter ignored the dog, it was as if he thought Blu wouldn't dare. All his angry attention was aimed at Callie. "So rather than marry me, you would prefer to—"

"Yes."

"—fuck a local hick?"

The insult didn't faze Tanner; God knew he'd been called worse things by his own father. But Callie didn't take it well. Lurching away from Tanner, she stumbled on her hurt leg without acknowledging it. "How *dare* you?" She thrust up her chin, her shoulders rigid. "He's a better man than you'll ever be! He's honorable and caring. Kind and strong." Almost vibrating with anger, she yelled, "He's *amazing.*"

Sutter's lip curled in disgust. "When you're done slumming, give me a call. Then we'll decide if we have a relationship or not." After that cutting remark, he turned to go.

Callie shouted, "I hope you hold your breath waiting!"

Okay, so yeah, Tanner knew his eyes had widened over that whole bizarre exchange. He was kind, strong, *and* amazing?

Like a bull ready to charge, Callie was still heaving. Sutter got behind the wheel, slammed his car door, stepped on the gas and sped away.

Gently, Tanner brought Callie against him. "Ease up, honey, before you blow a gasket."

She drew in one more sharp breath, and then whispered, "Oh, God." Her face contorted and she bent like an old woman who'd just suffered a painful blow.

It scared Tanner, thinking it was regret that caused that look.

Until she cried out, *"My leg..."* and clutched at him.

"Shit." He caught her against him, carefully taking some of her weight. "What can I do?" If he lifted her in his arms, it'd only hurt her thigh more. She was so bruised and battered, he wasn't certain what to do to help her. "I was nice because you asked me to be, damn it, and now I really wish I'd smashed his face."

"Me, too," she said brokenly. "Tanner, I desperately need to sit down."

He kissed her temple and helped her to turn back toward the house. "I told you adrenaline blocked pain."

"Then I wish the adrenaline would return." She hobbled forward a single awkward step...

And they both heard applause. They looked up and found Dirk and Lang at the edge of their property, their faces amused—until they spotted her left thigh and arm and got a good look at her face.

Dirk crossed the yard in angry strides. "What the hell happened?"

If he hadn't been busy holding Callie, Tanner might have slugged him for whatever insinuation he tried to make. "She fell."

"Out of a plane?" Lang asked.

"My attic, actually," Callie replied breathlessly, still struggling to get it together.

"Good God. You could have killed yourself!"

That Dirk sounded so enraged on her behalf surprised Tanner. "Get her door, will you?"

"Right." He rushed ahead and held it open, a frown of concern masking his usual cockiness.

One thing was certain: both of the brothers were appalled by her injuries. It would have been convenient to blame them for the broken window, but Tanner tried—whenever possible—to be fair.

Lang muttered, "I saw her asshole ex was here and told Dirk."

"Yup." Tanner hadn't forgotten seeing the brothers talking to Sutter in town. Now might be a good time to find out what that was about. Blu wisely stayed close, his posture still protective, as Tanner got Callie in the house. "Either of you know how to make coffee?"

Oddly enough, they each held up a hand.

Now that they had company, Callie was gritting her teeth trying her best not to groan. He needed to see to her, but he also knew she loved her coffee with a few cookies.

Pointing to the kitchen, Tanner said, "Through there. Coffee and mugs are in the cabinet over the maker. Put on a pot, will you?"

Dirk went utterly still, then his gaze shot to Callie and he frowned some more while nodding. "I'll see to it." He took off.

Lang followed him. "We'll have it ready in a sec."

Once they were out of the room, Callie gave him a wan smile. "See?" she whispered quietly. "You're completely amazing."

Tanner snorted. He got her settled, said, "Don't budge," and went down the hall to get aspirin and a couple of hand towels. From there, he detoured to the kitchen and saw the brothers side by side in front of the sink. Such an incongruous sight, the two of them working industriously to be *helpful*. It boggled his mind. "Six scoops," he told Lang. "She likes to taste her coffee, but doesn't want it too strong."

Dirk looked nonplussed for a moment, then he frowned in concentration as he carefully removed a scoop from the basket to put back in the can. He closed the lid on the maker, pushed a button and said with satisfaction, "It'll be ready soon."

Tanner was seeing a whole new side to the brothers, thanks to Callie. It was an odd realization and he wasn't quite sure what to do with it yet.

He handed Dirk the tray. "Get her a couple of cookies, too." He nodded to the pantry. "Napkins are on the table. I'll put her cup together in a minute. She likes it a particular way."

Lang asked, "Have her critters been fed?"

Tanner hadn't given a thought to the goats or chickens. That was a first for him, too. "No, they haven't. They need to be let out of their shelters, fresh water, feed—"

Slapping him on the shoulder, Lang said, "No worries, man. We got it."

Well hell. The reprobates were actually enjoying being helpful. Hating the brothers was a lot easier than thanking them, but he did it anyway. "Appreciate it." As they started out the back door, he added, "When that's done, we need to talk."

"Damn right we do," Dirk agreed.

"Past time," Lang said. "So don't go anywhere."

No, he wouldn't be leaving Callie today, no matter what he had to rearrange. Someone had put a rock through her window, and he suspected the snake had been planted.

Until he figured it out, he'd stay by her side.

That idea suited him just fine.

CALLIE WAS SO proud of Tanner, she almost couldn't stand it. Amazing was too mild of a word. He was unlike anyone she'd ever known, pivoting easily whenever necessary, holding his temper in check while keeping up his guard.

Being gracious when it was warranted.

He was one of a kind and she wanted him. Today, tomorrow, forever. Yes, it was fast—and she didn't care.

Now that she'd taken the pressure off her leg, the pain receded to a low but continual ache, still there but not nearly so sharp. Aspirin and ice helped, as did coffee. It was almost comical, sitting in her small, newly updated living room, Tanner on the cushion beside her, Blu stationed in front of her, and Dirk and Lang on chairs facing her.

It was so quiet she could hear herself chewing a cookie. She slanted a look at Tanner, who appeared in deep thought. "So."

All three men tilted forward, as if ready to jump at her bidding. Even Blu looked back at her, his head tilted.

She snickered. "Do you think you could all relax?"

Tanner countered with, "Feeling better?"

"Yes, I am. Thank you." She turned to the brothers. "All of you."

Lang actually flushed, but Dirk nodded. "Welcome. What the hell was that about, anyway?" Before she could reply, he sat forward, his forearms on his knees and said, "I don't like that guy. You shouldn't let him come around."

Callie touched Tanner's thigh. Honestly, he was so wired, she thought he might jump to her defense even when she didn't need it.

"First, I didn't let him. Sutter and I are through, but he seems to have a problem remembering that."

"Let Tanner remind him once and the bastard won't forget again."

"It's not Tanner's problem."

Showing his exasperation, Dirk threw up his hands and glared at Tanner. "Can't you do something about this?"

Tanner said, "I'd be happy to."

"Second," Callie interrupted, emphasizing the word so they'd all understand she wasn't done yet. "I don't need anyone to fight my battles for me. I told Sutter to get lost and that should be the end of it."

Lang snorted. "Get real. That prick...er guy, is pushier than you think."

"What do you know about it?" Tanner asked in a deceptively mild voice.

It shocked Callie when Dirk said, "He tried to make a deal with us."

"What?" How would Sutter even know Dirk and Lang?

"Go on," Tanner said. "Let's hear it."

"We met him a few weeks back when he was here. Said he was picking up her cousin or something like that."

"He was outside waiting on Glory," Callie recalled.

Lang nodded. "We saw him." With a shrug, he explained, "When he realized we were your neighbors,

he had a lot of questions for us, but Dirk told him to
fuck off."

Tanner nodded. "Good instincts."

"Thanks."

Now, after all this time, they were agreeable? Astounding.

Dirk continued. "He said he'd like to talk to us about
a deal. I knew right off he was trouble—and weak, too,
with his fancy shoes and turned up nose—but I figured
he wanted weed or something. That day, he didn't have
time to talk, so I gave him my number. He told me not
to mention it because Callie wouldn't understand."

"No," Callie stated. "I wouldn't have."

Tanner removed her ice packs and put them on the
tray. He was better at timing the treatment than she
was, but it felt good to have the prickling ice removed.

While he folded the hand towels, he said, "I saw you
talking with him at the sandwich shop near the tracks."

Swiveling her head, Callie glared at him. "You didn't
mention that."

"By the time I saw you again, it didn't seem like a big
deal." Keeping his gaze on the brothers, Tanner asked,
"I know he came here after, so what was that about?"

Lang seemed uneasy, but Dirk just rolled a shoulder.
"He offered us cash to keep an eye on her, let him know
how she was getting on, if you were hanging around,
stuff like that."

Damn. Callie wanted to close her eyes, but she made
herself face the humiliation. "You told him about the
tree, didn't you?"

A sardonic grin curled Dirk's mouth. "The tree you
climbed in the middle of a thunderstorm because you
thought I'd kidnapped your goat? Yeah, I told him."

"Jerk."

He laughed. "You weren't exactly an angel yourself."

No, she hadn't been. Callie blew out a breath. "I'm sorry for misjudging you."

"I'm sorry for repeating the story."

She supposed she'd have to be gracious about it. Didn't mean she had to like it.

Tanner forged on. "What else did you tell him?"

"That snakes spook her, that she was spending time with you, and that she was fixing up the place." He smiled. "And overall she was doing a great job."

Funny that a compliment from Dirk could mean so much. "Thank you."

"It's the truth. We see you working nonstop."

"And you never seem to mind much," Lang added.

She beamed at him. "Actually, I'm loving it."

Again, Tanner got them back on track. "Any idea what Sutter was planning to do with the info you gave him?"

"He's scum—worse than what you've always accused us of being," Dirk said. "So who knows? You can bet it won't be good."

Callie made a decision and she hoped Tanner would agree. "Thank you both for helping out today."

Taking that as a dismissal, Lang stood, but she didn't want him to go just yet. "I want to share something, and I hope you'll hear me out."

Slowly, Lang sat back down. Dirk only narrowed his eyes and waited.

When Callie glanced at Tanner, he gave one slight nod.

"Someone threw a rock through my attic window." She quickly held up a hand before they could get riled.

"I'll admit, at first I wondered if one of you had done it, but I couldn't see any reason why you would."

"Because we *wouldn't*," Dirk ground out, the clench of his jaw the only sign of his temper. "Whatever Tanner's told you, we don't hurt women."

"Not ever," Lang added. "That'd make us chicken-shit and we're not."

"I believe you."

"All you know about us is what Tanner's told you."

"All warranted," Tanner said.

"Most, maybe." Dirk let out a breath as he considered things. "I guess it makes sense she'd suspect us since she probably doesn't know that many other people yet, being new and all. There's no way anyone would accuse Addie of any wrongdoing, and since she's sleeping with you it's not likely she'd accuse you." He shot Callie a look. "Even though he had plans for this property and you mucked them up."

"Expanding his tree farm, I know."

Lang huffed. "More like he wants to put up a mentoring program or something for all those troubled kids he supports." Shifting uneasily in his seat, he muttered, "We always thought it was a solid idea."

"Kids like that need attention," Dirk said. "They gotta know things so they have options."

The bottom dropped out of Callie's stomach. Beside her, Tanner had gone still.

Dear God, she'd been wallowing in her freedom, enjoying learning new things, playing at life—and in the process she'd unknowingly disrupted Tanner's special dream.

Why didn't he tell me? His profile didn't alter, not

a flicker of guilt or anger showed, but she felt the new tension in his frame and in the very air around him.

"I didn't know," she whispered.

Tanner nodded. "I'll figure out another way."

But how could he? She had the perfect property for it, especially since it was right next door to his tree farm.

Once more, Tanner wrestled the topic back on track. "The lock was opened on her window, which makes me wonder if anyone got in her house that way." He hesitated, then said, "Or if the point was just to plant a big snake in the attic. That's why she fell. She heard the noise, went up the ladder to investigate, and the snake was there moving around."

With a shrug, Dirk said, "Snakes get in attics, usually looking for food."

"Sure, but they don't throw rocks or unlatch windows. Besides, there wasn't a single mouse or rat to be found. Other than some dust, the space is spotless. And now, after what you've told me about Sutter, I'm wondering if he planned it all."

It suddenly struck Callie, too. "Odd that he'd show up here so early the very next day."

Dirk worked his jaw a few seconds. "He has to have hired someone else. No way would that fancy pants hold a snake or skulk around at night."

"I agree," Tanner said. "But if it wasn't either of you, then who?"

"I might be able to find out." Dirk pinned Callie in his gaze. "But I don't want to be accused of any more shady shit. I don't give a damn what Tanner thinks. But you…"

"I would be eternally grateful," she said quietly. Now that she knew why Tanner wanted her property, she had some big decisions to make. That'd be easier to do without Sutter's interference.

To everyone's surprise, Tanner agreed. "Try telling him that you saw someone hanging around, and you don't appreciate him hiring someone else."

Dirk stood. "I'll crack my knuckles and act all threatening." He half grinned. "Usually works, just not with Tanner."

"Thanks." Tanner got to his feet and offered his hand. "We'd appreciate it if you got back with us on anything you learn."

The two men, recently bitter enemies, now shook hands.

Despite the low throbbing in her arm and the deep ache in her thigh, Callie enjoyed the moment. A lot had been accomplished here today, more than she'd hoped for. And likely more than Tanner had ever expected.

CHAPTER SIXTEEN

CALLIE HAD JUST finished dressing after her shower when Tanner tapped on the bathroom door. "How long are you going to linger in there?"

She'd come out when she was good and ready. Or… when she could stop crying.

Everything she'd planned, everything she'd thought she knew and it had just dissolved as if it never existed. Why hadn't Tanner told her?

She dried her eyes yet again. "Two more minutes."

"Honey, we need to talk."

Yes, they did. But it should have happened weeks ago. Of course, if he'd told her right off why he wanted Reggie's place, she'd have sold it to him and moved on and now she wouldn't have him at all.

Miserable at that thought, she opened the door and tried to look composed.

His gaze dipped over her, and he bent to take her mouth in a warm, leisurely kiss. "Holding up okay?"

It was nice having his attention and concern, but she wished it wasn't over an accident. "I'm fine, I promise. I was just stiff when I first woke up, then having to deal with Sutter…"

"You never need to defend me."

No, of course not—because Tanner didn't need her, he just needed her property. Drawing a shuddering breath and willing herself to stay dry-eyed, she leaned into his warm chest. "He's lucky I didn't smack him."

He tipped up her face, his astute gaze missing nothing. "You're upset."

"A little." *A lot.* "We could get that discussion out of the way. That is, if you have time to stick around…?"

"I'm all yours."

Oh, how she wished that was true. "Where's Blu?"

"Kam came by and got him."

Okay, then she could use more coffee. "Let's go to the kitchen."

"Wouldn't you be more comfortable on the couch?" he asked as she limped along.

"No."

"At least sit down."

She tried a smile, but she knew her frustration showed through. "That night we spent together was…" Astounding. Eye-opening. *Heart-stealing.* "Pretty awesome?" Ugh, how weak that sounded. "I enjoyed myself. And you. I mean, us together."

"In case there's some confusion, I enjoyed it, too."

She eased down into a chair. "Tanner, why didn't you tell me?"

He didn't pretend not to understand. He just poured the coffee, then sat across from her. "There didn't seem to be a point. I assumed you'd be gone soon enough."

Did he believe that still?

He looked down at his mug for a moment, then back to her. "Whenever you've asked, I've answered your questions."

And she'd had plenty of them. She wanted to know everything about Tanner. "Yes, you have."

"Now I have a question of my own."

She got as comfortable in the chair as she could. "Go on. I'm an open book."

He surprised her by asking, "How are you affording this?"

Her mind went blank. "This?"

"Far as I can tell, you don't have a paying job. Even though Reggie didn't have a mortgage, there's still insurance, utilities, upkeep, feed to buy for the animals, your own groceries—"

"Right. I get it. I have expenses." She'd have to address them soon, anyway.

Idly, he turned the coffee cup while scrutinizing her. "Seems every time I turn around, you're buying something new."

Settling in even more. Clearly it bothered him, but if Dirk hadn't shared Tanner's plans, she'd still be in the dark. "Early on, my parents started investing on my behalf. I think at first it was a tax thing, though I don't keep up on all that. Then when I turned twenty-one, I got my own investment counselor. He suggested diversifying some of my accounts, and to do that I had to sell a few things, move them around. Eventually, all of my accounts were well away from my parents' influence—and thriving."

"So you're independently wealthy?" His expression was unreadable as he asked for clarification. "Not just as part of the McCallahan family, but as your own entity?"

"Wealthy? No, it's not like that. I couldn't go out and buy three houses or a yacht or anything." She winced. "I am comfortable, though. Even when I worked for my parents, and later with Sutter's family, I was a saver."

"You're saying you did without?"

"No." She was starting to feel defensive. "I had nice things, but I've never really had extravagant tastes. Not like my mother or my friends." Probably because so much had been given to her. Throughout college, her parents had paid her way, including an allowance for food, clothes, and transportation. "Mom and Dad love to travel. They'll go off for a month or more at a time, but I'm more of a homebody. You saw my car versus theirs. And my wardrobe? Even when I dressed for business in designer suits, my casual clothes were just that—casual."

Skepticism narrowed Tanner's eyes. "You're saying you like living like this." He gestured at the kitchen, and even rocked the table, showing that it had an uneven leg.

Funny that she hadn't noticed that before.

"You like mucking out goat shelters and collecting eggs?" Forearms on the table, he leaned forward. "Living in a small, two-bedroom house with a damp basement, an unattached garage, and thugs for neighbors?"

Why was he being like this? Now that she knew him—and loved him—she figured he had to have a reason.

She tilted up her chin. "I've found it challenging and in some ways rewarding." Hoping to tease him out of his mood, she added, "Plus, I'd hardly call you and Kam thugs."

Instead of cracking a smile, his mouth tightened and he sat back again, putting added distance between them. "It's challenging, but the novelty of it won't last." While her heart ached, he said, "It's not the life you want."

That hurt more than she was willing to show him. "I decide what I want, not you, and I'll have you know I was trying to prove—" Hurt caught her breath, ending the words that she'd been about to say. "Never mind. Why should I explain anything to you when you obviously don't know me at all?"

"No, go ahead and finish." He challenged her with his gaze. "You were proving yourself to me?"

"Ha! Get over yourself." Shoving back her chair, she awkwardly got to her feet and went to the sink to dump the rest of her coffee. She'd suddenly lost her appetite. "I have nothing to prove to you or anyone else. Not a damn thing." Covering her heart with a fist, she struggled to contain the angry overdose of emotion so she wouldn't cry again.

A lifetime ago she'd learned that a smile disarmed people more than an outburst. And she'd witnessed it from Tanner many times, the way he tempered his reaction, calm when others tried to incite his anger.

At least in that, they were alike. Turning back to him now, she got her lips to curve. Not much, but it was the best she had at the moment. "I was proving to *myself* that I could do it. That's the only standard I have to live up to. Me and what I think." Saying it made her believe it, and that went a long way to illuminating the choices she now had to make.

Tanner said nothing, but he stood too.

The length of the admittedly small kitchen spanned between them. "Right now," she said, "I happen to like myself."

His voice emerged as a rough whisper. "No reason you shouldn't."

She wasn't about to get drawn in again. "If you and Sutter and my parents don't see me for who I am, I don't care." In truth, she cared too much and it disappointed her because she should have learned by now. "I see my-self. I like and respect the person I am."

"With good reason."

"You should go."

"No."

Her mouth dropped open. "What do you mean, no?"

"You're pissed, I get it. But I rearranged my day to be with you, so I'm not budging and you're in no shape to throw me out."

Flabbergasted, she stood there fuming until he slowly closed in.

"I told you once already, I more than like you. Hell, Callie. If you stay around I'm going to love you."

Whoa. She stared up at him, hoping she'd heard him right. "But—"

"Forget the property," he said, before she could bring it up. "Now that you're here, I don't want you to leave." Gently, he framed her face in his hands. "I didn't tell you about my plans at first because they didn't matter. I figured you'd move on soon so I was only delayed. Then I got to know you better. Not just the princess who seemed so untouchable, the girl I'd idolized through school."

"I wish I'd gotten to know you then."

He shook his head. "No. Hell, no. Everything might have been different. I'm glad you didn't know me. You said you like who you are now. Well, I feel the same. That scared, pathetic kid I was—"

"You were *never* pathetic," she insisted.

He lightly kissed her for that. "My point is that I'm a better man now. Faults and all, I'm the person I want to be, the man I want you to know."

Damn, those tears were back again. "I have great

respect for the person you are." Even knowing it was too soon, she said, "I think I started falling for you that very first day."

Humor and satisfaction made his dark eyes gleam. "Was it my big...chain saw?"

She laughed. "Your chain saw, your sexy body, how you are with Blu and Addie. That first morning we shared coffee, I realized how different you are from anyone I've ever known, and how different I am with you."

His mouth twisted. "I unloaded on you and that's not something I ever do."

"Maybe even then," she teased lightly, "you knew you were the one for me."

Breathing a little deeper, he put his forehead to hers. "I want to be—if you'll let me."

"Yes." Whatever she had to do, even if it meant handing over the house to him for free, she'd do it, because Tanner meant that much to her. Who he was, what he did for others and how he did it, made him the most lovable person she'd ever known. "Anything you need."

He tunneled his fingers into her hair. "I need you to please let me help you to the couch."

"Being with you like this, hearing what I want to hear, it made me forget my leg." Now that he'd mentioned it again, the ache intensified.

He huffed a soft laugh. "Well, I haven't forgotten. Come on."

FOR THREE DAYS, Callie hobbled around, hampered by discomfort as she eased back into her chores. Feeding the chickens was the hardest part because of the heavy bucket to carry, but she was determined to push herself.

And what a fit Tanner had. Addie, too.

That was almost reward enough for the pain her independence caused her. Neither of them was used to losing an argument. It was a wonder they got along so well.

The first time she'd insisted on feeding the hens herself, Kam, being the goof he was, had rolled his eyes at her and said, "Go on then. Make a point. I just hope you know what it is."

Of course she did. The point was, come hell or high water, she *could* do this. She didn't need them to do it for her, but she loved that they were around, concerned and caring.

Honest to God, she was starting to love them all. Addie was in her element when she could fuss like a mother—a mother very unlike Callie's own. Addie worried first about others, not herself.

Kam teased like a younger brother. At one point, when Callie was heading out to corral the goats, Kam had jogged past her, saying, "Race you," when he knew she was barely walking. His lighthearted joke had taken away the sting of his help.

Best of all was Tanner. Callie closed her eyes, thinking of how he spooned her each night. The warm, damp kisses he put on her shoulder and the back of her neck. How he came alert anytime she moved.

It had to be frustrating for him, but he didn't complain, and instead swore that he was right where he wanted to be.

She really loved having Blu around, too. And twice Percy the cat had come over with Addie to visit. It was like they were one big family—but living in two houses.

That was the problem. She needed to show Tanner that while she could hold her own, she'd rather live her life with him.

His plans mattered to her. They'd matter even more to the young people looking for a purpose, needing to feel valued and appreciated.

She badly wanted to discuss her house with him, but she also wanted a commitment from him. Proximity couldn't be the only reason they were together now. If she wasn't right here, next door, would he be willing to put out the effort to be with her?

On the fourth day, she awoke recovered enough to really tackle business—namely, her life, which included Tanner and his amazing family. As usual, she found him in the kitchen with coffee ready. She heard the goats and chickens and knew he'd already tended to them, too. He even had cookies on the table.

"You're a very domestic man," she said as she strolled in. She wore only the shirt and panties she'd slept in, and she hadn't done a thing to pretty up for him.

Didn't matter. Despite her messy hair and wrinkled shirt, he came to her for a warm kiss. "How do you feel today?"

"Ready to take on the world—or one large, sexy man." She bobbed her eyebrows.

"Is that so?" He guided her to a chair. "You're walking better."

"The pain is nearly gone." She flexed her arm and easily took her seat without a single grimace. "I'm a little stiff, but that's all."

"Seeing you like this"—he slid the back of one finger over her breast—"I'm getting a little stiff, myself."

That set her heart to racing. "Wait." She grabbed up her coffee mug and chugged back half, then got to her feet again and started out of the room. "Give me five minutes to freshen up."

Laughing, the diabolical man caught her waist and tugged her back against him. "Easy there." He nuzzled her ear, his breath hot, his morning whiskers raising gooseflesh on the sensitive skin of her neck. "If you're really feeling up to it, maybe we could shower together."

"Yes," she breathed, turning to cuddle against him, saying a little desperately, "I need you, Tanner." In so many ways. Now more than ever.

Both of his big, hot hands cuddled her backside, sliding over the slinky material of her panties. "It's been the best kind of torture, being with you but not having you, not loving you."

Her heart rapped harder. Forget the shower. Forget everything else. She looked up at him and whispered, "Love me now."

Thankfully, he needed no more encouragement than that. The kiss he gave her was far better than caffeine could ever be. With one hand he stroked her breast, his palm rasping over her nipple, and with the other he cupped her backside, urging her into delicious contact with his erection.

"You need to lose those jeans."

He smiled against her mouth. "Yes, ma'am." He opened the snap and pulled down the zipper, then hooked his thumbs in the waistband—and a split second later, a frantic knock sounded on her door.

Callie let out a groan of massive frustration. "I'm cursed."

"No, you're not." With yet another firm kiss of promise, he said, "I'll get it, okay?"

Another faster, harder knock rapped on the door, the sound insistent.

"What the hell?" He snapped his jeans as he strode out of the room.

Hoping it wasn't anything important, Callie trailed behind him—until he paused. "Babe, you aren't dressed. It could be Dirk or Lang."

She looked down, saw her nipples were pressing against the cotton material of her shirt, and huffed. "Go on. I'll be right back." As fast as she could, she went down the hall and found shorts, then a loose sweatshirt.

She was still pulling it on when she heard her mother demand, "Where's my daughter? Callie! *Callie.*"

"Mom?" Alarmed, she adjusted her clothes as she stepped into the hall. Both her mom and her dad met her halfway. "What's wrong?"

"Callie!" She got swept up into her mother's arms and squeezed too tightly, causing a strain to both her arm and her leg.

"Ouch, Mom."

Tanner stepped in, gently separating them. "Sorry, ma'am. Callie had a mishap and her arm and leg are still sore."

Tears swam in her mother's eyes. "Oh, my God. I hurt you?"

Her dad said, "Hush, Liz. You can see she's okay, but there's no way to miss all those bruises."

Callie realized her dad was staring at her bare thigh, and yeah, the bruises did look horrendous.

Drawing back, her mother gazed at her leg and her face paled. "Dear God, they look even worse now than they did in your video."

The discolorations had darkened to mustard yellow and a sick shade of green. They weren't pretty, but Tanner hadn't minded.

"Yeah, they're icky, but I'm feeling much better today." Callie tipped her head. "How did you—?"

"Let's all sit down." Her dad wedged himself in front of Tanner and put a hand to the small of her back.

Tanner trailed behind them, his expression wary until Callie pulled away. "Why don't you both go in the kitchen? There's fresh coffee. I'll be there as soon as I grab some socks."

Both parents stared at her, her mother clearly devastated and hurt, her father concerned. "Come on, Liz," her dad said, leading her mother away.

The second they were out of sight, Callie dropped against the wall and closed her eyes...until Tanner's lips touched hers.

"Hey," he said softly. "They love you and they're concerned."

"And they have lousy timing."

"Family is family." He took her hand and led her to the bedroom, then urged her to sit at the end of the mattress. Because he was now familiar with her house, he found socks for her and knelt to help her get them on. "We were probably jumping the gun anyway."

"No you don't." The second he stood Callie stepped against him. "We have plans, buster, so don't go changing them because of a minor delay."

"I won't." He stepped back to pull on a shirt. "Want me to head out until they're gone?"

"No!" She twined her fingers with his. "Do you mind sticking around?"

"I'd rather stay."

Relieved, she smiled at him. "Thank you." A few moments later, when they stepped into the kitchen together, her dad noted their closeness, but her mother pounced again.

"Glory posted your video and I saw it. Of course, I came right away." She pulled out a chair for Callie and then refilled her coffee mug.

Tanner got the creamer out for her.

"I called her to ask what had happened, and the girl was nearly hysterical. Now I can see why."

"I was hurt days ago, Mom."

"I only just saw it!"

Wow. Okay, that was very real upset in her mother's voice. Callie wasn't quite sure how to deal with it. "There was no reason for Glory to be hysterical."

Her mother flapped a hand in the air. "She sounded upset."

So *not* hysterical? Good to know. Gladly, Callie gulped down more coffee. "When I sent it to her, I explained what happened and told her I was okay."

"Okay, as in alive," her dad said. "Given how bad that bruising is, you had to be in a lot of pain."

"It was never that bad."

Tanner stood off to the side, coffee in his hand as he watched the three of them interact.

Callie wanted him to be a part of things. With her, in all ways. She smiled at him. "Luckily, Tanner makes a very attentive nurse. He and his family have been taking good care of me."

All eyes turned to him. Didn't faze Tanner. He moseyed over—the epitome of a man without a care—and took his seat at the table.

"It was bad," he said. "I wanted Callie to go to the hospital for X-rays, but she insisted nothing was broken."

"Stubborn," her mother said. "She's always been that way."

"I'm not a doctor, obviously, but she was able to move her arm and leg okay, and she swore that she bruised easily." For the next ten minutes, Tanner took over, explaining what had happened without mentioning their suspicions about Sutter. "Today, she really is much better, but yeah, she has bruises everywhere."

That sharpened her dad's attention. "Everywhere?"

Tanner met his gaze. "Yes, sir. Her left arm and leg took the worst of it, but her hip, waist, one shoulder— the drop from the attic left a lot of marks."

New tears filled her mother's eyes. "Why didn't you call me?"

"You aren't exactly close by, Mom."

"I am never too far away when you need me."

The sincere words hung in the air between them, going a long way toward softening Callie's usual, off-hand attitude. "I didn't know," she admitted simply. "I figured you'd be busy."

Her mother came out of her seat, cupped Callie's face, and then kissed her brow. "You're my daughter and I love you. Please, please promise me that if you ever need me, you'll call."

"Um, okay. Thanks, Mom."

"I mean it!"

That last sharp retort had Callie straightening. "Well, I *might*," she said, "but only if you don't push Sutter at me."

"Frank explained that Sutter was out." Her gaze moved to Tanner. "Now I see why."

"Oh no. Don't do that. Sutter was out well before I met Tanner."

"He said he knew us when he was a boy."

"He knew the family name, Mom, but I hadn't officially met him until the day I got here."

"You moved fast," her dad said to Tanner.

Callie jumped on that. "Actually, I'm the speedy one, Dad. I practically twisted his arm."

Tanner ducked his face, then ran a hand over his mouth, but he was still grinning when he faced her parents. "Only true to a point. I was interested from the get-go, but I wasn't sure if she'd actually stay."

Her dad slowly nodded. "Callie was sure."

"Yes, she was. She's a woman of conviction."

Intrigued, her mother asked, "So my daughter pursued you?"

"She takes after me," her dad said. "You remember how I chased you down, Liz?"

As the conversation shifted, Callie accepted that her parents weren't leaving anytime soon. She gave Tanner a look.

He winked at her. "I'm calling Addie so she can bring over Blu. I'm sure she'd like to meet your folks, too."

Until he said it, she hadn't noticed that Blu wasn't around! She was used to him greeting her, but she'd quickly gotten distracted with sensual promises from Tanner. Now she had to wonder if he'd had sex on the brain too, and that was why he'd taken the dog to Addie.

It seemed so, yet now it was all upside down.

Grinning at her forlorn expression, he reached under the table and curved his hand over her knee, his thumb gently stroking. "Soon," he whispered.

She wanted to hold on to that, but then Addie showed up, and naturally she hit it off with Callie's parents. Who wouldn't love Addie?

The surprise was that her parents were so warm and open. Of course they could be; their success in business depended on them being likable. The difference was, this seemed genuine. It was a side of her mom she hadn't seen lately. She immediately thanked Addie for taking care of Callie, and then she grilled her with a million questions. The two women ended up sitting on the sofa together, angled toward each other, knees touching, while they discussed the worries of adult children.

It was a novel experience for Callie.

Her dad was clearly in his element here, getting to know Blu in the confines of a small house while Tanner told him more about the tree farm and caught him up on the comings and goings of Hoker, Kentucky. There'd been a lot of changes since her mom and dad lived locally, but the vibe was much the same, and her dad loved it.

A few hours later, Kam came over. Then Nell texted and asked if she could visit. Addie insisted on everyone staying for dinner, and to Callie's surprise her parents agreed, extending their visit even longer.

Her day that had started with so much promise quickly turned into a family gathering.

WITH SO MANY people around, Tanner knew Callie had all the help she needed, so he took some time before dinner to wrap up a nearby job for a longtime customer. Now that he knew he'd have Callie again, leaving her for any reason was difficult. He felt primed, as if they'd indulged hours of sexual teasing, and it was only the promise of the coming night that made the wait bearable.

A few hours later he took a break and gave her a

call. She answered by saying, "I need an outside job so I can escape, but all I could do is sneak out to talk to the goats."

Just then he heard them bleating. He pictured her leaning against a tree, the soft sunlight through the trees playing over her skin. He saw the warmth of her smile. How the breeze teased her hair. Dropping his voice to a hushed whisper, he asked, "Is it really so awful?"

"Actually, no." Bewildered, she explained, "My parents are behaving…differently. Friendlier, more approachable, and my mother actually seems carefree instead of rushed and distracted. I don't get it."

"They like Addie."

"*Everyone* likes Addie, even Dirk and Lang."

Yeah, he'd noticed, and it had given him a lot to think about. Not that he'd fully trust them yet; years of hard lessons were hard to shake. Yet most of his reasons for disliking them so much were leftover from their late teens and early twenties. He couldn't think of a single thing the brothers had done in the last few years except spread nasty rumors and act like assholes—and Tanner was honest enough to admit that it usually started with him. "Maybe they're just enjoying themselves."

"It's just that the last time I saw Mom, she was abrupt and wired, insisting that I marry Sutter. Then boom, she says she knows it won't work and she doesn't seem at all bothered by it."

"Whatever her reasoning, I'm glad she's let go of that idea." Now that he knew Callie cared, he wasn't about to share her with that obnoxious ass. "They used to live in Hoker. Maybe they like getting reacquainted with the area. Your dad had a ton of questions for me."

"And now for Kam," she said. "They asked about

the ice cream shop. Apparently, they had a lot of early dates there."

He grinned. "It hasn't changed much, though the original owner retired and now it's his granddaughter running it."

Abruptly, she said, "There's something I didn't tell you."

That sounded serious, putting him on guard. "What's up?"

"My parents are overextended. Financially, I mean. Last time Dad was here, he said my marriage to Sutter, which would have partnered the companies, could have given them new opportunities so they could recoup."

Son of a—

"No one knows about their business troubles yet, but I expected Mom to keep digging in, to try to insist that I do what was best for the family." She let out a quiet sigh. "Dad said he wanted me happy, and he promised that Mom would come around. I didn't believe him though."

Tanner released a tense breath. "So you think she's had a change of heart?"

"Seems so…but now I feel a little guilty. I wouldn't marry Sutter—not for any reason—but I don't think I've been very understanding of their situation. Combining the companies would have been—"

"Good business. That's all," he said. "It wouldn't have been commitment and fidelity. It wouldn't have been love."

"I know," she whispered. "I want all those things."

"So do I." *But only with you.* He made a sudden decision. "I'll head home. I can finish the job another time."

"No," she said, the hint of a smile in her tone. "You

don't need to do that. I was just thinking things through, but thank you for listening."

"Anytime. I mean that, Callie." He wanted to share everything with her—including his future. "I'll be home before dinner. We can eat fast and then go back to your place."

"Well, about that… See, Mom loved Nell on sight, and so Addie invited her to the birthday party on Saturday."

"Okay." That didn't seem like much of a problem to him, as long as Nell was okay with it. Since meeting Callie, she'd really come out of her shell. "They'll be back on Saturday. Fine by me. I don't have a problem with your folks." As long as they weren't pressuring her to marry someone else.

"The thing is… Well, they might be staying with Addie until then."

Of all the… If it wasn't so frustrating, it could be funny. "Your folks? Staying with Addie? For *two* days?"

"I know! But at least they didn't want to stay with me."

Laughing, he shook his head. "Yeah, staying with Addie is preferable—as long as they don't have a problem with me sleeping at your house. I want to have you all to myself."

"You made promises, and no matter what, tonight you have to pay up. So yes, I'm all yours."

I'm all yours. For tonight, but Tanner figured it was time he set some things in motion—so that she'd be his forever.

LIAM ENDED UP joining them for dinner too, and the meal was moved from the eat-in kitchen to the dining room table in the great room so they could seat all eight people. Callie had never heard her parents laugh so much, and they weren't the least bit daunted by all the cross conversations, jokes, and personal stories that went around. In fact, they seemed to love them.

Even having Blu under the table, and Percy the cat keeping watch on the back of a long sofa, didn't faze them.

At one point, Callie said, "If only Glory was here."

"There isn't enough room," her mother said.

"Nonsense, Liz," Addie said without looking up from her meal. "There's always room for one more chair at the table."

Her mother paused in eating, then dabbed her mouth with a napkin and smiled. "What a lovely sentiment, Addie. I hadn't thought about it that way. For years now, Frank and I have had endless business dinners where everything was so formal."

Liam shrugged. "To me, this feels real formal."

"Me, too." Nell cast a shy glance around the table at all the decorative bowls of food. "We didn't exactly do family-style sit-down dinners around my house."

Liam agreed. "Closest I've come is sitting at a fast food booth with a few friends."

"This is great though," Nell assured Addie. "It's the best chicken and potatoes I've ever had."

"My first time having real potatoes instead of in- stant." Liam grinned. "They're *way* better."

"You're both so sweet. Thank you." Addie beamed at them. "Just wait until I bring out dessert."

Her mom turned to her dad. "Frank, do you recall when we were kids and we'd get together with all our friends at the diner?"

He lifted her hand and kissed her knuckles. "A dozen of us would squeeze into the booth. You shared your fries with me."

"You shared your milkshake."

"Those were wonderful, simpler times."

Callie ping-ponged her gaze back and forth between them, amazed at how they stared so lovingly at each other. It was almost embarrassing, except that no one else seemed to think so. "I can't quite picture you two smashed between friends and sharing food."

"I can," Addie said. "They were young and their love was new." She lifted a shoulder. "We get older and thankfully the heart settles down and gets comfortable. Otherwise, none of us would survive falling in love."

Her dad laughed. "Very true. Reggie used to harass me about being so lovesick all the time. What can I say? I knew Liz was the one within a few days of meeting her."

Callie thought of how she'd reacted to Tanner when she'd first set eyes on him. It was so different from anything she'd ever known, she hadn't been sure what she was feeling, she just knew her heart rioted anytime Tanner touched her. Sometimes if he just got close.

What Addie said made perfect sense. Love was sustainable. As a relationship matured, love changed to make it more bearable. Otherwise the excitement would wreak havoc on a body.

"Since you mentioned Glory, you may as well know that she flew back today." Dismissively, her mother said, "She told me, rather firmly, in fact, that she was done traveling for a while."

That was welcome news to Callie. "I hope you'll respect her wishes."

"Absolutely," her dad said, speaking before her mom could. "Glory is planning to stay with you. Liz and I thought it was a good idea, just so you weren't alone." He grinned at Tanner. "Now I'm wondering if that might be a problem."

Tanner denied that. "Family is never a problem."

That seemed like a perfect opening to Callie, prompting her to clear her throat. She hadn't planned to make an announcement this way, but everyone was mellow, enjoying the meal, and the timing just felt…right. "Actually, I've been thinking of moving."

A shocked silence fell over the table.

"Not far," she hastened to add, seeing the alarm she'd accidentally raised. She shouldn't have blurted it out like that. She wanted to be closer to Tanner, always, but she couldn't just invite herself to live with him— though she'd certainly love that. So she hoped to offer a solution. "Tanner had plans for Reggie's house. He was going to buy it."

Tanner abruptly leaned back in his chair. "We already discussed this and I told you to forget those plans."

"I can't," she replied softly. Then to her parents, she explained, "He helps to support disadvantaged youths."

"Like me," Nell said, drawing everyone's attention again.

Liam took her hand. "And me."

Tanner's expression shifted and his frown eased. "You're both friends."

Nell laughed at that. "I'm glad, but I know I was a real pain in the butt when we first met a few years back." To Callie's rapt parents, she spoke plainly and to the point. "I was rude and mean and I pretty much hated the world. I tried to hate Tanner, too, but he didn't make it easy."

"When he's offering help," Liam said, "he won't take 'no' for an answer."

Nell smiled at Tanner. "I didn't know anyone like him existed. Took me a while to realize he was the real deal."

"And now we're friends," Tanner insisted.

Addie added, "Like extended family, even."

Liam put his arm around Nell's shoulders and pulled her close to kiss her forehead. "He helped me to get my first job. I can't even tell you what that independence meant to me. I met him, got to know him—and then I wanted to be like him."

"Exactly how I felt when I was younger," Kam said. "Course, there were times I wanted to lose him in the woods, too."

Tanner cracked a grin. "Brothers."

Addie swatted at Kam. "You're *both* wonderful."

"All of you are." It was an odd, mixed feeling for Callie. She loved hearing the praise for Tanner, and at the same time her heart squeezed for Nell and Liam. Indeed, what would have happened to them without Tanner's assistance and influence?

To Tanner, her dad asked, "What would you have done with the house?"

"It doesn't matter now. I don't want—"

Kam interrupted. "The idea was to keep the animals, maybe even add a few more, and expand the garden. We'd have connected the two properties so the older kids could learn tree farming, gardening, caring for farm animals, along with all the related stuff."

"They'd have been paid, of course," Addie said.

"Best way to teach kids to manage money is to show them how to use a budget."

Tanner got in the spirit of it. "We'd have taught them the proper tools to use, maintenance of the shelters, yard, and even the house."

"Cooking, shopping, and housekeeping," Addie added. "But the house isn't available. Our sweet Callie is there and we love having her for a neighbor."

Kam lifted his tea. "And more."

Tanner took his brother's tea from him and set it back on the table. "Seems to me that Callie is already doing a lot of what I had planned."

"She is," Liam said. "The friends I brought over to help her paint, remove carpet and stuff—they all needed that work. Bad." He turned to Callie, his appreciative smile going crooked with emotion. "You overpaid. You always do. You treated them like adults, and it meant a lot. The guys left laughing with nothing but respect for you."

"You pay me to help with the animals," Nell said. "Even though I'm not an official vet tech yet."

"And you trust me with repairs," Liam added. "I like the responsibility."

Tears welled in Nell's eyes, but with her smile they looked like happy tears. "At the halfway house, we all watch you online before bed. You're so... I don't know. Real and believable, and fun. No matter what, you're upbeat. That video we did of your bruises—I figured if you could still laugh and joke with us, even when you could barely walk and you were black and blue, then I could stay upbeat too."

Addie smiled down the table at her. "Sounds like you're an inspiration, honey."

"She is." Her mother actually sniffled, and got a hug from her dad because of it. "I'm so proud of you, Callie."

Tanner took her hand. "You don't need to sell your house, babe. It's already being used the way I imagined."

For the rest of the meal, Callie stayed in a daze. While she'd been reinventing herself, she'd also been helping others—and hadn't even realized it. Or at least, to any great extent. She felt like a fraud because she hadn't set out to be selfless like Tanner. She'd just been determined to start living again.

Never, not once, had she imagined that her life would go this way. With so much personal meaning, not just for herself, but for others. It was invigorating and it gave her hope that she could, in fact, get it all.

A life of meaning, with a man she loved—and who loved her in return.

After they'd all devoured a homemade chocolate cake for dessert, Liam and Nell thanked everyone and left. It was clear to see they wanted time alone together. She might have worried more about Nell, except that Liam was such an exceptional young man, and Nell was savvy beyond her years.

They all pitched in to do the dishes, but that meant too many people were in the kitchen, making the large room feel much smaller.

When they finished, she asked Tanner to get the box of albums that he'd carried over for her.

"What's this?" her dad asked.

"Photos that Uncle Reggie had in the attic. I thought you might like to see them." She hoped it would soften their memories of growing up in Hoker, especially now that they were experiencing a financial strain.

Her mother snatched up a loose photo on the top, then caught her breath. "Frank, do you remember us this young?" The faded image showed a small house with shingle siding. On the sagging front porch was an old glider holding three youths. Her mom was in the middle, with her dad on her right side, Reggie on her left.

They were all three laughing.

"I can't believe Reggie kept this." Even her dad looked emotional now. He took the box from Tanner and tucked it under one arm. "We'll go through them all tonight. Thanks for bringing them over."

"There are more," Tanner said. "Reggie's attic is filled with old stuff, including more photo albums and framed photos."

"I actually miss him," her mom said softly.

"Come on," Addie said. "Let's let these young people get on their way. I'll show you up to the room you can use."

Callie kissed her dad's cheek, then hugged her mom. "Just so you know, he loved you both." When her mother went to follow Addie, she had tears filling her eyes.

CHAPTER SEVENTEEN

KAM WAS SOON heading out for a date, so Tanner told Addie they'd take Blu with them so she could visit with Liz and Frank.

With the dog at his side, and Callie's hand in his own, they started across the yards. The scent of rain filled the air, a warm breeze heavy with humidity. "I'm glad I got that job wrapped up. Looks like we're getting more rain."

"Huh." Callie stared up at the sky. "Another heavy storm, do you think?"

He shook his head. "Shouldn't be, but we better get the animals put up for the night."

Suddenly Blu stopped, his body going rigid. Back legs stiff, ears up, he stared ahead.

"What is it, bud?"

Blu didn't move, and that told Tanner something was wrong. He tucked Callie behind him. "Maybe you should go back to—"

"No." She knotted a hand in the back of his shirt. "I'm sticking with you and Blu. We have a date, remember?"

How could he forget? "Might be Dirk or Lang nearby, but stay alert."

"Do storms spook him at all?"

"No, but could be a coyote." He hooked the leash to

Blu's collar, just in case. They were close enough to her house to see the front and side. Nothing seemed out of place. Together, each of them watching the area, they moved closer, until Tanner saw the large boxes on her front porch. "Were you expecting a delivery?"

Immediately, she stepped around him. "Yes! That's my bedding. I can't wait for you to see it." She reached over to stroke Blu. "It's okay, sweetie. Just some packages."

But Blu wasn't convinced. Even after they'd reached the porch and Callie had the door unlocked, Blu didn't want to go in. He circled the packages, his scruff up, and when he reached a smaller box, he jumped back and then snarled.

Callie petted him again. "It's okay, Blu, That's probably something for the house, too."

"You don't know?" Tanner asked.

"I've ordered a lot." When she reached for it, Blu barked, making her hesitate.

And then the box shifted.

"Damn it." Tanner was already guessing what might be in that box, but now he'd have to inspect all of them and it was starting to drizzle. "You have a box cutter?"

"Yes." She darted inside and was back seconds later.

Tanner moved the box with his foot, but it was securely taped. Whatever was in there wouldn't be able to breathe. Snake or not, he didn't want it to suffer. "Here. Hold Blu's leash so he doesn't get too close. I'm going to take it across the street."

"I'm going with you," she said, holding the leash and following him out of the yard a good distance from the porch, until they reached the opposite side of the road. "What if it isn't just a rat snake? What if it's something poisonous?"

"Venomous," he corrected again. "Snakes are venomous, babe." He knelt down and set the box in the weeds. "Believe me, I don't plan to handle it if I can help it, but I have to get it out of the box."

Carefully, he turned the box until the end flaps were facing him, then he cut through the packing tape and stood. Again, using his foot, he tipped the box over and several rat snakes emerged. Not just one. Or three. It looked like five or six smaller snakes had been packed in there, crammed together, and now they angrily slithered away.

Callie whispered, "I'm going to have nightmares for a month."

No, she wouldn't. He'd be with her and he'd be damned if he'd let this chickenshit stuff continue.

"Enough." Furious, Tanner searched the road, hoping he'd see Sutter hunkered down somewhere. There were no extra cars or lurking ex-fiancés. From here, he could see that Kam hadn't yet left, but trees and honeysuckle blocked his view of Dirk and Lang's driveway.

"We're getting wet," Callie said, reaching out to touch him.

"Come on." He wanted her inside, and then he'd take care of rounding up the chickens and goats. The only problem was that Blu hadn't yet relaxed. In fact, he had his nose to the ground and was trying to lead Callie toward the side yard closest to the Garmets'.

"Do you think—"

Just then, Blu angrily lurched away and Callie not only lost her hold on the leash, she almost did a face plant. Tanner caught her, but Blu was on a mission. "Get inside and lock the door. Call Kam." He took off after his dog.

When Blu suddenly yelped, his heart stalled and rage imploded. *If anyone hurt Blu, there'd be hell to pay.*

Still running, he forced his way through the tangled honeysuckle—and found Lang on his knees, holding Blu tightly as the dog struggled to get free.

Worse, Sutter was there, holding a gun on Dirk. He wasn't a firearms expert, but the damn thing looked deadly, especially jammed against Dirk's ribs like that.

Tanner realized almost at once that Lang was trying to protect Blu. He could hear him murmuring, "Shh, shh, dog. It's okay. Settle down."

The problem was that Blu didn't like the brothers, and he really wanted a piece of Sutter.

Seeing him, Sutter cursed. "Why the fuck do you hillbillies have to hang out in packs?"

Tanner said, "Blu, stay," repeating himself twice before Blu, panting hard, subsided. His body remained tense and ready, and he was still emitting a low angry growl.

Keeping his gaze on Sutter, Tanner moved forward. He planned to happily rip the gun from his hand and jam it down his throat.

Sutter ground the gun against Dirk, making him grit his teeth. "If you make me shoot him, then I'll have to shoot the dog, too! And *you*."

Noting the tinge of hysteria in Sutter's tone, Tanner stopped. "That's a lot of talk for a dead man."

"I'm the one with the gun!"

Deliberately, Tanner curled his lip. "Have you ever fired one before?"

Sutter's mouth clamped shut and he didn't answer.

"I didn't think so. I'm a little doubtful that you handled a snake either, so how'd you get it in her attic?"

"Clearly, you don't understand the power of money.

It's easy to hire others to do your dirty work. To move goats, to handle snakes." He shrugged. "And around this shithole, people needing money are around every corner."

So that was how her goat had gotten into the woods? He owed the brothers an apology. "Is that what you tried to do with Dirk and Lang?"

For a single moment, Sutter looked confused, as if he'd never heard their names before, or had long since forgotten. "Wait. You're talking about this local trash?"

Seeing the way Dirk narrowed his eyes, Tanner half expected him to struggle—yet he didn't. He got the feeling Dirk was waiting for his moment to strike. "I'm talking about my neighbors. Callie's neighbors."

"You'll never convince me that Callie cares about either one of them, and I find it hard to conceive that you do, either. At first, they were willing enough to take my money."

"That's a lie," Dirk growled.

"Yes, yes, you have scruples." He smiled at Tanner. "He dared to be affronted that I wanted her scared."

"I'm more than affronted, you cowardly prick." Tanner edged forward again. "That's going to be a big problem for you."

Sutter's brows snapped together. "Stop acting territorial, you bastard! Callie is *mine*."

"She was never yours. She'll never be yours."

"Because of you?" Sutter laughed. "She might be indulging a walk on the wild side, but it doesn't mean anything. Normally I'd be fine waiting for her to get over her little snit, but unfortunately for her, I'm out of time."

Tanner paused. "What's that supposed to mean?"

"My parents are threatening to give the company to my uncle if the wedding doesn't happen in August, as planned." With a negligent shrug, he said, "They're absurdly old-fashioned and thought marriage to Callie and the ties to her family would influence me to settle down." His self-indulgent smile curled. "All because I'd gotten myself into a tiny bit of trouble."

To Tanner's mind, too many people had wanted to sacrifice Callie. "They're as delusional as you are." He took a bored stance, when in reality he wanted to plant his fist in Sutter's smug face. "Callie would never have married you. She's too good for you."

"But not you? Ha! Maybe you don't know, but if Callie doesn't marry me her parents will go bankrupt. Seems everyone wants the wedding—except you."

"And Callie."

Sutter shoved forward a step, making Dirk stumble and bringing Blu back to bristling aggression. "I was born to run that company! A few mistakes and they're…" Catching himself, he drew a breath and straightened. "I told them those women weren't important."

"More than one, huh? You really can't keep it in your pants."

"No one would have known about the other bitch if she hadn't gotten pregnant and come whining to my parents."

New anger surged through Tanner. It was damning enough that Sutter wanted to ruin Callie's life, but to make light of a woman carrying his child…

An enraged shriek cut through the quiet night and a body rushed up behind Sutter. Everyone seemed to move at once.

Sutter tried to turn as the lunging woman jumped forward, a fist-sized rock held in both hands over her head.

At the last second, Tanner recognized Glory.

The rock she wielded missed Sutter's head but hit him hard in the shoulder.

He fired the gun.

Blu attacked.

Tanner and Dirk both went after Sutter.

Pandemonium reigned for a few moments. Shoving Dirk aside, Tanner landed a hard punch in Sutter's gut, then another to his face. He was only vaguely aware of Dirk wresting the gun away.

Sutter staggered and would have gone down, but Tanner didn't let him. He'd threatened to shoot his dog. He'd been terrorizing Callie. He'd ridiculed a woman carrying his child.

A beatdown was less than he deserved, but for now it'd do. Even enraged, Tanner quickly realized that Sutter had no clue how to defend himself. He squealed and cried out and tried putting his hands in front of his face, but none of it did him any good.

In the corner of his mind, Tanner could hear Glory sobbing, heard his brother calling his name and Blu barking.

A small body practically landed on his back. He was about to throw it off when he heard Callie saying, "It's okay now, Tanner. It's okay."

She spoke to him much as Lang had spoken to Blu. He shot a glance at his dog, but Blu had subsided, panting hard while Lang praised and petted him.

The sound of his own harsh breathing filled his ears. Damn, he and his dog were acting the same.

Somewhere in the distance, sirens blared. By force of will, he opened his fingers and let Sutter drop to the ground. The sniveling bastard moaned and curled to his side.

Disgusted with the entire thing, Tanner took two

steps away. Since Callie was still clinging to him, he gently drew her around in front of him and cupped her face between his bruised hands. "You're okay? You didn't hurt your arm or leg again?"

"We're all fine. Well, except Sutter, but he deserved it."

Damn right he had. Tanner glanced around again and found Kam holding Glory, his hand stroking her hair. When his brother met Tanner's gaze, he said, "She's upset."

Yeah, Tanner could see that.

Callie's mom and dad were there, too, both of them looking around helplessly.

Addie was kneeling on the ground, checking Dirk's arm and using her lightweight jacket to dab at the blood. She looked up at Tanner and said, "He's been shot."

"Only grazed me," Dirk grumbled, appearing dumbfounded by her care.

"He needs to go to the hospital," Addie insisted.

Blu had calmed, and he didn't seem to mind that Lang was practically hugging him.

"Swear to God," Tanner said quietly. "It's like my world has gone upside down." Then he gathered Callie close, heard her groan, and quickly softened his hold. "Shit, I'm sorry. I hurt you?"

She snuggled closer. "Old bruises," she murmured. "Tanner?"

It was so damn hard not to squeeze her, to confirm that she was his and only his, but he'd have rather taken that bullet than cause her pain. "Yeah, honey?"

"I love you." She tilted her face back to see him. "I don't care that it hasn't been long enough. I don't care what house I live in. I definitely don't care what Sutter does or doesn't do. We can be arguing, or talking, or just sharing coffee, feeding goats or…or *even dealing with snakes*. I'm so happy when I'm with you." Tears welled up in her eyes and her lips trembled. "The kind of happiness I never knew was possible. I love Hoker, I love your family, and I love who I am with you. You're it. You're mine."

And just like that, she made everything right again. He touched his mouth to hers. "I love you, too." Nothing had ever compared to this. To the rightness of it. The completion and peace and sense of being where he was supposed to be. With the people most important to him. And with Callie.

He glanced at Sutter, at his battered, bloodied face. "I'm glad it's me."

She smiled. "It was always you—from the moment I saw you."

In August, a wedding took place. It wasn't at all fancy, but Glory insisted on a lot of beautiful flowers, and her mother wanted her to wear the designer gown that had already been altered for her. Callie didn't mind. In the dress, she felt like the princess Tanner affectionately claimed her to be.

Tanner made it clear that he didn't mind either, since Sutter had never seen the dress and he knew she'd chosen it with her own preferences in mind, not Sutter's.

He pulled her close now and kissed her, then grinned as they looked around at the one and only event hall in Hoker. Callie had to admit, it was pretty outdated with paneled walls, metal chairs with plastic-covered seats, and a worn linoleum floor. "This is their moment of fame, you know. The renowned McCallahan family, having the town's biggest event in their hall. They'll live off this for years."

She smiled. Her wedding had been perfect, and the reception was too, because all her favorite people were here. Her mom and dad were now seated with Addie. That had taken some doing, because Addie wasn't a sitter.

Kam, who'd served as Tanner's best man, was laughing with Dirk and Lang. She saw Tanner shake his head. He was still having trouble accepting that the brothers weren't quite as bad as they had once been. No, they weren't role models for young people, but they'd left their most unsavory habits behind in their late teens and early twenties.

Plus she knew Tanner would never forget that Lang had protected Blu, and Dirk had been trying to catch Sutter in the act. That's how they'd ended up in the woods with a gun pulled on them.

Who knew Sutter even had a gun? Of course, he'd gotten it from someone else, and hadn't known how to use it, but still, things could have gone very, very differently. If it weren't for Dirk and Lang, they might still be trying to prove Sutter's guilt.

"Glory looks stunning." Her cousin had taken her role as maid of honor seriously, and had worked with her mother to get everything arranged so that Callie didn't have to deal with it.

"She always looks perfect," Tanner said. Then he re-thought that and said, "Not as perfect as you."

They were alone for the moment, standing together and sipping drinks, so Callie shared something she hadn't before. "She was once in a bad car wreck."

"Who? Glory?"

Nodding at the awful memory, Callie explained, "Her parents died, and she almost died, too. She'd broken a shoulder, a leg, two ribs, her nose and jaw…"

"Damn." He looked at Glory with new concern. "You'd never know it to see her now. If she has scars, they don't show."

Thanks to multiple plastic surgeries, many of them pushed by her parents, Glory's physical scars were no longer visible. Now her scars are all on the inside.

Tanner took her drink from her and set it on the table with his own. "Can we leave now?"

"We need to make the rounds to tell everyone goodbye and thank them." Glad that he'd drawn her out of the sad memory, she said, "Maybe ten minutes more? No longer. I keep thinking that Blu is missing us."

She'd already moved in with Tanner's family. Funny thing was that Kam had plans to move out. Not far, just closer to town, but he swore he'd be back so often Addie wouldn't be able to miss him.

No one believed that.

Glory also had a place in town now. It was a house, as small as Callie's but more updated. Definitely not fancy. She claimed she wanted to simplify her life, but not in the same ways Callie had.

And good thing, because Glory had officially been promoted in the family company. Her recent rushed travel had netted several new deals with promised commissions from multiple sources. That had earned her favor, but also, Glory had wisely recorded Sutter's rambling threats and explanations—before she'd attacked him. For that, everyone was eternally grateful.

Knowing that Sutter's family would soon be embroiled in scandal and legal troubles, her parents had gone to them in person and shared the damning information. It was a sign of respect.

In appreciation for their discretion, Sutter's family had gone ahead with the deal, fully endorsing them.

They were shamed by their son's dishonorable behavior but they loved him and planned to stand by him through his legal ordeal.

Callie wondered if Sutter would ever learn his lesson, but he was no longer her problem.

"Blu isn't the only one who misses you. I still can't believe your folks want to relocate here."

"It'll be good for them to cut back." Despite the new financial promise, her parents had downsized and were even looking to have a moderate—by their standards—house built in the more upscale side of Hoker. According to Liz, both her girls were "based here now," and she wanted to be close to them.

Glory had spent so many years thinking she had to kowtow to Callie's parents, but now that she'd finally stood up to them, she'd gained new respect. Callie planned to encourage her every single day—after her honeymoon.

"You're *sure* you don't want to go to Costa Rica?" Tanner asked for the hundredth time. "I could squeeze out some time—"

"No way." She turned to face him, loving him with her whole heart and pleased that they'd spend the next two weeks in her little house for privacy. After that, they'd move right back in with Addie, and Kam would move out, and they'd begin the renovations on her house so it could be set up to accommodate more of the young people looking for security, guidance, and attention. It was Tanner's dream and she was thrilled to take part in it.

So far, they were planning to remodel the attic and basement for extra sleeping rooms, with an addition to the side for two more bathrooms. When it was finished, it would be perfect for what Tanner had intended.

"You have a tree farm to run," she reminded him, "and I have goats and chickens to feed. And Blu really would miss us if we were gone for two weeks. Plus, I love our plans and can't wait to see it all taking place."

Tanner put his forehead to hers. "I thought Reggie's house was a teardown. You showed me otherwise, and thanks to you there are so many more possibilities now—for the kids, and for me."

"For us." Feeling silly, she said, "You know, if Sutter hadn't been such a jerk, I might not have come here, and I wouldn't have met you. So in a way—"

Tanner scooped her up, making her laugh when he turned her in a circle, drawing everyone's attention and earning cheers from Kam, Dirk and Lang, and laughter from Liam and Nell. "I'm never thanking that ass, so don't you dare ask me to."

"We're together, and that's all I need."

"Wave goodbye. I can't wait a minute more."

Smiling, Callie waved to her parents and Glory, her new family, and her new friends.

Oh, she'd proved something all right—that life was better when you listened to your heart.

* * * * *